PURE LIFE

(or RIP BLUE RIDE X LUCKY SMASH ZERO NAKED GRACE SET GO)

PURE
LIFE

(or RIP BLUE RIDE X LUCKY SMASH ZERO NAKED GRACE SET GO)

EUGENE MARTEN

STRANGE
LIGHT

Library and Archives Canada Cataloguing in Publication data is available upon request.

ISBN: 978-0-7710-5176-0
ebook ISBN: 978-0-7710-5177-7

"The Rapture of the Athlete Assumed Into Heaven" by Don DeLillo. Copyright © 1990 by Don DeLillo. First performed at the American Repertory Theater, Cambridge, MA. First published in The Quarterly. Used by permission of Robin Straus Agency, Inc.

Book design by Kate Sinclair
Jacket art: (jungle) The Anio Valley with the Waterfalls of Tivoli by Cornelis Apostool; (cloud texture) max fuchs / Unsplash; (palm fronds) Chua Bing Quan / Unsplash; (football player) Kevin Dodge / Getty Images

Printed in Canada

Published by Strange Light,
an imprint of Penguin Random House Canada Limited,
a Penguin Random House Company
www.penguinrandomhouse.ca

10 9 8 7 6 5 4 3 2 1

Penguin
Random House
A HAZLITT PROJECT

For Kelly

And to the memory of my parents

. . . how super it must feel to achieve your biggest thrill as an athlete on the last day of your life, to know the perfection of the body even as your skin loses heat and energy and hair and nails, and now we're all enfolded in your arms, you are the culture that contains us, we're running out of time, so tell us quickly, time is short, tell us now.

DON DELILLO, *The Rapture of the Athlete Assumed into Heaven*

About 5 percent of love is romantic. The other 95 percent is something else.

STEVE YOUNG, NUMBER EIGHT, *QB: My Life Behind the Spiral*

Piuta yumuhka man,
Kiama lihnira man,
Tatahkukam dakbi
prak piram

MISKITU HEALING SONG

This is not yet the time of girls, it is a time of fields, diamonds, courts, fake leather; vacant lots and asphalt, broken glass and blood. It is Sunday afternoon in early autumn on the front lawn of a public school. Time to pick up a game, choose sides, five on five, the sidewalk out of bounds. The other border is a long hedge behind which boys go to pee, play with matches, learn to smoke, drink, sniff, abuse small animals and sometimes each other, under the blind windows . . . The boy whose ball it is hikes to himself, backpedals in the dirt. His brother stands in front of him, arms raised, counting: "One one thousand, two one thousand . . ." (Sometimes he counts battleships.) Now here he comes.

Streetlights flicker.

It is officially dark, a school night; boys have algebra, state capitals, late Mass, boys have baths. Now it is four on four, now three on three. (Across the street the mother of twins sings her sons home: "JoeyEddie! EddieJoey!") Two on two, then one on one, brother on brother, each trying to catch his own throw. But the boy the ball belongs to is the boy who belongs to the ball. He is shy, quiet, a bed-wetter, good with numbers, goes to confession, an altar boy—but a mother's boy with no mercy. Even when it is touch, he tackles . . . An argument, blows, tears. Now he plays alone, throwing and running, against no one, against himself, against the dark, against all.

Drags a garbage can into the middle of the field, throws to what only he can see.

Coach tells his kids, "You must choose the pain of discipline or the pain of regret." His assistant nods. The oldest boy is twelve.

They start with the three-point stance. Those who pick it up fast go on to snap drills. Some become centres; some don't pick it up at all. The grass, unmarked, is fresh-cut and smells like the end of summer. Then there are sprints, bear crawls, tumbling drills to see who has feet. He is the oldest kid there but slow and skinny; he doesn't have feet. They set up passing squares in the diamond. He stands on the pitcher's mound again though Little League was months ago. Four receivers run around the bases and he throws to each as they cut around the bags.

The assistant is paunchy, pasty, rheumy-eyed. Calls him Snake because he's left-handed like Number Twelve. "Just hit their hands. They don't even have to catch it."

He is four for four his first time out. Then the runners change direction and he is eight for eight. The assistant's hand on his back, boneless, like a leech.

First day in pads, bigheaded in helmets, they learn to sweat, hit, how not to cry, vomit behind the ash tree that shades their parents at the edge of the grass. Coach keeps them thirsty. When their mothers aren't there he speaks to them in the language of men, the language he used at the slab mill where he was a cinderman, where he ate carbon dust and iron like everyone else in the valley. But if you ask him he'll tell you this is his real job.

"Fire out! Fire out!" he says. "Good group! Good group!" Says everything twice.

The boys bark like dogs.

When their mothers aren't there some of them have no ride home. The assistant beeps his horn but the one he called Snake rides his bike. He has his number now.

Black Monday. A father arrives at Sheet and Tube, the Campbell Works, to find a sign taped to doors now chained shut. He and five thousand men and women turn around and go home or to the scores of bars that line the valley, and whose days are also numbered. He will not be the same.

Some fight back, but two years later the Brier Hill Works (blast furnaces named Grace and Jeannette) close. Then U.S. Steel's Ohio Works, then Haselton, then Sharon Steel. Unemployment in Y-town rises to twenty-four percent, and a building a day burns down in the valley, insurance the only income for those who must walk away from homes and businesses. Arsonists pay off the fire departments.

Homecoming.

After the game, reassuringly sore—pain is still a privilege, a token of accomplishment—Number Nineteen moves in another way under a different kind of light with the captain of the majorettes. His vest matches her ball gown, and though they are not in the Court—both declined nominations to make room for the less popular, the unattractive, disabled, bullied, minority, a practice that has yet to establish itself—they are the true king and queen of the evening, their corner of the gym its centre, and to almost everyone.

But in truth he is as uncomfortable in popularity as he is in this rented tuxedo, and declined the nomination for class presidency for somewhat the same reason, though also so he could focus on game tape and defensive alignments, and on English and Social Studies, his academic weaknesses. In truth a bit of a bore, shy with girls, good at math, drinks ginger ale at the parties he attends mainly for solidarity, fellowship of the varsity jacket, has a close friend somewhere out there among the absent and excluded who isn't a jock, whom he has defended against his own teammates, all of which is forgiven because he threw for five scores and put up nearly four hundred yards tonight and is starting quarterback for a high school in the middle of America.

He vomits before every game.

But if it is true that he is shy with them, kind of skinny and geeky around them, gangling, purportedly saving himself for marriage (though, with his dark eyes and curls and aquiline nose, on the verge of looking the part he has played tonight), it is also true that it doesn't matter, that they come to him, as the captain of the majorettes came, though perhaps in part because it was expected of her, and they believe they are in love, perhaps in part because it is expected, though perhaps he is truly in love with only one thing.

The deejay conjures Sade, smoke and velvet. Nineteen drops his hand to the small of her back, perfecting the embrace. Deep-sea slow. Streamers and balloons, colours bending over the polished wood floor and walls, over teachers relegated to chaperone, watching, policing, perhaps seeing themselves among the watched, recalling the cologne, the hair, the hush, the sway, the groping as for beauty just out of reach, the yet-unbroken promise of it all. Maybe as good as it got.

The King has cerebral palsy, dances knock-kneed with his mother at half court.

The captain of the majorettes looks up suddenly, not at Nine-teen but over his shoulder, as if into her future (community college, Where Futures Begin®), then tucks her blond head under his chin, makes a memory, and he looks over it to another uncrowned queen on the other side of the gym. No escort, no makeup nor need of it, neither cheerleader nor majorette but a fair gymnast, probable valedictorian, and foremost a violinist, bound for some school without an athletic program. We think we want what we already have; he turns away. Sees Number Forty-Seven, looking around as if for a better party, a fight to break up or begin, prematurely thinning, wearing the same full beard since ninth grade, probably too small for college though not for the girl he is dancing with, not saving himself for anything; sees Thirty-Six and Seventy-Four, with whom he has visited nursing homes and soup kitchens at Coach's behest; Coach in his tight suit and crewcut, lump in his chin, who has taught him humility as well as six different drops, that there is throwing and there is passing, that your eyes are more important than your arm, that there can be honour in losing but no winning without honour and every-thing else is just kicking stones.

Nineteen believes in almost all of it.

"I can't believe you drove all that way in this weather," his mother marvels at the Lightning's coach. The family sits in the family room, on the same furniture in the same duplex his parents moved into the day they married. You can smell it. You can hear the neighbours' TV on the other side of the wall.

"School jet can't fly in a snowstorm?" his father says.

The coach smiles. His nose is red, bulbous. "You must be think-ing of Alabama. Made sixty-some recruiting flights in six months."

"Right, I forgot. You're D-2." His brother and sister smirk.

"It's just a number. There's nothing your son can get out of one of those programs that he can't get out of ours."

"Televised games . . . Drafted . . ."

They have a week to decide. It is the only full ride on the table so far, and full rides are rare from Division 2. A partial from the MAC. The Buckeyes sent a letter but only invited him to walk on. And utter silence from the rest of the Big 10, the Big 8, Pac-12. Too slow for the Wishbone, not built for the punishment this would draw—not to mention the sidearm throw. Not to mention there are no left-handers in the Hall of Fame.

"The big schools don't care about intangibles," the coach says.

"Intangibles won't pay a house note," his father says. He has not worked since Black Monday, and he looks everywhere but at whom he is talking to.

"He threw for two thousand yards this year," his sister says. "He's All-State."

"With all due respect," the coach says, "the world is full of gym teachers who threw for two thousand yards."

"What's wrong with being a gym teacher?" his mother says.

"Kenny Anderson went to a small school," his brother points out. "Dave Krieg." And the coach runs a pro-style offense.

The coach enthuses over the athletic facilities, though he doesn't say the stadium is fifteen miles from campus and shared with two high schools. He talks about the renovated Fitness and Recreation Complex. Nineteen blanches at the subject of weights. He looks to his mother and speaks through his eyes: I will get you out of here.

His brother wears the jersey of The Only Team That Matters.

. . .

The school is a private liberal arts college founded in 1856 as a female seminary. Its main campus covers fifty-two acres in a small city two hours from Nineteen's hometown. The prime minister of Ethiopia is an alumnus. The school motto is engraved on a bronze seal embedded in the sidewalk at College Hall. Students are asked to walk around it; most do.

Lux et Veritas, and girls.

Nineteen is still in a committed relationship.

He meets the Lightning's starter outside the Athletic Training Centre behind College Hall. Number Eleven is a big friendly Italian kid who says, "If it ain't me, I hope it's you," and drives a convertible, shirtless, wearing sunglasses like he's Jim McMahon or something. He can bench-press three-fifty and runs a 4.7 forty. Nineteen—Associated Press's Mr. Football, played in the state All-Star Classic but here so did everyone else—struggles to lift one eighty-five and has been clocked at 5.4—about as fast as you or me. This must be some kind of mistake. He wants to transfer, play baseball, crawl home.

"How about fencing?" Coach says. "Or water polo?"

During rush Nineteen is invited to pledge Phi Psi but declines; he's heard things about alcohol poisoning and gang rape. Keeps himself on a short leash. Freshmen are required to take three credit hours in the humanities, and Nineteen takes a course in logic. He determines that the egg comes first.

Home games are broadcast on a thousand-watt AM station that plays gospel music on Sunday. There is no colour analyst and you can't hear the noise of the game, only the announcer's voice, eerily bare, as if he were calling it from a sealed vault.

Maybe two thousand in attendance if you count the pigeons

The Lightning have won nine games in five years, have dropped their first three so far and are down 20-0 in the third quarter of the fourth. Number Eleven confers with Coach at the edge of the track that rounds the field.

"Not one guy open. It's like they got our script."

"We string em out."

What we call Indian summer

Eleven attempts a naked bootleg just inside the twenty. The middle backer grabs him below the knee and doesn't just break his leg; his feet now point in opposite directions. Doesn't feel a thing.

"Could probably still outrun you," Coach says to Nineteen but gives him the nod and a play. "Just remember: it's a pocket, not a pitcher's mound."

He hears himself in the huddle, purposeful gibberish: "Scatter Wing One, Packer, on One. Ready . . ." Can't believe these words mean anything to anyone.

At first he just hands it off. A body squirting loose from a knot of other bodies. Then the Blue Knights put an extra man in the box and he can see downfield a little, goes upstairs. Just high enough but Eighty-Three drops it in the end zone. Coach is livid.

"You get two hands on that pig, hang on!" Swats him with the clipboard. "Secure the fuckin rock!"

Nineteen remains calm, recites more Dadaist poetry. Flow Tweet Packer on Two. The visitors' bleachers are tiny. Someone's mother exhorts the ref: "You blowin that whistle out your ass, get in the game!" God bless her.

Next time the wideout catches it in stride, scores, runs over a male cheerleader like he can't stop. Nineteen feels close to God. The mascot—arms, legs, a face embedded in zigzag foam rubber—plays air guitar. The game tightens, gets personal.

Helmets bang, exchange paint as in car accidents. Opposing players knock each other cold during a punt (one actually snores). The band plays *Carmina Burana*, gloriously out of tune.

BLUE AND WHITE! TRUTH AND LIGHT!

Soft toss across the middle He may not have a hose but he's got something

Nineteen is no dancer but never gives the ball away, gets rid of it in traffic, finds the gap with eight men in coverage. A play is a problem to be solved. The Lightning have a chance to force overtime at zero but the placekicker, somehow better at long range than close, botches the extra point. Nineteen stays at the throttle. Attendance improves. Number Eleven will become a sheep farmer after graduating and not own a phone or television.

Only the sure things throw draft parties. Nineteen spends the first day at the apartment he shares with his cousin on Liberty. They don't have cable but he knows only a half dozen or so D-2 players will get selected—usually linemen, backs, receivers, if any—and they won't go early so it's just as well. He prepares for an Actuarial Science exam. Keeps glancing at the phone till it becomes the black hole at the heart of every possibility. Dead plastic.

Next day he is at a dive bar on East Main, shooting pool with a loose collection of friends, all but one (former) teammates. Dark wood and beer breath. ESPN. Nineteen watches two guys playing chess in a booth under a stuffed antelope head. He pretends not to watch the ticker, pretends not to watch the Commissioner in his polka-dot tie reading off the selections from small pieces of paper.

The top picks are all gone. Chris Berman says, "The Colts are now on the clock."

"All about defense yesterday. Ismail went to Canada," the bartender says. He looks like a retired bodybuilder. "But Marinovich before Favre? Didn't see that coming."

Nineteen buys another pitcher.

Back at the table the former nose guard breaks, still in his varsity jacket. Near the end of the eighth round the Bills grab a wide receiver from Anderson.

The nose guard is incredulous. "Fuckin D-3!"

"Who the hell is Brad Lamb?" the former tailback says.

"Someone who never heard of you either," the former free safety says.

"Apples and oranges," the non-athlete says for some reason. Nineteen sees a girl at the jukebox eyeballing him. He is in a committed relationship with his career, goes to the bar for a refill.

"There's always UDFA," the bartender says. "Arena . . . CFL?"

"What are you, my agent?" Nineteen is feeling drunk for the first time in his life. "We knocked off Central Michigan last year. Central *Mich*igan." Like the Christians ate the lions. "All Ws."

The bartender offers a tautology: "It is what it is." He sighs. "I could change the channel." If only.

The free safety, a transfer from Central State, grabs Nineteen's arm and displays it to the Commissioner. "Show masr yer arm, boy. Good arm dat masr, he do a heap a work mo wit dat arm yet. Now walk aroun, boy, let good masr see how spry you be."

Nineteen elbows him in the belly and drifts toward the booths.

Back at the table the nose guard drinks from the pitcher. Spits in the non-athlete's beer when he isn't looking. The tailback is dancing for the girls at the jukebox and The Only Team That Matters takes a guard from Henderson State in the eleventh round.

The last pick is a quarterback from John Carroll. Who the fuck is Larry Wanke?

Size. Mobility. Leadership. So he's not the rah-rah type.

Finds himself looming over the chess game.

"What about the intangibles?" He can barely say the word. "What about first fucking team Kodak All-American? Fuckin Harlon Hill. Fuckin nine games with a broken thumb."

The chess players look at each other but not him.

"Hey! It's your shot," the non-athlete calls, but he has set aside his usual need to win.

"Bad move, White. You're letting Black grab all the space in the centre."

Black looks up. "Do you mind?"

But it is the fact that they're drinking Coke he takes exception to, inserts a little finger under the edge of the board and flips the whole game into the air.

"Hey, *I'm* supposed to do that!" the former nose guard yells.

"Big man on a little campus," the girl who looked at him says. He crushes a rook on the way out into spring light. Walks alone along the Grand River, which divides the world into the chosen and the left behind. He is afraid to go home.

He calls his agent, calls *her*. Only one of them answers.

Minimum wage plus a buck-fifty per delivery plus tips. You pay for your own gas. Unemployment in Y-town is still near twenty percent but he doesn't feel lucky. Has a degree in Communication Studies. He could try for an assistantship at his alma mater, definitely his high school, but that would be like an artist working at a paint factory.

He pays rent to his parents. Same wallpaper, closing in. Same smell.

No one has recognized him yet and that's good and bad. One night he delivers an extra-large double-cheese pepperoni to a small brick building on the upper south side, next to an abandoned house full of feral cats. Flattened roach in the hallway. Muffled drama, an eviction notice. It takes him a moment to recognize the man who answers the door, then they embrace like refugees who have found each other in a camp. Forty-Seven has shaved his head and reduced his beard to a goatee, works at a slaughterhouse in the valley. He doesn't invite Nineteen into the one-bedroom he and the girl he held at Homecoming share with their five-year-old son.

He asks after the captain of the majorettes.

Nineteen waffles. "I heard she's a paralegal. You still talk to anybody?"

Those who couldn't parlay their hand-eye coordination into manual labour have enlisted. Will the Hill rode a tank in Desert Storm. "Worked out with the Packers. He said something about some combine he signed up for. Elite something . . ."

"Meat market." Nineteen still throws to Lightning receivers once a week, hoping to impress an NFL scout on Pro Day. Lifts, throws through a tire swing. "Cattle call."

"Sure it is. They've gotten people signed." Forty-Seven names names.

Nineteen pretends indifference. "Only one team I'm interested in."

"Yeah, me too: GM. Lordstown. Cars are the new steel around here."

A dog growls somewhere inside. A woman scolds: "*Caesar.*"

Forty-Seven lowers his voice. "I kill pigs with an electric wand, man."

. . .

The Elite Pro Combine is held at an indoor college practice facility in the middle of Indiana in the middle of February. A green field with white stripes in an unheated warehouse. Must be five hundred guys there; guys on the bubble like Nineteen, guys who look like they played nothing but Nintendo, guys who were gods in high school then found themselves eighth on the depth chart. At least one ex-con. There's a soccer player from Germany, a long snapper who's fucking deaf and dumb but paid his two hundred dollars, a guy who runs a 4.3 forty but he's five foot one and they took his money. It's still dark out.

The offensive hopefuls are herded out to midfield and told to take a knee. They wear three-digit numbers. The Combine is presided over by a white-haired man with a clipboard, dressed in black, a former GM in yet another doomed alternate league.

"This is where you either keep your dream alive," he tells them, "or let it die with dignity and get on with your real life."

They start with calisthenics. The white-haired man in black moves through grunting, gasping, evenly spaced rows. "I know there's some genuine offensive talent here," he says, "but frankly, some of you are just . . . offensive," and Nineteen wonders how many of them could be eliminated in these first fifteen minutes.

Drill proctors take them to their stations in groups of eight. They are weighed, measured, photographed with their shirts off. Guys with tits still heaving from the warm-up; sometimes dignity dies too. Then the forty, the short shuttle (almost kills the dreamer), the broad jump, the vertical. A lot of waiting around, talk, eyeballing. Public Enemy and AC/DC leaking from headphones. Nineteen loosens his arm in the Player Holding Area, tries not to listen.

"I missed a funeral for this. I ain't leaving till I get my look."

"Tuck in your jersey, they check all that shit."

Three hours after the first push-up, the air horn blows again and position players are separated out for skill drills. Everything on tape. The evaluators are former pro scouts and coaches. Nineteen doesn't know why they are former anything nor does he care; he cares about the spread of his fingers, about using body momentum to make up for his lack of arm strength. He hopes to draw a receiver who can actually catch; if not, just get it between the numbers and shoulder. Just hit their hands. This is no place for intangibles.

It's dark outside again when they hear the horn for the last time, and snowing. Then it's just you and the phone again.

"That's not even on the team," his father says. He is watching the evening news. "Taxi squad doesn't play in real games."

"They call it the practice squad now." Nineteen doesn't have his own place yet but has never gotten used to it—farts, leftovers, rotting foam in the cushions. "Someone gets hurt or cut, I could get activated. And I get reps." Watches home games from the press box. And he wears the same number he's worn since high school, same as Unitas.

"Not even the fifty-third man."

"Three thousand a week," Nineteen's mother says, still not over it.

"What's he gonna do the rest of the year? Johnny U laid tile in the off-season."

She looks at the envelope in Nineteen's hand. "What's that?"

"Whatever you need it for."

Another mousetrap goes off like a gunshot.

"Lou the Toe sold insurance." His father stares at news of the past. "Jack Gregory was a farmer . . . They blew up Charlie Cadillac

14

in his Caddy. Vinnie D, Billy Naples. Called it a Y-town tune-up anymore." The past stares back. "Just leave it on the table."

He leaves when his father starts singing. He has a new agent now, sees a girl he met while looking for a place in the city, though she is not the violinist who was valedictorian.

Seven weeks into the season the third-string quarterback is pulled over for speeding on a Sunday night. A plastic bag containing what is determined to be a Schedule II controlled substance is found in his vehicle and he is suspended for the rest of the year. Coach only dresses two for games but Nineteen moves from his TV set to the sideline. The speed, the trash talk, brute utterance of impact; you hear the life of the game. A great privilege. The Only Team That Matters goes 4-12, and Nineteen asks his parents what else they need.

Next August he is still backup to a backup and Coach can't remember his name. Spends Thursday nights alone in a diner with the playbook—twenty chapters, two hundred and fifty pages, fifteen hundred diagrams in Coach's scrawl—commits over two hundred plays to photographic memory. If Peg dogs, the weak G blocks him and F checks Wanda. The waitress never asks. He studies the opposing sideline in his street clothes, looking at hand gestures, body language as they break huddle, anything he can relay to the DC. The backup quarterback, third year out of Harvard, pretends he doesn't exist but Number Fifteen, the starter, is impressed. Greying, beer-paunched, thirty-six years old, he has played for seven teams, married three wives, carouses, smokes, collects motorcycles. Takes Nineteen golfing and passes on a journeyman's wisdom, the game within the game: it's seventy-five percent mental . . . everything good starts in the huddle . . . look at the linebacker's feet . . . don't throw high over the middle . . . when in doubt, check her ID.

"And don't get old," he says, and breaks his right arm in Baltimore, four games in. Coach suffers the backup for six quarters, seven picks and a field goal, then down in Arizona says, "Say hi to those guys, Lefty. Just take care of the ball."

Jogs across two inches of actual grass to land the plane. The Sun Devil welcomes fresh meat. Nine-year-old giving him the finger. Semicircle of the huddle, hands on knees, hands on hips. The centre has to shut them up. Nineteen has to repeat the call. On Three.

He licks his hand.

Under centre, knuckles hard up against a moist crotch. The beginnings of a chemistry. Eighteen seconds. He looks over the defense (if Wanda doesn't dog, F is free to release). Bodies in colours, hands in the dirt. The nose tackle glaring or grinning.

"Somebody order double-cheese?"

Someone on his side laughs. At the snap he trips over his left guard's foot and doesn't take care of the ball. The tackle recovers it. The cheering is a knife in his heart.

"Hey, hold up. Here go your tip!"

Next series he completes his first seven passes. Up north the leaves are turning.

He is not a born leader. This, he knows, has always been a mark against him. Too reticent, aloof. Never threw someone out of a huddle. His trash talk is garbage. When he tries to bust balls in the locker room, his wit falls flat, his high five another awkward mechanic. He has teammates with bullet scars, who play with pictures of dead kids in their helmets. Fundamentalist Christians, a Rhodes Scholar, veterans who hear the clock ticking, whose autographs he sought when he was in middle school.

Not a born leader but a quick study. He watches twenty hours of game tape a week, ponders an opponent's tendencies in every down and distance, calculates percentages. The will makes the skill. On the field everything is information; if the cornerback shades just a half-step inside it's going to be man-to-man, a linebacker's eyes can tell you if he's going to dog. He prays for a blitz, lives to beat it with a deep ball, the breathless wobbly arc. (Who needs a perfect spiral?) Sometimes he doesn't beat it, but Fifteen has taught him there's a price for everything. He is not afraid to pay, to get hit, only to fail, to lose, and he plays a half with ten stitches in his tongue.

They start to call him brother. Cookouts in the empty littered lot, postgame.

He lives in the pocket, keeps ineffably cool at rush hour, both hands on the ball, eyes downfield no matter what. His field of vision spans both sidelines—one of his few gifts—but he doesn't look at his target till he throws, and hits receivers in stride. His strategy protects bodies, careers, he shares credit and assumes blame, argues respectfully with Coach and his coordinators but they cannot argue with his aim. When he throws his first TD the equipment manager offers him the ball and he gives it to the team. A quick study. Takes his line to a steakhouse because their game is his game, goes to the Flats on Thursday nights, Bible study with Eleven and Thirty-Four, learns poker so he can win and forgive debts (he gambles only for glory), suffers a strip bar once, finding it full of flesh but not what he thinks of as sex. He keeps the secret of a DE who is queer but a hired killer with 4.4 speed and nine percent body fat. Leads by calm example and performance; if you are going where they want to go, they will follow, and they follow him, Sunday to Sunday, in every weather, to their better selves.

But always there is a distance, the self he withholds. He is good with numbers.

The press, the League, take notice. The city, an underdog itself, stirs in the snow. Finds itself 9-7 (five late-game rallies, two of them technically miracles) and alive in January for the first time since . . . Wildcard, bottom seed—they'll have to win three on the road to play for the Ring but wouldn't have it any other way. No one knows quite how he does it but he is one of their own, blue-collar pretty, the left-handed kid from only an hour and a half away who doesn't make mistakes, and celebrates by preparing for the next one.

He doesn't feel like a millionaire. A three-year contract, twenty-five paragraphs of boilerplate with an eight-page addendum, papered out on the owner's ten-seat jet; the only guaranteed money on the team. An endorsement deal with Converse. A luxury box at the stadium for his family. He wonders what to buy, doing bench presses in March.

Starts with a house for his parents, a condo for himself overlooking a river where it mouths the great lake. His father is reluctant to move till a stray drive-by bullet kills his television. Other relatives are not so shy. Cousins, uncles, second cousins, some whose ties are even further removed, but here they come. With credit card debt, bad medical news, circling loan sharks, sure things: restaurants, story stocks, inflatable furniture. Riding Arabian horses, here they come.

He hires a financial adviser, forms an LLC to cover his assets. Buys a GMC Jimmy and drives north in the off-season for the

Stanley Cup. Brett Hull recognizes him in the seats and high-sticks the glass to say hello. At the afterparty a French-Canadian hockey reporter also says hello. In a four-star room she tells him the story of the scar on her thigh.

Zero Flood Slot Hat, he thinks, tracing it with his finger. 78 Shout Tosser.

Oh lordy, somehow he
   Wasn't even looking
No words

Velocity vectors, parabolas, his head full of arrows. His game has evolved through endless drilling and repetition; sight adjustments, footwork, muscle memory. Dropping back into his calculus. The pocket is still home but he can hurt you outside the tackles if he has to. His playbook is scrawled with pencil like a rough draft subject to revision in motion, but Coach, a disciple of detail, a system builder who cries when he's happy, bites his tongue because the will to win is the will to live. Everything else is foreplay.

Pro Bowl starter, probable MVP. He is indifferent to statistics, but one of the few categories which he does not own is fourth-quarter comebacks because his team rarely trails. Dark horse days are over, he drives a perfect meat machine engineered to generate the letter W. Cincinnati, Atlanta, Houston, 112-10. His deep threat an Olympic sprinter with a Muslim name and with whom he shares a faith of timing and pattern. A fullback with legs like a guard. A punter with a five-second hang time. The requisite contingent of sociopaths on defense who live in a dark place from which they pitch three shutouts. (What is it about Samoans?) Fifteen hundred pounds of O-line that not only gives him time to set his feet, but lets him stand in the backfield like a man watering his lawn because Nineteen knows how to take a hit but is not made to take a lot of them.

Defenses play to hurt him. Defenses do not win, they impose defeat. They are the anti-life. He doesn't take it personally.

Best record in team history. Fifty bucks per trading card. Women send him their underwear in the mail. He signs an autograph for the fan of an opposing team as he beats them. The press adores him though he rarely says anything interesting, because he is unfailingly polite, boring in the best way, sings every word of the national anthem.

At the podium after Pittsburgh, still in the endorphin glow, suit over an open collar, they ask him what It feels like.

"You make a series of decisions," he begins. They don't hear the singing inside.

After Pittsburgh he walks into a restaurant with his parents, no entourage, no Mystery Girl, and generates a standing ovation, the diners rising in waves as he moves past like some messiah healing the lame and halt. (He will have the chicken breast.) Eight percent unemployment, crack addicts throwing babies in dumpsters, thirteen wins and top seed in the conference; home field throughout the playoffs. Local musicians record songs about him that go into heavy rotation, The Only Team That Matters owns the rights to his face and erects a twenty-foot billboard of it over the interchange approaching downtown; he takes the shoreway the day before home games so he doesn't have to drive past himself en route to the hotel. Appears in a local commercial for an electric home heating fan, sitting in a suburban living room in full uniform, smiling his best imitation of a smile.

"Don't be left out in the cold this winter," he monotones. "Join a winning team." And he throws the ball right in your face.

. . .

You do not consider yourself a professional groupie.

You meet him at the bar where they hang out after the Friday walk-through. You're playing eight ball and he waits his turn to take winner. Everyone else seems to know what this might mean, but he is so focused on the game it is almost amusing. From what you've seen, he is like that with everything—darts, foosball, air hockey. You suppose it comes with the territory. You suppose it is the territory.

You're a good shot and you don't think he scratches on purpose, but you're surprised he lets you follow him home. You'd expect a motel, or maybe the men's room, or the room in the back the proprietor has reserved for such occasions. Or the parking lot, or nothing at all—you've heard he was celibate during the playoffs.

He says he doesn't do this often.

Professional groupies memorize rosters.

He seems proud of his building. Coral stucco, kind of Old Hollywood, overlooking a marina on the west bank of the river. Once a grand hotel, it was for some reason popular with aviators and he asks you if you know who Charles Lindbergh was. He asks what you do. You could tell him you're a cultural anthropologist researching the correlation between the athletic libido and something or other, but you dropped out after a year and now wear a nametag at DrugMart so you just say "'Credit or debit?'" as you look around. Chrome, glass, dark wood—jock taste but neat, almost old-lady fastidious. He tells you who else lived here. He tells you where the shower is. You'd like to ask him about The Rematch but you know better. You'd like to ask him if he knows who Amelia Earhart was but you ask about the reddish-brown patch that wraps around his back and side like an outsize birthmark.

21

"Turf burn," he says; it no longer hurts but will take months to fade. "I don't do this often," he says, and you almost tell him you can tell, but you give him points for trying. Pleasure is beside the point, and he doesn't ask you to let him choke you, which makes him a gentleman all things considered. Apparently, he's also a missionary.

When you wake up it is still dark and you're alone. You have to pee. The bathroom is *en suite* but, passing the living room flicker under the door, you can't help but take a look: there he sits in t-shirt and undershorts, scrawling in a notebook, watching tape.

You sit on the toilet with the light off, watching the tape in your head. He seems to feel obligated to let you spend the night but in the morning barely speaks—pre-game silence, you don't take it personally. Monday a customer asks about your weekend.

"I'm not sure who fucked who," you say. "Debit or credit."

You cannot watch. There is one second on the clock. There is a reason they call it a Hail Mary—five receivers and an empty backfield—so why are you the one praying? You are in the grip of destiny. You have done your part, done the seeming impossible once again, called your own number at the end of the drive and pushed between the centre's legs like a man giving birth to himself (and how can you have gotten that far without going the rest of the way, to Atlanta, the Roman numerals?) but it is out of your hands now, it is in theirs (if you get a play on the ball spike it for God's sake don't tip it) so you sit on this end of the bench alone, between the fortys, helmet on top of your head, sweating in the cold, finger bandaged (nail torn off), grass-stained, arms on your knees, looking at the ground, making a deal with God. So why not let them watch for you, the eighty-plus thousand, the how-many million, and let them let you know when the ball is snapped, shotgun, all go, only three rushing, the clock at zero but the play still alive, the only ticking now in your chest?

The owner's daughter says, "I've never dated a billboard." She asks him if he's been to the orchestra—he doesn't have to wear a suit.

"Not since grade school," he says, doesn't say he has sung onstage with Hootie & the Blowfish. The concert hall is marble columns, brass and bronze. The box has velvet curtains. The Triple Concerto. He kind of likes it at first, the building melody stirs like the soundtrack to a highlight reel. He sees Tony Dorsett breaking out in the secondary, end zone to end zone, no one laying a hand. But the soloists are just getting started when the point has already been made, and at the end of the allegro he almost claps in relief, then remembers there are two movements to go. The conductor, she said, is a fan.

Afterward he takes her to a trattoria on the outskirts of town to avoid fans. Checkered tablecloths, bottles wrapped in wicker. He knows the owner, who gives them the back room where Louis Prima once sat. He has been there with the starting offense, though they preferred the Olive Garden.

"I hate eating in big groups," she says, hair tied back and laid over one shoulder.

"It's important for a team to do things together."

She asks him how he liked the performance.

"I think I relate to the conductor."

She considers this. "The conductor interprets, he doesn't improvise. Jazz, maybe?"

"I like smooth jazz sometimes."

Chess, then.

"Till the pieces start moving and have ideas of their own." He tries to describe the pounding of cleats closing in from the blind side.

"'In the dark I would know thy step.'"

"What's that, Shakespeare?"

"I used to write poetry in high school."

He tries not to stare into the hollow of her neck. "All girls did."

"Did they write it for you?" The waiter opens a bottle of Pinot. "You seem the high school sweetheart type."

She will have the gnocchi and burro. He orders a steak and tries to show an interest. Poetry. An English major, then?

"I'm getting my master's in art history." She is not sure what she will do with it.

"I'm sure there's a place for you in your father's organization."

"What organization?"

He doesn't know if he likes her, reminds himself she's adopted. He doesn't like the wine but has some more. "I'm surprised he was okay with this."

She puts up her hand to hide the food in her mouth. "I was my mother's idea. My father and I live in the same house. I didn't ask him."

It surfaces that she likes the Breeders as well as Beethoven. And pinball. He figures the tip in his head and they go to an arcade. Tries to suppress his need to win while she mans the flippers of a machine called *Funhouse* in low heels, dark sheath dress, sleeveless.

Spying on her as if she were at the piano again.

This will be the year. Las Vegas likes them 6-1. *Sports Illustrated* agrees, puts Number Nineteen on the cover again, in uniform but unhelmeted, a profile that belongs on the side of a coin.

It is also a re-election year. The President is a fan but the feeling is not mutual, so it is his opponent who visits training camp on a tour stop. He and Nineteen connect on a hitch for the photographers. Nineteen believes in the sanctity of unborn souls.

He buys a farm, visits bald-headed children in a pediatric ward. "Really puts things in perspective," he chokes up on the evening news. He has had a reputation for coldness with the media.

Golfs with Numbers Seven, Eight, Twelve, Thirteen, the other Eight, with his new best friend the Hank Aaron hitter. Plays Ping-Pong with nobodies at home.

Is sacked on the first play of the season in Kansas City. Safety blitz. Lands hard on the tip of his shoulder and is a long time getting up. He walks off the field—in his career he will never be carried—but locker room X-rays reveal a Grade 3 separation—both ligaments torn from the clavicle. His season is over. Las Vegas adjusts the odds.

The owner paces the hall on his cane, past empty rooms—he has reserved the entire wing for privacy. This is not just any baby. Nineteen in scrubs, putting ice on her lips, asking questions. About a centimetre an hour, they tell him. A machine quantifies pain as if inducing it: the higher the number, the more it hurts. The room gets crowded. He is asked for an autograph. She is in active labour for just an hour and a half. The delivery nurse is amazed. ("How long was yours?" "Twenty-seven years and counting.") He looks into the pink ripeness and his squeamishness subsides, everything is amazing—even the turd she passes like a preliminary offspring before the head crowns. A tuft of black hair. She watches TV, *Why don't* you *fucking push?* The whole head now. Impossible. Wet, purple-grey, eyes shut, scowling. Something breaks with a snap as the shoulders emerge. *Was that me or?* Then he shoves the doctor aside and brings her into the room like taking the perfect snap. For one moment he is ready to throw everything else away.

It is the beginning of the end.

He is not the same. His shoulder is not the same. It is held together with a dead man's ligament and it won't listen to his brain. The team is not the same. They are not young, and Thirty-Four, their best blocking back, is traded for the future. The future weighs a hundred eighty pounds, brings his personal chef to the locker room. The right tackle, a left-handed quarterback's best friend, retires to get a Ph.D. in astronomy. So here they come, smelling blood. T-bone him, wrap him up and topple him, pull him down by his shirt, leg, face mask, shoelaces. Celebrate like children at Christmas (*just a three-man rush but for the sixth time this afternoon*). He hears his ribs crack, eats grass, coughs blood. Number Ninety-Nine in black and blue piledrives him like fake wrestling, but this is not fake and he bites off the tip of his tongue. Looks for his shoe.

There are hits he doesn't remember. A swarm of black stars, then a circle of blurred faces above him, trainers and doctors, asking him what one plus one is. ("Why don't you ask me something easy?") And always two fingers so you always get it right. The head team physician is an orthopaedist, silver-haired, his hands steady but his eyes cold—they see what the owner wants them to.

"Let's get you inside and take some pictures. It'll look better if you can walk."

Sprains, ligaments, torn quad, torn groin, bruised bone, bruised lung, broken fingers, broken jaw. All the Latin words for pain.

He takes to carrying smelling salts in his hand warmer.

"Let's shoot it up and get you back out on the grass. You know Billy Kilmer played a Super Bowl with one leg shorter than the other." A shot of Toradol in the ass. Vitamin T. Numbs you enough to let you play, but Tuesday it takes an hour to get out of bed. Sometimes the needle has to dig for the pain, makes a grown man cry, so he refuses it and plays through. Plays through sickness, vomit and diarrhea, two dislocated shoulders (in one game), wears a SWAT team vest to protect his cracked ribs.

He appears at a postgame press conference in a suit with his neck sandbagged like some litigant on court TV.

A former teammate, born again in Bronco blue-and-orange by free agency, plants him in AstroTurf and he swallows a tooth.

"If God can forgive me, brother, so can you." Helps him up, then does it again.

The head team physician writes for Vicodin, Indocin, Oxy, and there is a candy jar in the training room full of pills in the team colours. He also writes for anabolic steroids and Nineteen is tempted—he could use some of the speed, the muscle mass that nature has withheld, but the side effects scare him; the starting OL is a juicer and is taking a hormone derived from the urine of pregnant women to offset the shrinking of his testicles.

Novocaine. Xylocaine. Cortisone. Hike.

He can't run and he can't hide. Pisses blood from a lacerated kidney. Surgeries, rehabs, missed games, limbo of Injured Reserve. Bone taken from one part of his body and put in another. Every time he comes back the game has changed: dummy formations, false coverages. Chaos theory. His sidearm throws batted down, his magician's play-fake debunked. Sack-fumbles, the dreaded pick-six, altercations with fans and receivers: *Try throwin with the other arm motherfucker.* Rich kids with season tickets leaving at halftime. (His wife who hates football stays for every snap.) As he goes, so goes The Only Team That Matters; they sneak back into the playoffs just once, get shut out in the first round and there it is, the ominous hum of an angry hive, so deep you can feel it, but the seats are empty. There is pain and there is pain.

The camaraderie, the transcendent brotherhood gone to family dysfunction. Silence on the team plane. Maybe it wasn't love after all.

Regime change. His contract renegotiated, no guaranteed nothing. The next new coach wears The Ring and is also the *de facto* GM. His first order of business is to put up a sign outside his office that says TEAMWORK MAKES THE DREAM WORK. His next order of business is to call Nineteen's agent, who calls his client, lone wolf of the locker room, white in his beard at thirty-two.

The afterlife of the professional athlete is situated largely on the golf course. His favourite holes are in Florida, where he winters with his family. He plays with friends, former teammates and rivals, with Tony Robbins and candidates for public office, in charity tournaments (including his own because every ex-athlete must host a charity tournament), with business acquaintances who will become partners and associates, and he likes to joke that he makes more money on the links than he did on the field and for a long time this is true. Plaid shorts, white polo, white ball cap; deal flow, money grab, private equity. Philanthropy and real estate—industrial and mixed-use, and not just as investor, but as developer. He is also a Director, Senior Vice-President, Head of Operations and minority owner. Owns a steakhouse in Fort Lauderdale and is about to open another back up north.

Has a manager now instead of an agent, who manages his appearances and determines speaking fees, which are roughly equivalent to the cost per trip of the Learjet he leases for business purposes and family vacations.

His smile is bright and new; his Best Ball partner is a cosmetic dentist. He belongs to a Ring of Honor, a Rotary Club, sits on boards of regents and trustees, sits courtside with the local comedian on whose network show he has made a cameo appearance, sits in a box next to the bullpen during All-Star Week with his old friend the ESPN analyst and a grunge rocker who is standoffish but polite. Runs a football camp for disadvantaged youth because he believes in giving back, appears at scholar-athlete banquets, grand openings, ground-breakings, galas, fundraisers, because he believes in appearing. Owns six percent of a hockey franchise, horses for business and pleasure, an endangered animal resembling a cross between a giraffe and a zebra that his daughter saw on TV. He cuts ribbons.

"I make more green on the green," he repeats at the Professional Development Workshop. Goes to confession and supports the troops.

Another daughter. A nanny. Trust funds.

He belongs to a club in West Palm Beach, but his favourite course is in the Panhandle, right off the Gulf. Seven thousand yards in the middle of flat scrubland, pines, lined with brilliant white dunes thirty feet high. You can swing from the heels here, the ball almost disappearing in unlimited possibility. Here he plays just to play.

The rest of the year he spends up north on his farm, not an hour's drive from the city he played for. Four hundred acres, three hundred tillable. Swimming pool, tennis court, basketball, ATVs.

A restored five-bedroom Greek Revival farmhouse with a wrap-around porch. Trails, a creek, barn owls, deer. An encounter with coyotes.

Finally, a boy . . .

Nineteen plays chess with his wife in the family room, under exposed ceiling beams. Fieldstone fireplace. Outside the pounding of a ball—the girls playing one-on-one.

The boy sits on Italian leather with Dr. Seuss.

Nineteen moves a pawn. "He should start with lacrosse. Everybody can play lacrosse." He picks up his glass. "He must get something from me—God forbid my legs."

"God forbid he'll need hair plugs too," Mrs. Nineteen says. She prefers wine.

"Follicular grafts." Nineteen has trouble with the syllables, though not because of the scotch. He wears a hat in the house.

The boy is engrossed in his book, one page at a time. When two leaves are stuck together, he separates them before proceeding.

"God forbid my arm, for that matter. Does he read or just look at the pictures?"

Nineteen's wife wakes her sleeping bishop. "Do I even look like a soccer mom?" She hosts a reading group here once a week. Chess has little to do with the intelligence.

More pounding, now overhead—Amish carpenters putting shakes on the roof. Nineteen is in love with their work ethic. The farmhands are Amish as well—he grows soybean and corn in rotation—though they don't understand why someone would own his own planter and combine for what they consider a hobby farm. The girls' shouting outside, then a man's voice: "You only need three dribbles to make a move! You gonna let little sis school you?" Number Fifty-Two, unannounced. They don't see much of him these days but Nineteen's wife sucks in her breath. She likes them, just not around her girls.

"'Then he came to a dog,'" the boy reads. ""'Are you my mother?" he said to the dog.'"

"Sailboats are for cheapskates and Democrats," the senator says. His yacht is nearly sixty feet long. The transom drops like a tailgate to form a rear deck and this is where Nineteen stands with his wife, holding a rum and coke. He has been on vessels like private ocean liners, with white-uniformed crews, bodies in bikinis, trunks, hats to the back, but this is not the ocean and the senator is up for re-election.

The disgraced Hank Aaron hitter and the restaurateur lounge at the wet bar with the senator's daughter.

"A cap-and-trade bill would cost this state a hundred thousand jobs," the senator says. When he was mayor Nineteen's mother sat next to him at the fifty-yard line, fingering her rosary beads.

"Preachin to the choir," Nineteen slurs.

"Didn't you oppose the carbon tax?" Mrs. Nineteen is a registered Independent.

The senator smiles. His ice cracks. "How's your father these days?"

"You'd have to ask him." They haven't spoken since the day her husband was released.

Nineteen looks landward as if for the old stadium, sees only the sails, the gulls, the lake receding from green to blue to meet the bobbing skyline three miles away.

"Know your meat," the restaurateur advises the disgraced hitter. "An A-grade cut should be cherry red."

Nineteen moves toward the bar, where there is wraparound seating. He suddenly wants to talk to the restaurateur about aged prime, to the disgraced hitter about anything but baseball. He grabs for the deck rail, discovers there is no deck rail here. His wife's abbreviated scream. Cold slap on his back, barely liquid, and the lake seals him in itself. Strange how little panic he feels, still holding his glass as if he'd just stepped into another room. Dazzling underbelly of the surface. Somewhere below, fourteen thousand tons of his old house have been submerged to form an artificial reef. Imploded in sixty-two seconds.

In the mirror, shirtless, his gut forming a vertical crease as if subdividing. He leans forward, lets his arms dangle. The right is slightly bigger below the elbow. It won't hang quite straight.

He still has trouble saying no, and sometimes doesn't get the chance to. He is making payments on a hundred and eight credit cards, a hundred and twenty cell phones.

He keeps five teeth in a cup on a shelf in a room he calls his office.

Has trouble sleeping. Blue pills, white pills, the little pink ones when he's feeling his shoulder, or his hip, elbow, knee. He tapes electrodes to his back and sends electrical impulses to his spine from a little black box.

The tanning salons he opened with his sister have gone dark. He paid for her degree in finance but she doesn't return his calls. Some days it hurts just to shake hands.

He turns, twists his neck, left, right, looks at the scars that zipper his flesh like the seams of a creature constructed in a laboratory. Two fused vertebrae. Limps sometimes—played half a game with a broken ankle in Minnesota. Doesn't remember the other half.

He cries sometimes at tearjerkers. Cries now, not for the scars but what earned them.

His financial adviser says, "Wall Street puts the likelihood at forty percent," and tees off into a soft wind with a five iron. Par four. White glove.

"I've had worse odds."

"Think of it as a necessary adjustment, not a disaster."

"How much of an adjustment?"

"*If* there is a mild recession . . . say soft returns of about four percent on the year—but your NOI should remain positive."

Nineteen reaches into his cart bag for a sand wedge, finds his flask instead. They have no caddy. He used to wait till they got back to the clubhouse.

"And what if it's not so mild?"

"Well, then everything suffers. Office, warehouse, residential. No port in that storm."

Nineteen stands over the ball at address, the next hole five feet away. He is three strokes ahead. "But retail bounces the hardest."

"Think of it as an unwinding of excesses." The financial adviser's white hair is bunched in a visor cap, his face red but unworried. "Way to save par."

"I'm worried about Tampa. If I go vacant . . ."

"The bank converts the construction loan into a longer-term mortgage."

"Or they foreclose."

They drive left to avoid the big bunkers, white sand so soft you could drown in it. "I'm a fortune maker, not a fortune teller." The financial adviser never takes off his glove. "What is it your coach used to say? One play at a time?"

"Football is business but business ain't football," Nineteen says. "Advise me."

"I think you should think about tech. Jesus." The financial adviser is staring at what is basking between the flagstick and the edge of a salt marsh. It must be twelve feet long, nearly half of it tail.

"Don't you just love Florida?"

Glittering armour. Slit eyes. Pure life.

Disowned, disinherited, she still has in no particular order her children, their horses, her reading group, her Bikram, her animal rights, fossil fuels, genital mutilation, her Pinot Grigio; Toni Morrison, Henry James, Books Not Bullets. Her thickening neck. She talks about returning to school, finishing her degree, perhaps teaching.

In no particular order he has what he has, and sometimes she stands at his office door, knuckles poised to knock, hears ESPN and its countless iterations, hears the Bowls, the Tournaments, the Opens, the Cups, the Classics, the Invitationals, the Madness; he prefers baseball on the radio for Tom Hamilton's tenor: *Swing and a drive, way back and gone!*

She remembers the room before he called it his office.

She hears him now behind that door, alone or in company, shouting coverages from his leather throne, coaching his screen: "Eyes up! Eyes up!" Hears him crack open another dark ale, sixteen-ounce cans with his old younger self on the label, in action, in uniform; unsold cases fill the house.

Sometimes the room is quiet and she knows now what she might interrupt. She remembers when she was part of the silence on the other side, his face hidden in the hollow of her neck.

· · ·

"Remember Mile High?"

"I remember em all."

"The blizzard?"

"Got your bell rung a time or two."

"It's still ringing. There's always a price."

"Who you tellin."

"You gave more than you got."

"Yeah well, what goes around . . ."

"No one hit the A gap like you."

". . . can't even shoot hoops with my kids anymore."

"They grow up fast."

"Gotta ride one of those carts at the grocery store like them fat people."

"You are them fat people."

"Go ahead, make me laugh."

"You just need a good night's sleep."

"What's sleep?"

"Seriously."

"Seriously, either it ain't happening or I'm taking a twenty-hour nap."

"When I have trouble I just think about the tunnel. Coming out in that light?"

"Don't get me started on light. I'm wearing my Ray-Bans all the time. Wearing em right now with the TV off."

"Yeah I can tell over the phone. You turning into a vampire?"

"I'm turning into something . . . I don't recognize me. Start trippin over dumb shit . . ."

"Hey. Who was it got cut on Christmas Eve?"

"Can you tell I got a gun?"

"Was it . . . The hell you need a gun for, Fifty-Two?"

"No, a .44. Carbon mono wouldn't do it. Rat poison, Drano . . ."

"What are you talking about?"

"What am I talking about. Bitch turned em against me, says they're afraid of me. Says she caught me pissin in the oven once. Who does that?"

"There's only been you," he says.

"I know," she says sadly, having caught him at his keyboard in the act of fidelity.

The priest is a voice in darkness, behind a screen you'd use to keep out flies. "The Catechism teaches that the sexual function is meant to be enjoyed in the total meaning of mutual self-giving within the marital relationship of a man and a woman."

Nineteen requests an Act of Contrition. "Hails Marys, Our Fathers—just words," the voice says. He suggests Nineteen read Saint Augustine, and perhaps even consider psychotherapy.

"Think of what you learned on the field. The privilege. Life lessons and shit."

"Fuck that. What good are life lessons you can't use? Okay, how about: that which don't destroy you can still really fuck you up."

"I'd do it all over again."

"That's just the oxy talking."

"Johnnie Walker. But I'd do it for free."

"Yeah, okay. Me too—as a placekicker."

"You ain't weird enough to be a kicker."

"I'm getting there . . ."

"Who got cut on Christmas Eve? Was it Twenty-Eight?"

"Twenty-Eight broke both his arms so his wife had to wipe his ass."

"You do remember."

"I remember all that shit, it's the last two minutes I can't . . . Like my head sprung a leak. Gotta write shit on my hand like that guy in that movie."

"What movie?"

". . ."

"Fifty-Two?"

"So how is Tina these days?"

"Tina's *your* wife, Five-Two."

"Bitch turned em against me."

"Don't be that way. She was thinking about her kids. She still—"

"I just forget their names sometime. My head . . . eyes get so blurry . . . I just go off the grid. Gotta write shit on my hands like in that movie."

"Yeah, you said."

"Said what?"

"Forget about it. Forget golf."

"I don't want to forget . . ."

"I'll be down there and we'll just talk."

"We're talking now . . . I had my own dealership, man. Motherfuckers . . . How can you steal from yourself?"

"Some things they can never take away. Remember coming out of the tunnel?"

"I'd trade it all for eight good hours. Didn't even get a ring. Got two steel plates for an ankle. Thirteen screws. Walk like a fuckin pirate anymore."

"Thirteen? Hell, I only got two."

"Yeah I know how you hate to lose . . . I'm sorry about Indy."

"Fuck Indy. I'm over it. It wasn't life or death."

"Look who's talking. Man, look what time it is . . ."

"You there?"

". . . I'm sorry sir, you must have the wrong number. I'm a seller, not a buyer."

"Fifty-Two."

"Look at the time, I gotta get to the lot. Them cars don't move themselves."

The officer returns your license and registration. "Have you had any alcoholic beverages to drink?" he asks politely.

"Couple beers," you say.

"You sure it was just a couple? I'm noticing a strong smell—"

"Must be swamp gas."

"Excuse me?"

"I told you I was having dinner." You didn't say with whom.

"Would you mind stepping out of the vehicle for me, sir."

"Aw, bro. You said it was for speeding." But you comply. A warm night, muggy. Too dark to see beyond the mad strobe of his lights, but you hear the amphibian chorus, song of South Florida. Behind your SUV he asks if you're carrying any weapons.

"Just my cannon arm." The lights are unbearable.

"Excuse me?"

"Little joke . . ."

"I notice you're having a little trouble walking," the officer says.

"I got two screws holding my ankle together." But, actually, there is a smell. Marshy, vaguely flatulent. Down here there is always water nearby.

"Would you mind taking a little test for me, sir? Something we call a walk and turn?"

"I don't do too good on tests. I tole you—"

"Sounds like you're having a little trouble talking as well."

"Bit off the tip of my tongue. My offensive line couldn't . . . You know. Wide zone blocking scheme. You look like you played some ball."

"Can you walk a straight line for me, sir?"

"You said thirteen over the limit."

"Sir." A car passes.

"Come on man, I just lost my best friend. You know who I am. I won't even drive—I'll go sit in the swamp."

"Sir, let me remind you this is being recorded on dashboard video."

"Like you're on *Candid Camera*? Come on, bro."

"I'm not bro, okay? Are you refusing to take a field sobriety test?"

"I tole you, my line."

Tell him you had dinner with the mayor, the chief of police. His radio crackles.

"Are you willing to take a preliminary breath test?"

"I heard those things . . . don't always get it right."

"So you're refusing the PBT?"

"Just gimme a break. I'll go sing with the fuckin frogs."

"Watch your language, sir." His hand moves toward his holster.

"Man, I just lost my father."

"I thought it was your friend."

"He *was* my best friend . . . dropping like flies . . ."

"At this point . . ." On suspicion. Probable cause.

"God bless you, man. Do what you gotta do."

But the cuffs are appalling. "Do I have to . . . I'm not gonna hurt you."

You've talked to fucking presidents.

"Do you know who I am?" *10-24 (officer needs assistance)*. "Do you know who I was?"

"My client has become the latest victim of the economic down-turn and collapse of the real estate market," Number Nineteen's attorney says in a prepared statement. "He has misplaced trust and reliance on those closest to him to manage his business and finances."

On the LIST OF CREDITORS HOLDING 20 LARGEST UNSECURED CLAIMS, Nineteen's ex-wife is fourth with a divorce settlement of $3,040,000.00.

"Luckily we live in a country that believes in second chances, and my client intends to overcome this adversity as he has so many times on the field of play."

Nine point seven mill to Florida Bank on a foreclosure. A hundred and fifty-eight bucks to the City of Sunrise for a water bill. The IRS, lawyers who charge six hundred dollars an hour, reimbursements for car accidents, pool cleaners and lawn service, his chiropractor.

In Schedule F of the Summary of Schedules, he owes his sister and brother unspecified amounts for unspecified claims. Child support.

He is reputed to have forty-four dollars in his checking account, a reporter says.

"'The most effective and efficient method of liquidating these assets is through Chapter 7,' the Chapter 11 trustee appointed in October said in a prepared statement," a reporter writes.

Nineteen saw them every other weekend when he was still in Florida, but now that he's back up north for good he's at their mercy once a month. The oldest is of age now and elected not to come. There is not much to do. The ATVs are gone, and the horses, both ridden off by creditors. Some of the okapi were sold to private owners, the rest donated to zoos. The one she named Woody died.

His fields are fallow. He talks about converting to forestry. A bat drowned in the swimming pool.

The basketball court is still playable, so they settle on shooting games—Horse, Twenty-one, Thirty-three. The girl is a fair shot but softball is her métier. The boy, fourteen going on forty, is not unathletic but not interested. Doesn't believe in competition. "I compete with myself," he says, and his sister, batting nearly .700 this year and all but committed to Syracuse (D-1), says, "That what you do in your room all day?"

"Be nice." Nineteen had fifteen Vicodin for breakfast. Hasn't shit for a week. They go inside.

He lives like a child who woke up one day abandoned by his parents and must fend for himself. His attempt at tidying up before going to the airport (he remembered this time) served mainly to rearrange the disorder: clothes, fast-food wrappers, mail opened and not, cans of his namesake ale crumpled and fallen, reeking.

He promised to make them dinner, but when they see him trying to cut a loaf of French bread with a hacksaw, they decide to order in.

Sitting, they repair to their phones. "This place used to be filled with people," the boy says, scrolling. "Now it just smells." But how does he live in Florida and stay so pale? Computer tan, Nineteen decides and cracks open another can. He asks after his eldest.

"She has a tattoo on her back," the middle child says. His scarred old helmet sits on top of her head. "She got it the day you didn't have to pay her child support anymore."

"She's young, wild, and free." The boy says it like a catch-phrase of which he doesn't approve.

"How about you?" Nineteen asks him. "You discover girls yet?"

"Mom has. She wears braces now, too," his son says.

The girl doesn't look up: "Shut up, bitch."

Nineteen wants to say something but his mouth keeps filling with beer. Then he forgets why he wanted to say something. The doorbell rings.

They try to decide what to watch with dinner. "Let's see *The Notebook* again," the girl says. "I want to see Dad cry."

"I don't," Nineteen's son says and suggests the Lyrids, streaming for free in the eastern sky. They go out on the back porch, eat Chinese food and hear a coyote under stars that hide from the city. Some of them move, trail a thin blue flame, then disappear.

How could he not have known? Of course he would be the last but had anyone tried to tell him? Thinking back, there were whispers, intimations, exchanged glances, encrypted silence, but even if he'd picked up on it, even if he hadn't pretended oblivion, who could believe such a thing without proof and, once such proof were available, who could bring himself to examine the evidence?

But to find out the way he found out.

He hopes she is at least practicing some sort of safety, using something, protecting herself. He supposes she is an adult. (He is not always sure of their ages.) It is, after all, her body, or was, yes, age of consent, but this is what she consents to? What she chooses to do with the gift? (Is it what they call acting out?) He thought she wanted to teach yoga, Downward Dog. How he could not have known.

The name she invented for herself has five Xs.

But to find out the way he did: first-person from behind, finger on the touchpad, other hand fisted around himself, drunk, trying to synchronize his strokes . . . Straps and blocks, a full-length mirror . . . Petite, black hair, tattoo on the small of her back, the initials within, but when she finally looked up it was too late. Zoom into the mirror as he broke the plane and she looked up from the other side of it, the face he first saw not twenty years ago making its way to him, to this, on her knees, mouth open, grunting and gasping in fifteen inches of liquid crystal display . . . And him finishing in spite of it all.

From across the fields, howling at dusk. A lone creature separated from its pack.

Sober, he doesn't recognize himself; the antique mirror has become a door and he opens it.

His glass is still full—normally he takes it straight from the can, but supposes some decorum is called for—and he sets it on the soapstone countertop. Reaches for the brown plastic containers, the round blue pills, the long white ones. He pours the rest of them into his hand with great care, sits down heavily on the edge of the claw-foot tub, and is that how he will be found? In a cold dry bath like a porcelain casket?

He presses them into his mouth a few at a time like bits of candy, washing the bitterness down with his signature dark ale—last can in the house—till glass and hand are empty, his head not quite. Last thoughts appear in rather orderly fashion, like rolling credits. Pills are a woman's way out, they say, but that is the least of his worries now. Fifty-two held a gun to his heart. First he tried antifreeze—*Didn't work but I'm cooler in the summer and warmer in the winter.* Did he really say that?

43

Winter clamours for admittance.

He hears glass break. Didn't feel himself letting go, and that is how you let go. Hears the wind calling him and tries to call back. How he loves a blizzard, loved playing in them. Out here the snow stays clean. In Pop Warner Coach yelled everything twice.   Let it bury him then, not to be discovered till *Move the feet! Move the feet!*   She tied her hair back and hung it over her breast   He tries and falls to his knees, a numbness creeping up like a rising tide, his body betraying him one last time.   Fireworks in daylight girl in the bleachers playing the violin   reaching into the blur for something, the edge of any-thing, to pull himself   *Who's not moving the feet? Who's dogging it here?*   but wasn't it better before, no coach, no crowd, just whoever else wanted to play, even when it got too dark to see the ball?

A fter the treatment there was still time to meet an old friend for nine holes at a public course in Boca Raton. The Institute was an hour and a half from Fort Lauderdale but his flight didn't leave till evening. From Jupiter he headed south. Palmetto, cypress, guava; Walmart, smooth jazz. The interstate would have been faster but he took Highway 1 to stay close to the edge, crossing the canal when he could to South Ocean Boulevard to glimpse the beach between high-rise timeshares and hotels. You could smell it. He was still sober but fairly euphoric with well-being. Even passing West Palm, where in a previous life he'd held a membership, was relatively painless. There loomed a threat of rain but it was not yet hurricane weather.

In Delray Beach he turned west, drove through an upscale wetland of small lakes, polo fields, country clubs, twelve-foot hedges that concealed residential estates. Tuscany Lakes swung by on his left just before the turnoff to Southwind Municipal Golf Course. He had friends who lived there, in gated communities, but the house he'd shared with his family would have required considerable detour. It was not the third weekend anyway.

He was running early. He sat in the parking lot at Southwind trying not to argue with sports radio, contemplating his swing, then his treatment. He'd first heard about Doctor Q through the neurologist who had diagnosed him—more by way of warning than recommendation. The Doctor was a board-certified anaesthesiologist who'd started practicing addiction treatment out of his office in a Tampa Bay hospital. Patients spent four to six hours in anaesthetic sleep while he administered intravenous medications that averted withdrawal symptoms. Word got around—Ricki Lake, Dr. Phil, CNN—and soon prospective patients and their families were sleeping in the hallway outside his office. He'd leased another three thousand square feet from the hospital but when even this proved inadequate to hope and demand, Doctor Q and his wife bought a former sugar plantation in Jupiter at public auction and turned it into the South Florida Wellness Institute.

Four buildings on thirty-seven acres. A seven-member staff—three of them former patients—composed of Evangelical Christians who considered their work a spiritual mission. Their employer (the one who signed the cheques) spent more time on his phone than on Scripture, and in manner and dress resembled a Cadillac salesman more than a physician. But he claimed not only to detox addicts in four to six hours, but that he could cure certain forms of arthritis, reverse the effects of aging by fifteen years or so, treat autism, Parkinson's, Alzheimer's, MS, epilepsy, and other neurological disorders.

Nineteen had not come there to detox.

He wasn't sure who had come up with the sobriquet. And though his sojourns to Florida might have been described as quixotic, that was not what the Q stood for.

The initial therapy had taken two weeks. Its components were somewhat mysterious: serotonin, intravenous fluids, vitamin supplements, a pill under the tongue. Fifteen hour-long sessions during which Nineteen sat in an upholstered recliner in a room containing three rows of upholstered recliners, all of them occupied (conversation was not encouraged), an IV needle piercing the top of his hand, a coldness stealing in, watching meditative videos on flatscreen (running water, wind blowing through trees), Yanni and Kitaro administered shimmering through headphones. When someone asked what was in the bag hanging over their heads, the Doctor replied, "A better life" or "It's proprietary," but by the time Nineteen left, the worst symptoms had receded— the headaches, the ringing, the blurring, the sudden depths. Reprieve from the permanent hangover.

"The problem," he told the Doctor after his follow-up—just four days this time—"is that the good times don't seem to last." He didn't say anything about the blackouts.

The Doctor was wearing a tan blazer over a black turtleneck. A chain would not have been out of place, and he wore a ponytail. "Ever been in a car accident?" he began, and Nineteen held up a pre-emptive hand. He'd heard the analogy more than once: the brain banging against the inside of the skull as the head impacts the windshield . . . an "accident" endured multiple times every Sunday for how many seasons, etc. Had used it himself, in fact.

The Doctor took another tack: "Let's look at some pictures," and they went into the conference room. The long oak table, a cup of sharpened pencils in the middle. Nineteen sat while the Doctor switched on the lightboard where the PET scans hung like postcards from the phantom zone. The glowing misshapen fruit of the brain, the Rorschach symmetry of the hemispheres. Seat of his soul, before and after. Yellow patches of dead and dying tissue where blood vessels had bruised themselves against the brain case, scarring down, restricting the flow of blood and inhibiting the healing process.

The Doctor pointed rather excitedly. "Look at this. Left frontal lobe: seventy percent improvement." Nineteen tried to remember if pretty colours were good news or bad. "Right occipital: *ninety-seven percent*. Look at that fucker! My favourite shade of blue." Then the not-so-good. "But the right frontal lobe: only sixteen percent. Right anterior cingulate: twenty-two percent. And the right medial frontal"—a kind of sigh—"only a half-percent improvement."

Nineteen gestured at the pictures of his brain. "So that's why it doesn't last? Is that what that means?"

"It means reversing neurological damage takes time. PET scans can't tell us everything, but they do tell us we've made progress. What you might be thinking of as a relapse is just two steps forward, one step back. We'll get there."

Nineteen nodded slowly. "Okay. Who needs a right anti . . . whatever, anyway."

He thought he was being funny (another symptom) but the Doctor frowned. He looked at his phone and said, "You're free to try alternative treatments."

"You *are* the alternative treatment."

"Exactly. You've been to neurologists. I believe you've tried the oxygen?"

It wasn't a question. Nineteen had lain in the hyperbaric chamber Namath had sworn by, only to find its results even more ephemeral than those of the Institute.

Hypnosis, acupuncture, sensory deprivation, marijuana, fish oils. Alternatives.

"You heard of this GyroStim thing?" he suddenly remembered. A gyroscopically-mounted chair that could spin you on any axis in any direction at speeds used for training astronauts. An NHL wing claimed it had saved his career, and though Nineteen at the moment was at a loss for his name, *The Right Stuff* had been a favourite film.

The Doctor's smile could be infectious. "Tell you what. Get back on 95 and take the I-4 exit to Epcot. There's a ride there called Mission: Space. You can get the same effect for hella lot cheaper and you get to wear the suit and helmet. My kids love it."

Nineteen was unable to imagine the Doctor as Disney paterfamilias, posing with someone in a dog suit, but his point was taken. A thousand dollars a go and a waiting list of over a year, and the last time Nineteen had been to an amusement park he'd climbed into something resembling a giant mechanical spider, made the operator stop halfway through, and had to lie down on a park bench till he could allow himself to be driven home.

The Doctor was thumbing his phone again and Nineteen had used the interruption (or was *he* the distraction?) to hurriedly squeeze his hand and see himself out. He took a side exit to the parking lot. The waiting room would be filled with the variously afflicted drinking complimentary bottled water as from the taps at Lourdes, eight thousand miracles and counting, and there was the large framed photo on the wall behind the receptionist: Nineteen holding a football, the Doctor at his side holding a human brain. He'd been given a reduced fee for the endorsement. The contract covered an initial treatment and follow-up, and the subject of money would no doubt rear its head.

But sitting in his car in the clubhouse lot at Southwind, he was sure he was still feeling better. His phone hummed. He thought it might be the doctor but it was his old Lightning teammate and golf partner, a lower handicapper and now a high school coach in Coral Springs, begging off. Nineteen barely troubled himself with the explanation; down here they played football in the spring. He pushed the buttons. *No worries.*

So he went to the driving range instead, an aqua setup where you could drive balls directly into a lake. Afterward, nearing the airport, the highway took him across Northeast Seventh Street, where his steakhouse had briefly reopened after *E. coli* had shut him down for a month. The girl had recovered but needed a kidney transplant. She was four years old and the building was now an animal hospital. This heartened him till it made him think of horses, which made him think of the okapi, which made him think of his children . . . No train of thought was safe. Florida was a minefield.

After returning the rental and getting his boarding pass, Nineteen dutifully endured the security screening—he could not afford the extra hundred dollars for PreCheck but always thanked the TSA employees and often said "God bless"—then headed for the food court en route to his gate. Not long ago it would have been the cocktail lounge. At Burger King he bought a garden salad with Tendergrill chicken and a packet of Lite honey balsamic dressing. He asked for a cup of water; he had not had a drink, or any other kind of painkiller, in four months.

The only empty table stood within view of the outsize television screen hanging from the ceiling. The one next to it was occupied by a fortyish man, a slightly younger-looking woman, and an adolescent boy wearing earbuds. They all had phones out and they were all eating meat. A family. Nineteen sat and tore open the packet. A hundred twenty calories but he used only half of it. He tried not to look up. The draft was approaching and ESPN was evaluating the current prospects. Highlights from the

Combine, the League's annual meat market, young men in black pressure-wear like superhero costumes, running sprints, cone drills, lifting weights, getting timed and measured. Nineteen remembered his own combine performance, which hadn't required an invitation. Now they were using virtual reality goggles, wore workout shirts fitted with sensors measuring heart rate, respiration, acceleration. So much for intangibles.

He'd always thought the best way to scout players was to watch them play.

"Enjoying the underwear Olympics?" Nineteen turned. The man at the next table wore a floral shirt and held an expensive phone, had a thick tanned neck. Had some money but worked with his hands—construction, Teamsters, the kind of prosperity you didn't see much of these days. He nodded back up at the screen, at a quarterback from Louisville. "Kid ran a 4.38. With speed like that he could throw to himself."

"But can he play a 4.38," Nineteen said.

"Kid must've threw the ball seventy yards in the drills," the man said. "We're talking Vick, Newton, cannon on wheels. What's not to like."

Nineteen had an answer but was reluctant to share it. The purported dual threats did not impress him. They took away the middle of the field, which undermined the deep game, and they were exciting to watch but took too much punishment to sustain a long career, develop as passers. Maybe it was just too street for him.

"Ask me that in a year or three," he said.

"Be fantasy-friendly anyway," the man said. "You play? You don't have to win to win, you know."

Nineteen also had an opinion of fantasy football, which he also withheld. The boy with the earbuds made a sound. They looked at him but he was addressing the game on his phone, gun-shaped hand pointing at yet another felled opponent. He wore a hood over his baseball cap and looked effectively sealed off from the world. There were teenagers who'd become millionaires shooting zombies in tournaments.

"That your boy?" It seemed safe to speak in the third person.

"Till I can prove otherwise."

"He play sports?" He was sure the man had played in high school. A wrestler for sure.

"On his Xbox."

"Well there's this thing called depth perception?" the woman said. She wore nylon warm-ups and had not looked up.

"You can bowl with one eye," the man said defensively. "There's diabetic athletes. Look at Jay Cutler."

"Yeah, look at him," the woman said, a bad joke Nineteen would not have indulged. But he was not sure what they were talking about, only that he did not want to be audience to the re-enactment of an old quarrel.

"Maybe if he'd taken better care of himself," her husband said.

"It's not his fault, it's Type 2. They don't always catch it in time."

"The other one's no picnic either."

The boy's mother looked at Nineteen. "It's Type 2. They had to put one of those pumps in his stomach."

"Can you tell which eye is fake?" the father said.

"I'm sorry," Nineteen said, not just for the boy. He noticed the man staring at him. It was a look he knew well, one of hazy familiarity that was usually dismissed as error. He used half the packet, exercised, cleansed, used his right hand as much as possible to hide the tremor in his left, and the replacement option he'd purchased from the company that used the word "system"

52

instead of "hair" was not excessively full and was credibly grey, but he was rarely mistaken for who he'd once been. He looked forward to being nobody.

"So where you folks headed?" he felt entitled to ask.

The man nodded grimly in some direction beyond the food court. "The murder capital of the world."

"It isn't the murder capital," his wife said.

"Hell on earth. State Department says we shouldn't even be going there."

"That's the mainland. The islands are still safe." She kept Nineteen in her confidence. "We're going to the islands—the big one. Roatan. Ever been?"

Nineteen shook his head. His tropical destinations had consisted mainly of Barbados, the Saints Maarten and John. He supposed he'd heard of it. "I hear it's nice down there," he said.

"We're not going for the snorkelling, bro."

"They're doing some wonderful things there, medical things," she said. "Things that aren't FDA-approved up here." She made quotes with her fingers.

Her husband scoffed. "Eff the FDA."

"Things with stem cells," the woman said.

Nineteen repeated the words to himself. Like other terms and names—Benghazi, WikiLeaks, emissions tax—they were in the air and vaguely familiar, were waiting for him in that inexhaustible reservoir of fact that must be rescued from fiction to become knowledge and even wisdom, but must compete for our attention with pornography, gaming, what passes for social intercourse, videos of small animals, creators who create nothing but followers. Something did occur to him then, some controversy which he then warily cited; Nineteen believed all life was sacred, especially that of the unborn.

"Those are foetal cells," the wife and mother said emphatically.

"The ones from abortions," her husband said helpfully.

"These are adult stem cells," she reassured Nineteen. "They're from your own body." She glanced at her son and lowered her voice. "His what-do-you-call-it, pancreas, isn't producing enough insulin. So they'll harvest some of the cells from his blood, grow a few million more, then inject them back in and they know just where to go." She stopped whispering. "They've had Type 1 patients who have stayed off insulin for a year. It's documented."

"There's ziplining down there too," the boy murmured. He still hadn't looked up.

His mother was unabashed. "Nice of you to drop by."

"Thought you were playing with your Android," the father said, and seemed to find the remark worth repeating. He got into the spirit of things. "Seriously. You wouldn't believe what they can do with that shit. Grow organs, cure cancer, Parkinson's, that one where you start going soft upstairs . . . Old-Timer's Disease." That pleased him as well.

The woman was learning from her phone. "And it's not the murder capital anymore." She shared the screen. "Number three now, it says."

"God bless the Masturbation Highway," the man said.

"God bless," Nineteen repeated absently. He still wasn't sure what stem cells were. He glanced at the TV screen, then looked out into the concourse. Travellers pushing rollaboards ahead of them like leashed pets. A tattered man with plastic bags for luggage; there were homeless living in airports. The woman followed his gaze and seemed to realize something. "We really should be getting to our gate." She stood and began methodically organizing their fast-food trash, neither looking at nor speaking to Nineteen again. As if she had ended a call.

But her husband was staring again. The Look, and now he took it a step further and said, "Have I seen you somewhere before?"

"Not that I'm aware." The man came forward and offered his hand just in case. Nineteen took it carefully; he'd broken every finger at least once.

"Good luck," he called to the boy as they entered the stream of departure. He'd been unable to tell which eye could see.

"Same to you," the boy said, and said something else, and Nineteen thought he heard the man ask his wife what sounded like, "Think that's his real hair?"

He ate his salad in the company of his device.

She waited for him in Baggage Claim wearing a cowboy hat and a white blouse and a Bluetooth earpiece. They'd met at a Step meeting in a church basement (#3: Surrender), exchanged numbers and spent four hours on the phone afterwards. They'd rescued each other from drink, and then, tired of the semicircle of caffeinated confession and the fellowship's dismal five-percent success rate, rescued each other from AA, retaining only the Serenity Prayer and some dependable slogans. Neither had lapsed since, though she also credited her clean time to the Supreme Being, of course, and to His subsidiary, the Big Pink, for which she was now an Independent Sales Director.

"'Wherever you go, there you are,'" he said, snatching his bag from the carousel.

"'Let go and let God,'" she said.

They kissed and held hands on the way to Short Term Parking.

Nineteen's girlfriend drove the black Camry she'd earned supervising a twenty-six-member unit with nearly fifty thousand dollars of production in six months. (She could have opted for a Chevy Equinox, and though she was steadfast about buying

American, Japanese mileage was just too crazy.) Next level, if she doubled production, was the pearlized pink Cadillac SRX SUV with sun roof, OnStar, seat warmers, a cooler in the trunk. Twenty-five hundred lipsticks a month. You could keep it for two years, or opt for nine hundred dollars monthly instead but, at the end of the day, it was about neither car nor cash.

"Better put that in the backseat," she said, looking at his bag. The Camry had fifteen cubic feet of cargo space, but she'd retained the customer base she'd built as a Consultant and the trunk was filled with product, some of which had found its way into the faux-suede interior.

He did as she suggested and got in the passenger side. He preferred to be driven.

As an Independent Sales Director who wore the pin and enhancer and earned a Unit Volume Commission of thirteen percent, Nineteen's girlfriend no longer had time for part-time telemarketing or UberX or online classes, but was still his nominal manager—the position itself was nominal—and she debriefed him in queue at the exit gate, a blacklist of unreturned calls and withdrawn commitments, from youth organizations, event managers, a non-profit with the word hope in its name; from a producer of what is called reality television, who'd courted Nineteen when the wheels were falling off and he was in the news, going bankrupt, resisting arrest, slurring his speech on-air as a preseason colour analyst, backing his Range Rover into a mounted policeman in Miami.

Fathering a daughter who wasn't returning calls either, who'd given herself a name he couldn't repeat even in thought.

He unbit his tongue. "Anything else?"

"There's Akron next month." First pitch, possible autos after. "If you're still up for it."

"Who ain't up for Akron." He couldn't resist being the occasional Somebody, and there would be nothing to refuse soon enough. Sometimes they even paid.

She gave a dollar to someone holding a cardboard sign at the foot of the on-ramp, yelled: "This doesn't make you a bad person." We are all carrying signs, she'd learned.

They took 480 East. Noise abatement walls had been recently erected and for long stretches it was like driving in an arid canal lined with billboards. Nineteen's girlfriend docked her phone and instructed the car to play what is called Adult Contemporary through its six standard speakers. A compromise. Her own tastes ran to Patty Loveless and Patsy Cline, and once upon a time, in pursuit of a dream that did not require wholesale monthly minimums, she'd spent three years in Nashville, waiting tables, tending bar, renting a room in a house, then sharing it, singing to brown-liquor drunks and rowdies at open mics where only other singers and songwriters were listening. The Bluebird, the Orchid Lounge, someone's cabin in the Smokies ("Just you and me, writing songs, making music. No strings"). She'd miscarried, auditioned for the last season of *Star Search*, was passed over, moved to the other side of the bar, moved back home, was briefly, violently married, enrolled in flight attendant school, lost her job after 9/11, lost a hair salon, enlisted, was medically discharged after a nervous breakdown, reinstated by United, laid off again during the recession, drank all the while and by now had something to sing about but started instead going to meetings in church basements, discovered the Pink Dream (more often cause than cure), Nineteen, and now drove a shiny black sedan you could talk to with eight-way adjustable seats and Entune Premium Audio, which she would have the use of for two years or until re-qualification.

Nineteen hated country music. He heard her sing only once, at a karaoke fundraiser. Faith, faded wallpaper, loss. Alcohol and tribulation had tempered her voice, not ruined it, and he'd wiped his eyes, though he cried easily these days.

She taught him to line-dance. She'd been a fan of his when so was everyone else, and when everyone else wasn't. Her loyalty was unconditional; she knew what it was like to sing to empty seats.

"Hey stranger," she said, and why did she call him that? She asked about Florida.

"We talked on the phone."

"You gave me your flight number."

"I was thinking maybe . . . We talked."

"So let's talk some more."

He sighed. He was not used to her undivided attention nor did he want it now. "After this I can't afford him anymore anyway," he said flatly; he'd drawn his player pension early and was getting half of what he'd have gotten had he waited another ten years.

A pickup overtook them, swung in front fast and close with no signal. She flashed her brights, touched her heart, then touched Nineteen's hand. "'Surrender doesn't mean giving up,'" she quoted, "'it means coming over to the winning side,'" and he thought she was going to bring up The Lawsuit. Class action. Six thousand brain-battered former players versus the League whose initials meant Not For Long, so they used to say, and Nineteen had been invited to participate. The neurologist who'd inadvertently referred him to Doctor Q had declared him eligible, but Nineteen refused to join and in this he was unequivocal. It wasn't just a game, never had been, and now it was under siege. He'd let his own son play, if he played. He was sure he'd known what he was getting into.

He expected her to bring it up and was going to mention the family at the airport pre-emptively, but then she said, "Incoming," and told her phone, "Answer call." She no longer said, "I have to take this."

Nineteen looked out the window. They were crossing the monumental overpass that spanned the river valley named by the Iroquois, beneath them business parkways, an old drive-in, the vast white dome that looked ominously science-fictional but housed an indoor driving range. The obligatory bike path. He heard his girlfriend talking to an Independent Beauty Consultant, or a Star Consultant, or a Star Team Builder about offspring units, wholesale purchase volume. He looked back inside, at what his suitcase shared the backseat with: wrinkle filler, lifting serum, spot reducers, toning lotion. The liniments of rejuvenation. She used them and swore by them and sold them, went beyond them to the knife, to lower-lid blepharoplasty (they scraped the fat out of your eye bags), had undergone firming and augmentation—not that he was complaining, but he understood it wasn't just vanity; he knew as well as anyone that your body is never quite your own.

She was otherwise petite and wore sunglasses and from a distance passed for thirty.

"Remember what she said at Seminar," she said to whomever she was saying it to. Sisters in success. "It ain't frontloading, you just can't sell from an empty wagon." Her little-girl voice could harden into a kind of ruthlessness and Nineteen found this out of character but hardening in another way. He thought about putting a hand between her legs. Unit Volume Bonus, Unit Circle Bonus, Star Consultant Bonus—it seemed to have nothing to do with customers, but you couldn't use the P-word; she preferred to call it dual marketing. A free country. No one had a gun to anyone's head. He'd gone to the doctor of his own volition and if he wasn't sure what the plastic bag was dripping into his veins, it probably didn't matter anymore anyway. But to whom or what would he turn when it was empty?

"So there was this family in the food court, at the airport," he said carefully. The call seemed to be over. "They were going to Honduras."

"Not even a Red Jacket and she's talking pink suit." Smiling. "Silly bitch."

"Well, sort of Honduras."

She grew fond: "Such a sweetheart though. Honduras."

"Actually I think they said it was an island around there." He tried to remember. "Starts with an R."

"Aruba. No, that's . . ."

"Central America."

"Starts with an R." She instructed her phone to look up Honduras.

"Yeah, this family. They had this kid."

"Oh right, all those kids."

"No, they . . . What kids?"

"Crossing the border."

"You're talking about Mexico?"

"Well, coming *through* Mexico, these kids. I mean like ten years old. Alone. Nine. Their parents are . . . Is that where they're coming from?"

"Is *where* where they're coming from?" He struggled to hang on to his thread.

"Well they're poor. Starving? Like the ones you can sponsor once a month?" He tried not to see the ads, the barefoot brown lives you could save for the price of a cup of coffee a day. Changing the channel before the tears came. "You've heard about it. The President?" Her phone had become an infotainment screen. "'Illegal alien children.' Really?"

"What? But *these* parents, this family I'm talking about, the son has diabetes."

"No jobs, gangs—just don't bring that shit up here, thank you. We're so lucky, you know. We should send money." Then she began to think Pink aloud. It usually went there.

"There's some kind of clinic down there."

". . . and such beautiful skin."

"The parents, they think they might be able to cure him there. Or at least—"

"Authorized distributorships in Guatemala, El Salvador . . ."

"Are you reading or driving?"

". . . a free facial. I'd even spring for a starter kit. A woman can have an empty stomach but she's got to have her lip—" She sounded alarmed: "Your son has diabetes?"

"No, this kid! They're taking him to a clinic on this island! Roanoke or something." He knew it wasn't Roanoke. "They're using—"

She spoke to her phone.

Nineteen turned away. It had almost happened. He'd given himself a headache—or worsened the one that never quite abated. He looked at his own phone, then out the window again. The interchange was coming up and they were passing the vast tract of land where the world's largest indoor mall had once stood, where a portion of it remained, though not for long. Bulldozers, monuments of rubble. What would grow there? He'd heard rumours of an Amazon fulfillment centre—order pickers trying to keep up with robots, miles of conveyor belts. Fourteen football fields. How about nothing instead? Leave it at zero, plant some grass; Number Nineteen, former real estate developer and erstwhile farmer, found a measure of relief in open spaces.

They segued smoothly onto 422. He would be on his farm in twenty minutes or so and he wondered if she'd mention selling it again.

"Roatan," she said suddenly and he looked at her, pretending to know what she was talking about.

It did not call itself a nursing home and was located on a state road near a country club and a junior college campus and not much else. Sometimes passing traffic had to stop for deer. Canada geese. It resembled a small upscale resort and in the back was a courtyard with a putting green, closed-circuit TV cameras, and a seven-foot brick wall.

Nineteen met Coach's wife in the parking lot, a compact, red-haired woman in a long fleece vest who barely came to his chest when they hugged. He remembered when her hair was another colour but, except for that, she'd allowed herself to grow old.

"Ernest and some of the boys have been out. I'm sorry you missed them."

"Me too," he said. He would see them at the reunion. He didn't mention Florida.

"He asked about you and I thought, while there's still time . . . I can't guarantee anything, though. He called me Priscilla Presley the other day."

"Maybe he'll call me Elvis," Nineteen said, to his horror.

"It's really pretty swanky inside, you'll see." She faltered, looked down. "I hope you don't think I'm being a cunt."

Nineteen had never heard her use the word on herself before. He said he understood, regretted that as well, and they went inside.

An elegantly appointed lobby. Long carpeted halls, chande-liers, wallpaper, stuffed chairs. Their footsteps were soundless, the staff wore dark blue scrubs. She primed him as they walked through: use a kind voice, don't quiz. Don't pretend you under-stand. There was a beauty salon. Grand piano. Activities in the activity room—board games for the memory-impaired. Two living rooms with fireplaces, big windows. A circle of empty chairs. There were private apartments, semi-private apartments, companion apartments—doors were open and Nineteen tried not to look as they passed. It was not the nursing home his mother had worked in; you almost couldn't smell it.

The patients—or were they to be called residents?—were neat and clean and wore dignified new clothes regardless of how ill-fitting, how palsied or bewildered the wearer, some gripping walkers, moving in laborious considered steps.

They heard an invisible machine beep. Meaningful Moments, trademarked.

"And not a single rocking chair," Coach's wife said.

Her husband sat in a sunroom wearing a fedora and a sweater vest. Nineteen had never seen him dressed that way. An attendant sat nearby.

"He used to wear the colours, then all of a sudden doesn't want them anymore. He got quite . . . insistent," she said. "Tried to set them on fire. That was one of the reasons."

They weren't alone; Nineteen glanced briefly around with a fixed smile on his face. The attendant rose and said something about dentures in a low voice.

"I'll take care of it," Coach's wife said and the young man left.

Coach was looking out the window. They stood before him and he looked between them. His glasses had slid down his nose.

His wife fixed them and kissed him and said, "I brought someone to see you. Look who I brought."

"Someone to see," Coach said out the window.

"We should sit," his wife said, and Nineteen moved a couple of chairs.

"You asked about him the other day."

"Sure." He was still looking out the window.

"Coach," Nineteen said. He looked at Coach's wife.

She kind of smiled. "What else are you going to call him. I do."

"Coach, we used to . . . We worked together. I played for you, remember?"

Coach nodded. "You prayed for me."

Nineteen didn't correct him; he tried to remember you weren't supposed to use the word remember. "Can you look at me?"

He looked at his wife instead. "Sure."

She laughed sweetly, a practiced sound. "No babe, look at *him*."

"Coach," Nineteen said. "How are you?"

"I'm itchy," Coach said, and Nineteen could have cried.

His wife tried to reboot his memory. She asked him if he knew his name. He did, and the year he was born, but when she asked him how old he was he said he was sixteen.

"Do you know where you were born?" she asked.

He pondered, then said, "In the hospital!" as if at a revelation. They laughed and he with them like he'd been in on it all along.

What he'd had for dinner. The names of his children. What year it was. The state he lived in.

"Sure I don't remember," he said, and Nineteen thought of the questions they'd ask you on the sideline, after the smelling salts.

"Did you like the ice cream we had yesterday?" she asked.

"Did you speak German as a child?" someone else said and Nineteen half turned.

There was another family in the sunroom, conducting another gentle interrogation: an old woman clutching a doll, answering questions while her inquisitor held a camera.

"Do you know what you did before you retired?" Coach's wife asked.

"Sure," he said, reasonable and matter-of-fact. "I dug up spuds in Idaho."

You could hear the piano in the activity room playing the "Ode to Joy."

"That's not all you did, Coach," Nineteen said now. Coach looked at him. "Do you know why I call you that?"

"Sure."

"We all did, Coach. The team. I wore number nineteen. I was your starter till—" He didn't want him to recall everything. "Do you know who I am now?"

"Sure," Coach said. "Brian."

"Brian's your son," his wife said.

"Brian was Eighty-Six!" Coach said with sudden vehemence, then looked at Nineteen for a moment as if he would wink. "Women."

His wife chuckled but Nineteen was afraid he'd shut the door. Coach was right about the other Brian, a wideout from Boston College. He tried to mine the vein.

"That's right, Brian was Eighty-Six. Can you re—Can you think of anyone else? Do you know who Forty-Four was?"

"We had ice cream," Coach said, and Nineteen looked away. He'd wanted to hug him but was afraid to.

"Did you like the ice cream, sweetie?" Coach's wife said.

Nineteen reset. "'There's only the next play,'" he quoted. "Remember that? You must have said it a hundred times."

"A hundred times . . ." Coach laughed. He put his hands in his pockets.

"'The heart ain't just a muscle,'" his wife said.

"'There's a gleam, men.' How about that one?" Nineteen said. "Three Rivers? Halftime?"

Coach smiled. "There's a gleam?"

"Monday Night in Three Rivers. We pulled it off. Remember the fake spike?"

He looked at Coach's wife and apologized. He'd forgotten again.

"It probably doesn't matter," she said.

"Three rivers," Coach said. "Tie my own flies."

Nineteen persisted. "Then on the plane ride back, we had to turn around. Do you know why, Coach?"

"There is a gleam," Coach said, seeing it through the window. An engine had caught fire.

"We probably shouldn't pile it on," his wife said gently.

Nineteen apologized again and excused himself to the men's room. He didn't really have to, it was temporary shelter. His father had been lucid till the end, and that was no blessing either. When he got back Coach was inventing a new language, taking parts of words and mixing them with parts of other words. It was not quite gibberish; it brought something back.

"You don't have to make sense, Coachie," his wife was saying.

Yes, sense was definitely overrated, and Nineteen said, "Pro Right Fox 2 Okie, on One."

"One . . ."

"What comes after one?" Coach's wife said. Her husband looked at her but didn't count. He moved his hand in his pocket like someone feeling for his car keys.

"Pro Right Flip, Hare 2 Flip Dig," Nineteen said. She looked at him.

"28 Grace. Rip Load Jet Fullback Counter Joker Right," he said, and Coach looked up for a moment as if he'd heard an invocation whose ultimate meaning was finally within his grasp, a code only he could decipher. Then he said, "'Four and twenty blackbirds baked in a pie.'"

His wife sighed. "He still knows it by heart. How about your ABCs?" she asked him. "A-B-C-D—" Were they piling it on now?

"—E-F-G," Coach sang. They continued in agreement up to the letter U.

"What comes after U?" his wife asked.

"'Sing a song of sixpence, a pocketful of rye. Four and twenty blackbirds. Four and twenty blackbirds.'"

The piano had stopped. The old woman asked her doll, "Kann ich rausgehen und spielen, Mutter?" while her visitors talked to each other.

"What about the other blackbird? The one in the song," Coach's wife said. "Do you want to sing it?" She didn't wait for an answer, and didn't seem to need one. Nineteen felt as though she'd forgotten he was there, but didn't mind. She was no singer but she sang.

Now the other family was looking over. Now Coach joined in, getting just enough of it right.

Firestone Tire and Rubber Company built the stadium in 1925 for the recreational use of its employees. Iron girders, an arched brick entrance. It sat less than five thousand spectators in bleacher-style benches, and sat less than half that today. Nineteen hadn't thrown a ball before a crowd this small since high school. Still, he did not want to disappoint; his right arm felt like hard rubber and he wasn't sure he could get it over the plate, let alone at seventy-five miles an hour. He had a hose, alright.

He prayed and had a sort of inspiration.

From the pitcher's mound, wearing a Racers jersey with his number on it, he took a few steps toward the plate, quieting the curiosity of the crowd. Then, bending his knees, holding the big green ball in both hands, he extended his arms and leaned forward as though he were riding centre once again. In a hoarse unaccustomed voice he barked out signals, and in response came scattered applause, shouts, whistles.

"Omaha! Omaha!" he called, head swinging like radar, reading an invisible defense. "Set . . . hut!" and he dropped back three steps, his shoulder singing as he delivered a lazy floater not so far outside the plate that the catcher had to leave her box to grab it. Hardly anyone laughed, and his shoulder would quiet by end of day.

He and his girlfriend watched the rest of the game from the grandstand, behind the home dugout, with Nineteen's younger daughter, his old friend the local radio personality, and his slightly newer friend the restaurateur. More support group than entourage. Nearby, a kid with muscular dystrophy shouted from a wheelchair decorated with team gear. He was something of a local celebrity and at the bottoms of innings called every batter by her first name. He had been on TV.

Threat of rain. "Eye of the Tiger" playing between innings. The sand had been watered to keep down dust and was reddish like Martian soil. They sat behind first base but Nineteen liked watching third, the hot corner. She was fearless in red and black and pinstripes, fielding line drives point-blank, projectiles that could kill. He liked the way she barehanded bunts, positioned herself to each batter; liked watching women wear eyeblack, play drums, enter pleas, ride motorcycles, fill out uniforms made for men, while his girlfriend watched her phone.

His daughter, who would be a sophomore and was planning to major in architecture, had been invited to the game by the team's general manager, who sat beside her. The league was expanding to Australia, he told her, would include a Beijing travelling team. A player's average salary was six thousand dollars a year. The first pitch had been her idea.

They beat Chicago with a walk-off homer: off the glove, over the fence, gone. In spite of his girlfriend's insistence, Nineteen hadn't planned on autographs afterwards, not after the debacle of the last year—was it last year?—sitting at a folding table behind a somewhat motley display of t-shirts, sweatshirts, jerseys, mugs, bobbleheads—where had she got it all? eBay?—holding a fine-point permanent marker and not knowing where to look. For a hundred dollars you could run a route and he'd throw to you. Her idea, no takers. He'd scrawled his name a few times, sold nothing, chatted with someone wearing number four, that of the top draft pick, the latest hopeful of The Only Team That Mattered. He couldn't remember precisely what the preceding event had been, only the security chief coming by to politely remind them that their allotted half hour was up.

Someone called his number.

He turned. A man in his forties wearing his jersey, holding a pen and a twenty-year-old program from a game Nineteen still remembered; he remembered most of them.

"Can I bother you?" He was pleasantly if not completely surprised, and though he hadn't planned on it his girlfriend had brought a Sharpie. No bother at all. A small crowd had formed. My pleasure. How do you spell that? How humble now, how eager to please, the cool comportment of youth gone the way of the curls, the steady hand, the Roman nose. The former player, former star, his sometime team, a onetime wife. A present of past states and relations. An ex-life.

Was that with a C or a K?

Most of them men, his age or older. Guts, jowls, rookie cards, throwback jerseys. The old songs, the old stadium, its crumbling grandeur. He knows what's coming but they are quick to hold him blameless. *Brought us back from twenty-one down. If he doesn't shank that kick.* (He feels no need to remind anyone that the point after would have guaranteed only overtime. But not even the years can diminish The Hail Mary.)

"Fouts never got there either," the local radio personality says. Nor Cunningham, Moon, Peyton's father Archie.

"Who's next?" Nineteen's girlfriend says, though she doesn't have to.

You had Miami's line we're not even having this conversation.

He jokes that he lives closer to the Hall of Fame than anyone in it. Signs a kid's copy of Madden NFL 12. Gives a high school backup advice.

Glad you stuck around. (After the game or in this world?)

Now we only beat ourselves.

If I could of stood in your shoes for one day.

"It might not be what you think. And make sure it wasn't Tuesday." Tuesday you felt Sunday . . .

A fifty-year-old woman with his number tattooed on her chest. "Still waiting for another you."

His girlfriend laughs: "Next!"

It didn't take long. The last was a serious-looking guy who'd waited till everyone had their turn. He had a small boy with him and was dressed head to toe in composite loyalty to every major local team: an MLB fitted hat with visor to the back, an NBA track jacket, the jersey and sweatpants of The Only Team That Mattered, NBA slider sandals.

"What sport does his underwear play?" the restaurateur murmured.

"I drove seventy miles for this," the man said, and handed Nineteen a blank sheet of paper.

"We should pay for mileage," the local radio personality said and Nineteen said nothing, signed his name using the bleacher seat for a surface and returned the sheet. The man wore number four and so did the boy.

He studied the autograph briefly, then commenced to tear it to pieces.

"You were marginal at best," he told Number Nineteen. "That's why some special teams scrub wears your number now. You rode the running game and a stud defense to your win total, not to mention the rule changes, and you should thank God every day of your life you played for a fuckin genius who could make anyone look good."

The next part sounded rehearsed, and first he tossed the torn bits into the air. "The only confetti you'll ever see," he said, and walked through the exit wound, child in tow.

Nineteen's girlfriend was looking at his sweatpants—"Fucking stupid ugly"—and then looked at everyone. The restaurateur, once a Golden Gloves boxer, was moving, following the man through the gate.

"Hey. Guess whose dad drove seventy miles for an ass-beating."

Nineteen's daughter carefully removed a bit of paper from the top of his head.

"If his kid wasn't with him," he thought aloud. Someone was pointing a phone at him and he slapped it out of the grandstand to reassure himself.

She rode him in the lunar light that bent into the bedroom. Her childless body. He moved his hands up. Swore that if you held them a certain way you couldn't tell, and then it didn't make any difference. The sounds she made were real enough. He felt himself drawing down to a singularity, that itch that scratches itself, the sin that absolves. She rode him to the moon, flattened herself as in supplication to it, let him lick them. Used words she didn't use on her phone. The sounds, the musky disclosure, her hair brushing him, bearding him, how he didn't mind that at all, how it helped the rest of it happen. How it happened almost too fast.

It hadn't been so long that he had to think of the girl on third.

She remained bent over him like that for a moment, ribs heaving against his while he softened and withdrew. Then she rolled off and in unbroken motion swung off the bed and went to the adjoining bathroom, her hair slipping from his mouth. (His own at rest on a faceless Styrofoam head.) He dripped, dabbed at himself with a tissue, broke some of the wind he'd swallowed. When she returned he'd struggled back into his boxers and they lay side by side, fingers loosely entwined, breathing. Breath became speech, after-words—things offline and on, family, her team leaders, the black bear in the windbreak, were the doors locked?— but their phones stayed off unless he fell asleep first. Words became infrequent then, became breath again, the sound of sleep. Limbs twitching in the disorder of dreams.

Sex squelched the grey noise in his head, and sometimes sleep followed with a kind of violence, eyelids crashing down, but tonight there was something else keeping Nineteen awake. He rose with it, carefully removed himself from the sheets and, after putting on the habitual polo and pulling the door to, took it downstairs with him.

He stood in his living room without turning on a lamp. The moon was stronger here and in its frozen blue cast his sensible new furniture looked like a photograph of itself. There were creatures who lived in that light, and some who could see in the dark. He heard them now, midsummer sounds filtering through window screens. He felt an urge to unlock the door again.

He looked down. Something on the long oval of the coffee table (Target), printed matter, informational. He knew what it was: after she'd moved in, just before she'd become a Consultant herself, he'd let her host one of her parties here—she thought it might bolster attendance and just look at all the room. He'd lurked at the top of the stairs, listening with unexpected interest as the product came out and the IBC explained the order of application, that the skin around your eyes was different than the rest of your face, that your left side aged faster than the right, that you should always apply it with your weakest fingers, ring or small. Then, as scripted, he'd made his appearance, just passing through, a wave and a word to which there'd been ensemble response—those who didn't know sports had been primed—not stopping on the way to his office or—he couldn't remember now—was he on his way outside, to chase hunters off his property on a used Suzuki four-wheeler?

Now he let them on the acreage for a fee.

He sat down on the sensible charcoal weave of the sectional sofa and chaise lounge (IKEA) that had replaced the Italian leather.

Looked up at the TV, a modest (45-inch) off-brand rectangle hanging over the fireplace as some watercolour blandscape might have in another era. There were no eras now, just a continually unfolding and transmuting moment, one decade blurring into the next. Streaming.

Sometimes he caught himself staring at the blank screen, remote in hand. Now he got up and fled to his office, a smaller version of the living room with dark wood panelling, an oak desk, bearskin rug. There were no windows. Trophies stood on shelves, walls were splattered with plaques, certificates, clippings, photos. Smiling with the playoff teams of two decades ago, shaking an ex-president's hand, at the Tahoe celebrity tournament with the man who'd been machine-gunned in *The Godfather*, a math achievement award from the seventh grade. There was a pool table and a bar over which an electric Budweiser sign had once shone; the table was still racked and he'd been meaning to restock the bar with soft drinks and mineral water.

Nineteen switched on his laptop, closed the door, switched off the light and sat at his desk, lit only by the screen. The keyboard's luminous alphabet. Oh the places you'll know—and the things you didn't want to; like the dark matter that comprised most of the universe, the vast majority of the Web, it was said, was not publicly visible, was protected by passwords and hidden servers, hundreds of billions of pages not found by search engines. If you went deep enough you were advised to cover your webcam. Alphabay, Darkbay, Dream Market, Valhalla. Not just guns and drugs and pedophile fan fiction, but jihadist recruiters, the services of hitmen, recipes for human meat, appointments for bestial acts, live feeds of torture and murder. Sites that could see you—so they said.

The last item Nineteen had sought to purchase online was a manure spreader and did not require use of an encrypted browser. He had not farmed since Chapter 7. He was selling ten acres to the township, which they would add to Shadyside, the public burial ground, and at the rate he was leasing parcels to his neighbours, he would be living off the land without planting a seed.

He had difficulty concentrating sometimes, had to remember why he was here; tonight was about a different kind of harvest.

He started typing, stopped, looked at the dropdown below the search bar, his computer a step ahead: Basics, for dummies, FAQs. Click . . . Undifferentiated cells with the capacity to become those of any kind of . . . Two types—no, now there were three, the third being tricky to pronounce but you didn't have to murder unborn generations to obtain them.

He watched a rat's heart being grown in a laboratory, beating, then being installed successfully into a rat. Then again, this time a pig. It was serious mad-scientist shit but in a good way. Young women in Mexico born without sex organs, surgically equipped with laboratory-grown vaginae. "They have normal levels of desire, arousal, satisfaction," a spokesman said. Nineteen opted not to watch the video.

Somewhere an owl called, and he felt a shiver of privilege. The impending marriage of science and nature, for better or for worse. He narrowed his search.

Head trauma. Brain injury . . . Another white lab coat, this time worn by a woman, shiny black hair pulled back tightly from her face. In high school he might have harboured a secret crush. She spoke with an accent: "We are hoping that, by manipulating this particular family of proteins, we can encourage the cells to show a higher percentage of neural markers, indicating that they would mature into neural cells rather than" the sludge he now carried around between his ears that passed for a brain.

He thought of the family in Florida again; it was where they were going that he had trouble remembering. Haiti? Hong Kong? He started typing again, each letter a sown seed, and the computer remembered for him . . . called it a failed state. Sounded catastrophic but there was an island, something with an R . . . Type it in the box, press ENTER and

a red light flashing. A wheel in his hands. Then more, the world composing itself around him as if after a dream, though he hadn't been dreaming. Is he now? Upholstery beneath and behind him, the flashing red light above and before, through the windshield. Hands on the wheel. Still wearing his shorts and polo, but now there are sandals on his feet. He isn't moving. He doesn't panic—if only because the rest of the blanks have yet to fill in. The dashboard clock says three-twelve but it's dark. The window is open.

Someone says, "What are you waiting for?"

He turns. Puts her together in the intermittent light: the full breasts, tank top, the unwashed hair like the woman in the lab coat rousing cells like sleeping children.

"No one's coming. D for drive, right?"

He hears nocturnal chirping, sees the signs now through the windshield. A four-way stop, a junction of roads. Two unfamiliar numbers, coordinates for somewhere in nowhere. Beyond that his headlights see only black asphalt, white stripes, wild grass. He does not yet panic, if only because it isn't the first time.

"You're not changing your mind, are you?" She leans over, puts her hand on his knee. The oily greyish pallor, sores around her mouth. His dream or hers? "Come on, let's go chase that white dragon."

The red light flashing. The signs. Her hand.

"**A**quí, por favor," Nineteen's girlfriend said, her face in her tablet. She'd downloaded the guidebook, her translation app notorious for its derangements of speech.

They'd begun their preliminary descent. Nineteen had the window seat but when they came out of the clouds he was watching the U.S. Open on the screen in the seatback in front of him, didn't notice the sun spattered across the sea, incandescent, the lone ship just beyond trailing the white gash of its wake. The Americans were pulling off an upset in the quarterfinals, though he kept forgetting the players' names. Flying was hard on his head.

"A cuánto está . . . ?" she pretended to ask someone. Chances were excellent they would pass their entire stay without having to utter a word of Spanish, but she believed in thorough preparation and the FCC would not let her conduct Company business in the air. Fuck their GPS.

Nineteen belched through his lips and tasted breakfast again, his mouth remembering what his mind could not: some kind of quiche with three colours of potato, and mozzarella sausage . . . fresh fruit, warm biscuits, juice. (She'd advised him against coffee or tea; they never cleaned the water lines on planes.) He didn't necessarily crave the taste of business class, its four-page menu with suggested wine pairings, but couldn't refuse the extra legroom for his surgically-modified ankle, the additional recline and lumbar supports for his back, the hundred-plus channels of DirecTV. Nor could he have afforded it on his own; in addition to being a Future Executive Senior Sales Director, his girlfriend was a virtuosic travel hacker, exploiting hotel stays and credit cards, minimum spending requirements, airline shopping portals, category bonuses, accumulating points and air miles to the moon. He couldn't remember the last time he'd flown aft of the curtain, where the passengers didn't compare airline chefs.

He adjusted his noise-cancelling headphones, finally glanced out the window. Prize monies at the tournament totalled over fifty million this year, but the island was coming into view, its long dark shape, and Nineteen started thinking again about the clinic.

"*Papel higiénico,*" she said. Toilet paper, in her country accent.

He'd thoroughly explored the website, read the paeans of grateful patients and loved ones, watched video testimonials, familiarized himself with clinic staff. He'd filled out the eight-page questionnaire and agreed to conducting the initial consultation online—Nineteen hadn't Skyped much since his bankruptcy, had never been comfortable with it in the first place, but doing so meant he could start his treatment as soon as the clinic opened Monday, with only routine preliminaries in the way. Today was Saturday.

The staff was exactly half Honduran but the neurologist was American. Late fifties, with round-frame glasses and white hair parted in the middle, reassuringly tanned. He wore a Hawaiian shirt and spoke with a Georgia accent from what must have been his office—some kind of certificate framed on the wall behind him, the plastic anatomical cross-section of a human brain on a shelf. He did not sound like a team physician and Nineteen had liked him almost immediately.

"Instead of medicating or replacing, why not use your own body to do what it naturally does?" the doctor had said. He turned out to be a Gator and Dolphin fan but had some flattering if painful familiarity with Nineteen's professional history. He'd then recommended the only golf course on the island "in case you were wondering if I'm really a doctor," and also recommended flying Avianca—they tried harder, the amenities were better, and his voice had thickened when it mentioned the red uniforms.

The cabin bell dinged. The captain spoke. They were crossing the north shoreline, a submerged grey-and-rust mass below that must have been a reef, then the aqua shallows. Seatbelts belted, seats uprighted, garbage collected. Another crew member repeated what the pilot had said in Spanish, and Nineteen's girlfriend listened in vain.

"No pre-arrival beverage?" somebody said.

The neurologist had discussed the MRIs Nineteen had had taken stateside and shipped to the clinic. He held the scan prints before his webcam and pointed to Nineteen's frontal lobes. Reduced blood flow, brain shrinkage—that was something new. There were other scans as well, more advanced, something Dr. Q hadn't tried or mentioned.

"Diffusion tensor imaging," the neurologist had said. "Based on the movement of water molecules in brain tissue. Measures microstructural changes in white matter."

"White matter?"

"Fibres that connect different areas of the brain."

Nineteen felt his stomach drop a hundred feet. The island now filled his window, all green, all trees, hills and valleys now defining themselves, few buildings and no roads yet that he could see but, as always, the eminence even the humblest destination assumes on final approach, the sudden enlargements, intimacy of detail, so much so soon, the accelerating rush as to some ultimate moment if only because it might be the last. And her voice, murmuring in practice or prayer.

He'd watched the treatment video. Somebody's torso discreetly covered in sheets except for a circle of exposed skin at the base of the spine. The iliac crest—a feature of bodily topography he had some familiarity with. They used a drill that looked like a screwdriver to extract the bone marrow, then a centrifuge to separate the stem cells. A narrator assured him the entire procedure could be accomplished in a single visit.

"You'll be under conscious sedation when the cells are reintroduced through a catheter in the groin area, up to the carotid artery in the brain," the neurologist had said. "Virtually painless." Nineteen was not afraid of pain, but there was the matter of disappointment. The cells would act as drug factories in the damaged areas of the brain, secreting substances that repaired tissue and encouraged growth. And then?

And then.

"We had thought they would transform into neurons and brain tissue, but with bone marrow cells that doesn't seem to be the case. The main effect seems to come from supportive or nursing functions."

Nineteen's stomach had dropped then, too. The doctor doctored.

"But that doesn't mean there isn't every reason to believe you'll see progress, that at the very least the degeneration will be arrested. The remaining challenge is to find dormant cells most suited to a particular disorder, then find a way to release the neural activating factor. I can tell you it's just a matter of time—it's already been done in the laboratory. The defined steps needed to translate this to the patient's bedside are within reach, here at the clinic."

There was more—they'd cured Parkinson's in mice and monkeys—but Nineteen had already renewed hope like a driver's license. It would be a gradual miracle, then, with steps, stages, corners. One play at a time—the lessons of a life in professional sports continued to apply.

The clinic also had financing, low monthly payments. There was only the matter of side effects left to discuss. Risk.

"I'm coming to that."

He'd read things, seen things.

"Adverse effects are rare."

Tumours. Dark masses. A woman with a bone growing out of her eye.

"There's a lot of exaggeration," the neurologist said, "but shit happens and we're going to make sure you know about everything going in."

The shit that happens included transplant failure, organ damage, infections, cataracts, infertility, cancers . . . pretty routine stuff, and what was more routine than death?

The golf course was in French Harbour, about ten minutes west of the clinic.

"You'll use every club in the bag," the neurologist had said, after they discussed the blackouts—possibly hippocampus-related, he thought—of which Nineteen's girlfriend was still unaware. She'd co-signed his application, and now squeezed his hand as she had on takeoff. They'd crossed the southern shore and were over the water again; boats and small ports and marinas, a rusting half-sunk hulk left to attract fish and diving tourists. A sort of highway just inland running parallel to the shoreline. The water was very close now and just as you started to wonder the runway appeared and Nineteen remembered landings on the team plane, guys drunk on smuggled booze, playing cards, playing Monopoly with real money, grabassing attendants, Twenty-Nine standing up in his seat with his arms out like a surfer just before the plane touched down.

"¿Cuánto la debo?" she said.

The resort the clinic was partnered with had free shuttle service from the airport. A small air-conditioned white bus driven by a squat, serious man who did everything with one hand while speaking into a phone in the other. They were the only passengers and this was not necessarily a surprise; it was not the high season and most of the action was concentrated on the west end of the island anyway.

A twenty-minute ride during which they hardly looked up from their screens. The driver sounded as though he were being kept on the defensive.

The resort was situated about a half mile below the highway, off its own winding red-brick road and beside a ferry terminal to the west. A cluster of Spanish Mediterranean–style buildings facing an artificial lagoon, a three-hundred-and-twenty-foot pool behind them. A marina to the east and, once again, beyond the lagoon, the selfless blue sea.

They pulled into an unpaved lot up to the main office. Felt the heat as soon as the shuttle doors opened. The driver planted their suitcases in the gravel and resumed pleading his case; it sounded utterly futile. An orange cat appeared and rubbed itself against his legs. Nineteen's girlfriend took her wallet out of her purse. She'd changed currency at the airport and leafed through bills that always seemed damp. Held up a twenty-lempira note, named for a Lenca Indian warrior who'd posed a considerable problem for Spanish invaders in the sixteenth century: "How much is this again?"

"About a buck," Nineteen said, still pretty good with numbers.

She added another note and proffered them to the driver, who kicked the cat out of the way and reached for his tip. Nineteen's girlfriend revoked it in the same instant, stone-faced, shoved money and wallet back into her bag, zipped shut, turned her back and strode to the office.

"Kick *him* in his . . ." Her tentative grasp of Spanish failed her and she pushed through the door. Nineteen looked at the driver, attempting an expression between reproof and apology, wanting to get in out of the heat. She was angry enough for both of them. He decided he would see to the luggage himself. The driver stared after them.

Inside they were checked in by a pleasant young woman with a slight accent who did not look Hispanic. She wore black pants and a green polo shirt. There was paperwork to sign and Nineteen's girlfriend saw to it. Another young woman appeared with two cold cocktails for the guests. She also wore dark trousers but her shirt was pink and she looked to be a local. Nineteen's girlfriend complained about the driver and the girl at the desk took note. The drinks were sweet and the guests were adamant they contain no alcohol. While they sipped them the woman in pink fastened red bracelets to their wrists. The desk clerk explained what the colour entitled them to. She gave them two magnetic key cards and said someone outside would help them with their bags. She spoke Spanish to the other girl.

In the heat outside, the air conditioning had been a cruel dream. The shuttle driver and the cat were gone, replaced by a small group of employees whose polos were tan. One of them, a small and slender young man, picked up the larger suitcase—hers—and hefted it against his chest like a box. Nineteen showed him the wheels and retractable handle, and some of the young man's coworkers laughed. Another stepped forward for the other bag but Nineteen raised his hand. He could pull his own.

"Teamwork makes the dream work," his girlfriend said, disapproving of their laughter.

It was a long walk over hot gravel to Villa Two, Unit One. They sipped their cocktails, the ice chiming but melting rapidly. Nineteen's girlfriend mentioned the girl at the desk, in whom she had detected a slight edge. Attitude, you could even say.

"I don't think she really cares about that cat."

"Was she holding a sign?"

"What? I can't believe we have to walk all this . . . How's your ankle?"

The villa was at the end of the lot. At the opposite corner was the beginning of a promenade, and there a sign with an arrow pointing the way to the clinic. The latter had partnered with the resort so patients and their company could enjoy the amenities with the treatment facilities within convenient walking distance. The amenities did not include beach access. The place seemed a work in progress.

Nineteen had trouble with his key card. His girlfriend tried and opened the door on the first swipe. The air conditioning was on at its most aggressive setting. She gave the shuttle driver's tip to the young man and said, "Please be kind to animals."

"Thank you," he said in a heavy accent without expression and left.

"You wonder what they're thinking," she said.

It was an open floor plan. King-size bed, ceiling fans, kitchenette. Granite, marble tile, Tommy Bahama. There was a spa tub in the bathroom, dual sinks, washer and dryer, the toilet enclosed in a water closet.

The flatscreen was almost as wide as the one he'd once owned.

After they'd unpacked they discovered that the jets in the tub were not in working order. Empty sockets where buttons and a dial should have been.

"We'll call the desk after lunch," Nineteen said.

"Oh, let me," his girlfriend said. "They can fix it while we eat. Can you find the thermostat? My nose is getting cold, I hate that."

But somehow he became engrossed in the wall switches; lights came on in unexpected places, ceiling fans blurred and rocked in their moorings. He looked through the sliding glass doors off the sitting area. There was a small veranda on the other side, furnished, then bright sand, palm trees, the restaurant-bar, the lagoon. Nineteen had taken Caribbean vacations before, had encountered water closets and bidets in settings far more exclusive, private islands furnished with flamingos, served by chefs as renowned as their guests, not a native in sight, but that was another Nineteen, an ancestor from an alternate past; the current incarnation found the accommodations more than pleasant, all things considered, and was trying to remember exactly what it was he was supposed to be doing when he heard his girlfriend behind him.

"Well I guess that's that. We're in a Junior Suite." She held up her bracelet. "Jacuzzi comes with Premium only."

Well. Pool, lagoon, ocean. "How much water you need anyway? She have edgitude?"

"What? Did you figure out the air?"

He didn't hesitate. "We'll call the Amish."

"I love the way you fix things." He couldn't tell if this was ironic. The kiss was not. "Fuck it. Let's eat."

She advised him to change his shirt so he didn't look like an employee.

The restaurant-bar was a round structure called the Palapa, two-thirds open to the sea with an enormous conical thatched roof. They took an umbrellaed table just beyond the shade of the roof, facing the lagoon but not so close that the waitstaff would have to hike. Nineteen had been in the business. Not many other guests were about and he reminded himself this was the low season. A family were swimming and receiving service from the Palapa. They wore blue bracelets and Nineteen was slightly surprised to hear them speaking Spanish. Then, though not in the habit of second-guessing himself, he wondered why he was surprised.

Their waitress wore a tan polo and was very pretty with slightly blemished skin. When she'd taken their orders and gone, Nineteen's girlfriend thought aloud that a perfecting concealer would help, light ivory perhaps; though Mary Kay had invaded El Salvador and Guatemala, she had yet to establish a beachhead here.

"If that doesn't tell you what a fucked-up country this must be." She'd changed from travel mode to arrival—denim shorts, tank top, open chambray blouse, straw hat. Nineteen suddenly longed for her long thigh under the table. He wore a short-sleeved tropical print now and had exchanged his system for a ball cap— there was a good breeze but the hat was cooler. They ordered the lobster quesadillas, comfort food. An orange cat appeared, skulking under tables, but they couldn't tell if it was the one who'd been kicked. Nineteen, who thought of all cats as female, felt sorry for her but to feed her would give the restaurant a bigger problem. His girlfriend took a picture instead and posted it; the cat moved on, still hungry. Nineteen looked at the shadow of palm leaves silently brushing the white sand. He took no pictures.

The waitress returned with apologies: they were out of lobster. The chicken, then. They charged the meal to their room, the tip already figured in. As they stood to leave, Nineteen's girlfriend noticed a version of her sombrero on the head of an elderly woman sitting near the bar. She was with an elderly man who wore a tropical print shirt and swimming trunks, though his pale spotted skin looked as if it might ignite upon contact with the sun. A bug under a magnifying glass. The woman, probably his wife, was also dressed for the beach, her flesh far more tanned and none the better for it.

Nineteen's girlfriend tried to look away but it was too late; the woman wiggled her fingers and said, "Nice hat." Nineteen's girlfriend returned the smile meant for non-recruits.

The lagoon was made by men but was big enough that kayaks and paddle boats were available for rent, and had the same translucent colour they'd seen in the shallows from the plane. It was inviting but Nineteen and his girlfriend thought they should walk off lunch first and started on around it. They held hands, smelling of insect repellent. There was furniture at water's edge, chairs and chaise lounges and beach beds with four-poster canopies, most of it unoccupied. A couple of young men in boardshorts wading ankle-deep with bottles and British accents. Nineteen nodded at a security guard, a man raking the sand. No cats here but there were seagulls and big black vultures with grey heads and necks like the mantles of medieval knights. They heard cruel laughter.

Three men sat at a table littered with empty bottles. Grim-faced, loud, they wore trainers and sleeveless hoodies, dark expensive clothes that looked cheap on them. One of them, small, wore a big shining watch and rings and a chain and spoke abusive Spanish into a leather-backed phone. Nineteen nodded but they looked only at the gringa and one of them said something and another laughed into his hand.

"Same to him." It took a while to leave them behind.

They rounded the west end of the lagoon and started along its far side, atop the retaining wall that faced south. It was cool here. There was no beach access because there was no beach to speak of, just a narrow shoreline of smooth stones, moss, debris the sea wouldn't have. Further on, two small footbridges beneath which the Caribbean fed the lagoon through two small openings covered with bars and mesh; just water and salt, not its soul. Nineteen looked out across the real thing, tasted the wind it pushed into their lungs. Grey clouds floated on the horizon and you could make out a squall line, a thin curtain of rain like a mourning veil. But the sky above the island remained clear blue, as if the horrors that haunted the mainland could not reach them here. They couldn't even see it.

"*El mirador el mar*," his girlfriend said carefully, reading her phone.

"Right," he said.

At the far end they crossed a long curving bridge, the beer-commercial blue now dark and secretive, a man paddling a kayak beneath them. Passed through a shady grove of trees that were not palms and found themselves at the edge of the resort parking lot. To the left, the villa where they were staying, to the right, the resort spa. Five types of massage, seven body treatments (honey and papaya, green tea–mint algae), facials, manicures, yoga.

"Do you mind?" she said. "Just a look-see?"

He looked across the lot at the arrowed sign indicating the clinic. He was sweating and near-limping but did not want to be in tow. He said he would take a walk along the promenade and meet her back here. She let go his hand.

A landscaped flagstone path, a row of buildings to his left in the same style as the rest of the resort but larger, some having a third floor, some adjoined. Stuccoed in tropical pastel. Curves and arches, red clay tile roofs, balconies, courtyards and patios. Ironwork. He passed a conference or party room into which workers were bringing long tables and chairs. They looked at him as if to question his presence. Next door was a Century 21 office where perhaps the clinic had arranged its lease.

Now he was alone, the buildings deserted. Nineteen looked to his right. The marina; sailboats, power boats, cabin cruisers, a few yachts. He'd been on all of them, and more, and all he could do now was take a picture.

He looked back toward the buildings and stopped. He was facing an arcade and on the wall through the arches was a mosaic of the God and Goddess of the Sea. The latter deity stood on a half-shell like Venus herself, attended by squid and octopi and nameless fish. Her counterpart was at the other end of the wall, his chariot a scalloped shell pulled by outsize seahorses, his court a frenzy of sharks. Nineteen looked at the gap between them and felt alone.

He thought of his children. Took out his phone but was unable to get a signal, then looked up at the hills mounting over the resort; they'd been warned about dead spots on this part of the island. He took another picture.

The clinic was at the end of the promenade and you might have missed it were it not for one last arrow pointing from the edge of the path. Nineteen walked up two steps through another arcade to the entrance, glancing around, thought of the workers who'd stared at him a few minutes ago. He'd expected something more annunciatory in the way of signage, not a sheet of letter-size paper printed in inkjet and taped to the other side of the glass double doors. The blinds were half-closed and Nineteen squinted through the darkness between the slats, tried to make out the reception area he'd seen on the website. The gleam of upholstery could have been anywhere.

There were other levels and he walked up a curving stairway with hand-painted tiles on the risers meant to evoke the glyphs of a lost civilization. There were ruins on the mainland. The solid balustrade curled into a discreet round niche into which had been deposited a mop and bucket, backpack vacuum, wet-floor signs saying *Cuidado*.

At the top of the stairs a tiled patio with a pair of round tables and chairs, potted bamboo trees, a pleasant space for staff and perhaps patients between therapy, a place to consult and console. Signs warned of surveillance and security but he was a patient, not a trespasser, pre-approved for financing and entitled to the lay of things. It was just so hot. There were other doors and windows but all the blinds were drawn except for one set, and through the glass he saw only an empty room and wondered if it was still part of the clinic, said to be expanding, some adjunct space as yet undefined.

He saw another staircase now, straight and steep, and he resisted the urge to sit and rest his leg, and climbed. On the third and highest floor he stood catching his breath, tropical print clinging to his back, on a long covered balcony behind which rose a hillside buried in riotous overgrowth of purple wildflowers, thorns, a wild fragrance filling his head. He imagined phone signals trapped like prey. Along the back of the building, more wood-framed dark glass through which he might glimpse something, anything. There was nowhere else to go.

Moving slowly from window to window, he heard a rustle and flapping from the ceiling, realized he must have disturbed a nest. But he was seeing things now, the affirmation he must have come here for, what looked like an examination table, anatomical charts, edges of shelves, spines of reference books, volumes. And vaguer, gleaming shapes of metal, plastic, maybe porcelain.

He touched his phone and heard the flapping again, insistent, almost violent, looked up and saw wide black wings, long finger-bones like ribs, feral snouts. A dozen or so flying fast and straight in either direction along the ceiling of the balcony, a foot or so from his head. They were not birds.

Hand pressing down on his cap, Nineteen fled down the upper stairway, not quite falling, then the curved one and back onto the promenade where he looked back before slowing to a limp, heaving and sweating, looking back again. He tried to collect himself then, appear calmer than he felt, for he saw he was no longer alone; heading back toward the resort, he passed a short, dark stocky figure at the edge of the marina, facing seaward, hand at its ear, and thought it might be one of the loud men from the table by the lagoon, though he seemed to be listening more than talking now, though you couldn't see his jewellery. Then Nineteen heard a moaning in his pocket and reached for it.

She was done. Where was he? She wanted to get wet.

In the morning they had an early, American-style breakfast at the Palapa, also not included in the Junior rate, then returned to the villa and tried to decide what to do. The golf course the neurologist had told Nineteen about was closed on Sunday. Nineteen's girlfriend was disappointed; she'd improved her swing considerably, having been coached by her boyfriend. ("It's all about making a circle. The ball just happens to be in the way.") There was still plenty else to do on the island, though diving was probably out of the question. But there was still snorkelling, riding, fishing, jet-skiing, ziplining, parasailing, glass-bottom boating, encounters with dolphins or forty-foot whale sharks who were gentle and ate mainly plankton, and whom Nineteen had confused with captive Sea World predators who sometimes became psychotic, like abused children, and tried to devour their trainers.

Snorkelling, then.

Another short bus ride, then a five-minute boat trip to a tiny private island called Little French Key, almost adjacent to another private island called Big French Key. They signed waivers. Nineteen and his girlfriend had snorkelled before, but it had been some time and they were given vests and told not to stand on the coral. Ten minutes in another boat. There were three other couples but they were very young and kept to each other. Everyone was instructed to stay within the natural channels of the reef. If you saw a barracuda, just go the other way, but attacks on swimmers were extremely rare. They were warned about lionfish who, though beautiful and succulent, possessed venomous spines sometimes fatal to tourists, and posed almost as great a threat to the health of the reef as did humanity. No one saw any lionfish, or barracuda, or much else due to a strong wind and murky water. But weightlessness, like sex and marijuana, called truce in the war of attrition Nineteen waged with his body. Her thigh touched his. The guide followed in a kayak. The coral was reddish brown and its layered, convoluted architecture made Nineteen think of brain tissue, as if within its recesses was seated an alien intelligence, the mind of the sea, though this was perhaps due to the purpose of the trip.

Lunch was included in the excursion fee, and back on the Key, whichever one it was, they had grilled chicken, red snapper, plantains, coleslaw. Nineteen and his girlfriend sighed at the rum punch. It took only a drop to drown. The fish was excellent but immediately afterward one of the young visitors experienced tingling in her hands and the appearance of a rash. No one else suffered an adverse reaction, and when Nineteen's girlfriend suggested taking a picture of the irregular raised patch, she also remarked on the girl's otherwise healthy dermis and asked what she did for a living.

Back in the villa they showered together and lay on the wide bed, still aroused by the proximity of young flesh. His body yearned for hers, his mind for more, the oceanic union; they settled for sex. A half hour or so in the present tense, her tongue speaking in his mouth. Afterward he revisited the confusion of the lights and fans, then watched TV while she showered again, then lay beside him with her phone, the latest iteration.

"If there's still pushback don't forget about Happy Hour," she said. "It's just an hour and they still get hostess credit." Nineteen read and composed cellular text and watched Joe Gibbs's NASCAR team in the Mid-Ohio 200 qualifying. Before racing, Gibbs had coached the Redskins to three Super Bowl rings with no-name teams and middling passers, along the way perfecting the triple tight end set that had stopped Lawrence Taylor. Maybe, Nineteen thought, sleepy, he'd played for the wrong genius.

Days near the equator run from approximately six to six year-round, and it was full night when they had dinner at the Palapa. Three or four other couples were there, and several cats though none was orange. No one dined alone. It was pleasantly warm but the wind had picked up and the clouds over the sea intermittently filled with soundless lightning. The weather had still not reached the island; above the open roof was star-bright dark, and the luminous ribbon of galactic haze that marks the arm of the great spiral.

The evening's other entertainment was provided by a fairly handsome man with a goatee and an amplified acoustic guitar. He played and sang in loud, impassioned Spanish, then in smooth, accented English between songs would ask couples where they were from, artlessly incorporating this information into his chat.

Nineteen and his girlfriend started with the conch ceviche. "I'll try anything once," she said, though she didn't care for it and neither did he. She moved on to the slow-roast pork shoulder with coconut rice for the entree, and after brief deliberation he chose the ribs. It was a simple menu. The performer announced he would take a short break before his next set and Nineteen's girlfriend was grateful.

"You'd think we were at a bullfight," she said. "Maybe some nice Spanish guitar."

". . . so talented," Nineteen said, the last hand clapping. He was always impressed by anything combining speed with precision.

An elderly woman's voice nearby said, "You should have been here Friday. It was karaoke night." It did not sound like necessarily a good thing.

They turned. The old couple they'd seen at lunch the day before were sitting at the next table. They were dressed casually for the evening and having less exposed flesh made them easier to look at. They'd apparently finished eating; the woman sipped blue liquid from a tall glass and the man sat behind a hollow pineapple on which bits of fruit had been arranged to make a happy face. A straw poked up out of it which he looked at blankly.

"Well, hello," Nineteen's girlfriend said, reprising the smile she'd used at lunch. "Sorry we missed it." And she was; she had no time for karaoke these days but occasionally sang "Stand by Me" at the Saturday Success Meetings.

"We just got in yesterday," Nineteen explained.

"Well I don't know how long you're staying," the woman said, "but FYI Tuesdays and Thursdays they let the cruise ship animals in here." She shook her head.

"We're only staying till the middle of the week, actually," Nineteen's girlfriend said.

"Just as well," the old woman said. "It's a nice place but there's not a lot to do here. You need a car." The creped skin of her arm trembled as she raised her drink. She wore a wedding band.

Nineteen's girlfriend said they'd gone snorkelling.

The woman looked at her husband, covering his hand. "We rode in the glass-bottom boat, didn't we? We swam with the dolphins, left side and all."

"Did you really?" Nineteen's girlfriend seemed pleased. "I did it in Florida. Isn't it great? Did you touch them?"

"When they let us—they don't always want you to, you know. They only look like they're smiling. They liked Marvin, though. Guess they couldn't tell what a shark he is." She laughed, pleased with herself, and hugged him. She seemed quite drunk. "My little slumlord."

It was hard to imagine him swimming in anything but his own urine. "Did you kiss one?"

"Like getting kicked in the mouth with a wet boot." She sighed. "They eat thirty pounds of fish a day. I guess that's why they charge so much."

Another crooked flare of lightning. The clouds had crept closer to the island. Not to be outdone, an enormous gibbous moon would glow through a gap, then hide its beautiful scars till the next window.

"I was hoping to get a little golf in," Nineteen said. He tried to address the couple as one. "Know anything about Black Pearl, by chance?"

The old man looked at him as he had his drink.

"He talks about as much as he golfs right now," the woman said. "Aphasia. You can't always tell if anybody's home."

"Oh. We're sorry," Nineteen's girlfriend said, though neither she nor Nineteen were sure what aphasia was. When there was no further explanation, she went on tentatively, "So that's why you're here?"

"What do you think? The hundred-thousand-mile warranty is up, right?" The old man made a sound. The wife decided it was a request and put her hand gently on his back, pushed the smiling fruit a little closer. He bent forward and put his mouth to the straw. Nineteen wondered if the drink was as harmless as it looked.

"Last week he couldn't even do that." She nodded at the walker parked next to their table. "That was a wheelchair." She spoke matter-of-factly, then lowered her voice. "He still can't talk but he doesn't drool anymore. And he sure can float. Maybe I should quit while I'm ahead?"

Nineteen and his girlfriend couldn't help looking at each other. He thought of Coach. He'd watched the videos, heard and read the testimonials of John, Mark, Kathy M . . . Cancer, burns, chronic pain, psoriatic arthritis. But nothing close to his own condition, and not in the flesh, such as it was. He measured out his voice, not wanting to betray his desperation.

"How many treatments have you had?"

"Me? None." It was hard to tell if she was being coy or just drunk. "What about you? Don't tell me you're here for the fake beach. And you look too young for diapers." She looked at

Nineteen's girlfriend, specifically her chest. "They do facelifts here without surgery."

"Head injury," Nineteen said. His girlfriend looked at him but he felt he owed the old man this disclosure. Maybe some of the miracle would rub off.

"Well that's serious. You say you had an accident?"

"You could say I had an accident every Sunday."

"Racing cars or something . . ."

Identified as a possible athlete, Nineteen was encouraged to say, "Football."

The woman looked at him, nodded, touched her husband. "Marvin owns property."

"Yeah?" One vocation was as good as another, Nineteen decided. "Tried my hand at that. Recession kind of had its way with me."

"What recession?" Again, it was hard to tell. The woman looked at the man she called Marvin again but somehow the name wouldn't stick. He could have been a war criminal fled to the equator, hiding behind a woman's drink. "He had to cut back, and he's already a cheapskate . . . doing our own mainte-nance . . ." She pulled the straw from her drink and drank. "Tenants—they're all from hell you ask me. I think that's what gave him his stroke. Here's yours."

Nineteen would have liked to steer the subject back to the treatments but dinner had arrived. The musician, who had remounted the small stage, tuned his guitar to a rumble from the clouds. The wind rose. Lightning and stars.

"*Buen appetito*," the woman misspoke. She finished her drink and let her neighbours eat in peace, then rose carefully, embark-ing upon the process of exit. A waiter approached to help and she shooed him away. Nineteen held a shiny red bone and said, "Good luck, Marvin."

"Marvin says back at you but it ain't about luck—it's science," the woman said. "There's nothing they can't do. AIDS, make the blind see . . . they can stop the aging process." The new old Marvin rose like a shaky Lazarus; the pineapple was empty.

"That's how I know he's still with us," his wife said. She turned to Nineteen's girlfriend and spoke to her chest. "Have you had work done, dear? They can make your face lift itself here. We can all live forever some day."

"Some of us, anyway," Nineteen's girlfriend said, annoyed; she'd not been asked what she did. And immortality might be bad for business.

The singer sang "Samba Pa Ti" as the old couple lurched off. "Come on, look alive. Those vultures aren't here for the sea breeze, you know." She somehow said it with love. Over her shoulder she issued a warning about scorpions in the shower.

They shared dessert and made it back to the villa before the storm broke. Nineteen doubted he would sleep, energized by the encounter and a slight case of diarrhea. Later they were disturbed by someone trying to get in through the sliding doors; it turned out to be the child of the family next door, who'd lost his way.

By morning the rain had stopped but the sky had not cleared. Nineteen was nervous and they had just a continental breakfast at the Palapa (included) before heading to the clinic. She reminded him to take his passport. There were more people on the promenade than he'd expected, and everyone seemed to be looking toward the east end. Cadence of Spanish in the air, a sense of something going on. People turned their way as they approached, as if the Americans might have a clue. She took his hand. The crowd thickened the closer they got to the clinic, and then Nineteen's girlfriend said, "Uh-oh."

Three bands of yellow police tape stretched across the width of the promenade, just beyond the God and Goddess of the Sea as if to mark the border of their kingdom. On the other side of the tape, where the clinic proper began, stood four members of the National Police, holding assault rifles to their chests with the barrels pointed at the ground. They were dressed like soldiers, stormtrooper black, with helmets and balaclavas over their faces, and even with the bright yellow POLICÍA stencilled across their bulletproof chests, they seemed beyond mere law and order.

The police tape was printed in two languages; neither was necessary.

There were more military-style police at the entrance. One was a dark-eyed woman and Nineteen felt a vague provocation of taboo. Militant burqa. He saw civilians on the forbidden side of the tape, some in blue scrubs, thought he recognized faces from the website video. One of the police officers seemed to be interviewing them. A man in a suit was acting as some kind of mediator and Nineteen knew a lawyer when he saw one. He looked toward the marina where insigniaed watercraft were moored under guard. They'd come across the sea like a small armada, under cover of night.

He heard his girlfriend's voice. She was talking to a tan, grey-haired man who wore Bermuda shorts and sandals and spoke with an accent Nineteen could not identify.

"He doesn't know anything either," she reported, and someone else said, "Whatever it is, this is Central America, so it can only mean one thing." The speaker was a squat bulldog of an American, with a gut and an unlit cigar he used as a baton of emphasis.

"I don't see the DEA," Nineteen said. Nor was the local constabulary represented, with their bicycles and whistles and hand-sewn shoulder patches. They reminded Nineteen of mail carriers.

"Would you know em if you did?" the American said. "They don't always wear badges."

"Please don't let it be hostages. Are you a cop?" Nineteen's girlfriend asked the American, who wasn't, but had friends who were.

"*They* maybe know something," the man with the accent said, pointing at the news crews idly chatting over paper cups and cigarettes before the mural. Casually flirting. Cameramen, street reporters in business attire holding familiar microphones with strange logos: 45TV, MayaTV, MasTV, VivaTV.

"Hey," Nineteen's girlfriend said. "Isn't that your doctor?"

Nineteen shook off thoughts of an anchorwoman he'd almost become engaged to. Yes, there he was, white-haired, arms folded, standing among the other staff not fifty feet away. Nineteen called his name. People turned. He called it several times, each time raising his voice. The neurologist looked around wearily; it was not the first time he'd been shouted out today. Finally he saw Nineteen, unfolded his arms and waved. He did not smile. Staying where he was, the neurologist turned up his hands in yet another helpless shrug, drew thumb and finger across his lips.

"They won't talk to you," someone said. "The guy in the suit won't let them."

"Someone should say something," Nineteen's girlfriend said.

"Somebody better say refund if they're closing up shop," the man with the cigar said, and Nineteen almost told him to shut the fuck up. He did not want a refund. He had gathered that most of the crowd on this edge of the promenade were tourists (he did not think of himself as a foreigner) and probably patients, but unlike the cast of characters in the video, none looked Hispanic.

He did not see the old couple from the Palapa.

Time dragged them imperceptibly into the next stage of waiting. It was hot. The cigar waved—maybe more badger than bulldog, Nineteen thought. The news anchors updated their feeds, standing before the yellow tape under artificial light, stiffening into their TV personae. Cameramen shot B-roll. Someone tried, again, to speak Spanish to the four policemen and was, again, rebuffed. The medical tourists began to exchange ailments—arthritis, cartilage, back pain, complaints with unfamiliar acronyms.

Someone confessed to incontinence. ("They do that here?") Conversation turned to real estate, a hundred feet of white sand for a hundred fifty thousand, American. Nineteen tried to participate, but could not distract himself from the nascent despair driving its slow punch in his gut.

Activity at the clinic entrance. The doors opened and a procession of National Police accompanied by a civilian wearing an ID badge on a lanyard filed out. They carried PCs, laptops, banker boxes. No one was in handcuffs. The news teams came to life.

"You need body armour to arrest a computer?" the man with the cigar said. "I'm telling you, drugs." Onlookers seemed disappointed; given the special ops production values of the raid, a few suspects in custody averting their faces, even a body bag, seemed not too much to ask. A chorus of further conjecture: tax evasion, malpractice, fraud, asset seizure. Rat-a-tat Spanish peppered the air. Worst of all, the sun was coming out.

The policemen carried the evidence like pirates' plunder across the promenade and onto the dock. Transparent plastic bags filled with shredded paper. Nineteen had heard the Israelis used autistic children to reassemble documents. Boots thumped on wood toward a waiting launch, halted. Someone wrote on a clipboard as if generating a manifest. It was going to take some time. Another man in black walked out of the clinic and headed toward the yellow tape. He was dressed like the other police but the patch on his shoulder bespoke rank and the reporters now diverted his way, hurrying to the tape and jostling for position, shouting questions, proffering microphones on outstretched arms without looking.

"¡Por favor, por favor, todos!" The spokesman, mouthless behind his mask, raised his hands. "¡Tranquilo!"

The press obliged. He spoke in a calm and practiced way, approachable but assertive. Nineteen and his girlfriend watched, she picked out a word here and there. People held out phones with translator software.

"When does someone talk to *us*?" But Nineteen was no longer in a hurry. Someone would be along, another spokesperson or someone else. There would be apologies, assurances, English. Everything he was afraid of.

He thought for some reason of the man he'd seen at the marina two days before, and the bats.

"What?" he said, tumbler in hand.

The bar at the Palapa was a circle, and crowning it were three television screens configured in a triangle so you could watch something from anywhere in the round. Men exploring caves on a Spanish-language nature show, a Latin pop star with no surname prancing onstage to adolescent frenzy, a soccer match with its own brand of mob hysteria. On another occasion Nineteen would have watched from the safety of a table, but this was not that occasion and he'd asked the bartender for a shot of Johnnie Walker Black and whatever was on tap.

"'If He brings you to it, He will see you through it,'" she said, looking at her phone. A few guests sat in the restaurant for a late breakfast, but he recognized no one from the clinic. They had the bar to themselves.

"'Don't quit five minutes before the miracle happens.'" Like she was checking them off a list. She drank water with lemon, and would barely look at him. "There's always a price to pay," she said then, and that was one of his own.

"Now that ain't even fair," he said.

"Six months," she said.

"Five," he corrected her.

"Your hand is shaking."

"This'll help that."

". . . but you're a grown man."

"A grown-*ass* man," he corrected, and looked at the glass he held. It was filled with gold, filled him with anticipation, the long-deferred pleasure of an infidelity. If she wouldn't leave he would make her disappear.

"We make choices," she said, and in tone and cadence might have been talking to one of her consultants, team builders, one of her sisters in scam: "It's called a setback, but it's really a test— we all get tested. You sure you want to throw all those good days away?"

"I'm not throwing anything away. Not a drop." Nineteen was not by nature impudent but lately his nature was subject to change without notice. He switched hands and raised the glass. "To Dry Drunks and Earth People." Twelve-step jargon for non-addicts. "And to the clinic. Innocent till proven . . . who gives a fuck."

It tasted as it looked. She took a deep breath. It was just a sip and he savoured the burn before taking up with the beer.

That morning one of the administrators—the president of the board of directors, it turned out—had approached the yellow tape after the National Police spokesman had addressed the media. He had assured the bewildered gathering on the other side that this was only a temporary closure, that the clinic was a victim and had not knowingly committed any wrongdoing, that some of their needs (though not Nineteen's) might conceivably be met at the hospital on the other side of French Harbour, a facility with which the clinic enjoyed what he called a synergistic relationship.

When the question of financial reimbursement had reared its importunate head—probably the American with the unlit cigar—the administrator had answered, "That will be handled on an individual basis. But let's not get ahead of ourselves."

Nineteen wished he'd thought of it then, wished he'd said it aloud. Cancer, pain management, erectile dysfunction; Nineteen wished he'd thought to suggest updating the clinic website so that its list of treatments and services now included money laundering as well.

"Now *this* is interesting," his girlfriend said, pressing virtual keys with her thumbs.

He looked up at the screen as if she were talking about the match. "No fans like soccer fans . . . Riots, stampedes I heard in Brazil where they cut off a ref's head once. I can think of some zebras I'd like to cut their head off." He belched silently, warmed his nostrils. Bad calls were part of the game. "You talking to me or your phone?"

She glanced his way briefly, as if at a stranger who'd asked was this seat taken.

"You're kind of funny when you've had a few." She sounded genuinely entertained.

"I'm not even there yet."

She showed him her phone: his DUI dashcam performance. He snatched at it. "I'll throw that fucker in the fake-ass lagoon." She pulled it away and he shot the rest of the shot. The warmth infusing his belly was rising to his head like a yogic ascent through chakras. A forgotten song recalled, a gift you give to yourself. Fuck YouTube.

She made a sound and quoted Mary Kay Ash, having apparently exhausted her cache of AA wisdom: "'When you come to a roadblock, take a detour.'"

Tell it to your car, bitch. But he was grateful she hadn't invoked the class action again, though money was in as short a supply as time. What detour? Costa Rica? Panama? China? India? Plastic surgery franchises in the States were injecting stem cells for you name it like a side dish on a menu. Meanwhile he felt the icy advance of tau proteins spreading across his cerebral cortex like a glacier of death, entombing living cells, tangling nerve fibres, obliterating the self. Meanwhile paranoiac rages, violence. What they called suicidal ideation, the thought of thought engendering pain. He remembered Coach, his wife dressing him like a doll. How many last chances do you get?

"And why do they call them tau?" he thought aloud. Till recently his experience of the Greek alphabet was limited to the letters of fraternities. (He hadn't pledged but he'd gone to parties.) He ordered another drink as he pondered. If your self was to be obliterated, you might as well try to enjoy it; the self, he had reason to believe, was overrated.

Nineteen's girlfriend leaned over the bar. "Excuse me! Excuse me!" The bartender, pouring, held up a finger, but she went on. "Excuse me, this man has an issue. He hasn't had a drop in six months. Just so you know." The bartender was young and had gelled hair. "You know you look like Mario Lopez?"

He smiled at the gringa, shrugged and served his customer. "I don't know who is this."

"A grown-ass man," Nineteen said, and drank. Admittedly, he saw the resemblance. "To grown-ass men," he toasted. The bartender looked at the soccer game, then his phone, either to verify the likeness or rejoin the collective conversation.

"I have things I should be doing," she was saying. "I have a Career Conference."

"Still here? You keep saying that but there you are. So go troll up some fresh meat."

"We empower people."

"God help em." And he drank to grown-ass women.

She said something else but he was contemplating the bottle of Johnnie Walker Black, which made him think of Johnnie Walker Red, Ken Stabler's drink, which made him think of Ken Stabler—not loitering flat-footed in the pocket with all day to throw, but repeating the same story every five minutes, which made him think of Ken Stabler's brain, which made him think of Fifty-Five, who'd shot himself in the chest so as to leave his own intact, which made him think of Andre Waters, who'd shot himself in the mouth, which made him think of Jovan Belcher, who'd shot himself in the head after he shot the mother of his child nine times, which made him think of Terry Long, of Mike Webster tasing himself to sleep, of Forrest Blue, Mackey, Morrall, Ali, which made him think they used to call it punch drunk which made him drink his drink which made him realize what his girlfriend had said though he asked her to repeat it anyway.

"I said what if you don't even have it." She used a different voice now.

He couldn't tell if she was being ingenuous, and spoke slowly: "So you're not actually trying to piss me off?" He chased the whisky. "I checked all the boxes. They think Stage Two . . . the fuck!"

"But they can't know for sure, right?"

"Well Jesus Christ," but it was true. The only definitive way to diagnose it was direct examination of brain tissue, post-mortem. There was certainty only in death.

"So what do you want me to do?" he said. "Put one in my heart so they can have my brain in one piece?" They'd freeze and fix it, pickle it blanched and rubbery like a soft-boiled egg. Halve it, quarter it, cut the lobes into slices exactly five millimetres thick. Then mount them in wax for further thinning, the substance of fear, love, aggression, your children's names, in slivers measured in millionths of millionths. Not quite nothing.

She sipped her water. "Don't look at me like that," she said, though she said it to her phone.

"Look at you like what? What are you talking about?"

"That doctor in Florida. That whatshisname."

He tightened up. "You gave him his name."

"He got famous for helping drug addicts."

"He helps a lot of things. People branch out."

"There's lawsuits."

"Show me someone famous who doesn't get sued."

"I'm just saying."

"Stupid people say they're just saying."

"There were other issues going on—you told me yourself. Lots of drinking. There was the oxy thing going on." The Xylocaine thing. Decadron. Problematic appearances on TV and radio. Slurred speech, rambling . . . incoherent, they said, and dropped him.

"Are you talking about . . . ? You think I was just lit all the time?"

"Where do you go?"

"You weren't even there."

"Were you? You take out the garbage and don't come back till five in the morning."

He barely heard. The stranger he could become was arriving, he saw it on her face. Let it. Let self-pity have its say, then paranoia and rage, in that order; he was entitled.

"Or maybe you just think I'm faking this shit."

The waitress who'd served them the day before came to the bar to put in an order and left. She might have been twenty-two and Nineteen watched her come and go as if no one were watching him.

"Only God loves ugly," his girlfriend said. "Who is this man?"

Nineteen had turned and was addressing the bartender. "You know, some people should just know when to mind their own fucking business."

Another dredged-up homily he'd heard before: "'Words are seeds planted in the hearts and minds of others.'"

"Fuck that old bitch. Didn't she take that shit with her?"

"'Only sow what you wish to receive in return a hundredfold.'"

The vaguely biblical tone further enraged him; even her bullshit was stolen. "Why don't you get a real job anyway? Direct sales my ass. Call it what the fuck it is."

". . . real enough to get your Chapter 7 ass financed here," she murmured. It was true; somehow, through all the tribulations of drink and despair, she'd kept her credit intact.

"All you did was sign your name. Didn't cost you a penny." He decided to sow some more seeds. "But while we're here . . ." He tilted his head in the general direction of the clinic. "They got a plastic surgeon over there. Once they set up shop again, why don't you use that credit score to pump up that skinny ass like those fake cans of yours?"

He reached for her chest and she slapped his hand away. She looked at the top of his head. The response sat there on a skin-coloured polyurethane base but it now took the form of pity. It was his turn to unrecognize her; no Ladder of Success, no Queen's Court of Sales, just flesh and blood—the real pink thing, wounded and demanding. Kind of beautiful and a little scary. The stuff of song. Fuck her.

"Alright," she said softly, and took up her bag. "It's your shit-show." She stood. "Here's not looking at you."

The security guard had edged over. Nineteen ignored him, called the bartender Mario Lopez. "I thought she'd never. Let

110

the wallowing begin." He ordered another beer and asked the bartender to change the channel. The bartender said his name was Ephraim.

"On second thought," his girlfriend said, "I'll have what he's having."

"You don't want what I'm having." She'd stood but remained at the bar. Nineteen glared at her, then sighed. "Fuck it. I'll drink that motherfucker too." He grabbed the remote and clicked. Serena Williams speaking French over Spanish subtitles. The security guard cleared his throat. The bartender pulled a draft for the gringa and placed it on a coaster in front of her. Nineteen had formulated a toast, and when he raised his glass to propose it she tossed the contents of hers in his face.

He shut his eyes reflexively as it washed over his head, his shirt. A scream nearby, then laughter. There was a roar in his head or in the air. His face dripping, a cold spray. Wind. The floor heaved. The light almost hurt. He gripped the rail and opened his eyes.

They were crossing the wake of a container ship, its stern receding to his right—starboard, he still knew. Towers of bright-coloured steel boxes stacked on its deck. The ferry rocked again, sent up another burst of spume, then was out of the freighter's wash and back in the blue-green chop of the Caribbean. He tasted it.

Nineteen stood in the curved peak of the bow, fairly soaked. He looked dead ahead. Only sky and sea that way, but to the left he saw distant land, faded hills—islands, perhaps. He looked around and saw only a young couple at the rail nearby, grinning at him, not quite as wet. They looked away. So did he. About ten yards aft (he still measured distances in yardage) along the sun-bright deck of the prow, a set of stairs rose to a narrow-railed deck that curved around the passenger cabin. There were people up there, out of reach of the spray, but she was not among them. A child was expelling something into a paper bag while a woman stood patiently beside, hand on her heaving back. The words PRIMO CLASE were stencilled on the cabin door next to them. The terror of another blackout was somewhat mitigated by its having occurred in first class.

The boat was looking familiar to him now, its aerodynamic curves and clean white lines; it was the ferry from the dock just west of the resort. Was he heading for the mainland, then? The thought carried no particular impact. He faced front again. To port, clouds had formed and the waves were grey with clots of black like ink in the crests; on the other side the sun shone and there were seabirds white against the dark sea, dark against the white sky.

He heard Spanish and felt alone. He was starting to feel certain she wasn't on the boat at all. There'd been an argument.

The last time it had happened he'd been traumatized. Now the feeling was one of intense curiosity, the beginnings of anticipation. He looked down at his dripping self, still wearing the navy polo, white pants. Bulges in his pockets: wallet, passport, phone. It occurred to him she might have left him a message, but his phone was wet and wouldn't even light up. It was kind of a relief. He briefly entertained the idea of dropping it overboard, then put it back in his pocket.

The wind roared, the deck hummed. He knew the throb of an engine and this felt different, smooth and high-powered like some kind of jet propulsion. Wherever they were going, they were getting there in a hurry. It suggested purpose, relieved him of decision. He looked around again. The couple were gone. He supposed he must look a little scary, planted in the utmost stem like some figurehead incarnate. It wasn't his fault. Let the brutal wind dry his clothes if not clear his mind; he'd find a bar to take care of the latter but for now he hung to the rail. His right hand still bore the sting of salt water. He looked down and saw that his knuckles were split, a little bloody. A flap of skin. He didn't panic, though he felt a brief swell of nausea he attributed to the vessel. Looked up again and now thought maybe land was verging on the far horizon, though he wasn't sure.

When Nineteen debarked at the terminal in La Ceiba, his clothes were almost dry but his phone still wouldn't work. He briefly considered taking the next ferry back, then discovered the next one didn't leave till seven in the morning. It was out of his hands.

Outside it must have been nearly a hundred degrees and even the cab drivers seemed reluctant to be there. Most of them drove white Toyotas in various repair and few spoke English. One was so far along with child Nineteen was afraid she might break water en route. A short, neatly dressed man nearby wore a thin moustache and a baseball cap with the letter C stitched above the visor. He leaned against his car with his arms folded. "El centro," he said calmly at intervals. "Doscientos lempiras."

Nineteen was drawn to his composure, and to the cap. "Speak English?"

"Downtown. Ten dollar." The driver gestured at his vehicle. "Aire acondicionado." Nineteen got in.

He rode up front for the legroom, listening to Spanish news. Traffic was dangerous but purposeful; familiar red octagons said

ALTO and were regarded as suggestions. There were more bikes and motorcycles and scooters than cars, bicycles equipped with lawn-mower engines. A car without doors. Ancient American school buses repurposed as local transit, still bearing the names of the districts they'd served. Wild palms. A woman on a rusty moped cut them off at twenty miles an hour without glance or gesture. She wore a house dress and hardhat and drove with a child on her lap and one behind, lashed to her waist with a length of hemp. There were surprisingly few horns and Nineteen felt insulated from tragedy, glad he wasn't sober, witness to a form of natural selection.

"What?" he said, but the driver was talking to his radio. Traffic thinned and they were in a neighbourhood, a loose grid of dusty backstreets and squat houses of painted concrete or wood or plaster, or no paint at all. Cinder block. Slack colourful laundry hung everywhere. Bars on windows and razor wire. Two boys with buckets and rags operated a car wash under a sheet mounted on four crooked sticks. Their handmade sign said EL PRIMO. A leg hung off a hammock.

They rode in. Further downtown was a soldier with a machine gun guarding a Chinese restaurant in the middle of Central America. People boarding a bus being wanded for concealed weapons—even the children. Martial law or just another day. Traffic stalled and vendors wandered among the vehicles in the hot hazy light: "Pollo! Pollo! Agua! Agua!" The driver bought a plastic bag full of water like a small transparent pillow. Nineteen had another thirst, other hunger. They drove past a vacant trash-covered lot and in the middle was a tattered figure, a discarded human being sitting on a canted discarded toilet, pants down, reading a discarded newspaper as if ingesting its content and excreting it. Nineteen looked at the driver. The driver spoke to his phone.

The city centre was congested, static. As they crept through it the driver became impatient with Nineteen's lack of destination. "¿Donde? ¿Aquí? Where you want?" Then he said "Hotel?" and Nineteen eagerly consented, because he recognized the word and because there would be English at a hotel, maybe a bar.

His money was not as dry as his clothes but didn't have to be. He was calculating percentages when the cab rode off, the tip already figured in, or the driver just glad to be shed of him. The hotel was called the Iberia, a name on a smoked glass storefront. A man lay face-down on the sidewalk near the entrance. A puddle had seeped from beneath him and run down the sidewalk to the gutter in a divided stream so that passersby had to step twice over it. A broken vessel. An enormous flattened cockroach lay just beyond and between these two cautions Nineteen was persuaded to move on.

He walked, low on cash and daylight. At the corner someone shoved a mottled yellow object up at him: "Bery good, bery good." An old woman cross-legged on the sidewalk, hawking half-rotten fruit out of the bell of a hat. So buy a piece and throw it away, help her out. It was too much too soon. He stepped into the street. A horn blared and he was jostled.

"¡Cuidado!" a voice yelled and for a second he felt like hitting someone. He saw a dirty white van, a small air conditioner sticking out the back like you'd see in someone's window. People here walked and talked and drove all the same way. It was nothing personal. He finished crossing.

Faces, furtive dark-eyed scrutiny. Nineteen looked around for a destination. A shoe store, auto parts, another hotel, a business that bulletproofed cars, all crammed together in low shabby buildings painted in pleasant watercolour. Spanish curves of colonial balconies, relics of a wretched past, and whose purposes did they serve in this second-hand present? Signs tried to tell him: PICO RICO. SANDÁLIA. TIENDA IMPORTADORA. The barred windows, but no bars or banks. Someone's brakes squealed. He passed a cell phone store and wondered for a moment if they could help him. *Cómo dice* "My phone is wet"? They say bury it in rice for a while. No shortage of rice here, and he wondered if he really wanted it fixed.

Another street, another sidewalk. A little man with no shoes or hair or teeth jumped in his face. He had wizened reddish-brown skin and for some reason a blue tongue.

"Hey, American? You know where you're going? You lost?" Were both so obvious? This person looked as though he would have spoken a tribal tongue on the verge of extinction, but his English was perfectly clear.

Nineteen pointed vaguely ahead in spite of himself, slowed but didn't stop.

The man kept pace, backpedalling without looking. "I'm not from around here, either. I'm from Costa Rica." Nineteen had been there, remembered only that it was legal to urinate in public. He walked faster. "Hey, I got important information for you!"

The blue tongue—a child eating candy, or maybe a medical condition. Nineteen felt pity and disgust. He tried to keep his voice low. "I'm just trying to—"

"Right on your way, just keep going! Banco Atlántida, on your right."

Nineteen was too startled to thank him.

"*Grassyass*," the man said in mock Yankee twang. "De nada, my friend. God bless America." Finally, he looked where he was going. "Hey, can you help me get something to eat? I take dollars." A small joke, a little laugh.

Nineteen did not want accompaniment to the bank, and they stepped into a doorway. People glanced and kept going. His last two singles. "Pura vida," the man said before he disappeared like a figure in a fairy tale. A note of ironic disappointment; tourists were supposed to be rich.

The bank consisted of an ATM behind a scuffed glass door but it was where the man said it would be. A short line, a kid in uniform with a pistol-grip shotgun. He nodded. Nineteen was ecstatic when his swipe unlocked the door. The machine asked him if he wanted to transact in English, and then it was just a matter of zeroes. He was always amazed at the sums foreign currency required. He drew his limit, off the credit card his girlfriend had co-signed for.

Armed with cash he could look them in the eye now, if not answer the question he saw there. They were taller than he'd expected, some with features somehow ancient—not old but of another time, another world. Indigenous. Boys in wife beaters or clean white polos tucked into dollar-store jeans. Girls gifted with song. He kept seeing the word *baleadas*—something to eat? He'd forgotten about the woman with the fruit. He saw one sleeping on cardboard, barefoot, hand open as if dreaming in want. He thought he might drop some money in it, decided on prayer instead. People living in their clothes, shoes for a pillow.

Power lines and palm leaves, the sidewalk buckled like a drawbridge. He came to a park and stopped. There were concrete benches in shade and he thought about sitting on one. Pink flowers sprouted from bark. Empty brick planters and concrete fountains drained of water, but the place looked well-kept and the only sign of disorder was another drunk asleep at the foot of an enormous tree. Its trunk was limestoned white at the base and wide as the man was long, vast outspread boughs crooked and leafless with long flat vines pending like strips of withered flesh. A bronze statue of a man in uniform stood in the middle of the park. He was called the George Washington of Central America, but George Washington had not supervised his own execution by firing squad. There was also a statue of Lempira but the soldier had pride of place; the tree was there before either of them were born and had given the city its name.

Nineteen saw the black vultures now and decided against the benches. He looked across the street. A small cathedral with two belfries and an electric cross between them. The cell phone tower behind was taller and the mountains beyond rose above everything. Then a Texaco station, Wendy's, and the signs continued to speak American English. Popeye's, Pizza Hut, Burger King (La Casa del Whopper). He had not eaten since that morning, and he was starting to wonder if this was still the same day. He went in.

The air conditioning disabled him, and so did the smell. He squinted; the sun had rendered him half-blind. He was sweating. He stood six feet from the register and a girl in fast-food dress said, "¿Puedo tomar su orden?" His head began to ring, his mouth hung open. Just look at the pictures. HAMBURGUESAS A LA PARRILLA. POLLO Y MAS.

"¿Qué te gustaría ordenar?" She sounded impatient. Someone behind him cleared his throat, a predatory growl. He saw jagged lines, the lights began to flicker, and he fled.

Outside he walked fast, as if to outrun the migraine's aura. He noted the cross streets were numbered and the numbers were getting bigger. Calle 10, Calle 11 . . . Like many athletes Nineteen was superstitious, and when he got to twelve he turned and crossed the avenue.

At the corner children played in a fenced yard. JARDIN DE LOS NIÑOS on crumbled brick. On the next building someone had painted a man on his knees, hands behind his back, gagged and blindfolded and awaiting execution. NO MAS ASESINATOS. The barrel of a gun tied in a knot. Plenty of bad luck here. Then the smell of fried chicken, SUPER POLLO, but his thirst had overtaken his hunger.

He turned the corner. Avenida de Julio. Started making the numbers smaller. Across the street two boys were being detained by two cops. One was holding on to a telephone pole, the other had his hands against a wall the colour of dried blood. He wore a backpack and a policewoman had opened it and was methodically sorting its contents. The officers wore ball caps with embroidered insignia and latex gloves as if dealing with a disease. Doing a dirty job in clean blue uniforms, and how dirty it must get here. God bless.

But the boys were also clean-cut and looked like schoolchildren, though Nineteen knew they could be anything. The one by the telephone looked very young but very calm, as if accustomed to someone else's hands in his pockets, between his legs, probing. Nineteen couldn't see the other boy's face. God bless everybody.

Further up he saw what he took to be an ice cream stand, then an enormous sign with the picture of a brown bottle looming over it. The label read Salva Vida—sobriety was apparently a state from which to be saved, in increments of approximately one dollar.

He headed for the window. In front of it four men sat at a dirty white plastic table and drank from brown plastic bottles, looking at him till he looked back. The small parking lot beside them was crammed with white Toyotas and he stopped in apprehension. Off-duty cabbies. What if the one who'd driven him in appeared? He didn't know why this should unnerve him except that he didn't want to be confronted by the past in any form; lately there was more to it than he remembered. He felt his skinned knuckles again.

On the same block he saw a small, neat wooden shack with a sign on its roof and he tried to sound it out: "*Pul-per-i-a*." There was no door, just a big window where an old man served customers, but there were no customers now and in the dimness behind the man Nineteen caught the promising lustre of liquid and glass. There is a gleam, men.

"Liquor," he said boldly.

"Licor," the man said. He wore a cowboy hat. "Sí. Alcóholica." Nineteen was filled with affection for him. "Whisky?"

"No whisky," the man said. He dropped his voice. "Tengo guaro."

"Tango . . ." The proprietor reached back and retrieved a clear half-pint bottle with the picture of a rustic town on the label.

"El Original," he said, looking around as if the transaction were questionable. The transparent liquid promised clarity and Nineteen took out his wallet. The man had to write out the price. Out of sight of the store he opened the bottle, sniffed, discreetly tasted it. A burning neutral sweetness. Rotgut. He was not disappointed, things were falling into place. "There's only the next drink," he paraphrased, then heaved up a great sob from nowhere. It was supposed to make him laugh. He looked around furtively and took a bigger swallow.

Shouting. He was in the open-air market now, green wooden stalls lining the side street. Traffic looked impossible, knotted with pedestrians. BIENVENIDOS TURISTAS A LA CEIBA stencilled on every stall but Nineteen saw no one who looked like a tourist and felt more in exile. The vendors were of every description as was their merchandise. He moved deliberately, through the guaro. Familiar and unfamiliar fruit in wooden bins and crates. Scales, shapes and colours, the dirt smell of produce. Someone held a cluster of live white crabs on a string, clacking in his face, and old people selling lottery tickets from wooden chairs under an umbrella.

She would like it here. She would haggle. He wanted a drink and went to the sidewalk to have one. A warm cloud expanded in his brain. Bery good bery good.

Here the row of stalls conjoined with storefront awnings and balconies to form a long, dim passage. Clothing—denim, t-shirts, ball caps—displayed in ensemble, a ghostly absence of wearers. Glitter of cheap accessories. Honduran flags, their own stars and stripes. The vendors here were younger and called to the gringo slipping past, dripping dollars like a tree shedding leaves.

"¿Qué quieres? ¡Lo tengo!"

"Tango stem cells?"

"¿Qué?"

"Show me how much."

He bought a pair of sunglasses to ward off future migraines and a chain for her—it might make up for what there might be to make up for. He held the money in his flat open palm, trusted them to take what they needed.

At the corner he put on the shades though he didn't need them. As if they might reveal more than obscure. LA PRENSA, LA TRIBUNA, the signs sang so beautifully now. He passed a bar, a dim wooden grotto without pretense of atmosphere nor decoration, filled with deafening Latin pop and stale beer fumes. The space was divided into two levels, with all the men downstairs and the women drinking over their heads. At some appointed time they would meet. Some would rise and some would fall. The smell reminded him of spring break, the main drag of Daytona, and it also reminded him of the taverns where he would be sent to fetch his father, and he left it behind.

It was hard to see where he was going now and when he took off the sunglasses there wasn't much difference. The streets were deep in shadow, the sky above darkening blue. A breeze carried sea salt and Nineteen headed into it with amphibian instinct. He entered a small park with a white gazebo in the middle and sat to soothe his aches from the inside out with drink. The park was named for a long-dead president who had been more than accommodating to the American companies establishing banana plantations in his country. It looked like a children's playground. There were large, friendly plastic animals to climb and ride, worn from use, but as evening approached the activity was of another nature and the voice that accosted Nineteen as he left the bench was not a child's.

"Something wrong with your leg?" He almost stopped.

"Hey, there you go. How you doing?" Just a slight accent and Nineteen thought at first of the man with the blue tongue but didn't turn. The sound of English here was more warning than welcome. Maybe he was talking to someone else.

"Why you don't hear me? I saw you at the hotel. You hurt your leg?"

A little closer now, a voice of the street but not the blue tongue. He turned his head just enough to make out a figure three or four steps behind, big. Maybe a white t-shirt.

"Man, you got the . . . Just trying to get someplace." Past a grinning lion's head.

"Me too!" the voice said, then, "Come on now, don't be like that."

Nineteen almost stopped again; the panhandler tactic of familiarity enraged him. He wasn't that drunk, and drunk, he wasn't that stupid. Thought of cleats pounding in from the blind side. Sometimes you stand in, keep your eyes up, take the hit. But here taking the hit meant something else. Here, ninety-six percent of homicides went unsolved.

He saw a holstered guard at the edge of the park like his right tackle. "*Hola*," Nineteen said to the cop, sounding as American as possible. Being an American usually helped.

The voice muttered and fell behind.

He crossed the *avenida*. At the next corner he saw the street sign bore the number one and celebrated with a drink. The bottle was almost empty. Looking for another store, he went in the direction the sun had gone and after a couple of blocks came to a big white Art Deco hotel with curving wrought iron balconies. It was well-lit and looked expensive, and beside it was a waterfront park with a brick esplanade and planted palms and guards and kids at a stand selling overpriced fruit in plastic bags. He had to piss.

In Costa Rica you could piss in public but this was not Costa Rica and behind the hotel he found a narrow dirty beach and the seclusion of dusk. Pelicans, gulls, kids shouting. An old wooden pier thrust its broken bones into the sea. It was sagging and gapped with missing planks but a gang of boys had made it to the far end and were attempting backflips into the water. Nineteen looked down the pier as down a bridge into the past and boyhood. Closer in, a lone fisherman had cast out against the fading sky and must have done so from a submerged reef because he seemed to be standing on water.

Nineteen toasted them all generally and finished the bottle. He turned and relieved himself behind an old customs house in the same condition as the dock. ADUANA. Peeling letters at close of day: 1917. If he'd had anything left he would drink to it as well, one ruin to another, still standing.

He wanted more. On Calle 1 he heard festive music to the east and redirected. Found another pulpería and another bottle, identical to the first except twice its size. He used the empty to clarify the purchase. The songs grew louder but street traffic had thinned. He passed under a banner declaring TÚ NO NECESITAS DROGAS, crossed a small yellow bridge over an estuary. Then a street with no name, a building that called itself INSTITUTO DEPARTMENTAL, blandly ominous, and Nineteen thought of secret police, interrogations, disappearances, and kept the bottle in his pocket. He was glowing.

The music originated at the corner of a street named for Victor Hugo, from a two-storey pink building, the second floor embraced by a veranda on three sides. At street level a big open window faced the sidewalk with two stools beneath it. Nineteen took one of them and a thick-bodied young woman in a tight glittering dress appeared in the window. Her lip was moustached with tiny beads of sweat. Nineteen said "Salva Vida" to her and realized he'd been waiting to use those words since he'd seen them. Horns, percussion and voice assaulted him from a sidewalk speaker four feet away but he did not have to repeat it. He looked inside the window. It was Monday night and the dance floor was empty except for the whirling lights of a mirrored disco ball. There were tables to the side, one occupied by a cadre of Honduran bikers. Black leather and denim vests with LOS CORSARIOS stitched across the back. One was a woman. Another girl stood over them in a cocktail dress, conversing or taking orders. The ball matched the barmaid's glitter.

Nineteen finished his beer. The girl in the window, who regarded him as some sort of anomaly, tilted the bottle and said "¿Una más?" A useful expression. He would have to adopt it, and he did. Then again. The barmaid wrote nothing down, apparently did her arithmetic with the empties. There was movement in the street. He turned and saw three mariachis on three bicycles, single file, wearing identical black sombreros and red shirts with their guitars strapped neck-down to their backs. A picture seemed called for but his drowned phone wouldn't come back to life. When they'd passed he saw another bar across the street, open on three sides with a low pitched roof, a competitor returning fire with its own barrage of sound.

After the third beer he went inside to use the men's room, walked through the coruscating light to be confronted by two doors. One said *Mujeres*, the other *Caballeros*. A common sink between them. He scrounged up the few words of Spanish he'd heard her practicing on the flight but could only surmise that one room was intended for horses.

He would be a horse then, and entered. A narrow room with plastic plumbing. The toilet had no seat, nor water in tank nor bowl. A back-alley smell. He used the toilet anyway, took two hits from the bottle and went out to use the sink.

There was disco light and deafening music but no water in the taps.

"No . . . *agua?*" he asked the barmaid back out on the floor. She asked him something back and he stared at her, then she rubbed her hands together and he nodded "*Sí*" and she yelled across the room.

The young woman he'd seen talking to the Corsarios came toward him. She was pale and slender and her dark curls sat heavily on her shoulders (if they were real and who was he to judge). She greeted him strangely with a high five.

He shook his head, hands at his side. "I don't think you want to do that."

The bikers had gone.

"What can I do for you?" she said, almost without accent. He showed her his hands, surprised, and she said she'd be right back, then was with a bottle of hand soap and a small plastic bowl, a towel over her arm. She led him back to the sink, squeezed soap into his hands, and when he was done she poured water from the bowl over them into the sink.

He asked, of course, how she'd learned English, shaking drops from his hands.

"Same way you did." Her smile was kind. "I grew up in the States. I have family there."

He took the towel but didn't use it. "So . . . you came back . . ."

"I have family here, too." She looked at the towel. "It's a long story. You're going to stick around to hear it?" He was currently the only customer.

"Maybe." She hadn't made him forget his hunger. "You serve food here?"

"Only on weekends."

"Is that when all the action is?"

She nodded. "The capital thinks, San Pedro works, La Ceiba dances—especially Saturday. That's when we turn on the water in the restrooms." He couldn't tell if she was kidding. "But Monday . . . Zona Viva is Zona Muerta."

She asked him if he'd ever had baleadas. He thought he'd seen the word on the street, said, "I'll try anything once," though it wasn't exactly true.

She smiled as though to herself and told him about a place a block over, drying his hands for him as you would a child's and with such care his eyes welled with gratitude and he thought he might choke up another sob. It was at odds with his erection.

"No cerveza there," she said. "Come back and you can hear my story. Then tell me yours."

127

A baleada consisted of a length of spicy sausage wrapped in a tortilla with beans and crumbly cheese and some kind of sauce. Nineteen ate two out of a red plastic basket in a bright open room, nearly half of which was occupied by a delivery truck. Across the street he saw the word HOTEL in glowing multicoloured letters attached to the tallest thatched roof he'd ever seen. He wore his sunglasses. A young family ate at the next table and a small boy stole glances at the gringo. The gringo looked distracted. He kept hearing something—a whistle, shouting, the sound of sport, and when he'd finished he went off to find its source. A drink first.

Around the corner from the restaurant was a painted concrete enclosure with caged windows set at intervals in its cracked and peeling walls, and within it men were kicking a ball. Nineteen stood at one of the openings, hooked his fingers in the wire mesh and watched. Patchy turf, bald in places and roughly marked. He thought with affection of the old stadium shared with the baseball team, the painted sand of centre field. The red zone. Here the field was called a pitch, he knew. There were defenders, midfielders, forwards who did the scoring, reaped the glory, but Nineteen would have been a goalkeeper. Goalkeepers got to throw the ball as well as catch it, and direct the defense. God how he would have directed the defense.

They were just practice drills—passing, sweeping, feinting—but Nineteen didn't care. He was a fan of everything. Thudding weight, pumping lungs, bodies in opposition. He thought of training camp and took the guaro from his pocket. *Get there! Get there! This as fast as we can move?* He raised the bottle to them and drank. A man inside looked at him and he realized he must have been remembering out loud.

The man was at least forty, wearing a windbreaker, shorts, and a whistle. His players called him *Profe* but a coach is a coach. Nineteen smiled and nodded as if in mutual understanding. He meant well. The team reconfigured into passing triangles. Another ball had been produced but it was still necessary to take turns.

"Good squad, good squad!" Nineteen toasted them. "Gotta be all day now."

"Agua!" The manager whistled a water break. He seemed to have no assistants. Then he walked carefully over to the window where Nineteen greeted him: "Hola, Coach."

"Hola," the manager said. He smiled carefully. "American."

"That's what my passport says. Hungarian on my father's side, God rest him."

"Hungria team win bronze in . . ." The manager thought.

"Abla English, Coach?"

"A little. Some."

Having eaten, Nineteen decided that sports had replaced food as the universal language and more or less said so. What was not to get?

"I see this, yes," the manager allowed, a little uncertain.

"But soccer, bro. *Fútbol!*"

The manager watched him drink. "You like it, this game?"

"I like it all. *Love*," Nineteen amended. "Love it."

The careful smile. "But soccer is number one in the world."

"No shit. I mean somebody has to be, right? But *soccer*." Nineteen capped the bottle, put his hand on his chest like he was saying the Pledge of Allegiance. "Fuckin A. Riots, stampedes . . . I mean, wasn't there, like"—his cheeks puffed with a small belch—"some kinda war once?" He was dimly familiar with the Soccer War of 1969.

"Wasn't about game. Was about land," the manager said.

Nineteen felt reproved. He meant well. "Hey, I'm not meaning to bust your balls here. You're doing The Work here, Coach. Shaping young lives. Give em structure, order, all that shit . . . System, process, you know? Anything else you're just kickin stones."

"Well . . ." The manager looked back into the crumbling arena at the lives he was ostensibly shaping. They had splintered off into loose one-on-ones. Some were younger than others, some had pot bellies, silver in their hair. They were not wearing uniforms and their average income was less than a dollar an hour. He looked at the scant audience of friends and family and said, "I'm driving truck, in my work."

"It's about loving something you do. It's about being part of something." Nineteen's eyes shone, voice quavered with what else it might be about. Drunk, he'd never met a cliché he didn't like, but he didn't quite say that life is a game.

"Is no FIFA but we have fun."

"Fuck Feefa," Nineteen said, more bluntly than he'd intended.

"It's maybe more different fun for you."

"Eggzackly." He seemed not to realize they may not have been in agreement. One of the players was spinning the ball on his toe. What was not to get. "So sweet."

The manager said something else but Nineteen was looking at the battered dirty ball, its cracked black pentagons; according to legend, the game had had its start in medieval England with a mob kicking someone's head around after an execution.

"What?"

The manager frowned and glanced back at his team, gave them some kind of signal. "So. What is it you job? In America."

Nineteen had thought he'd never ask.

"Ah. Not fútbol; *football*."

"What'd I say?"

"You . . . coach?"

"*Played* it . . . I played . . ." He raised his hand in increments. "Youth, high school, college. Nine years pro."

"You play professional."

"Nine years." He named the team, then the position.

"Ah," the manager said. "Tom Brady." He smiled. Saw the puffy face, the bottle, what passed for hair, and didn't ask Nineteen's name. "Is something."

"It is. Was. Till it wasn't, thank you." Nineteen didn't try to discern whether or not he was being believed. He brought his thumb and finger not quite together. "This close," he said. "Twice. We knocked on the door . . . I did everything right. Nobody home." He shrugged, uncapped the bottle. "Hail Mary, full of grace, Mother . . . fuckers. I'm over it. Did I say it wasn't just a game? Fuckin free agency kicked our ass. So did everybody else. Went down *eleven* times in Indy—team record, not a good one. Cheque, please! How many fingers I got up?" He didn't wait for an answer. "It's always two so you always get it right. But you know what?" He started to raise the bottle, lowered it, instead reached into his face and took out six front teeth. The manager looked away. "It catches up, then passes you by, no hard feelings. Time numbs all wounds—with a little help, right? But you know what?" A black leer. He raised the bottle with one hand, restored his smile with the other. "I'd even let em do it all over again."

A man had approached the window, waited for Nineteen to finish. "Profe."

The manager turned, had a few words. Then he looked cautiously at Nineteen. "We have a small game now—to practice."

"Don't say small. Scrimmage." Roughly half of the players were taking off their shirts.

The manager looked at him. "You watch us."

"It'd be a privilege." He was still in need of rescue. "Live go. Best on best."

"I ask you for something."

"Anything, Coach."

The manager gestured. "El guaro." Nineteen stared at him, cap in hand. "Por favor. To put it away, this botella." He glanced back, pointed with his thumb. "For them. It makes nervous. To respect."

Nineteen looked at the manager, the bottle, the players, the few spectators, as if defining a complex relationship. Then he screwed the cap back on and put it in his pocket.

"Whatever you say, Coach. Sorry. I had no idea."

"The policía, they don't want this drink. En público."

"I don't know what I was thinking," Nineteen said, ashamed, then angry at being ashamed.

"Is no problem. Thank you."

Fuck the policía. He was a grown-ass man.

"Was nice to be talking," the manager said. He started to back away. "Cuidado."

"Same to you," Nineteen muttered. "My pleasure." But it was fully dark and the damage was done. He'd meant well. "No problemo."

Fucking amateurs, fucking field fairies.

He didn't stay for the kickoff.

The wind had picked up on the calle. Ferns, signs and weed trees waved. QUEEN'S BEER STORE. PIZZA EXPRESS. He drank and walked. A car beeped him off the smooth unmarked street and yelled something and he yelled back, "*Yo la tango!*" A man in a doorway smoked, black shirt open on a thin gold chain. Behind him the green felt of a pool table and the Honduran bikers playing a game Nineteen was not familiar with. The woman was tall. She leaned over the table, exposing the small of her back and you could almost read the ink there. Walk in, put your change on the rail. Take winner. There was a time when he would have, when he was rarely alone and was up for any encounter, but even without his line, his pads and protection, it wasn't her friends he was afraid of.

He passed a cadre of German backpackers on the sidewalk. Their store-bought dreads, their patented shabbiness. Want of soap. He shouldered one into the street and, when he heard one of them yell "Asshole! Only an American!" yelled back "*Sieg Heil* wash your ass!" and kept going till the incessant Latin beat dissolved into country-and-western and he saw two men in cowboy hats nursing drinks at an open-air bar. The singer referred to himself as a truck-driving fool. Nineteen only liked country when *she* sang it. When he started to move on he almost walked into a horse in the middle of the street. It was big and brown and moving in the opposite direction with neither rider nor saddle, as if in slow flight, and he got out of its way but stayed close enough to smell it. He'd had horses once, took an almost perverse pleasure at the smell of manure.

"If you need to know where the bathroom is," he told it, "I got you."

The Zona became desolate. He thought he heard someone behind him. *In the dark I would know thy step.* The wind was stronger now. In a brief blue flash Nineteen glimpsed a miniature golf course, weeds sprouting from the holes, the blades of the windmill motionless. Broken masonry, decapitated palms, pylons supporting nothing. Failure in a failed state. He felt a drop on his face, heard reggae. Saw a row of coloured light bulbs slanting on a string. A grey-haired man in blue let him into a Jamaican club after a brief once-over. A couple on the open floor chasing the elusive beat. People would dance to anything. The bartender spoke English but was reluctant to use it on Nineteen, save to tell him about a place where foreigners hung out—"American expatriate," he enunciated in his brogue, pointing.

"Only ex-Pats I know used to play for Belichick," Nineteen said, proud of his drunken wit, then became suspicious. "Whatsamatter *mon*, you don't want my business?"

The bartender didn't speak to him again and Nineteen drank his beer slowly, thinking about Bill and Brady and their unbeatable system with pure resentment unadulterated by his usual good sportsmanship; it was good not to be yourself for a while. He looked into the street. The threat of rain had abated and he left without leaving a tip.

The hotels at the edge of the Zona were low-rise affairs with pools, salons, gyms, tennis, had European-sounding names like Rotterdam and Versalles and Partenon. Nineteen saw a dog at a dirty puddle snapping up water. A short dead-end road led to the beach and a big restaurant-bar with two levels and a champa-style roof. Relatively upscale. A valet stood outside amid a faint smell of sewage. Inside, the tables and booths were not exactly packed, the stage and deejay booth unoccupied, but the place was doing more *viva* than he'd seen elsewhere; he would actually have company at the bar. He told the attractive English-speaking hostess, as obligatory as the armed guard and flatscreen TVs, that he was headed there, and her eyes dropped below his waist, but it was the bulge in his pocket she was looking at.

He sat on a wooden stool at the wooden bar, glanced without preference at the TV, having progressed to the point where everything was interesting, for better or for worse. The bartender wore a Hawaiian shirt against his tan and looked younger than the bits of grey in his hair and beard. He set a napkin in front of Nineteen, heard him order an American beer, then smiled and said in an accent that might have been Bostonian, "Haven't seen another gringo in here for a while."

Nineteen was too far gone to be surprised. The word made him think of bandoliers and sombreros. He repeated the remark he'd made at the Jamaican club and the bartender laughed professionally. Patriots aside, Nineteen had always liked Easterners.

"I was told this was something of a hangout," he managed.

"Used to be." The bartender put a bottle in front of him. "Before the Peace Corps pulled out. Want a glass?"

Nineteen shook his head. He had a rough idea what the Peace Corps did, so instead he observed, "Not a lot of action around here."

"Monday night. Saturday they even pat down the white people." The bartender did something behind the bar having to do with ice. "You should be here around the third week of May—la Feria de San Isidro. It's like Carnaval, Mardi Gras . . . half a million Hondureños cutting loose for three days. Hemingway without the bulls."

Nineteen thought of men in red scarves running for their lives, which made him think of the end days of his career. "Not much on crowds these days."

"How about half-naked women on floats?"

"I'll take half-naked women on . . ." He trailed off witless and the bartender told him what he owed.

Nineteen laid some paper in a dry spot along the drip edge. He looked around, wondered if this was the kind of place where young women sat down next to Americans and struck up conversation. "So why'd they pull out? The Peace Corps."

The bartender made a mojito. "Not long ago this was the murder capital of the world."

"So I heard." Scaring off business was apparently not a concern. Nor serving someone who's probably had enough. "Somebody got murdered?"

"Not quite . . . Rape, robbery. No murders, though. That was West Africa."

"Shit happens." Nineteen drank, trying to swallow his words. "What do I know."

"Not just here—El Salvador, Kazakhstan. They got out of Malawi because of lynch mobs—lynch mobs hunting vampires."

Nineteen shook his head. He hadn't heard of Malawi but he'd heard of vampires. "They got them here too?"

"In a manner of speaking."

"So how do you know so much?"

"I was a volunteer. PCV."

"You were in the . . ."

"Twenty-seven months—closed my service." He gave the drink to a waiter, folded a cleaning cloth. "I was in La Moskitia."

Nineteen looked at him.

"You heard of the Mosquito Coast?"

"Yeah. That movie. Whatshisname." He could no longer snap his fingers.

"Harrison Ford."

"Hairson yeah, he's great. *Docta Jones!*" Nineteen thought he might have met him at an after-party. Or backstage. Or in an owner's box.

"Jungles. Villages. Mountains. A lot of jungle—used to be, anyway."

"I bet. So what'd you do in there?"

The bartender answered deliberately. "I was a water, sanitation, and hygiene extensionist." Then, "I built outhouses."

"No shit." Nineteen smiled but the bartender didn't. "I mean, somebody has to."

"No shit is right. No movie, either. It's a matter of life and death there. Literally." A matter of typhoid, worms, dysentery, cholera. "Built thirty-one in a little over two years. Formed a latrine committee. They were ready to start composting."

Nineteen started to say God bless but amended it to "More power." He was moved by service to others but it usually involved sexier forms of sacrifice. "You go to school for that?"

"I have a degree in psychology—the Corps trained me. One more?"

Nineteen nodded. "Think they'd have any use for me? Mine's in communications."

The bartender served him, took bills from the pile. "What did you do with it?"

"Hung it on the wall." He did not want to follow this thread. "So you stayed on, right? You like, live here."

"Four years."

"Huh." Nineteen looked at the new bottle. "This how you make your living?"

"Among other things." The bartender seemed to be trying to decide something. "I've started my own business, actually."

"Building shithouses?" Nineteen said, and wondered how to take it back. Someone said "Por favor" and the bartender stepped away. When he came back he'd apparently decided it was Nineteen's turn and said, "So what brings you here, if I may? This ain't exactly Antigua—or Belize, for that matter."

"Well since it ain't the murder champ anymore."

"Still got to watch your back here, brother. State Department doesn't even want you here. You're supposed to stay on the island with the other gringos."

"That's where I was." He mumbled to no one. "Found myself on the ferry . . ."

"It's a long swim."

"Tell me about it." Nineteen belched softly. "Just checking it out."

"Checking it out." The bartender sounded either slightly disappointed or skeptical. "Guys like you come here, they're usually either building or buying."

"Guys like me." Nineteen decided to be flattered. The bartender asked where he was staying and Nineteen paused, the bottle en route to his mouth. "Good question." Resumed.

Another customer sat down and the expatriate bartender saw to him. Nineteen heard them speaking Spanish and felt slightly abandoned. He decided this warranted a real drink and stole to the restroom.

This *baño* had working pipes and Nineteen washed his hands before and after. He'd just unscrewed the cap when the guard stuck his head in the door.

"Can I help you?" Nineteen said, and the guard said, "Is lady room," looking at the bottle.

The mistake of gender was forgivable but not the illicit booze. In middle age Nineteen was a more docile drunk, but might not have been so easily ejected if they hadn't let him keep the guaro. He forgot all about the former volunteer. Outside the warmth came in a soothing breeze and the smell of the sewer had been replaced by something more fragrant. No hard feelings. He thought to try his phone. It glowed encouragingly now but none of its functions were available. He looked at the valet, who wouldn't look back. He was thinking of half-naked women for some reason. Their curves curved so Spanishly. Then they were all naked except for a girl in pink washing his hands. She wanted to tell him her story. He heard the sea. Had his drink and started away from the beach toward the street.

The immediate past recurred, dimly recalled, as he headed back. The reggae bar, the country-and-western bar, both quietly dark. To his right at another corner, over a wooden fence, the word HOTEL again, now glowing in a void as if the building to which it was attached had dematerialized, its guests now quartered in limbo.

Headlights keeping a distance behind. Nineteen wondered if he was being followed.

He drank and crossed, heard the music again; he was almost there. In the street he saw the horse, standing still as if waiting for him to mount. Behind it, across the calle, the window where he'd sat saying *una más* was shuttered and mute, the story he'd come back to hear untold. The building had no colour. Had it once been pink?

Nineteen was relieved in a way. He stood now before its rival on the opposite corner. Its three sides still open to the night, to him, still singing its songs. The headlights were gone. He drank without discretion and went in.

A variegated dimness. The floor crunched under his feet and he saw it was made of gravel like a parking lot. The bar was small and had few seats and he took one of them. There was a dance floor but no one was dancing; the few patrons were scattered among tables along the outer edge and they were all men. Seated shadows clutching bottles. Ball caps, cowboy hats, shaved heads. A waitress sat on a lap, holding a round tray. Her coworkers congregated in a corner behind the bar; trays and cigarettes, cotton tank dresses in different colours. More servers than served. Nineteen watched their high-speed exchange and marvelled at their ability to speak without apparent breath. They ignored him till there was a break in the music and one of them came over. Wide shoulders, hair tightly pulled back from an unsympathetic face. She stared at the gringo without saying anything and apparently would have done so until he said, "Salva Vida."

A back door with a palm frond waving in the dark just beyond it.

She held the beer and made a sort of peace sign and he realized he was meant to insert money there. He had plenty left, and felt a spasm of guilt. He would try to call her. The beer was warm. It was starting to seem like a mistake.

He finished one mistake and ordered another. The music started back up.

The heavyset waitress returned with his beer, this one warmer than the first. Nineteen asked did she have any colder.

"¿Qué?"

He tried futilely to make her understand, and she him. A voice behind him said, "Refrigerator's busted. No *frío*."

The speaker was about thirty and trim and dressed neatly in slacks and short-sleeved button shirt, wore a neat trimmed goatee and had neatly combed hair. He stepped forward and proffered his fist, said something else you couldn't hear over the music.

After a moment, Nineteen presented his own knuckles and said, "What?"

The man leaned forward. "I thought I heard Gringlish, no offense. Thought I might be of some help . . ." His gesture encompassed the bar, the waitress, the scant inventory. "You don't speak Spanish?" It wasn't a question.

"I can say Salva Vida," Nineteen said. Drinking usually made him affable but even in his state he doubted this establishment would provide the service of an in-house translator. He couldn't tell if he'd heard an accent. "You American?" He took another swig.

The man apparently took this for an invitation, helped himself to a seat and smiled at the waitress, who looked provoked. "I was born here but I'm not from here, know what I'm saying?" Nineteen said nothing. "I come up in L.A., South Central. You ever been? Where you from, *papi?*"

"I've been to L.A.," Nineteen said, but didn't say where he was from. He'd played in the Coliseum but didn't tell him that either. He was so neat and clean.

"We don't get too many gringos around here anymore, no offense." Nineteen wondered why he should keep saying it if he meant no offense. "Just hearing it, I'm there. Figueroa, Central-Alameda, Florence . . . Crazy."

Nineteen wasn't sure if these were women or neighbourhoods of nostalgia. "South L.A.?"

"South *Central*," his visitor insisted. "I got stories to tell, papi. A lot of the guys I come up with, man I'm just lucky to be standing on top of the dirt so I can tell em."

He kissed his fingers and pointed heavenward, where his compatriots now resided.

Nineteen nodded. He'd beat the black and silver in front of ninety thousand in their own house. Lost five pounds of water weight in near hundred-degree heat.

"Sorry?" The man was looking at him. Had he thought out loud again?

"Just my brain talking. No fence," Nineteen elided. "Got a nurlogic disorder."

"How's that?"

"I'm drunk."

The man smiled, then pointed at the label on the bottle. "You know what that means?"

"Sure," Nineteen said. "Boy do I ever." His face felt red to bursting.

The waitress came back then but spoke to the visitor. The exchange quickly escalated, came in short bursts like a gunfight. Nineteen was impressed; these people did not equivocate. He heard the words *dinero* and *comprar* and *salida*, saw the woman point outside as if she would throw the man out, but he said something that seemed to mollify, if temporarily, and she went away.

"Everything okay?" Nineteen asked, but could have guessed the import: buy or fly.

"Don't worry about her," the man dismissed. "I told her she reminds me of the woman who used to carry around a car door. You ever hear that one?"

"What?" Against his better judgment, Nineteen was always up for a joke.

"Someone says, 'Hey, senorita, why do you carry that car door around?' And she says, 'In case I get hot I can roll down the window.'"

Nineteen laughed genuinely, another mistake.

The man pointed. "Made you smile. Now you're having a good time." Another fist bump. He leaned into the little window he'd made. "You having a good time? To be honest you look a little bored. Monday night Zona Viva is Zona Muerta, right?"

"It's fine. I'm fine." Nineteen was wondering when the fist bump had replaced the high five.

"You sure? Hey, you just got to know where to go, right? If you want I could show you around a little."

Not a translator, then—a concierge. Nineteen didn't answer, because he doubted he could say the word, and because he suddenly believed this asshole had been nowhere near L.A. He remembered the man who'd followed him through the little park, the crawling headlights, watched another waitress park her lit cigarette behind the bar and walk into the grim perimeter beyond. He tried not to picture her carrying a car door.

"You checking that out?" The man was incredulous. "That bitch sits on your lap you might not get up again. Forget about these zungas, I can get you something a whole lot better." He shifted in his seat. "You been to L.A., right? You know Figueroa Street?" Touched his beard. "Where you say you were from, papi?"

"Coliseum's on Figueroa," Nineteen remembered aloud. Dirty sunshine. Bleachers with the peristyles of ancient Rome. He decided he preferred gringo to papi.

"There you go." The man seemed impressed. "All kinda shit on Fig, my friend. You should see it at night. Hey, during the day too for that matter." The music abated momentarily and he lowered his voice. "We got that here too, man. Zona Culo. Zona Bona. Legal. What do you say? Can I interest you?"

Nineteen looked at the back door, thought the beach must be close. He didn't think he could even finish his beer, thought it might have finished him. He shook his head. What had happened to the music? He tried to hear the sea.

"What you down for then, man? Whatever you need. I could take you around, show you a better place. They don't even have TV in this hole." The music resumed. The man who'd had the waitress on his lap was dancing with her now. She held his intervening gut with both hands.

The man from South Central whistled, would not be distracted. "Hey, over here. So talk to me. You smoke *juanita*? You like the happy dust? What are you into?" He smiled. "The night is young and here it's cheap." He leaned in again and was as covert as the music would allow. "How young you like it? Before the hair maybe?"

Nineteen turned his head. "Fuck is wrong with you."

The man put his hands up as if he were under arrest. "Hey, whoa! Don't get me wrong now. That ain't me. I'm just making sure it ain't you either. I mean come on now."

He took great pains to perish the thought, looked around guardedly. Nineteen shook his head again, longed to lay it on the counter. He put some words together: "Jus   lemme   be here."

He was somehow understood. "Alright, okay," the man said, as if he were the one pressed. The big-shouldered waitress swung by to look at Nineteen's bottle and glare at his company again. The latter waited till she'd gone. "I'm just trying to be friendly. *Bienvenidos*, you know? I thought, you know . . . but that's cool. No problem. No problem, right? Todo está bien."

He raised his fist and it occurred to Nineteen how it looked like a snake rearing up. He could not bring himself to return the gesture again. Another response seemed called for. He allowed a quantity of beer into his mouth but didn't swallow. The man didn't leave.

"You're just gonna leave me hanging," he mused in a wounded voice. Didn't wait for a response, nor would he leave. "Hey. Can I ask you for a favour?"

"I can't do any favours." It came out easier this time.

"What?"

"I don't do any favours."

"Can you just hear me out?"

"I can't."

"Alright," the man said rather quickly. "No problem. Fuck it." He considered. "Just buy me a beer then. Salva Vida." His pronunciation was emphatic, nasal, soft on the d. It was almost funny. "Just buy me one and we'll call it even, okay?"

"I can't."

"You can't." He sounded reasonably curious. "How can't you buy me a beer?"

It didn't occur to Nineteen to say he was out of money. He just shook his head.

"You can't buy me one fuckin beer."

He gripped the bottle. A couple of times during his breakout year, drunks trying to impress someone or themselves got in his face down in the Flats. He'd back them off without backing down but in his state couldn't remember how. In his state couldn't tell if the bottle was plastic or glass.

"Okay. No problem." The man sighed, shook his head at what the world had come to. "Just one. Play me like that. Not even this panther piss." The waitress was watching again but he seemed no longer to care. "That's alright though. All fucking right."

"I know it's alright," Nineteen said.

The man sat up. "What? You say something, pendejo? You think it's alright?" Just like that, zero to a hundred. "I come at you with an open hand and you leave me hanging? You better hope it's alright, chimba. You're gonna need Salva Vida, play me to the left. You're gonna need someone pull that bottle out your ass."

A burst of ugly Spanish. The waitress added her own but she was addressing one of her coworkers: "¡Llamelo! ¡Llamelo!" and the girl started pushing buttons on her phone.

The man stood like he'd been sitting on wet paint; Nineteen climbed out of his seat somewhat slower, putting it between them, brandishing the bottle though he was having trouble seeing straight. He thought he heard voices behind him. But the man spoke to the women, hands raised again in that placatory gesture. "Está bien, está bien. ¡Cheque!"

The waitress spoke and the other one lowered her phone. The man backed away toward the front door, looking at Nineteen. "I got you little bitch, little pussy." He paused to speak to the men in back on his way out. Then: "Bienvenidos, maricón." The music went well with invective. You could still hear him out in the street, in Spanish; *chimba*, *raja*, *puta*. Nineteen thought he heard *perro* and was sure that meant dog.

Even when you couldn't hear him anymore the barometric pressure in the room wouldn't drop. Nineteen sat down, somewhat galvanized, not sure whether it was braver to leave or to stay. He thought he could finish his beer now but the barmaid was shaking her head. She was pointing to the back door. When she spoke it was not to him, but over his shoulder. She no longer looked angry, but afraid. Voices behind him.

Where r u? You ok? If I dont hear from you this morn am calling police.

He woke to the sound of hammering in a bed in a small white room, clothed but uncovered. A ceiling fan turned slowly. The hammering sounded distant and was outdone by that in his head. His tongue bloated like a little corpse, filling the dry tomb of his mouth. When he sat up the pounding became worse, then slightly better and he swung his legs off the bed and stood to look out the small window in the opposite wall. His feet were bare.

Sparse grass, tropical plants. A fence of stone posts connected by a turquoise wooden rail, a dirt road on the other side that took him nowhere. He turned and saw his wallet, phone, and passport neatly arranged on a chair next to the bed. In a certain kind of movie the bed would be bigger and a woman asleep in it. There was no other furniture. He checked his wallet, turned on his phone and took it all with him into the hallway outside the room, looking for his shoes and a toilet.

Police cant do anything for 24 hrs. Someone thot they saw you at the ferry station. For gods sake call!!!

There wasn't much to the place. Tile floor, pale walls. A second, larger bedroom, fully furnished, a small bathroom with an open electric shower. His phone had now completely revived and trembled urgently in his hand, but first things first and he put it in his pocket and stood over the toilet. A note above the tank requested guests not to flush toilet paper but to use the provided receptacle, thank you. Nineteen looked at the lidded metal trash can in the corner next to the bowl, and his queasy stomach turned a little more.

He read her words but didn't listen to her voice.

He came upon himself in the mirror. His system was mussed and speckled with sand and this somehow made it more convincing. A lump on his forehead covered with a blood-caked Band-Aid, and a dried patch on his shirt that was not blood . . . Puking on the desolate littered beach . . . something in his hand . . . rock, bottle, shell . . . He was grateful he could remember things but afraid of what they might add up to. His stomach revolted again and he dry-heaved painfully over the toilet as if in bodily recall.

Im in la cieba. Im ok. Theres a ferry back later.

OMG where are you staying? Call me so I know its you. We have to talk.

The little hallway elled into a living room that was of a piece with the kitchen. Another ceiling fan, motionless. Bland mismatched furniture—dining table, loveseat, armchair—except for a handsome carved mahogany table atop which stood a television and a small framed photograph. In the picture, the expatriate bartender he'd met the night before stood smiling with his arms around a young Latin woman. He might have been consoling her. Nineteen looked around. The place was generally spartan and lacked what he thought of as a woman's touch.

There was a water cooler in the open kitchen and he drank six paper cupfuls before he saw the handwritten note taped judiciously to the wall above. The expatriate would be back for lunch; he apparently did not just tend bar.

He drank another cup and his thoughts turned back to his phone. Then they turned to his shoes and he went outside.

Warm and breezy and not uncomfortable; he thought it might have rained. The bungalow was painted light green. Nineteen found his shoes on the front porch—a concrete slab flanked by white fluted columns—and evicted a gecko from one of them. The front door was also hand-carved and painted—waves and fish beneath a palm tree beneath birds and five-pointed stars. A child's world. Alongside the porch was a tiki hut, a small patch of bright tropical flowers, and next door another bungalow, yellow, windows and door yet to be installed. Between them stood a coconut palm and in the distance the green-grey mountains, always having the last say.

Do you know what you did?

Nineteen looked the other way. A grove of trees growing defiantly out of sandy soil blocked his view, but he knew what must lie on the other side.

Felll off the wagon

149

U jumped off that mfer. Call!

He was aware again of the hammering, now accompanied by the smooth metal scream of a power saw, and walked toward it, climbed a mound of excavated dirt twenty yards or so from the green bungalow. He assumed it would afford better reception. From the top he saw a Honduran flag flying on a pole, and beneath it another flag, white, blue and red, in that order, but didn't know which state it stood for. Then a development of beachfront properties extending to the east in a rough line as far as he could see. Thatched-roof tropical bungalows smaller than the one in which he'd woken, a three-storey Spanish villa with antenna dish, custom pool, a rooftop terrace. Stages of completion. Stacked bags of cement, pipes, lumber, rolls of rebar. Nineteen heard someone singing to Spanish radio, saw men hammering, sawing, digging and hauling, but could not find the expatriate among them. No one saw him on his little mountain.

He summoned her name on the screen, his finger hovered over it. His knuckles had started to heal and he was almost disappointed; if someone had raised that lump on his head, he would have liked to have returned the favour. He looked up. The sea was now visible over the trees. He remembered the access the resort had denied them and he started down the dirt toward it. Clouds intermittently hid the sun. A trail led through a gap in the trees. The shoreline was dark with silt but clean of garbage and he stood looking. Sand crabs. The sea smelled alive, loosened the metal band fastened around his skull. A kid drove by on a minibike and waved. You were supposed to be mindful of kids on minibikes at the beach but Nineteen waved back. Then he switched off his phone and returned to the bungalow.

He'd figured out how to turn on the TV, and when the expatriate returned he was watching a Mexican soap opera in which attractive people with no discernible employment spent their time in mansions, scheming without subtitles.

"¡Hola! ¿Cómo está?" Nineteen fumbled with the remote; he hadn't heard the door.

The expatriate was accompanied by a workman wearing a hardhat, muddy jeans and a muddy t-shirt. He was called Tom and he was a pipe layer, and he shook Nineteen's hand with considerable gravity, seemed not to notice the mess on his shirt. He was young and muscular, probably athletic, and he spoke no English. Nineteen looked at him without envy; even in top form he'd never had a body like that.

"Es un honor conocerte," the piper layer said, then said something else Nineteen didn't understand, though the tone was familiar. He seemed in a hurry to leave. When he'd gone, the expatriate did not explain, but again asked Nineteen how he was, in English.

"Better. Thanks." He put down the remote. "Hope you don't mind."

"Make yourself to home—you get my note?" He'd left his shoes outside and wore a bandana and white coveralls spattered with light blue. Some had gotten on his tan and looked like war paint. He could have been a Chargers fan.

"Honduran national colour," the expatriate explained. "We get a tax break if we use it wherever we can."

Nineteen thought of the flags. "What's the red for?"

"Not Honduran. Guy who owns this development is a Russian national. Owns the bar I work at too. Matter of fact"—he gestured around—"this used to be his place."

Nineteen had done business with Russians. They had not golfed. "I just know the hammer and sickle."

"Right? Red usually stands for blood. I can understand these people wanting to keep it off their cloth. Ready for some lunch?"

"I'd hate to abuse your hospitality." Nineteen was starving. "I'll be catching the ferry back this afternoon."

"Then you have plenty of time. Just let me wash up a little. I'll find you a shirt." He switched on the fan and on his way to the bathroom pointed at the TV. A woman crying beautifully. "Those people are huge stars here, like Hollywood." Nineteen thought he'd changed the channel. He'd known players as addicted to soaps as they were to painkillers.

He stood in the kitchen while the expatriate made scrambled eggs, sausage, beans. "Hope you don't mind tortillas. I can't remember the last time I ate toast."

"When in Rome."

"This ain't Rome." The expatriate laughed. "But since you mention it, you mind putting your shoes on the patio? Outside's always trying to get inside here."

Nineteen was embarrassed. He'd intended to and forgotten, the way he forgot all the little things anymore. When he came back in the smell of food filled him with such gratitude he could barely thank the expatriate for whatever he'd done for him the night before—he was still nervous of the details.

"Don't mention it." The expatriate sounded as if he meant it literally; for a second the subject seemed closed. "Sometimes my wife meets me at the bar and we walk home together. It's like a few hundred metres." The mournful smile in the picture. "We were out back with some friends when you went by. You were in pretty bad shape but I didn't think much of it till I saw those bolos behind you."

"*Bolos.*" He remembered the cries of birds he couldn't see, which made him think of bats, which made him think of the man on the promenade at the resort. "Like, muggers?"

"They weren't looking to rob you, though it might have come to that." The expatriate's tone was even. "Someone told them you were looking for little boys to fuck."

The metal band tightened again. His hand went to the bloody knot on his head.

"That wasn't them, dude—you stumbled into a palmetto." The expatriate took plates from a cupboard. "I talked them down, told them I knew you. Hell, they were about as drunk as you were. But people here think Americans are capable of anything."

"Not that. I mean, you can't think . . ."

"I don't think. If you were a pedophile that's the last place you'd go. And you don't even speak Spanish? It's not an unheard-of tactic around here, though. People use it sometimes to get even." The sausage smelled more like beef than pork. "Someone trying to get even with you?"

Nineteen thought about the guy who said he'd grown up in L.A. and shrugged. "I honestly don't remember."

"Maybe it'll come to you." The expatriate was plating. "Or maybe better it doesn't." He opened the silver stainless fridge. "All we have is agua to drink. Sorry."

"God's gift," Nineteen said. "*Gracias.*"

They carried out rattan chairs from the kitchen and placed them under the tiki hut by the patio. En route they passed a hairy brown coconut fallen from the tree and the expatriate kicked it as far as he could toward the beach.

"Those things take root wherever they land," he explained.

"Goal," Nineteen said. "You play soccer?"

"I hate sports."

The eggs were quite good. Apparently everyone else was at lunch as well for the sounds of construction had abated and there was only the faint tinny music of phones and the skreaking of gulls. Heat and flies. The mention of soccer had made Nineteen think of the pipe layer who'd shaken his hand. Something he meant to ask.

"That guy you came in with. He work for you?"

"Sometimes," the expatriate said. "Sometimes I work for him. We both work for Oleg."

Nineteen recalled his body. "Bet he lays a lot of pipe. Tom, was it?"

The expatriate smiled. "Try Tomas Jefferson de Stallone de la Rojas."

"Seriously?"

The expatriate nodded. "That ain't the least of them. When he was born this country was running a serious pro-American fever. I'd have asked him to stick around but I think he might have been intimidated."

Nineteen asked why the pipe layer should be intimidated but already suspected the answer; it was in the look on his face as they'd shaken hands.

"Full disclosure: after we got you into bed last night, I took the liberty of checking your passport."

Nineteen chewed. "Well, you might have been harbouring a sexual deviant."

"Hope you're not pissed," the expatriate said.

"Not pissed about you saving my skin."

"About me shooting my mouth off to the guys, I mean."

He'd said he hated sports. "I wouldn't think you followed the game."

"I don't. My father did, though. Only sport he watched but

on Sundays he could be tough to be around. Maybe that's why I feel the way I do."

"Who's his team? Pats?"

"Cowboys." America's team. "But it's literally what he did instead of going to church—I think he actually saw it in religious terms. And he was a big fan of yours." The expatriate didn't say if his father was still alive. "He used to record games and sell them. There was one he always talked about . . . Kansas City? Said it not only proved God exists, but what a shitty sense of humour He has."

"Maybe he should have just went to church." Nineteen slapped his arm. Things so small they were invisible kept biting him, a ghostly torment.

"Sorry." The expatriate shook his head. "Maybe you'd rather not talk about it."

"I forget everything but what I want to," Nineteen said, digging back in. "You sure got the eggs right."

They finished and stuck their napkins under their plates for the wind. The expatriate reached into the bib of his coveralls and retrieved a stick of twisted paper. "You mind?"

"Not if you don't mind sharing." Nineteen had recently discovered its medicinal value; these days it was one of the few things that brought relief.

"Relief from what?" the expatriate asked him and, when he'd heard, said in a grey cloud, "Is that why you were on the island? Isn't that where the medical tourists go?"

"I guess. Yeah." Nineteen might have stopped there but could think of no other way to repay his host's benefaction; he didn't think cash was an option.

The expatriate spoke with held breath as he passed it. "I take it this is some kind of treatment you can't get in the States."

"Not for brain damage. Not at these prices."

"From your playing days?"

"Back then the trees ran into me." Though on principle Nineteen still didn't approve of its recreational use, he'd always liked the smell. He passed it back.

"So how'd it go?"

"It didn't," and he told the expatriate about the raid.

"Narcos." The expatriate inhaled without irony. "This is a troubled land."

"And that's why you came."

Exhale. "Another full disclosure: I used to do more than smoke this stuff. Sold some to an undercover cop in the Yard. Judge gave me a choice: the military or the Peace Corps."

"So you chose to help people."

"I chose not to go to jail."

"Still." Nineteen felt entitled to pry a little; it must have been the weed. "So why do you stay? The girl in the picture?"

"My wife." He said her name as if it were all the explanation required. "My *de facto* business partner."

"Business." Nineteen gestured around. "This?"

The expatriate shook his head. "I don't even get paid for this. I do a little supervising, a little painting . . . I get free rent." He nodded at the green wall. "This casita was the owner's—first place he built when he started the development."

"Nice," Nineteen said, thinking about the toilet paper. He sort of remembered something else. "Last night at the bar, you mentioned . . ."

"I don't think I went into any detail." The expatriate extinguished the joint and returned the burnt end to his coveralls. "Some people call it 'adventure travel.' I don't."

Nineteen slapped his arm. "Like . . . ziplining, rafting, hiking?"
He thought of mild brushes with danger.

"We take people into La Moskitia." The expatriate's phone
rang and he silenced it. "The Mosquito Coast?"

Harrison Ford. That much he recalled.

"Did my service there as a PCV. Lived with some of the Indigenous people for two years."

"Indians."

"If you like. Careful, though. To some that's like calling them
niggers. They're Pech and Miskitu, mainly."

"They're named after a bug?"

"Probably not—mosquitoes over there are called *zancudos*.
Nobody knows for sure, but it might come from the word musket;
when the English started using the Tawahka to fight the Spaniards,
they turned out to be pretty handy with guns. Too good, maybe."

"So much for spears and whatnot."

The expatriate couldn't quite hide his annoyance. "You might
still call them primitive by our standards, but no." He took out
his cell phone. "Some of them even have these."

Nineteen looked at it and muttered. "They can have mine."

"Signals are pretty hard to come by, though. Go deep enough
and you're completely cut off. There are parts so remote no
one's set foot in them yet. Practically inaccessible. And archae-
ological stuff—ruins, artifacts, things they've only started to
document."

"And you take people there."

"While it's still there to get lost in. Before the loggers, cattle
ranchers, fucking Google fuck it up like they have all the other
hidden places. Landsat—you know what that is?" The expatriate
didn't wait for a reply. He was no longer the affable bartender.

"People, look up from your phones. They're tearing out the heart of darkness!" He was suddenly aware of himself, swallowed, sounded almost contrite. "We have different packages."

Nineteen could forgive him for saying he hated sports; unlike most people he was not uncomfortable in the presence of true passion. "Ruins . . . like, Mayan ruins?"

"The Maya stuff is in Copán. Near the Guatemalan border. Very impressive." The expatriate did not sound impressed. "The stuff they've found in the Moskitia doesn't point to any civilization we know of. You've heard of the White City?"

"You mean Seattle?"

"That's funny." The expatriate did not sound like it was funny. "La Ciudad Blanca."

"You take people there."

"It hasn't been discovered yet. We go into the Biosfera, but not me personally. I have guides, interpreters—I use local people exclusively. Like I said, I have ties there."

He started to describe different tour packages but his phone rang again and this time he picked up. Nineteen heard the power saw again. He heard the expatriate speaking Spanish, and it almost sounded like an argument—"*No ahora,*" he kept saying, and Nineteen felt his own in his pocket, waiting mutely.

The expatriate hung up and stood with some reluctance. "Gotta get back to the office." He looked squarely at Nineteen. "So what are your plans?"

Nineteen was also on his feet. "Ferry leaves at four-thirty . . ." He asked what time it was. "Might as well get an early start. Call me a taxi?"

"Sure. Or you can let me drive you to the *muelle*."

"The who?"

"The ferry dock. I have to pick up Cristina from work this afternoon—it's sort of on the way."

The girl in the picture. He would not let himself be haunted by a photograph. "You've done plenty. I don't even know how to repay you for last night."

"It's not about balancing a ledger." His host sounded slightly annoyed again. "Up to you. I can call a car or you can take a hot shower and watch *Guerra de Pasiones* while you wait for me. I'd change that Band-Aid."

The expatriate demonstrated the *ducha electrica*. He would try the TV again—there is always a game being played somewhere. He would call her when he'd cleaned up.

The expatriate's fledgling business did not yet provide a living and his wife worked in a maquiladora, making apparel for Liz Claiborne, Old Navy, J.C. Penney, Nike. The fabric she used was imported tax-free, the products she made from it were exported tax-free again. They would pick her up and double back to the ferry terminal; the expatriate said he wanted Nineteen to meet her.

They took his dusty Toyota pickup and drove along the estuary Nineteen had crossed the night before, pleasant middle-class homes with porticoes and concrete fences on either bank. It had rained briefly. Abruptly they were in the outer *colonias*, a confusion of shacks and houses deposited on a slope as if by avalanche. Sheet metal patchwork, shower curtains for doors. Girls in blue-and-white school uniforms threw gang signs at them, and in an alley they passed a kid huffing something out of a Pepsi bottle, the vessel flattening and inflating like a plastic lung. An old woman sold homemade juice from a cardboard stand and the expatriate pointed and said, "Tercera edad."

"I still don't speak Spanish."

"The third age." He downshifted but didn't stop. "Finding a job here is hard enough for young people. And for her? But she has to live."

"She has to live," Nineteen echoed.

"Won't stop the mareros from extorting their war tax from her."

Nineteen thought. "Gangs?"

"Nobody gets a pass."

They drove by a lone cinder-block wall on which had been sprayed two abutting fists, long-nailed forefingers raised like horns. Five or six shirtless boys in their early teens sat or leaned on the wall, mimicking the painted gesture, shouting, "¡Dieci-yoyo! ¡Dieci-yoyo!"

"Think they want their picture taken?" Nineteen said.

"I think they want to be remembered," the expatriate said. "Most of them will probably be dead in a year."

Nineteen felt compelled to justify himself. "I always tried to give back," he said. Ran a football camp for inner city youth. Sponsored charity golf tournaments for abused kids. Saw them now sifting refuse with stray dogs in a smouldering rubbish dump, arcane longhand on walls. QUEREMOS PAZ.

He'd talked with his girlfriend before they left.

The embankments rose and there were ads painted directly on the rock face in place of billboards. They seemed religious in nature. Then they passed a water park and were back in a commercial district. Nineteen was relieved to see a megamall. Ahead the road forked into a highway under green signs. "Won't be far now," the expatriate said, and Nineteen asked him how he'd met his wife. The expatriate said they'd met in town, where she was living with an aunt who owned a cleaning service, that before

the maquila she came to the development once a week to clean
the casita he stayed in; he didn't say that before that she'd lived
in the capital, where her father had driven a cab until he was shot
twelve times for refusing to pay the war tax, where her younger
brother was drowned in a toilet after refusing to join his father's
executioners, that the marero they called Mister decided he
wanted to make her a *paisa* but she'd seen what happened to the
girls who said yes (pushing a stroller with that number tattooed
to your face, forehead to chin like a stain) and the ones who said
no, and had decided not to decide, but to head to *El Norte* with
a cousin, though she'd never even heard a train before, that
mournful brass chord, pronouncement of both hope and doom,
hello and goodbye, let alone seen one, miles of boxcars, tankers,
hopper cars, ore cars, scribed with graffiti streaming past like a
single endless sentence that would tell you nothing but everything, let alone ridden on its back for countless miles with countless other *desconocidos*—Hondurans, Salvadorans, Guatemalans,
Nicaraguans—penniless, nameless, without papers—who couldn't
pay for transportation, couldn't find an open boxcar or even an
undercarriage, who are less than passengers, less than coal, ore,
grain, less than livestock. The expatriate also didn't say, and
didn't know, though she had tried to tell him, how it was to lash
yourself to whatever strut or grating or fitting can be found so as
not to slip off the roof while sleeping, though some did anyway,
were crushed, lost limbs or heads, or were thrown off defend-
ing against ambush by thieves or kidnappers who boarded like
pirates after paying engineers to slow the train down, using
sticks, pipes, rocks, bare hands, whatever weapon could be found
or fashioned, or simply, finally, threw themselves off in defeat
and despair, under the wheels or into the desolate wilderness
they crossed, to be found only by wolves and vultures and other

scavengers for once not in human form; as she had tried to tell him how it was to endure days without food or water or sleep, to ride past a living volcano and into the mountains for two days of snow and twenty-degree nights, through countless tunnels so utterly dark you could only lie flat on your belly clinging to the ice-slick roof as if born to it, a night within the night. Nor did the expatriate say, because he couldn't be sure, because she could no longer recall either, though it might have been Querétaro, because she knew they weren't halfway there, so it might have also been Irapuato, where she became separated from her cousin whom she never saw nor heard from again, where the train, while stopped at a station, was boarded by operatives of a cartel who traffic in drugs and engage in other activities some of which can be observed in videos you can watch from the safety of your computer but are advised not to if you wish to remain the person you were before watching them, who knew she would fetch a higher price than the Guatemalans or Salvadorans because she was taller and had fairer skin, and took her to a city whose name means "true cross," to what they called a safe house, the ultimate misnomer for a place where you are set upon by men who brush cigarette ash from your back as they ravage you, tattooed with the letter Z like branded chattel, where they warehoused her and others and took their pictures and posted them online, then took her to hotels and sold her, a unit of merchandise in the blackest of markets, sometimes beating her for lack of enthusiasm, want of a smile (anywhere but the face), the customers sometimes doing the same if she asked them to wear protection, which the expatriate didn't relate, nor did he that one of them, a woman from San Salvador, finally escaped, dug the tracking chip out of her foot with a piece of glass, got away and turned herself over to Mexican immigration officials, who for five hundred dollars

sold her back to the Zetas, who made an example of her using
baseball bats, then gasoline and a match, leaving what was left
on an altar to Santa Muerte, Lady of Shadows, after which came
not a plunge into despair but a creeping numbness, slow collapse
of one day into the next, the lost track of time, of the bars and
hotels and the drunken sweat-stinking flesh until she must ask the
man who has purchased her what day it is, what month, what
year; acceptance of the unacceptable, resignation to being used
till she was used up, then used in some other way, a drug mule
perhaps, or a body from which to harvest organs, or as a pro-
curer, a deceiver to lure other *migrantes* into the maw with promises of jobs, papers, a new life, and to which she shook her head
no, just like that, not sure if it was to save another life or just end
her own, but no, and awaited the final beating, the perfunctory
bullet, or worse, but was instead given three hundred pesos—
the only money she ever saw from them—taken to a bus stop
and told to disappear, just let go, just like that, never knowing
why it didn't go the other way, though it might have been that
the *Federales* were closing in and too many bodies would be an
inconvenience, but she would never know for certain, only that
she had beat them by surviving them, by refusing, by luck or
God's grace, that the bus fare took her as far as Monterrey, where
she wandered into an emergency room, where the hospital notified Immigration, who eventually sent her back to Honduras,
where she lived for a time in La Ceiba with an aunt who owned
a cleaning service, where she met the expatriate, who said his
wife's name was Cristina and that she had come once a week to
clean his house, who told Nineteen the palm oil plantation they
were now passing was owned by a Palestinian, that there were
some hundred thousand Palestinians in Honduras, that the country was changing from a banana republic to a palm oil republic,

and Nineteen, who listened with half interest, might have clung with greater appreciation to the merely informative and mundane had he heard what the expatriate hadn't said.

The maquila lay just beyond a bridge over a nameless river where kids played a variant of King of the Hill, deposing each other from boulders into the water. One of them wore a towel like a cape. The bridge was narrow and you had to wait for oncoming vehicles before you could cross. They idled behind a Mack truck, breathing diesel.

Nineteen leaned over and looked at the fuel gauge. "Why don't you let me fill er up on the way back." He'd seen a gas station called Uno before they got on the highway. "It's the least I can do."

"Actually," the expatriate said, "if you insist, maybe there is something."

Nineteen wondered if it might involve buying a beach house, but the expatriate said, "Moskitiaventuras."

"You got it, whatever that is."

"My guide company, the one I told you about." He shifted into neutral and pulled the emergency brake. "You could take a tour."

"The jungle thing."

The expatriate nodded. Nineteen looked toward the bridge. "I don't know. Sounds kinda gruelling." He thought about the parts of his body that had been replaced by hardware. "I'm not in the shape I used to be, and even the shape I used to be in . . ." One of God's little jokes.

"It's not so hard," the expatriate said. "I've had people in their seventies do it. Arthritis and all."

Nineteen, who'd drawn his NFL pension early, was about to ask how much it cost when the expatriate said, "How about this:

if you like it enough to give me a little shoutout, let me drop your name, I'll eat the fee. Call it even."

"My name." Oncoming traffic had run its course. Nineteen tried to sound good-natured about it. "My name means something to a guy who hates sports?"

"Not for lack of respect. It meant something to a lot of people."

"You want some has-been plugging an expedition into the unknown?"

"You were a star."

"The hell do you know." The expatriate's presumption irked him. Let the going rate for saving his life be a full tank. He hadn't been asked to endorse anything in years, but had never lent his name to something he hadn't tried at least once. When they lurched forward he said, "I'll have to think about it," but was only postponing refusal.

The expatriate leaned over the wheel, intent on negotiating a bridge riddled with gaps and with nothing in the way of barriers at the edges. "What was it like, anyway?"

Nineteen asked what he meant, though he knew. "Honestly, had my clock cleaned so many times I'm a little fuzzy on the details." In truth he remembered nothing as clearly, but he couldn't convey it to someone who hadn't played the game, any more than he could have known what it was like to cling to the ice-covered roof of a train roaring through thirty-one tunnels in mountain dark.

At the maquila a young guard checked the expatriate's ID then seemed to take special interest in Nineteen's presence, thoroughly examining the foreigner's passport before, with obvious misgiving, opening the gate. God bless. They pulled into the neatly marked lot and waited. The factory was a long building with interlocking aluminum wall panels and a peaked roof. It looked prefabricated but not as shabby as Nineteen had expected; there were picnic benches outside. It didn't look like a sweatshop. The back door opened but only two men stepped out, Asians in business suits.

"Koreans," the expatriate said. "They own the place."

"What do Hondurans own?"

"Their pain." The expatriate gestured at the suits. "They live in the Zona Americana. Kind of a walled city, houses like the Garden District in New Orleans. Got a nine-hole golf course where they hold a tournament once a year. Management only."

A compartment of Nineteen's brain wondered what par was. Another asked the expatriate what his wife did in that building.

"Lately she stitches the number twenty-three on NBA jerseys. Seems a very popular number." Nineteen braced himself for minors working fifteen-hour days, etc., but the expatriate just pointed and said, "Here they come."

The back door was open. Workers spilled out, most of them in jeans and company smocks, some with blue medical face masks pulled down below their chins. "There she is." A serious-looking girl, if not quite as serious as the one in the picture, not someone who bore the scars of cigarette burns on her flesh, or other scars not visible. She was saying goodbye to someone, an older woman.

Nineteen and the expatriate got out of the truck. "Buenas," she said, not shaking hands. She was slender and composed, had a strong nose and narrow mouth which may have curved into a faint smile when she glanced at the Band-Aid and what else was attached to Nineteen's head. He felt measured. She apparently spoke no English, nor much Spanish for that matter as she rode impassively between two men out of the parking lot and back across the *puente*, not saying anything till they were back on the highway. Nineteen felt her hip against him, static of arm hair, then she seemed to press discreetly against her husband to avoid touching this gringo she didn't know.

"She wants to know what it was like to be a football star," the expatriate said. "I told her you were too modest to brag about it."

Nineteen forced a smile; so he'd told her as well. A shantytown rushed past in green overgrowth, impoverished of everything but colour and Nineteen took this as evidence of happiness. He could not imagine her asking that question.

"Mirave," the expatriate said; they were talking to each other again, at length.

"El curandero," she said, a little impatient, and Nineteen checked his phone. Another message from the sportswriter, another from Number Thirty-Four about a charity game of touch with a former divisional rival. (He found such games too painful in all ways.) He texted his girlfriend first, told her he was on his way to the ferry.

The Muelle de Cabotaje, the terminal, was not as busy as it had been when he'd arrived, and Nineteen was briefly amazed it had only been a day. They pulled up to the curb just short of the entrance.

"Well," he said. The sky was grey and looked like soft metal. "So what do you think?"

"Sounds like it'd be amazing." There was no point in pretending.

"Five days, four nights," the expatriate said, hopeful. "Have you back by Monday. There's some hiking but you'd spend a lot of time in a boat. Rubber boots are a must, though."

"Sounds like a fantastic time," Nineteen said, "it really does," and the expatriate held up a finger.

"Something else: you'd be staying at an Indigenous village. They don't have doctors there but there's someone who still practices traditional medicine. A healer, you could say." He shrugged. "Cristina thought that might be something you'd be interested in."

She was looking through the windshield. Nineteen couldn't see what she saw but, English or no, she looked as if she understood everything. A business partner. He turned in the direction of the sea, across which lay the island where his girlfriend waited, then looked back at the expatriate.

"Is that what *curandero* means?" he said, and still she didn't look at him.

The gringa is sitting alone at the edge of the lagoon, holding a drink called a Blue Parrot in one hand, her phone in the other. She is wearing a one-piece bathing suit and a sun hat and is sitting at a table and chair next to one of the beach beds. The drink, a truer blue than the lagoon, contains no alcohol. The beach bed is unoccupied. On her phone she is watching a live feed of the Career Conference in Louisville. The keynote speaker is an Independent Future Executive Senior Sales Director who opens her keynote address by reciting her life verse—all sales directors are encouraged to have a life verse—which in this case is Psalms 37:4. "'. . . and he will give you the desires of your heart,'" the Independent Future Executive Senior Sales Director is reciting when the gringa's phone rings. Of course phones don't ring anymore, they sing, recite catchphrases, and you can assign a particular song to a particular caller, for example Hank Williams Jr. demanding to know if we're ready for some football, as he is now, and she stabs the screen with her finger as much to kill the music as take the call and says, swallowing, "Finally. You get your ticket?"

The waitress passes in her beige polo, carrying a tray. She smiles and keeps going; the gringa, who sounds like someone

trying to sound casual, wears a bracelet which does not entitle
her to table service and she has already gotten herself a drink
from the bar, but you would think a woman in her situation
might consider an upgrade to Premium.

"No," the gringa says. "Still closed till further notice. You
buy your ticket?"

The weather has been more or less perfect all day. The resort
seems almost deserted now; some of the guests were mainland-
ers taking advantage of the seasonal prices, now taking the ferry
back to their weekly lives. Even the black vultures have gone,
along with most of the medical tourists, but the cats are back,
looking for table scraps.

"Really," the gringa is saying. "Kind of a . . . What kind of a
change of plans?

"Who's that?" the gringa says. "Is someone there?

"What kind of a little trip?"

She tries to maintain her voice but everyone—the waitstaff,
the bartender, security, even the custodian—is a little nervous of
her after yesterday. Her companion will not be permitted back
on the premises. He struck only the wooden post beside her
head, but the mark remains, and if he returns he will be asked to
leave. She has been informed.

She is smiling now, not in a good way. Now she laughs, even
worse. "Seriously, is someone holding a gun to your head? I
don't . . . Are you even in any shape to do this?   Maybe *we're*
now or never, you even think of that? I notice I'm not invited.   Oh
right. I'll bet you never even   Oh. How brave, how . . . what's the
word? I guess it's easier to run off into the jungle than come back
and face what you   For someone who missed you sure did a lot
of damage. Who's paying for this, anyway?

"What does that even mean?" the gringa says.

"Your name.

"If you have to ask.

"You mean like a . . . Hello?"

The waitress the gringo ogled at the bar passes by again. This time she moves a little faster and does not look at the gringa, who laughs again through that smile.

"Whatever," she says. "I don't care what they call them. You're going God knows where for   Oh, is that all?   Well thanks for giving me the option, that's really   You got that right. I wouldn't if I could, but I can't. I don't have a week. I don't have a day. I have responsibility, I have fucking offspring units. I can't run through the jungle chasing witch doctors. I don't sit around on the farm all day harvesting nothing but good old days while someone else buys the groceries.   Professional has-been, that's   Fucking coward . . ."

The gringa stands but manages to lower her voice slightly. "Not a drop. Not like someone.   You wish I was, don't you? Well sorry. I'm just a two-stepper but when I start something   Hello?"

She dips her toe into the water, then her foot, then kicks it out in a splash. A small family of bathers—there aren't many—head for their villa. An orange cat watches.

"Listen!" she says, pacing. "Listen to me listen to me listen to me.

"Say something.

" . . . "

The waitress speaks quietly to the security guard, who has acquired a degree of notoriety having tussled with an American professional football player.

"Who do you keep talking to?" the gringa says. "Is someone there? Are you with someone? Is that what this is about? Healer my ass! Is she *muy linda*? Bet she's healing the shit out of you right now! Put her on. I'll heal her ass. Put her   Can't she talk now? Is her mouth full? Put her ass on! Maybe she can show you a thing or two because, to be honest with you   What?"

She is looking at the waitress, who speaks fluent English and whom the gringa finds very pretty and agreeable (though privately she finds her complexion in need of sealer), comparing favourably to the girl at the front desk.

The conversation continues though it seems there is no longer anyone on the other side of it. The waitress is nervous and annoyed but relieved the gringa has stopped smiling. The waitress is not unsympathetic. The gringa, probably in her forties, is not bad-looking (though the sun is doing her skin no favours) and should have no trouble finding someone else if she goes looking (though a woman should not look to a man for her happiness). Still, she might think about upgrading and changing the colour of her bracelet, all things considered.

The plane to Brus Laguna had two propellers and fifteen seats, some of them duct-taped or bleeding yellow foam, the majority occupied by an American mission brigade. The brigade were young and white and wore blue t-shirts bearing an image of our planet cradled by an enormous pair of hands, presumably those of its creator. Among the other passengers were a Garifuna woman nursing a baby in the front seat, and a man behind her wearing a suit and holding a briefcase. The pilot had had to step over the woman to get into the cockpit.

Nineteen sat on the narrow aisle next to the interpreter so he could see out of both sides of the plane. Through the windows across the aisle was the long northern coast, the bay islands passing out of view. On the interpreter's side there were green mountains under a flat layer of clouds, scattered towns and farms in cultivated patches or in the hills themselves so there seemed no way to reach them except from above.

They would meet their guide in Brus Laguna, as well as the two other participants in the tour.

The ride was noisy and did his head no good, but smoother than Nineteen had expected. He hadn't heard from her since their last conversation. He'd returned to the island the morning after; she was gone but had packed his suitcase and left it in the office. The desk girl's demeanour was no different than when they'd arrived. Back on the mainland he bought rubber boots, a poncho, bug spray, a lantern. The expatriate, who would not be accompanying them, recommended anti-fungal powder for his feet but Nineteen never travelled without it. He'd forgotten to buy a hat.

He looked out and down again. The clouds were lower now and there were no more roads or towns, just mountains and forests and the shiny brown-orange rivers convolving endlessly through. Nineteen asked the interpreter which one they would take to Las Marías. The interpreter shrugged apologetically.

"Honest, is hard to say for me. It look all the same for me up here." He was a trim, serious man who seemed young in age if not disposition, and he spoke English with a moderate accent and occasional disagreement of subject and verb. He was half Miskitu and half Pech, which by his own description meant that some of his ancestors were cannibals, and some had been eaten by them. He said the former had also intended to make a meal of the castaway slaves they'd encountered early in the seventeenth century, but the Africans, strong enough to survive shipwreck, had other ideas and were soon mixing blood with their hosts instead. Something similar occurred with the English sailors and pirates who happened along later, and by the turn of the century a new people were being born. They detested the Spaniards, but now spoke the language of the enemy almost to the exclusion of their own.

Someone said, "'Lord, when saw we thee hungry, and fed thee? Or thirsty, and gave thee drink? When saw we thee a stranger, and took thee in?'"

Nineteen turned. The team leader of the mission brigade had turned in his seat and was reading to his charges from the Gospel According to Matthew, his voice cutting the buzz of the engines. He was a wholesome twenty-something who reminded Nineteen of ROTC students he'd known in college. He seemed aware that he was being watched and glanced at Nineteen without pausing. "'And the King shall answer unto them, "Verily I say unto you, inasmuch as ye have done it unto one of the least of these my brethren, ye have done it unto me.'"

He stopped there and gave his full attention to Nineteen, with a smile that seemed to say, Can I help you?

Nineteen asked, "Are you on a field trip?" It looked to him like an airborne Sunday school class.

"We're on a mission. RCA."

"You don't just make records?"

The team leader's smile was tolerant. "Reformed Church in America. The New Era, Michigan church, to be exact. Never hear of it?"

"I have not, but full disclosure: Red and Grey, all the way."

"Well, Go Blue then," the team leader said. "But at the end of the day, we're all on the same side, aren't we?" He was well-spoken and Nineteen would find there was nothing you could say that he couldn't repurpose to his own end.

He looked at the other brigade members. They were as young or younger than their leader, and equally wholesome. Three were girls, who did not look back. "I guess that makes you missionaries, then."

"We're starting a chicken farm at the Bible Institute in Brus." Nineteen thought the interpreter said something then, but couldn't hear it over the engine noise. "We've partnered with the Moravian Church here."

"Well God bless," Nineteen said, thinking of outhouses.

"Did somebody sneeze?" The team leader smiled again. "We prefer not to tell the Lord what to do. We do expect to be used by Him in unexpected ways." He gestured out the window. "You know this department we're flying over is called Gracias a Dios? Isn't that appropriate? I mean, it's His will alone that's holding this plane up."

Somehow the brigade leader's words did not seem intended to reassure. Nineteen experienced a moment of vertigo. He'd been mildly rebuked and tried to backtrack. "So you're working with another church down there."

"We were blessed to find a mission partner that was training Indigenous leaders to spread the gospel of Christ. The Moravian Church has been sharing the good news in the Mosquitia since about 1930. You should see a Miskito worship service. They're a people who sing, and it is the Song of Songs." He was a living brochure.

The interpreter made another sound and it was not singing. Nineteen did not know what to say. "Well it's great you folks get along."

"God wills the existence of different churches to address different spiritual needs," the team leader said. "Do you attend a place of worship?"

"I haven't been to Mass in a while but I consider myself Catholic—if they'll still have me."

"*He'll* have you. All one team." The leader sort of frowned. "Catholics didn't have such an easy time of it here at first. I'm talking 1500s—the Inquisition would have been in full swing. When the first Spanish priest—Domingo something—tried to spread the Word in Guatemala, the Maya shot him in the throat with an arrow. Then they skinned him alive, passed his heart around at a banquet and everyone took a bite."

Nineteen almost smiled. He was moved another way now and this time found words: "All one team." He almost added, Go God. The brigade leader affected not to have heard. "So, you do this for a living?"

"I'm rewarded in other ways." The leader seemed to ponder whether to humour this impertinence. "Since you ask, I'm a relationship manager for the church in New Era."

Nineteen was thinking he had once been taken to a strip club by the same name when one of the girls said, "Excuse me"; she had a question for the leader. Nineteen didn't hear what the girl's question was but he noticed that the hands holding the Earth aloft on her blue shirt also seemed to be cupping her breasts.

He turned away. "Chicken farm," he said to the interpreter. "Sounds like God's work to me. You gotta eat, right?" He was quoting a fast-food slogan.

"Brigades." The interpreter had a sour look. "Cost maybe ten thousand each to bring those kids here. Do work the locals do better themself. Then they go home. They should just stay there and send the money. We have plenty of chicken."

Nineteen looked at him. "You go to church?"

"We are the people who sing."

"Moravian, then."

The interpreter nodded, spoke carefully. "'In essentials, unity; in nonessential, liberty; in all thing, love.'"

"More power." The interpreter looked out the window. Nineteen turned back to the mission brigade but the conversation was apparently over. He looked ahead. The Garifuna woman wore an African headdress of riotous colours, so tall it bent at a right angle against the ceiling of the plane. The interpreter tapped his arm; he was pointing out his window. Nineteen leaned over and looked. A faint yellowish swath of cleared land like scar tissue in the rainforest below.

"What am I looking at?"

"Airstrip," the interpreter said.

"That where we're landing?"

"I hope not. Is for narcos. Drug traffickers bringing shipment from Colombia. On the way to your country."

"Jesus. Don't the authorities . . . ? I mean if *we* can see it." He was probably being naïve. Narcos was a TV word.

"Not much authority in Biosfera." The interpreter smiled wryly. "Can't trust them anyhow. But the government know. Army blows up one pista, narco build two more."

Nineteen shook his head and looked about the cabin again. The Garifuna woman was now holding the infant to her shoulder, patting his back. He looked at the *ladino* behind her and noticed he was handcuffed to his briefcase. Heard the mission brigade in prayer and silently joined them; he was still, after all, a team player.

It had stopped raining in Brus Laguna. The plane taxied off what passed for a runway onto a muddy field. There were no buildings, no terminal, just a barbed-wire fence guarded by a kid in a baggy uniform with a machine gun. A ground crew in rubber boots unloaded luggage from the back of the plane and from a bin in the nose cone, piled it under the wing in case the rain started again. Cardboard boxes and paper bags. Nineteen's suitcase was back in La Ceiba at the expatriate's bungalow; the expatriate had given him a dry bag of heavy plastic and welded seams he could use as a backpack, though Nineteen couldn't see himself wearing one. He had an aversion to backpackers.

He stood in the mud under the bright grey sky with the interpreter and the other passengers, some still waiting from the previous flight. The only signs of transportation thus far were a motorcycle and a horse tied to a tree. Both were on the other side of the fence and Nineteen idly wondered which belonged to the guard. He checked his phone.

A horn blared. The guard opened a gate for a big black GMC pickup, brown-spattered but surprisingly late-model. "Taxi," the interpreter said and everyone converged on the truck. The mission brigade quickly filled the double cab along with the man in the suit—apparently they'd made an arrangement—while the woman with the baby argued with the driver. Everyone else rode economy: a pair of wooden planks fastened like benches across the width of the bed. Nineteen climbed aboard painfully, refusing the interpreter's hand. The passengers sat in two rows facing each other; he squeezed in at the edge. The luggage was stacked and lashed behind the cab and inside the tailgate. The whole process was interminable. The woman continued to argue until the brigade team leader surrendered his seat to her and a place was made for him in the truck bed. They lurched off, everyone sweating on each other.

It was slow going. They drove along a vast pine savannah in the middle of which stood a privy on stilts with its door open and white porcelain toilet showing, so far from the road or any visible building it might have been someone's idea of art or a practical joke, which Nineteen often conflated one with the other. A woman in a long dress walked along holding a lump of smoking charcoal on an ashtray for the mosquitoes. The driver said something and she shook her head. Then a woman carrying a load of laundry on her back with a tumpline strapped across her forehead, keeping pace with a man ten or so steps ahead carrying only himself. The driver said nothing and the interpreter, tight beside Nineteen, said, "Garifuna. Miskitu woman don't do this." He took out his phone. "Good people though. The door are never lock."

Children appeared on either side in school uniform though no school could be seen. It started to rain. A blue plastic tarp was bolted to the back of the cab and the passengers unrolled it over their heads and held it in place at the edges. When the rain abated and the plastic was rolled back, they were in the town proper. Elevated wooden houses, some with porches and picket fence railings, others just boxes of rough boards. Corrugated tin roofs. Fences made of twigs and wire, choked with vegetation, but what met the eye first was the gauntlet of brown faces lining the sides of the muddy street, locals staring in the direction of the truck in grim silent reception.

A one-armed man with a machete in an Arizona Cardinals sweatshirt, blood-red. BEASTS OF THE EAST.

"Don't get a lot of visitors here?" Nineteen asked the interpreter.

"They wait for their children to come home from school." Apparently a safe return could not be taken for granted.

"God's Acre," the team leader said, pointing, and they passed a cemetery on a ridge, all the vaults above ground for the same reason the homes of the living were on stilts.

An old cannon in a field, a cell tower with its antenna array like a candelabra. The truck stopped, started, gradually emptied. The mission brigade debarked at a relatively clean white building, a hotel with an internet café but no hot water. Beyond it a glimpse of the lagoon—a real one—for which the town was named; the mouth of the river they would take to the jungle was somewhere on the other side. A horse and a cow shared a patch of grass at the side of the road. The truck started and stopped.

The police station was an impressive yellow structure with wooden trim and stood on the only paved street in town. The man with the briefcase got out there. Nineteen and the interpreter were not quite the last passengers. The driver let them off in front of a large house that bespoke prosperity with a big veranda furnished with tables and chairs and a sign that read COMEDORA. Nineteen climbed out rather more deftly than he'd boarded, slung the dry bag over his shoulder and followed the interpreter.

Three people waited for them in front of the comedora. Two were a white man and woman, dressed similarly in shorts and windbreakers as if to affirm their status as couple. The woman wore a bucket hat and was probably in her mid-twenties. Her husband's face was still boyish in late-middle middle age, his wavy white hair uncovered to offset a pinkish tan. They gave Nineteen their hands and first names as identical as their clothing and which he immediately forgot. They said they were from Saskatoon.

"The Paris of the Prairies," the man said amiably, and never quite let up.

The third person was a compact, young-looking woman wearing a plain baseball cap and a t-shirt with loose-fitting trousers tucked into calf-length rubber boots. A machete in a scabbard. Nineteen could not have guessed her age. She had the narrow eyes and cheekbones he thought of as Indian, but there was something African there as well, and something not, and he realized that she too must have descended from cannibals, slaves, and pirates.

The interpreter introduced them. Nineteen lightly took her hand and said it was nice to meet her.

"Nice to meet," the guide said. There were faint black hairs above her lip. A short scar below one eye. She smiled demurely, said, "No more Inglis," and opened her hand. Nineteen imagined a glimpse of sharpened teeth.

"So you flew," the Canadian man said to him. "Where'd they put the chickens?" He nodded at his wife. "She wanted a more authentic experience"—made virtual quotation marks, pointed at the departing truck—"so we took one of those. Same deal but all the way from El Porvenir. Nine hours." He winced as if still in pain. "My *bum*."

"They must have crammed two dozen of us into that thing," his wife said. "And the roads. We're not talking the QEW here." Nineteen nodded, though he wasn't sure at what.

"Roads. Half the time we were on the beach, driving in the bleepin surf."

"That was a blast. Oh, and then there was the mysterious package . . ." She infused the last two words with such intrigue Nineteen recalled something the expatriate had said, that land travellers in the Moskitia were sometimes unwitting participants in drug smuggling. He wanted to know more but the interpreter pre-empted him.

"If you want authentic experience, then you come to the right place," he said. "You have been to Copán?"

"Meh," the Canadian woman said. "Very touristy. Too many reconstructions." She made an apologetic Canadian face: "Sorry . . ."

"Yes, are many reconstruction," the interpreter agreed. The guide said nothing but looked patiently on. She seemed to be waiting.

"I liked the stairs," the Canadian husband said.

"Hieroglyphic Stairway," the interpreter said.

"And the ball court."

Nineteen felt something like interest. "Ball court?"

"Like a field between these two slanted walls." The husband gestured. "They're not sure how they played but sounds a bit like soccer. They think they used their hips." He glanced at his wife.

"For royalty only," she said.

"But sometimes the loser . . ." The Canadian drew his finger across his throat. Blood coursing through runnels to a sacrificial bowl.

"Or sometimes was the winner," the interpreter said. "Was consider a great honour."

"Thank you, no," the Canadian woman said.

"We're talking Mayans?" Nineteen said.

"You want Mayan," the husband said. "Try Guatemala. Tikal. Pyramids up to here."

His wife rolled her eyes. "Everyone goes to Tikal."

"Guatemala . . ." Nineteen was still thinking about the ball courts.

"We're working our way down to Panama," the husband said. "We took one of those chicken buses across the border. Driver couldn't have been more than fifteen."

"And he chain-smoked," the wife said. They were like a conversational tag team.

Nineteen felt his headache returning.

"This poor guy fell out the back and they just kept going," she said. "He was drunk out of his mind."

The Canadian man tried not to laugh. "Must have been his stop."

"It wasn't funny," the woman snapped and her husband quickly asked Nineteen, "So, you come up from the capital? Or the islands?"

Nineteen decided not to mention Roatan. "La Ceiba," he said, not sure what to expect, but it was the guide who finally spoke, through the interpreter, who said, "Is everybody hungry? Why don't we all sit down to eat?"

They went up on the veranda and sat in a corner next to a water cooler. A checkered tablecloth. Small black flies. No other customers, but in the opposite corner a pale-skinned boy on a hammock sat up and greeted them ecstatically, and the Canadian man awkwardly tried to respond till his wife took his shoulder and whispered something. The boy reclined again and smiled with great love for them or something beyond them, showing jagged broken teeth.

The proprietor welcomed them. A weathered woman in a house dress, possibly the boy's mother, and she and the guide seemed to know each other quite well. She was introduced to each of her guests in turn and she asked who wanted coffee. It was black and very sweet.

The Canadian man had not wound down. He'd been a software salesman, sold artificial intelligence that detected hidden emotion in facial expressions. The Chinese had been very interested—so much so he was able to retire early, began frequenting the coffee shop where his future wife was a barista. They lived in a cabin on a lake and in the spring or summer or fall would rent it out through an online platform while backpacking in places like Cambodia and the Himalayas, staying in hostels and sleeping in hammocks and meeting people. He loved to meet people. His wife had a degree in popular culture.

She asked Nineteen what he did for a living.

He'd insisted the expatriate not say anything about his playing days, had an answer of sorts prepared. Much of it was true and involved real estate, the beachfront development in La Ceiba, meeting the expatriate . . . He professed interest in "the adventure travel thing."

"You two venture capitalists should have a lot to talk about," the Canadian woman said.

"Not sure I see the long-term growth potential in this market," her husband said, and glanced at the top of Nineteen's head. "Have you thought about crypto?"

"Not without going into a coma."

The guide said something to the interpreter. Nineteen heard the word sombrero.

"She says you should have hat," the interpreter said.

"Got everything but," Nineteen said. "Maybe I can buy one?"

"There is a general store near the town pier." The guide spoke again. "Did you bring boots?"

They had. The guide went down a verbal checklist and as she did their lunch was served: scrambled eggs, rice and beans, a slice of some kind of sausage, tortillas, a small crumbly wedge of the local cream cheese. The guide and interpreter ate with one hand fluttering, waving off flies. They seemed unaware they were doing it. The water was not cold.

"Is there a meal in Central America that doesn't include rice and beans?" the Canadian wife said.

"There's always beans and rice," the husband said.

The boy on the hammock spoke vacantly to the ceiling. Or perhaps he was singing.

"Carbs might come in handy," Nineteen said, and thought about game-day meals, linemen eating eight chicken breasts. (His own ritual ran to peanut butter and jelly.) He looked at the interpreter but was speaking to the guide. "I heard there's some kind of medicine man in this village we're going to."

"There may be a person there," the interpreter said. He sounded curious. "You have interest?"

"Thought I'd make an appointment." He was sort of joking.

The interpreter turned to the guide, then told Nineteen, "There is a *sukya* there, an old man. Are you sick?"

"I get headaches. Migraines." The Canadians were watching him. Was it Marlowe and Marlo? He would have to ask.

The guide spoke. "Sukya treats many ailment," the interpreter said. "Headache, depression . . . diarrhea, bad luck . . . He believe illness have supernatural cause."

"I guess diarrhea is a form of bad luck, eh?" the Canadian husband said.

His wife made a face and looked at Nineteen. "We don't have awkward silences in Canada. Eh."

"Does he have a fee?" Nineteen asked.

"Nothing. Anything. Whatever you care to pay." The guide spoke at length, and the interpreter said, "Sukya is not what used to be. Used to dance in fire, handle snake . . . he is very old. He might recommend to see physician."

Nineteen waved at the flies circling over his plate, trying to choke down his disappointment.

"It's not like it's the only reason I'm here," he lied.

There was the sound of fireworks, which they realized was distant gunfire. Just the locals letting off steam, the interpreter reassured them. The guide ate her lunch.

When they'd finished their meal she carefully counted a stack of bills onto the table. The Canadian picked up a one-lempira note and pointed to the image on the back side to Nineteen: "Ball court."

The slanted walls, the narrow field between. The long steps facing the gap.

"Bleachers," Nineteen said. The note was worth a nickel.

On their way out the strange smiling boy sounded exactly as he had when they'd arrived. He could not be healed of his happiness.

The streets were still muddy but the rain had held off and the sun tentatively appeared. There were not many people about. On the way to the general store they passed an empty lot with a square burnt patch in the middle. The guide explained there'd been a fire there presided over by naval officers burning a pallet of confiscated shark fins. Even after the rain you could smell it.

"Shark fins are illegal?" Nineteen asked.

"Depends how they catch them," the Canadian wife said. "Some fishermen cut off the fins in the boat and throw the fish alive back in the water. They sink to the bottom and drown, or other predators eat them."

"No more soup for us," the husband said. "They've discovered sharks in the North Atlantic that are five hundred years old. Not sexually active till a hundred-fifty."

If this were bait his wife did not take it. She looked at the guide and the interpreter. "Are there sharks where we're going?"

"There are some in laguna but not as many as was. Net fishing reduce the population." Sometimes the interpreter didn't wait for the guide. "Plenty of crocodile and alligator," he said, and they moved on.

They saw a motorcycle but there seemed to be no cars in town. The pulpería had a tax-deductible blue roof and a long porch festooned with merchandise. On the street below two barefoot children were playing a version of tic-tac-toe, drawing in the dirt with sticks.

The Canadians stayed outside to take their picture. They already had what they needed.

The store's owner was a corpulent man installed in a motionless hammock, its underside bulging tautly three inches above the floor. He climbed out quite nimbly to greet his customers and two teenagers who might have been sons and were dressed like city boys led them into the crowded darkness. Creaking floorboards with an inch of blackness between them. "Tengo sombreros, tengo gafas de sol . . . tengo todas." It was true: Frito-Lay. Tools. A few DVDs. *Aspirina*. You could buy a plane ticket here, make an international call, rent a hammock in the breezeway for a few dollars a night. Two old men sat drinking coffee in a corner of the fetid gloom, and one of the boys shined a flashlight into their cups to see if they'd added cream for which he would charge them five lempiras. And there were condoms.

The hats hung from the ceiling on a wire, bunched like fruit. The boy tried to sell Nineteen an Anzac bush hat but a camouflage baseball cap with a swoosh was much cheaper. The swoosh looked homemade and Nineteen didn't think it the product of a maquiladora. He bought a litre of water; the guide bought more in long plastic bags.

The town pier was a simple boathouse with louvred windows and jutted out over the edge of the lagoon on round posts. Three young men on the landward side were selling raw chicken out of a metal tub. Next to the tub was a basket of cassava, and one of the boys had a very uncooperative iguana on a string you could take a picture with or, for a somewhat higher price, buy for dinner. When they saw the tourists they yelled, "Bery good! Bery good!" and the Canadian husband said, "Well it's just a big canoe, ain't it?"

He was talking about the narrow boat run aground on the shore next to the pier. It was at least forty feet long and had an outboard motor but except for the gunwales looked to have been carved whole out of a tree. The iguana hissed and lunged.

"*Cayuco*," the interpreter said. The guide gave them life vests but advised they should be sat upon rather than worn—it was a six-hour journey. Here the lagoon was muddy brown. A broad-chested, pockmarked man with no front teeth was introduced as their captain. He had a brutally friendly grip. His lone crew, the bowman, was also his son, a skinny boyish man with whiskers at the corners of his mouth and no shoes. A machete in its sheath. Nineteen boarded first; the boat rocked unexpectedly. They were still half on dry land but he began to suspect that nothing would be easy from here on in.

He sat on a crude legless chair resting loose on the floor of the cayuco. The captain sat at the motor behind him and between them were the dry bags, the big canister containing their meals, and a burlap sack, all partly covered in weathered black plastic. Nineteen wondered if the sack might qualify as a mysterious package. The Canadian sat in front of him with a small backpack in his lap. The bowman offered the wife a helping hand (declined), then gathered with the guide and the interpreter at the prow to shove off.

A scraping underneath, then smoothness as the water took hold. They were all in. The bowman stood and with a long pole pushed them beyond the pier. A screened porch at its back faced them. The screens were dark but seemed watchful. The bowman poled them around and land was behind them. The captain pull-started the motor. The cayuco rocked and they grabbed the gunwales.

The sky was equally sun and cloud. For a while they manoeuvred around shoals of weeds, the lagoon deepening in colour. Then it spread itself before them in all its size. The word made you think of a lake but this had the reach of a sea, with swell and horizon, and Nineteen let his fingers trail in the water, forgetting what the guide had said about sharks and crocodiles. A puddle ebbed at his feet.

B efore swallowing the pills, Number Nineteen called his ex-wife in Florida and left a voice mail. It was not the drunken rambling monologue he occasionally submitted, and which she would delete without listening to in entirety, but was disturbingly calm and coherent. It was goodbye. Eschewing 9-1-1, she dialled the ten-digit number to the sheriff's office of the county in which Nineteen resided—the township itself had no police department—and told them who she was. Of course they remembered—there'd been previous visits. They would send someone out. She then prepared her children, notifying her older daughter via direct message.

The responding sheriff's deputies found evidence of occupancy (lights on, vehicle present) but no response to the doorbell or repeated knocking. Upon hearing glass break, officers determined there was sufficient cause to force entry, which was effected by kicking in the front door, which was later determined to have been unlocked. After a brief investigation of the premises, the attempter, a known male approximately in his mid-forties, was found on the floor of his bathroom, unconscious. Attempter's breathing was shallow, pulse faint, lips and fingernails blue, and he "seemed to be having convulsions" (first responder). Finding an empty prescription pill container nearby, officers determined that an overdose had occurred and administered ten milligrams of Naloxone with a pre-filled auto-injector through attempter's outer thigh. The Fire Department was called for assistance. (Cost of auto-injector: $800. Billed to attempter's insurance.)

In the emergency room at a hospital he'd never been to, Nineteen was intubated, filled with intravenous fluids, subjected to a battery of cardiac tests, dosed with activated charcoal through a tube in his nose. Bloodwork. He did not regain consciousness for three days, during which time he had dreams of bodies impaled live on huge burning tumbleweeds. Their voices were familiar. He woke with a runny nose and a feeling in his throat like he'd swallowed a pencil. He was also sweating, itching, shivering, nauseous, diarrhetic, racked with stomach cramps, body aches, and severe agitation (his dreams felt prescient), symptoms consistent with an acute phase of opioid withdrawal. A Level 4, medically managed inpatient detoxification was advised, to which Patient responded, "Can I have my hair back?"

He was moved to a fifteen-bed unit in the Alcohol and Drug Recovery Centre where he wore a buprenorphine skin patch to offset the worst of the symptoms, which is to say everything still hurt, swallowed phenobarbital for the accumulated debt of pain in his back and neck, *pro re nata*. Alpha 2 agents. Screaming at the med window. He shit himself. Yawned uncontrollably as if bored with his private hell. Kept his private room dark and the heat on high for the chills. Neuropsychological assessment, twenty-four-hour observation: Patient complained of fatigue, depression, and general malaise but made acceptable progress toward less restrictive level of treatment. *Refuses group but takes visitors readily* (two of three children, former spouse, friends who'd worn numbers, or hadn't). *Was observed twice to terminate visits with little or no warning* (brother, former spouse, who'd taken the red-eye to his side, held his hand when he was under like he was hanging off a cliff but couldn't say one right thing to him awake). But Patient was generally cooperative until informed that (sister) had obtained a temporary order of detention and Patient was to be transferred after a week to the Adult Psychiatric Centre ("What else you got here?!") whereupon restraint and sedation were indicated.

He spent the next fourteen days in a ward of about thirty people. They lost his clothes. It was quieter than he expected; almost no one talked to themselves. His roommate believed his thoughts were being recorded and broadcast on television and had jumped off a bridge. Group sessions. Chemical restraint. A rec room where there were puzzles with pieces too large to swallow. Donated magazines. He was there two weeks but refused all visitors; he would not be seen here, bald in hospital scrubs, doing word searches with a crayon.

"White birds taught me to fly before I hit the water," his roommate said.

The unit clerk was disciplined for requesting an autograph. Friday was Pancake Day.

The psychiatrist was a Pakistani woman whose name he found difficult. Patient was observed to have a somewhat shuffling gait probably due to recent medical emergency and subsequent detoxification. Eye contact was appropriate, attitude somewhat evasive but generally cooperative, language production occasionally impoverished with slight impairment ("Bit off the tip of my tongue"). Mood dysphoric but no evidence of suicidal ideation.

"How is your appetite like at the moment?"

"Today's Pancake Day." He enjoyed her accent.

Axis I indicated adjustment disorder with mixed anxiety and depressed mood. Axis IV listed financial, sexual, and professional difficulties as other psychosocial environmental stressors ("Strangers watching her fuck other strangers. She never even visited"), and Axis III suggested that repeated head trauma incurred as a professional athlete should also be investigated as a possible contributing factor. Neurological examination and cognitive behavioural therapy on a voluntary basis were recommended.

Nineteen went home to his farm. Experienced symptoms that had nothing to do with drugs. He missed his pills, missed being able to stare at some random object for hours under their spell— dust motes, a vase—and just totally get it. He rejected therapy and was referred to the neurologist who accidentally referred him to Dr. Q. There'd been a brief outburst of journalism at the discovery of his attempt, then another, shorter-lived, when he was released from the hospital, but he avoided the internet longer than he had to. A ten-minute interview on local news ("to hell and back," etc.) after which he could be safely forgotten again. He deactivated his social media, attended several AA meetings, met someone there, stayed off Oxy, and didn't have another drink until Roatan.

From the lagoon they entered a narrow channel lined with reeds and then mangrove trees, prop roots high out of the water like the legs of wading figures. The water turned black, and if you put your hand in it would you draw back a stump, the limb consumed by whatever had swallowed the light? The guide explained that the water was black from the decay of the roots, that the mangrove had adapted to living in salt water, how it breathed through pores in its bark or aerial roots like snorkels, and she sounded as though it were the trees' idea or was it the interpreter who made her sound that way.

Salt crystals on the leaves.

Then there were the ones she called white blood trees though their roots were dark and knotted like malformed tentacles, one of which came to life and detached itself like some offspring, and then the Canadians exclaimed and the tourists were reaching for their phones as the big black snake coiled up the tree trunk, the guide telling them it was an indigo snake and that it was not venomous, that it constricted its prey and was immune to the venom of other snakes.

Nineteen wondered if, when he got a signal, he would send her the picture. He could do better for a signifier of repentance, he supposed; he could send the snake to his children, then, or his chiropractor, or to Number Twelve, who'd owned an albino python and was wide to the right of their last chance in K.C., no hard feelings, though to an athlete mistakes are the worst sins of all.

Or send it to his ex, who'd saved his life, and whom he'd scared away for good when she came to visit.

They were on the Río Plátano now. The ride was smoother than on the lagoon and Nineteen was glad for the life vest to sit on; you could lean back in the wood and even swing your leg over the gunwale; the guide had taken off her boots and he watched the river clean her feet. The boat had a slow leak and the bowman would bail with a plastic bowl cut from a two-litre Pepsi bottle. Once he started to sing in a language that was not Spanish and the guide spoke sharply and he stopped. His father laughed.

"A very dirty song," the interpreter said.

They rode toward mountains, skirting rocks and the boughs of drowned trees nodding in the current like something alive. The banks curved one way then the other, and sometimes at the bends the water would eddy in countermotion so that to look there was to move in both directions at once and in this Nineteen found strange remedy to the vertigo that lately assailed him. He felt the back of his neck reddening and turned his hat around. The humming, biting clouds. Smell of woodsmoke—a fire smouldered in a small clearing where a bamboo hut stood four feet off the ground with a thatched palm roof. It was not the last. Corn and beans grew in small plots, sometimes rice, cacao, and everyone had a boat because the river was the only road, and sometimes you saw them at the bank, bathing or swimming or washing clothes, and if you waved so would they but never first.

Nineteen was surprised. He'd expected isolation in wilderness, but the forest on the banks looked stunted, interrupted, not the heart of anything. He waved.

The sky went cloudy to clear and over again like time-lapse photography. The Canadians wore earbuds. Then the clouds stayed and kept their dark promise and the passengers stretched the black plastic from the stern over their heads while the crew donned ponchos. When the downpour commenced they heard a deep-throated roar from the jungle so near and ferocious Nineteen might have gone overboard but was so petrified he could only listen.

"Howler monkey." The interpreter didn't wait for the guide. "His voice is much bigger than he is. Probably few hundred metres away. They don't like the rain." No shit.

The Canadians had encountered them before. "Cute little buggers actually," the husband shouted. "Like an organ grinder's." The plastic sagged, a sheet of sound.

"I think those are capuchins," the wife shouted back.

It howled again. "Takes some getting used to, though."

Nineteen wasn't used to it. Fucking King Kong, and the trees his highway.

The rain stopped and the river was a deep, rich brown colour. A hint of blood. They didn't see the monkeys but the mosquitoes were gone for a while and there was no end of birds: herons and cormorants, toucans with long rainbow bills, birds with nests that hung long and basketlike in the trees. The Canadians shared binoculars. Those they didn't see they heard, and the guide would identify each by its call, with flawless imitation, to which they responded as to one of their own.

Nineteen was impressed, but he hadn't come here for the birds.

They passed other boats on the way, coming and going, some with small motors that made a *tuk tuk* sound that gave the craft its name, others with outboards like their own, others propelled by men or women or children standing and pushing off the riverbed with long poles. Brown Indian faces, and black, and they too would only wave back. They carried various cargo, bananas and plantains, sacks of seed, infants, a slaughtered hog, a young palm tree in the middle of a boat as if it had sprouted there. A dog motionless in the prow like a carved figurehead, once a rooster in the same station.

The guide would have conversations with the passing traffic, in Spanish or a language belonging to no world with which Nineteen was familiar. She might as well have been talking to the birds again.

A bare-chested boy with a harpoon poised over the river. Waiting.

But when they passed the bigger farms, ranches, with horses and cows and bigger houses on concrete posts with galvanized metal roofs, the guide would neither raise her hand nor speak but turned away and said in bitter English, "Cowboys."

"We have them in Calgary," the Canadian said, as if they were talking about the same thing.

The guide pointed to the bank. Her voice had changed. "Their methods are not sustainable," the interpreter said, and his voice had the same hard quality. "Look how they clear-cut the trees to the river edge, how the bank is eroding . . . There used to be mangroves there." His grammar was briefly impeccable.

"Termito humano," the guide said as though she were cursing. A punching bag hung from the underside of a mahogany porch. They saw no people.

"I thought the Biosphere is protected," the Canadian woman said.

"Is hard to enforce," the interpreter said. "Law are piece of paper here. Indigenous not full citizen."

"But that's trespassing," Nineteen said. He considered himself a kind of farmer, though someone else had done the work.

"The government encourage settlement but . . . what they don't own they pressure the locals to sell."

"So they're not doing anything illegal."

"They fish with dynamite, with poison," the interpreter said. "They are eating the forest alive." The guide had not spoken but watched the conversation as if the interpreter were relaying her thoughts. Nineteen looked at the scar by her eye. A permanent tear.

"I've done a little farming," he said.

"You don't look like a farmer," the interpreter said.

He hadn't looked like a quarterback either, Nineteen reminded himself, and no one else said anything for a while.

After they had been on the river about four hours there was only jungle on either side. It was very hot and the air was thick with water returning to the sky. They pulled up on a sandbar for a late lunch and no one was more grateful than Nineteen to be able to stand. His neck, his back, his ankle, but he managed not to make a sound. There was a family of huge mossy boulders in a row, somehow ordered by size, and tall grass and then the forest into which the guide disappeared after a few words to the interpreter.

"If anyone need to relieve themselves," the interpreter said, and gestured at the possibilities of privacy. He advised them to avoid fallen logs, where snakes like to hide.

When she returned, the guide washed her hands in the river with the watery organic soap they'd all been advised to buy and opened the canister from the boat. She distributed slices of bread and American cheese and an unidentifiable brand of lunch meat. Dried plantains with salsa for the side and they ate in the wooden seats from the boat near the edge of the sandbar where the water was pooled clear and deep and flickered with darting silver bait fish. The captain and his son were gone.

"Where's the crew?" Nineteen asked.

"They have their own," the interpreter said.

"I saw them go into the woods," the Canadian woman said. "They had a little rifle."

"Having it their way," her husband said. He toed the pebbles. "Wonder if there's any arrowheads in there."

Nineteen looked at the guide, then the interpreter. "So how did she get into this line of work?"

The guide spoke deliberately.

"Her father teach her."

"Does he still do it?" the Canadian wife asked. "Is he in Las Marías?"

"Her parents live in Brus. Hard to make living as guide—he was also lobster diver."

Crack of a gunshot in the jungle. The guide ignored it. No one had noticed how noisy the jungle was till it wasn't. For a while there was only the river.

"Is dangerous work. When lobster are become less, diver has to make more dive . . . has decompress from returning to the surface too fast." The interpreter pointed to his head. "Like a stroke in the brain . . . Boat captain gives alcohol, *cocaína* for the pain . . . but more and more . . ."

On the lagoon they'd seen the white buildings of a training centre where Korean divers were showing Hondurans how to catch jellyfish instead of lobster. The Koreans were great lovers of jellyfish and had almost depleted their own waters.

Koreans, Nineteen had noted, were a presence.

The guide's father spent most of his day lying on a pallet in Brus Laguna, years of nitrogen in his joints, barely able to walk. Nineteen thought about the healer.

"Does she have family of her own?" the Canadian husband asked.

"Does she mind being in the third person here?" his wife said.

"She has husband and six children in Brus," and the Canadian wife said "Oh my God" but not at the guide's maternal status; the boat crew were returning to the sandbar. The captain carried a .22 and his son wore a dead monkey draped over his shoulders like a macabre stole. It was black and appallingly precious till you saw the small blooded fangs in rictus, its languid half-lidded eyes, and wondered how dead it really was.

"This is King Kong," the interpreter announced.

The bowman retrieved a ragged towel from the boat and went to a flat rock near the weeds. He wrapped the towel around the body below the neck like a barber and laid it on the rock and took his machete from its scabbard.

"He isn't going to," the Canadian wife said, and the guide spoke to him sternly in Spanish. The bowman looked at her, then everyone, and answered.

The interpreter said, "He want to know if anyone mind him to eat the brain before we go."

The jungle was coming back to life. "I'll pass," the Canadian husband said. "How about we just hear the dirty song?"

"They eat what they kill," the interpreter said. "They'll take the meat to the village."

"I hope that's not what we're having tonight."

"I'll try anything once."

"The hell you will. You want Mad Cow or something?"

"It's hardly a cow."

"Mad Monkey then."

"Good name for a cocktail," the Canadian wife said, but took it no further. Flies were gathering for the banquet of blood.

Having satisfied the requirements of etiquette, the bowman raised the machete and hammered artlessly at the monkey's head. Blood appeared. Keeping the towel bunched at its neck, he turned the body one way and the other. The top of the skull flipped open on a tiny hinge of bone. The bowman held the animal upright, peered into the braincase as with profound curiosity, then with a corner of the blade spooned out a portion of its fruit and archly offered it around.

Pale under the blood, striated. The Canadians and the interpreter declined. The guide took it delicately between thumb and forefinger, put it in her mouth, took a swig of water. Tilted her head back. The bowman excised another bite of tissue, and now it was Nineteen's turn.

He'd expected to refuse. But a kind of logic had obtained: cannibal tribes ate the brains of the dead to consume their souls. His brain was sick, he was being offered the essence of a small creature with the voice of a giant. On a spoon of sorts. He looked at the guide, a spot of blood at the corner of her cannibal's mouth. To taste what she tasted.

He took it.

"Let me get my phone," the Canadian woman said. Her husband turned away, then watched with everyone else.

Gelatinous . . . somewhat metallic, almost rusty . . . was that the blood? Not much of a taste, really, only slightly awful, so was it the thought that made him gag it back out? The bowman and his father laughed. Nineteen covered his mouth and forced it back inside. When he had barely mastered it, he grabbed up his bottle of water and swallowed it all.

They heard the jungle. The bowman washed his down with a Pepsi product.

Las Marías was purported to be the last outpost of civilization before the plunge into the verdant unknown. As last outposts went it left something to be desired, in particular electricity, and the only running water was the river. The healer was not there. He was downriver, treating a man with severe abdominal pain said to be caused by an animal spirit, in this case that of an alligator. He would be back in a day or two, it was said.

Nineteen was not surprised, nor at his lack of disappointment; his life had been defined by near-misses. He supposed it could have been worse. Could have been money laundering, or your secondary allowing a Hail Mary with no time on the clock after you've led your team to the threshold of the Magic Kingdom. Or inadvertently jerking off to your daughter, a minor internet porn star with breasts as fake as her name.

He wondered on what animal spirit he might blame his own affliction.

The village was scattered above the west bank of the Plátano but there was no landing as such, just a flattening of the bank and then a steep path of mud and clay that led to high ground. A group of children had gathered there to watch the arrival. It was late afternoon.

Getting out of the boat was trickier than boarding had been. Nineteen wore the dry bag on his back and let himself take the bowman's hand. The guide looked up where the children were and admonished the visitors.

"Whatever you do, don't fall," the interpreter said. "They will never stop laughing and you always will be The One Who Fell. We are their entertainment."

Nineteen was undaunted. He was already The One Who Fell, had fallen face-down in mud to exponentially greater mockery. He summoned the old cool and made it to the top without incident; leading by example.

A weathered, authoritative woman received them in a long skirt and head scarf and a sweatshirt with its sleeves cut off. "Mamika," the guide said, embracing her as if they shared blood. She was hostess of the *hospedaje*, the interpreter told them. She was also the captain's wife and the bowman's mother, and she and her family lived in two buildings next to a stick-and-wire fence beyond which horses and cows grazed in a muddy pasture. Nothing more of the village could be seen.

"Buenas," the hostess said to her guests, and that was all, and then began a discussion with the guide. Nineteen, though beyond loincloths and grass skirts, was mildly cheered that her sweatshirt read MEN DO THE YARDWORK, WOMEN DO THE HARD WORK. The discussion sounded like business.

A black iron cookstove in a doorway. The curved back of the cook: Josepina.

A man approached. It was the boat captain, but now he wore a new-looking Saints jersey, number nine, Super Bowl MVP, and he was holding a book. Number Nine had thrown the equivalent of over three miles that year, a record that would probably stand in time like the relics of ancient people, and he would one day wear the gold jacket in Canton, where Nineteen was only a visitor.

The captain reintroduced himself: "Soy El Presidente del Turismo de Las Marías." With the change of clothing came a change of office. He wanted them to sign his book.

"Well," the Canadian wife said. "Captain *and* President."

"And they must be the Chamber of Commerce," her husband said at the children.

A student's composition book in a handmade leather cover, pages filled with the names of visitors. Nineteen signed in his trembled hand.

The rest of the hospedaje was a few steps downriver of the pasture. The children followed loosely. Stray pigs and chickens. A square shack with a flat slant roof and two doors in front. The boards that comprised the shack were vertical on one side and horizontal on the other, as if nailed by carpenters at cross-purposes.

"Señors and señoritas?" the Canadian woman suggested but only one side was the privy. Behind the other door was a barrel of water with a pail floating on top, a tablecloth covering the barrel. The water would drain through the floorboards.

"Bucket shower," the Canadian husband sang.

"Done there, been that," his young wife sang.

The guesthouse was more impressive, built higher off the ground and of heavier timber with all the boards in agreement. The room doors were in front along a railed veranda ten or twelve feet above the riverbank. The guide addressed a wide gap in the middle of the rail and the interpreter said, "Watch your step at night."

"Don't tell me we get DirecTV," Nineteen said; a dish antenna was fastened to the rail in a corner, but the attached cable hung unconnected and nobody could explain whether the fixture had a future purpose or was some ornamental irony.

There were three rooms. Each held two beds with not a foot of space between. Narrow sponge mattresses in wooden frames. A stub of candle in a dish and a box of matches. A window with diagonal slats in place of screen or glass. Damp wood smell and a cockroach two inches long.

"Jesus," Nineteen said at the cockroach. He and the interpreter would share a room. The guide, who had grown up in the village, would sleep alone.

A cardboard box outside for garbage, crawling with ants. The room doors were equipped with hasps and small padlocks. The guide gave them each a key and advised them to lock their doors and leave nothing outside.

"People steal here?" Nineteen asked.

"If not secure your possession," the interpreter said, "is assume you don't want."

"People steal here," the Canadian wife said.

At dark they went to their dining hut, across a dirt clearing from the host house. The guide led the way by flashlight. A mutt with basset hound in it lay at the top of four or five steps in front of the door. It wouldn't move and the guide kicked it in the ribs.

"Really?" the Canadian wife said.

Nineteen looked at the guide but didn't say anything.

"We're not sentimental about animals here," the interpreter said. "Only children give them names."

"We could learn a lot from children," the husband said, staring at the guide. She had entered the hut.

"I could give her some names," the wife muttered and lingered behind to comfort the dog, who seemed quite indifferent. She would mention this in her review.

They ate by candle in a small room with a plank table and chairs, a counter, a large latticed window. Glass or wire mesh seemed unheard of here. The food was already tabled, in bowls covered with cling wrap. Roast chicken, tortillas, a version of the cream cheese they'd had for breakfast, plantains, and this time the rice separated from the beans. The Canadian husband found this amusing. To drink there was water at room temperature and a savoury juice made of banana and coconut. A delicately beautiful girl of about ten brought coffee, and she was their only visitor beside the geckos and insects. She was also the bowman's daughter.

"Her mother is Pech," the interpreter said, answering a question no one had asked.

Nineteen dug in hungrily. The name sounded familiar. "That another tribe?"

The interpreter nodded. "A little upriver. They were here first—no one is sure how long." He poured sugar as if he'd forgotten to stop. "They are quiet, reserve. Not like Mıskıtu."

"But you get along."

"I get along with myself," the interpreter said. "I live in Ceiba. Who else want coffee?"

Strange cries outside, an eerie ululation. Utter dark at the window. Three candles.

The interpreter was not inclined to talk further about himself. The Canadian husband looked at Nineteen. He was vegan, though not when abroad. "The monkey to your liking?"

"Actually," the wife said, "I was hoping for something a little more . . . Iguana, maybe?"

"We almost had beating cobra heart in Thailand," her husband said.

"That was Vietnam, old boy. We did have the fried worms."

"Does it taste like chicken?" Nineteen said and the Canadians laughed politely.

"Capybara maybe tomorrow," the interpreter said.

Nineteen looked at him.

"Like a giant rat."

Nineteen had had his fill of exotica, though he enjoyed the deference it had earned him. He liked the food and said so, then asked exactly where they were heading tomorrow; he hadn't yet decided if he would stay behind to wait for the curandero. Some watered-down shaman rolling an egg on his head.

The interpreter spoke with the guide, who took her coffee as he did. "In the morning we walk out of the village to meet the polers."

"Polers."

"They push the pipante upriver. Are too much rocks to use the motor."

"They push us all the way to the petroglyphs?" the Canadian husband asked.

"No, the river get too rough. We hike the rest—little hike."

"Define 'little hike.'"

Nineteen didn't want to think about hiking. "Define petroglyphs, exactly?"

"Like inscription in rock. Pictures. Some think maybe map—Inca map. Inca looking for gold."

"Those bleepers were always looking for gold," the Canadian man said.

"They not the only one." The interpreter listened to the guide. "But she doesn't think so. Map yes, but what kind? Maybe map that tells a story."

Another sound outside, not of nature.

"That a boat?" Nineteen said.

"Sounds like the generator at our cabin," the Canadian said.

"It is generator," the interpreter said.

"I thought they didn't have electricity."

"Only for pulpería," the interpreter said. "On special occasion. Sometimes they show a movie inside. Everyone is welcome."

"Is our dance still on?" the Canadian wife asked. At the guide's recommendation, the tourists had pooled a thousand lempiras to see a genuine Miskitu round dance to be performed that evening. Nineteen's contribution was already accounted for.

"Sí." The guide slapped the table, crushing a bug. No one was sentimental about flying cockroaches.

After dinner they returned to the clearing in the middle of the hospedaje. Several lanterns now burned at the edges, and a boombox sat on a crate. Nineteen borrowed the guide's light and went into the outhouse. Spiderwebs brushed his face and he couldn't stand straight. The toilet was a small, round repurposed sink with no seat. A plastic pipe jutted from the back and you flushed by pouring a pail of water into it. When he emerged an audience had gathered. The tourists sat on a large wooden stoop at the base of the guesthouse stairs. Someone pushed a button, unleashing a racket not at first recognizable as music. Guitar, Caribbean-sounding percussion that carried the beat and melody at the same time. Over this a man's voice, everything raw and loud, a recording of a recording, not live but alive. A song starting somewhere in the middle.

The dancers emerged from the darkness around the corner of the guesthouse. First the women, seven of them, young, all shapes and sizes, barefoot in skirts and halters, tubes or tanks. Applause. Light, halting steps, arms swimming in air. They circled the clearing then formed a line. As a group they were loose, almost sloppy, no two performers doing things exactly alike, but the motion of their hips rolled one body to another as if they were both swimmers and sea.

Unmindful of the mud, they went to their knees and brushed one another's hair with empty hands. They stood as the men came, also barefoot, shirtless in shorts and rolled-up dungarees. The men circled the women with their hands in fists as if gripping something, swinging them side to side.

"Pescadores y sirenas," the guide said. The interpreter spoke and Nineteen realized the men were holding oars. The music drowned out the rest of the narration and he let it; the dancers would tell him their story.

The fishermen and mermaids faced each other in motion. It was a simple song, a single verse repeated without beginning or end. The men cast their nets and haul them in. Wipe their brows. The sirens depart, spreading their arms underwater, but for one, caught in the net of the dancer closest to the guests. She writhes in struggle, then in a spiral around the fisherman, seducing him with circles of promise till he releases her, but at the touch of her hand he collapses as if struck dead. The audience howled, children among them. The mermaid dances down the line, touching each man in his turn to the same result and same reaction, under the stars.

She returned to the shadows, leaving the fleet prostrate in the mud and music, but the show was not over. Someone changed the cassette, and in the abrupt interval the Canadian woman could be heard to say, "Fifty bucks for this?"

The music rejoined, faster now, with horns, the singing drunk and urgent. It summoned the mermaids back into the light, but now their principal, though dressed the same, had broad shoulders and muscular calves and wore a crude cloth mask on which was painted a red mouth and wide blue eyes with lashes like spokes. A yellow rag of hair. For a moment the song was lost to hysteria. This grotesque new siren carried a leafy branch and a plastic bottle of water, and she filled her mouth then spat down into the face of the first smitten sailor as with the kiss of the sea itself, brushing him with the branch till he was miraculously revived and on his feet, dancing with the vitality of the reborn. The act was repeated six times, till the entire fleet was resurrected and moving with its counterparts as men and women, joined hand in hand, and Nineteen was stricken with the sudden awful thought that this witch was the shaman he'd come all this way to see, the healer he'd been told about just that morning in Brus Laguna, and was it just that morning?

There was shouting, movement. The dancing was becoming general. El Presidente del Turismo de Las Marías was there in his Saints jersey and encouraged the guests to join. An old man simulated buggery with the spurious sea maiden, who remained in character, and the Canadian woman, swaying shyly with her husband at the edge of the revel, wondered, "Should kids be seeing this?" Then the interpreter pulled her in. One of the dancers with her muddy feet and brown shoulders grabbed at Nineteen's hand but he begged off, not so much because of the screws that fastened his foot to his leg, but because she reminded him of his first-born child. He could not see the guide.

The mermaid still on her knees, under the old man.

After the dance there was a movie in the pulpería: *Rambo: Regreso al Infierno* on flatscreen. The store was above-ground but smelled like a root cellar. The stacks and bins and displays had been rearranged to accommodate a general audience, who stood or sat on the floor. The management charged no admission.

John Rambo, past sixty and bloated with self-hate, dubious black hair held in place with a headband. A hammy Spanish baritone issued from his scowl, and when the Canadian wife giggled the other viewers looked at her as if she'd farted in church.

"Fuck the world," Rambo says. They left before the carnage began.

The guide led them back toward the hospedaje but stopped just short of the dining hut. They stood where the riverbank was low but steep and thick with brush while she aimed her lantern at the water.

"What are we doing?" the Canadian wife asked. "Should we all have lights?"

"She want to show you something," the interpreter said. They could still hear gunfire and explosions in the faint glimmer from the store.

A rough circle of light played over a gently turning eddy. The guide sighed and turned away. "No crocodilia esta noche," she said, and led them back to the guesthouse.

He heard them fucking over the rain.

He couldn't sleep. The headache came in layers now—could you have more than one at a time?—and the ringing. He heard the rain, and the pigs and horses sheltering under the guesthouse, grunting and snorting as in some interspecies dialogue. He heard them in the next room over the ringing and the rain. There were walls but no ceiling, just rafters and then a common open space under the sloped roof. A conduit for voices. You could hear them trying not to be heard—thumping, panting, small gasps, an abbreviated moan. He thought at first it was a child having a nightmare. Another animal language. Interpret that.

Canadian sex. Three downs and no fair catch. He almost laughed . . . The backs of her legs, round and tan. Was it Leslie and Lesley? He wondered if they'd pushed their beds together.

A soundless flash of lightning then and in it he saw the insect still clinging to the wall under the window, big and flat and long-legged. He'd thought it a kind of spider but it had six legs and the guide told him they ate cockroaches. He thought of her now, at the other end of the guesthouse. Wondered if she was awake, hearing what he heard, sharing it like what they'd shared on the sandbar. If she slept in clothes.

Earlier they'd seen a blue lightning bug, floating in the air like a star unmoored.

The interpreter snored.

It began to rain harder. A pressure on his bladder. After the lightning it was blind dark all over again and the rain came so hard and felt so close like it was pounding the lid of your coffin and he thought he understood now why the *monos* roared.

If he could just get an hour.

The rain had gotten inside him and he had to let it out. He could wait for daylight, but did not want to stoop in the outhouse again. Did not want to disturb the netting he'd so laboriously tucked under his mattress, nor grope for the lantern he'd put somewhere under the bed, not knowing what his hand might close on.

There was a taper in the corner by the window, but the box of matches was empty.

He tried the old tricks; he couldn't remember a conversation he'd had fifteen minutes ago, but he could recall an entire play-book, its myriad variations, and sometimes courting sleep he would recount all the possibilities of a single scheme. X runs a

211

hook, Y runs drag. Z runs middle read or breaks inside and leads you to oblivion but it wasn't working now, he couldn't focus, and there was the fear of where else it might take you, some dim flickering vault of the mind, beyond the book, where someone laughs behind you and the lights go out for good.

It seemed to be letting up. Fuck it. Fuck the light. He would find his way outside and just go off the porch, fuck the dark. He turned on his side, clawed the netting up, swung his bare feet onto the bare floorboards and lifted the mesh over his head like a veil. Squeezed sideways between the beds and found the door easily enough. Anxious moments feeling the damp splintered wood for the little bolt that secured it. Then he was outside in a cooler openness, a different shade of dark, in his underwear, closing the door carefully behind him.

He wasn't sure if he could see anything but felt strangely accomplished to be here. He waited, then reached, trying for the rail or one of the posts that rose from it at intervals. Fine drops on his face. Where was it? He moved sideways from the door a few steps, then forward. Then forward again, his foot hovering, and the lightning showed him what he'd forgotten: the gap in the railing and that he was about to step through it and off the edge of the veranda.

He seized the post he'd seen in the flash and, when he'd calmed, felt for the edge with his toes. With his other hand he thumbed down the front of his briefs and did what he'd come to do, thinking maybe the opening before him had been made for just that purpose.

A sprinkling on the tops of his feet but he couldn't tell if it came from him or the sky. He remembered the bats on the island but wouldn't the rain clear the air?

Another flare. The river below was the same shiny smooth colourlessness but now there was something in it. He stopped. When the sky lit up again he saw them, what the guide had tried to show them and what he'd almost stepped into: red, floating just out of the flat motionless surface. Unblinking, impenetrable, no translation required. Saw them seeing him through eighty million years of implacable reptile hunger, not caring what number you wore nor whom the confetti had fallen on. You were perfect.

Now he saw there were more of them, but he would finish what he started.

Right in the eyes.

In the morning after breakfast the guide conducted a brief class in building a lean-to shelter out of bamboo and ferns. Then they walked out of town in rubber boots toward the forest and mountains, carrying backpacks and dry bags and bags and bottles of water. The Canadians wore wraparound hydration packs. The guide and interpreter had machetes. There was an occasional path. They passed the wooden schoolhouse where the bell they'd heard at breakfast was an old scuba tank struck with a pipe. Walked through pastures where the grass was sometimes submerged in clear flat pools. Stilt houses widely spaced. Two pigs sharing a puddle. Brahman cows with their long ears and baggy white skin, one of which had recently been slaughtered and skinned and its hide lay curing under the sun like a shiny red carpet, dogs and chickens tentatively nosing its edges. The Canadians did not take this picture.

They saw a girl pounding rice and singing, a washcloth on her head for the sun. She smiled, and the other villagers they passed always said "Buenas" or "Hola"—these were cannibals and pirates with good manners—and sometimes the guide stopped and engaged them in conversation, and sometimes the men spoke to her a certain way, called her *pantera*, and she wouldn't answer. She had a way with silence. The children liked being photographed. A loose group of them, shirtless and too young for school, giggled from a porch with mahogany floorboards. The guide pointed and said two of them were Miskitu princesses.

They heard hammering. A new Moravian church was under construction, a long building with a raised stone foundation and many windows, Gothic arches cut into heavy wooden beams. Its long roof resembled the hull of a capsized ark, a vessel whose survivors would be its congregation.

The Canadian man, who had built his own cabin, watched two men on either end of a crosscut saw: "These people are good carpenters."

"Like the Saviour," the interpreter said. "Every man is a carpenter who build his house." You couldn't tell if he was speaking generally.

Beyond the churches stood a brown horse with red wounds gouged in its flank, which the guide attributed to vampire bats.

Now they came to a steep hill with wooden steps embedded and at the top was another store, too small to accommodate a movie audience but well stocked. Behind it an enormous black man was burning a pile of termite nests and yelled "¿Qué tal?" to the guide. While they spoke Nineteen gratefully marked time with the others, sucking air and water. The smoke smelled almost like incense.

The Pech lived on the higher ground upriver. They were friendly (and, Nineteen thought, better-looking) but didn't want their pictures taken. Their dwellings sat on the ground and were not made of plank boards but woven wood lattices filled in with yellowish mud. Metal chimneys. Some had no walls at all, just thatched roofs or canopies on poles stretched over rude pallets or woven straw mattresses and Nineteen wondered at how much can be done without, if it isn't a matter of getting but getting rid of, if you are born to a burden and should live your life leaving it behind, day by day, piece by piece. Sleep on the floor of the earth, pound rice and sing. Define poverty. Maybe he wasn't bankrupt enough.

The visitors walked through a field of sugar cane and the guide hacked off lengths of the segmented shoots and told them the best way to eat it was from the side—less fibres to spit out. The Canadian wondered aloud if this wasn't stealing before he tried it.

"You can't steal from God," the interpreter translated, and it tasted like sweet tea.

They passed an abandoned hut and then there were no more buildings. The polers were waiting for them on the high bank. There were five of them and the biggest seemed to be in charge, wore a machete and calf-length cutoffs and a sleeveless buttoned shirt. They were all young. One was very dark and was whittling at the end of an uprooted sapling with a pocketknife, shaping the tool of his trade. Another was eating a yellow-skinned pink fruit from the tree he was leaning against, and the other two hung back.

Greetings, introductions—*¿Qué pasa? Pasa nada*—but only the *jefe* shook hands. The guide said something to one of the men who stood off. He did not reply. She repeated herself, and so did he. The big one interceded at length. Lineman, Nineteen thought. He seemed to be explaining. It was not quite an argument but the guide had folded her arms.

The interpreter turned to the passengers. "The one she talking to is call Erwin. He been doing this since seven years old."

They looked down at the two pipantes which had been dragged onto the riverbank. The other poles were in them. They looked back up in unison.

"Is there a problem?" the Canadian wife asked.

"She doesn't know this man, who doesn't talk. The jefe say the one who usually does is quit. The new man is Erwin brother-in-law. He is a fisherman but he want to learn palanquero too."

The new man spoke quietly now, looking at the ground. With his slight build and whiskers he resembled the bowman of the cayuco, but no relation was mentioned.

"We have a student driver?" the Canadian wife said. "Is that a guava tree?"

"We're still going, aren't we?" her husband said.

"Oh yes. She just want to let them know this is not regular," the interpreter said.

He invited them to help themselves to the fruit of the tree before they left, but not the ones that had fallen. This wasn't stealing from God, either.

Upstream. Nineteen rode with the guide, the interpreter, and three polers, one of whom was the apprentice. He proved a quick study. Stood in the bow with his brother in law, the engine, the steersman in the back with his sapling. They held the poles high and pushed down and back till they were almost squatting, then pulled them quickly up and let them drop through their hands next to the gunwale, let the river bottom bend them forty-five degrees so they could push again. It looked too easy to be easy. The jefe shouted instructions about low-hanging branches, rocks and what only he could see. He shouted to the other boat trailing twenty feet behind. They would lose each other around the bends.

"Has to read the river," the interpreter said. Nineteen sat in the back—a stern-heavy trim was required and he was the biggest of the passengers—the steersman behind him, using his pole like a rudder. They heard the Canadian man, holding forth to his wife about whitewater and rock gardens, and Nineteen looked back. He flipped off the husband with a grin, regretted it when the gesture wasn't returned. He hadn't tried to bust balls for years.

The jungle moved past in stops and starts but somehow they seemed to make time. The river was narrow at first, branches interlocking overhead in a green tunnel, then became very wide in places and they watched the canopy on either side grow a hundred feet, then more. The Canadian husband shouted. The polers kept close to the banks where they could, ferrying from eddy to eddy, the mild shallows. Birds perched and flew, called, and the guide pointed and identified bright-coloured parrots and toucans, trogons, tanagers, sunbirds and owls. Nineteen wished they would see some of the animals they'd been promised—monkeys, tapirs, anteaters, sloths, God forbid a jaguar—but all they saw were more birds: social flycatcher and melodious blackbird, names more interesting than what was so named.

The Canadians came temporarily alongside and asked if they would see a quetzal. The guide said this was not the right habitat for quetzal and the couple drifted back, muttering about the website. The sky greyed and a soft rain fell and the Canadians covered themselves. Nineteen looked back with mild scorn at how easily they sought protection; then the rain hardened and he sought his own. They came upon rapids, the up-and-down of small waves rolling under them. The jefe yelled "¡Derecha!" and the crew shifted their weight. The boat tipped to the gunwales and shipped water and the guide and the interpreter bailed furiously. Twice they were wedged between rocks. The first time they muscled through with the passengers helping, Nineteen shoving off slick mossy boulders and boughs by hand and watching a dragonfly drown, unseen forever by anybody but him.

The second time they could not get through and everyone had to get wet and push back out. Nineteen turned and couldn't see the second pipante. He rose to help but the guide wouldn't let him; it would be easier to reboard if he stayed where he was. He obeyed and sat resentfully, drops clicking on his cowled head; princess in a fucking sedan chair. But he was moved, as he always was, by team spirit and hard work, by timing and rhythm in coordination, and resolved to tip the polers when they got back to Las Marías, then wasn't sure how much spare cash he had and resolved to consult the guide as to what might constitute an appropriate gift. Or maybe the tour operator had already figured it in.

He looked back and could not see the other boat. A crude face was carved in a rock. A hard scraping under his tailbone and they were free. He yelled to the interpreter—where was the other boat?—and the interpreter yelled to the others and they all stood still in the current breaking around them, looking. The face was smiling. Then there was shouting from the second canoe as it reappeared; they'd run aground and had to do some pushing as well.

They left the smiling rock behind. "Was that a petroglyph?" Nineteen asked, pointing, and the guide muttered, "No es importante," without looking. Maybe it was laughing.

It was late morning when they arrived at the drop-off, and sunny for the moment.

"Looks like someone got our parking space," the Canadian man said, and a small canoe was tied off on the bank where they were headed. Its owners were nearby. A stream running down from the jungle had carved a deep culvert into the red clay of the bank and a family of three were panning it. A man and a woman and a boy Nineteen thought should have been in school. They were barefoot and wore cutoffs and the father and son were shirtless. The clay had dried on their skin, and was almost the same colour.

A dog cavorting in the water stopped to look at the arrivals.

"Hola," the guide called to the prospectors, who called back. The polers poled them ashore, and after the pipantes were unloaded the guide and the interpreter conversed with the parents whose son continued to work as though there'd been no interruption. The tourists watched, and the Canadian husband asked Nineteen if he'd ever invested.

"Too volatile. All gold's fool's gold, they say."

"Don't tell *him* that," the wife said, watching through her phone.

Crouching in the silt of the stream just before it emptied into the river, his small dark-haired head, focused and aware of nothing else, holding the pan, a wide wooden bowl, just under the surface, shaking it side to side, twisting it like a wheel, letting the larger rocks rise and skimming them off with the edge of his hand, picking out roots and moss bits and rolling them in his fingers before discarding them, shaking the pan again.

"It's heavy, always sinks to the bottom," the Canadian husband said, and Nineteen realized it wasn't just erosion that had deepened the culvert.

The contents of the pan dwindled, darkened with heavier materials, black and purple sands, concentrates. The boy now shook it back and forth, tilted it, dipped it again, working water with water, losing only what he wanted to lose, swirling what remained in expert hypnotic circles. Reducing, purifying, panning it down.

"I'm not sure what he's doing, but I could watch it for hours," the Canadian wife said. She wobbled—the clay slicked the surface of the bank and even just standing still was uncertain. Nineteen reached out and steadied her, then quickly let go her arm. She glanced at him and said nothing. Her eyes were grey.

"The Greeks thought it was made of water and sunlight," her husband said.

The guide was hacking boughs off a dead cedar with her machete.

"¿Algo?" the prospector said to his son. The boy was picking through the dark residue at the bottom of the pan. Stood and took something to his father. A delicate invisible transfer. The man spoke and showed his wife, then positioned it carefully in the palm of his hand, inviting everyone to take a look at something born in an exploding star and ferried to Earth by meteor two million centuries ago.

"How big?" Nineteen said, squinting for the tiny yellow glint in the intermittent sun.

"Maybe quarter of a gram," the interpreter said. The Canadian wife wondered at its value. She smiled at the dog.

"Let's see, about thirty grams to a troy ounce . . ." Her husband looked up. "Say about ten bucks. American."

The man put the nugget in a small clear vial where it had scarce company. The polers kidded his son, who remained grave.

They heard the guide's voice. She had made them walking sticks from the dead tree, leaned them against the trunk and now gestured.

"Okay, let's," the interpreter said and Nineteen reached for his dry bag. The polers would meet them at the petroglyphs. The rapids above were too strong to push passengers and cargo upriver. Downstream was a different story; the river would do the work.

The crew was gathering wood. They would fish for their lunch before leaving.

The trekkers chose their sticks. "Buena suerta," the guide told the family, who repeated it in reply. She told the tourists it meant good luck.

"Should we need it?" the Canadian husband asked, and the guide took them in.

There is a way to walk in the unfamiliar, she told them. The feet must have eyes. She demonstrated, lifting a foot; touching, probing, turning, planting. Like fitting a key to a lock. One step. Floor of leaf litter and mud, green stems, twigs, soft rotten logs, ferns with spiky leaves. Nothing ever quite died here, but found its afterlife in this world, fed by fungus and lusting for light. Plant sex. Black mossy rocks. Always touching, brushing, scratching, poking. A mouldy, verdant rankness in moist heavy air that seemed to rub the skin raw. Not the smell of a northern forest. Ants. Wood vines thick as your thigh and half a mile long, creeping across the ground then twisting up trees on their way to the canopy. Nineteen understood the competition for daylight. *Matapalo* growing from the top down, encasing tree trunks as in cages of bone, earning its name. Strangler fig.

There was a way to walk in the jungle, to stumble and slog, hope that the vine you reached for to arrest your fall was not bristling with thorns, or insects disguised to look like them, or what she called bullet ants for the pain their bite inflicts. If the feet don't have eyes keep the ones in your head on the ground for snakes— the coral snake, for which they had no serum, the pit viper, which can spit venom six feet, whose bite can penetrate rubber boots and cause a foot, a leg, an arm to liquefy and rot off with necrosis. Also known as the fer-de-lance but which the guide called *barba amarilla*. Yellow beard.

Sometimes a path only she could see. She and the interpreter led with machetes on lanyards looped to their wrists, swinging at shallow angles. Then the Canadians, wife first, and Nineteen. Thin metallic slice of the blades through the insect buzzing inside and outside his head. The floor rose steeply and became more climb than walk and he was grateful to God and the guide for the sticks. Not just his ankle, his knees and hips and back; he almost felt like an athlete again, living in sweat and pain. Then the drop on the other side and the hike became a half-controlled fall. At some point it started all over again.

They didn't see a single snake but saw a moth with eyes on wings the size of your hands, and when it flew by they felt the breath of its passing. Ants everywhere in vast, selfless societies. A procession of leafcutters crossing the trail, each marcher carrying a fragment like a tiny green fan, and the tourists paused as if to give them right of way.

Each could carry five thousand times its body weight, the guide told them.

"White man's burden. What do they do with the leaves?" the Canadian husband asked, pulling water from a tube, grateful like the others for the pause.

They fed a garden of fungus, the guide said, which fed them in turn. Fungus gave the forest its life, she said, and sometimes a living death and they came across a spider with strange growths fruiting in spurs and stalks from its body, lurching spasmodically across a leaf, zombified, a puppet enacting the imperative of an alien life form.

A spider web grabbed their faces, invisible but thick as fishing line, infinitely tensile and stronger than steel. It seemed alive as its maker.

There were crossings. A streambed with a couple of planks embedded in quickmud. A log bridging a ravine, about the width of a telephone pole so that they had to cross sideways, feet flat, and the fall probably wouldn't kill you but any misstep here could mean slow disaster, the beginning of some improbable end; months later, writhing with seizures in a suburban hospital, some parasite's larvae lodged in your brain.

"Has it been a couple of hours yet?" the Canadian man said, not for the last time.

Termite nests high on tree trunks, big and dark and tumorous. Kissing beetles, stingless bees, poisonous caterpillars, scorpions in the matapalo who defend but never attack. Plants that eat meat, or look like they do. A butterfly with transparent wings that drinks human sweat, and if you squatted and defecated where you stood, fifty species of beetle would have it gone in an hour.

Still, there was more flora than fauna. The guide showed them hoofprints, wild boar tracks, but they didn't see the boar, nor deer, tapirs, armadillos, nor monkeys, and when they questioned this absence the guide spoke on the predations of hunters, the genius of camouflage—the jungle is a hiding place—so they saw neither a sloth nor the harpy eagle that would pluck it like fruit with claws as big as a man's hands. Its seven-foot wingspan.

They didn't see the eagle but saw or heard other birds— macaws, cotingas, toucans, and there are Miskitu stories and songs about them, about the Hummingbird Woman and why the vulture is bald, and they heard the metallic cry of a red-winged blackbird and the guide told them the story of a German boy shipwrecked on the coast centuries ago, who was so young he had never known a woman, who was alone and had no food and would die a virgin, and who, as he lay near death and filled with desire, could only cry his want, and whose soul then shattered into a thousand pieces, each shard flying off to become the bird that sang his story, and the guide cried "¡Quiero! ¡Quiero!" in mimicry of this unrequited plea.

"Germans and sex," the Canadian woman said. "Fassbinder."

"*Quiero una cerveza*," her husband said. "Canadians and beer."

"It's a lovely story, though," the wife said. "Is there a book, maybe?"

"We are the book," the interpreter said, and did not submit her question.

A bridge made of hemp like a tightrope with handrails, so frayed and unsteady only one could cross at a time. Nineteen volunteered to go first; the guide wouldn't have it.

"Define 'short hike,'" the Canadian man said. "Define 'easy to moderate.'"

More flora than fauna. The canopy now high and full, shading the floor which was clearer, walkable, the trees tall and widely spaced. A dead mahogany, killed by lightning, a hollow grey tower with a great black fissure like a wound near its base, and when they looked inside there was a terrible ammoniac smell and they saw a pile of bones and feathers covered in dried blood and droppings, but not the creature who lived in the tree and whose appetite these remains enshrined.

Another mahogany, alive, buttress roots like fins slanting twenty feet up its trunk, its wood so prized loggers would cut down an entire stand to get to it, for here trees rarely stood with their own but in a mix and the guide pointed out oak, cedar, laurel, almond, cacao, a tree with strange knuckled roots like organ pipes, and Nineteen thought he recognized, in its wide trunk and spread canopy, a younger relative of the one he'd seen in the park in the city, and the guide said the spirits of the dead resided there, that in native cosmogony the forces of nature were governed by supernatural beings who caused illness and were the source of all evil in the world. Wind, water, the animals, this very tree. The Canadian woman asked if she shared this belief and the guide touched a fern that folded its leaves over her fingers. She told them the story it told her. Showed them Bitter Broom Weed, remedy for snake bite and rheumatism, Dutchman's Pipe for dysentery, something for respiratory ailments, a root that induced labour, and she showed them a plant that made a picture of a flower on its leaf to deceive insects into pollinating it, spoke of it and its ten thousand kindred species here as if their sentience and agency were matters of fact.

But she could also be scientifically pragmatic, could kick a dog without hurting it, describe complex natural processes and recite statistics, identify the life that surrounded them by order, family, genera, species. *Epiphytes*, she said. *Bromeliad*, and the interpreter relayed this knowledge tirelessly, as if privileged, and when the Canadian man asked where the guide had studied, the interpreter simply gestured around them.

The forest fed them. "*Passiflora quadrangularis.*" Passionflower, the guide told them, and told them Spanish missionaries thought the flower represented the suffering of Christ—the crown of filaments, the five stamen, the glands of the leaves like pieces of silver—that to partake of its fruit was an act of communion. It was purple and full of seeds.

"Our Lord tastes like apricot," the husband said. Nineteen bit his tongue and almost crossed himself. He looked about at the crowding green formlessness that was everywhere and went nowhere, engulfing and entangling, so dense the mind couldn't distinguish where tree left off and bush began, nor discern the shape of the land, but he knew it could bite, lay eggs in your skin, devour your lips and nose with white leprosy or cure your cancer, and he wondered what of him it might kill or cure, and if there was any difference.

Two yellow frogs fucking on the tip of a leaf. Their bright poison skin.

The canopy had dropped and opened and they came upon a small grove of coconut palms, one heavy with fruit. The guide wasn't sure how they'd gotten there—*Cocos nucifera* needed help to grow inland—but she knew that fifty-five million years ago, when the earth was warm and the forests born, there were palm trees in Alaska. She and the interpreter knocked down the ripe green drupe that is both fruit and seed with their walking sticks. The guide hacked a flat spot in the shell with her machete, then pierced it with the corner of the blade—she'd taped it off near the handle so she could use it like a knife—handed the fruit out and everyone drank the sweet cool milk while she returned to the grove to look at the palm leaves. One was bent inward at the rib, tentlike, and the guide peered carefully under the fold. She signed the others to come look but to do so quietly, and when they had they saw within the palm a colony of tiny white bats, asleep.

They moved on. The jungle closed. Thornscrub. It narrowed to a passage, a tunnel of vines and leaves and lashing branches. The footing tangled, obscured; even looking down you couldn't see what kept tripping you. Couldn't see through the thickets on either side, couldn't use the walking stick for lack of room and couldn't entirely ignore the Canadian wife, now behind her husband, the switching hemispheres of her buttocks still apparent through the baggy pants she'd sensibly worn.

"Pure jungle," the interpreter was saying, the rest lost to the incessant rustling and crackling, the ringing of steel. Harsh breaths. Nineteen pushed on in claustrophobic torment, drenched and parched, his spine burning to unbend, unable to escape the feeling they'd been swallowed. Something fluttered near his shoulder. It was small and its wings were black on one side and blue on the other, so that as it flew you saw both colours as one. It moved along with them, keeping pace as if trapped, and Nineteen anticipated the Spanish, the English, the Latin, maybe Miskitu, but he heard nothing and began to wonder if only he could see it, if it was perhaps the product of delirium, or another symptom of a defective brain, choosing finally to take it for a sign; he could not accept an indifferent nature, interested only in sucking his sweat and stealing his shit, because nature was God and God was not indifferent. Invisible, yes, hiding in His furnace of chaos and creation—cosmic tough love, then, yes, but not indifference.

Then they were out. The sky had darkened, and something was coming. They heard it at first, a low rush like wind in the trees, distant at first, growing, deepening, enveloping. The guide told them to cover themselves and everyone did but her. She told them it had rained for two million years before the time of the dinosaurs and Nineteen was struggling into his plastic skin when he heard the first slap of leaves, saw the foliage tremble with myriad impacts and then it fell with such weight and force they almost knelt to it.

Dama Alwani: Grandfather Thunder.

They were going uphill again. The guide had taken two big fronds and held their stems so that they overlapped, then held this green parasol over her head. The trail now like climbing a muddy waterfall. The sticks sank deep with each step, each step a lurid sound in the mud which sometimes sucked the boot off your foot. Sweating in plastic. The Canadian wife kept slipping and her husband would catch her but not always, his hand on her bottom. She slapped it away. Nineteen looked ahead at the guide and interpreter, keeping their boots on the edges of the path to optimize footing. A veteran move.

Going up you dropped on hands and knees, crawling, going down you fell to a sit and rode your ass. It had ended that way, on his ass in the rain and mud in the old stadium, the last play of his playing days, sacked and stripped before the third step of his drop, sitting on his ass in the mud and rain, front page, just able to see the numbers of the weak side linebacker who'd ripped his heart loose and kept it, dwindling into the end zone. Still remembered that sound, that low reproach, denunciation, felt it in the centre of his breastbone as if it emanated from that hollow. Then it came from everywhere and not even the jungle could kill it.

The rain had lightened. They crossed a stream and climbed again, then arrived in a flat clearing where they stood and looked and drank and breathed. A view of the river.

"Is it a little hike yet?" the Canadian husband said and his wife rolled her eyes. For all their trekking they seemed curiously untravelled. Nineteen wondered if that was why he liked them. He looked at the river curving below and was grateful they would be taking the boats back; he was sure he couldn't do this again. Beyond the Plátano the tops of the trees receded in a series of fading hills, among them a lone rocky peak upthrust like a tooth or talon.

"Pico Dama," the guide said. She was sharpening her machete with a file.

"If that ain't Spanish for Dog's Dick . . ." the husband said. Nineteen smiled; it was a fairly accurate description, and he advised the interpreter not to translate.

The guide asked if they wanted to eat lunch or wait till they got to the petroglyphs. "How much further?" the Canadian woman asked.

"Another camel's hump," the interpreter said—it was how the guide described the hills they'd climbed.

"Hump is right," the husband said. "Isn't there a camel with three humps?" and his wife said something inaudible, as was his response, and the ensuing exchange, and Nineteen realized it was the quietest argument he'd ever witnessed.

The husband looked at him and tried to smile. "We are not the proverbial bickering couple."

The words were just out of his mouth when they heard what sounded like a gunshot. The tourists looked around, then at each other. It was not close but difficult to say how far or where it came from. The guide was looking downriver. The Canadian man was about to speak when they heard another one.

A small flight of birds rose from the trees in the distance. They flew a short way and settled. The guide was pointing.

"Isn't that where we're headed?" the Canadian woman said.

"Cazador," the guide said. She was not naming the birds, and spoke in the tone she used for ranchers and loggers.

"She think hunter," the interpreter said.

"Well." Nineteen had taken off his poncho, preferring a light rain to his own trapped sweat. "Is it a problem?"

"That's why we don't see any monkeys, right?" the Canadian wife said. She thought. "Could it be the polers? That little guy on the boat to the village had a rifle."

"I don't know much about guns," her husband said, "but that didn't sound like a .22."

Nineteen looked at the guide. "Is this a problem?"

The interpreter shook his head. "You can go here days and not see anyone. But when you do is usually hunter. Is problem," he said, "but not for us."

"Maybe we should eat by the river," the Canadian wife said.

Everyone seemed to be waiting for the next one. When it didn't come the guide spoke, running her blade across a tree trunk for the burrs. She didn't sound concerned. "She think to have lunch at Walpaulban Sirpi," the interpreter said. "Are more place to sit."

"Isn't that what I said?" the Canadian wife said.

"Fine by me," her husband said. "But where there are hunters there are accidents."

His wife sighed. Nineteen was only thirsty. Before they left, the guide asked if anyone had personal needs to attend to.

It had stopped raining when they got to Walpaulban Sirpi, Miskitu for "small carved rocks." It didn't seem like a place at all, just more of river and trees with a difficult name. The boats weren't there.

"This happen sometime," the interpreter said. "The rain maybe swollen the river, make delay."

They looked to the guide for more but there was none. If she wasn't worried, Nineteen decided, neither was he. He was content to have arrived, everything would be easier from here on in—even his head felt better, though his ears were ringing as if he still heard the machetes. The river here was banked with big flat rocks; he dropped his dry bag on one and sat on it. The others took his example. After they'd rested awhile the guide took them to see what they'd come for.

The petroglyphs were carved into the flat side of a large boulder standing just a few yards from the bank. The water was not deep and the tourists waded in their rubber boots to a broad ledge at the base of the rock on which they stood and looked at the markings.

It was hard not to be disappointed. Even the Canadians, who'd been decidedly out of the national character during the hike, found it difficult to revert to type.

"It's only one line," the wife allowed. The husband said nothing.

Nineteen nodded. After the ordeal of getting here, they could have at least used the whole page.

The guide touched a figure on one end of the carving and said a word.

"Deer," the interpreter said. At the other end was something fiercer, dragon-like. Hungry.

"They think this is some kind of map?" the Canadian husband said.

"Some archaeologist think, yes, maybe was Inca make." The guide ran her fingers from one glyph to the other, slowly, speaking as if reading some ancient braille. "Some think it refers to creation myth . . ." The creature at the end was a two-headed crocodile. The world sits on its back.

"So it's a story or a map," the Canadian husband said.

"She says a story is a map of time."

"I'm still having trouble with the deer," Nineteen said. It looked like nothing but a knot of grooves.

"I think I can see it," the Canadian wife said. "But what does our guide think?" An abrupt change of tone, as if the dog had replaced the deer.

"She thinks maybe warning. Or a challenge." Nineteen thought of things he'd seen on nature TV, delicate mammals trying to cross a river teeming with jaws and scales, teeth. He asked how old it was.

"At least one thousand years."

The Canadian wife considered this. "The Maya Postclassic period."

Her husband nodded. "Not bad for someone with a degree in watching TV, eh?"

"Fuck you, eh?"

"Is not Maya," the interpreter said.

They took turns touching it. Traced it from one end to the other as if this were the only understanding there would be, along the engraved path smoothed and rounded by water, wind, a thousand years. To touch, to have touched. You were There.

"I'm sorry," the Canadian man said, "but those glyphs are starting to look like Today's Special to me. Anybody else?" Nineteen smiled. He didn't mind a smartass with purpose.

They ate on the bank and the sun came out and the polers still did not arrive. It was the same lunch they'd eaten the day before on the way to Las Marías but after the jungle and the mud and wings with eyes it was not the same at all.

The guide closed packages as they ate but didn't put them away. She exuded a faint underarm musk which Nineteen did not find unappetizing. The Canadian wife sat cross-legged in an open chambray shirt and sports bra, watching.

"Shouldn't she call someone—about where they are, I mean." She held a sandwich but it was still whole. "She has a satellite phone, right?"

"She call after we eat," the interpreter said.

"Should she wait that long?"

"If you insist, she can call now."

"Let her eat," the husband said. "Maybe they stopped off at the White City."

Nineteen looked at him. Where had he heard that before?

"If Ciudad Blanca exist," the interpreter said, "probably is way upriver."

"I saw something online—*The New Yorker*, I think." The Canadian husband dipped a plantain. "Said they found ruins. Some laser mapping thing."

Nineteen remembered now, the expatriate tour operator had spoken of it. He even recalled his Seattle quip and thought he might reprise it but the interpreter was talking about something called lidar.

"Sounds like the acronym for a bullshit detector," the Canadian husband said.

"From aeroplane," the interpreter was saying. "They find evidence of settlement—pyramids, plazas, canal, maybe ball courts, yes—but no one has been yet."

"Ball courts," Nineteen said. Perhaps there were shamans as well. *Curanderos.* "Where is this place?"

"Government don't reveal location, but probably the deep jungle, maybe inaccessible. Are places in Moskitia no person has stood. Maybe last places on Earth."

"Why doesn't the government . . . ?" The Canadian wife sounded distracted, speaking just to speak. "Looters?"

"So who is the looter," the interpreter said.

"La Ciudad Blanca," the guide said, and said more. Nineteen had wondered when she would enter the exchange. He'd gotten the idea that on some level she required no translation. Or maybe she just wanted to finish her sandwich.

The interpreter chewed, swallowed. "She thinks there is no just one city, but many sites, most undiscover. Not Maya, not Inca; something not seen before. Maybe ancestor to Pech."

Nineteen considered this. The Pech were a gentle people, the

Maya brutal, blood-soaked. Human sacrifices flayed and roasted alive, hearts carved beating from chests.

Where were the boatmen?

"Why do they call it the White City?"

"Probably because of limestone in the area." The interpreter listened to the guide. "But there is Indigenous stories about a city with white stone building, ramparts. A place where Indians take refuge from conquistadores."

"Cortez, that lot," the Canadian man said.

The interpreter looked rather slyly at Nineteen. "Was also called City of the Monkey God. Pech say Place of the Ancients. Maybe they know where is but they don't tell outsiders."

"Who can blame them," the Canadian wife said, still seeming distracted. "I wouldn't tell us either. We're only worth our weight in shit."

"¿Qué dice ella?" the guide asked him, reaching for her bag. The interpreter told her. He smiled coldly. "Says maybe it doesn't matter. Says at present rate of deforest, won't be Moskitia for secrets to hide."

The jungle would lay bare its mysteries for all to see, like sunken ships in a desert.

The Canadian touched his stomach as if the thought made him ill. He whispered to his wife, who fished from her backpack a travel-size dispenser of toilet tissue. He took it without a word and slipped back into the rainforest.

"Don't get lost," his wife called, then muttered what sounded like, "Time to feed the beetles."

Nineteen, still recovering from the hike, watched him go then looked at the Canadian woman. "He's in pretty decent shape, isn't he?" He was afraid to ask his age.

"He sold software to dictators so they can tell if people are lying." She seemed to have heard another question, then corrected: "He bitches sometimes, but only on principle. Now he's talking the Iditarod, Pacific Crest. A gorilla trek in Uganda. I don't worry about him, I just try to keep up." She was worried about something, though, and glanced at the guide, who was looking through her dry bag. "*¿Qué pasa?*"

They heard the guide's voice. The interpreter answered. It was not Spanish, but sounded like what they'd heard at times on the river. The language of the land. The wife looked blankly at Nineteen and the guide and the interpreter went back and forth until Nineteen said, "Is there a problem?"

"She can't find the phone," the wife said, nodding to herself.

Nineteen looked at the interpreter, who shook his head. "Is not in the bag."

The guide had emptied the dry bag and was repacking it in the methodical way she did everything. It was usually a pleasure to watch. Nineteen stood up out of his pain, looked around. "Maybe she dropped it . . ."

The wife did not stand. "Jesus, what if she dropped it in the jungle."

"It was secure in the bag. Couldn't just fall out."

"When did she see it last?"

"This morning. When we leave Las Marías."

"Is she sure she packed it?"

They were speaking Spanish. "Only one time it was out of her sight, when we stop to portage. When we talk to the family."

"The prospectors," the Canadian wife said. "She thinks somebody stole it?"

"She thinks maybe." The interpreter sounded more reticent

236

than the guide had. "She think was maybe . . . She don't want to say without proof."

The wife looked briefly to the woods where her husband had gone. "That guy she didn't know."

Nineteen remembered. The people who sing were also a people who occasionally stole. He would have preferred the river had taken it.

A slight tremor in the Canadian wife's voice. "If she didn't trust him she shouldn't have . . . That's on her."

For a world traveller she seemed easily rattled. Nineteen felt fatherly; for a moment he remembered her name. "So we don't have a phone. So what then?"

"She can't call the tour operator, let him know we don't have the way back yet . . ." Another long discussion in Spanish. The Canadian woman huffed, retrieved her own phone, pushed buttons. Stood suddenly and shouted into the jungle, "Are you okay in there?"

Nothing, then a hoarse yelled reply, barely intelligible.

"We wait one more hour at the most," the interpreter said, and Nineteen imagined for an absurd moment he was talking about the husband. "Somebody might still come."

"Somebody," the young wife said.

"They have been late before but not like this. Is possible was flood downriver, mudslide. The rain is unusual this time of August. It's usually our little spring, we call."

"We've heard," she said. "Is it unusual they steal phones too? What happens when they don't come?"

"Can't wait too long or will be too late." The guide hadn't hesitated but the interpreter, the messenger, did. "We will start hiking back."

The Canadian woman stared at him, then looked at Nineteen as if waiting for him to say something useful. For her and her husband the walk back would be a strenuous inconvenience; Nineteen could only pray the polers would arrive. He looked at the river. "Hike back to the village."

The interpreter shook his head. "There is Pech settlement downriver. We can spend the night there if we get before dark. Get a boat in the morning."

"That pushes everything back a day. People might have connections to make. *People have people waiting for them.*" The Canadian wife looked at Nineteen again. "Do you believe this shit? They shouldn't bring anyone out here if they can't . . ." She swallowed it.

And if they couldn't get there before dark? Nineteen wondered.

"Then we spend the night in the jungle."

The wife looked momentarily as if she might laugh. "It just keeps getting better. Spend the night. Okay." She looked toward wherever her husband was, then back. "Is she serious, spend the night? We don't have a tent, sleeping bags. What happens if it rains again in your little spring?"

"We will make a shelter. We will have fire, there is still food."

"Food. What if we *are* food? There are jaguars in there."

The interpreter spread his hands. Surely she'd roughed it before.

"That isn't the point!"

The guide opened her mouth but the tourist held up her hand. "I think I've . . . no, I've definitely heard enough." She took a step toward the trees. "Shelter. She better show us how to build a goddamn boat is what. Fucking Moskitia Misadventures. My ass itches."

She wasn't quite hysterical but Nineteen felt his headache intensify. He turned to his past for something he might bring to bear, turned to the guide for calm. He would have liked to see her make fire. She was looking downriver in an attitude of listening while the Canadian woman shouted into the forest.

"I'm sorry but are you almost done? You're not gonna believe what they want us to do." She said his name. There was no answer and now she sounded fully American: "God damn it hurry up and wipe your ass, they want us to walk!"

He didn't answer. She said his name again and he did not answer.

A plane flew over their heads.

Small, single-engine, fixed landing gear. It flew low, crossing the river, continuing upstream and seeming to get lower. He had not heard it over the river, but Nineteen wondered if that was what the guide had been listening to.

"There's an airfield around here?" he asked the interpreter.

"Not supposed to be," the interpreter said, and the Canadian wife turned and watched it sink out of sight, her arms half-raised in a belated signal of distress. She turned.

"Is that for us?" The hope in her voice was not on the face of the guide.

"Can't be," the interpreter said. Nineteen remembered what he'd seen from the plane over the Moskitia.

"Shouldn't we head that way anyway then?" the wife said. "How far can it—"

The guide held up a hand for silence.

"I'm sorry! Excuse me am I talking too much?"

The guide was now looking toward the jungle, pointing. "Su esposo," she said.

The Canadian husband had returned.

"Thank God!" His wife almost ran. "Did you see the plane? You know what they want us to—"

He stood at the edge of the forest as if it would reclaim him. His pink face had whitened, mouth open, his hands shaking as they tried to finish buckling his belt.

"Sweetie," his wife said, an endearment they hadn't heard before and Nineteen felt a small embarrassment. "What's wrong?"

She made a face between puzzlement and disgust. He seemed to be trying to say something. They all stepped closer and smelled it then; he'd either hitched up his pants too soon or hadn't dropped them. Snake bite, Nineteen thought, but whatever had bitten him hadn't left a mark.

His wife was touching him. He had given up trying to speak and raised his arm, pointed a crooked tremulous finger behind him.

"What?" his wife said. "What happened?"

"¿Qué es?" the guide said and the interpreter said, "What was it? A snake?"

"A . . . Oh God, is there antivenom?"

The Canadian man looked at them with a kind of dazed patience and carefully shook his head, still pointing. The guide looked there. The wife lowered his hand for him. "No es una serpiente," the guide said but it did not sound like a good thing and she looked upriver where the plane had gone and spoke a Spanish they hadn't heard before.

"She say to start packing up. We take a look, then we leave right away."

"Oh Lord, what happened? What did you see?" She was buckling her husband's belt. Nineteen wanted to follow the guide and the interpreter, but didn't want to, then heard her voice—"Help me with him? Please?"—and he took the Canadian's arm while she had the other and they guided him back to where the food still lay on the bank and sat him on a rock.

Oh fuck now what, she said and Nineteen started gathering the bread and lunch meat and little packets of condiments and dropping them into the canister with no attempt at order nor to expel the flies that followed them in, glancing at the jungle while the Canadian woman tried to coax her husband out of his stupor, but he just kept looking back as if for the part of him he'd left there.

The canister now sealed and latched and still the guide and the interpreter did not return. Nineteen looked at the Canadians, then turned and shouted into the forest. He received no response and tried again, provoking only a deeper silence that seemed to consume his voice. He looked back once more and they were both looking at him now, and without another word he faced the deep green quiet again, about to step into it, but then no longer had to for the guide and the interpreter were coming out and they were not alone.

Listen to the laughing rock.

The *liwa mairin* is a spirit who presides over and protects the creatures of water. She is also beautiful and capable of great evil, seducing men and then drowning them in the sea, in rivers and lagoons. Lobster divers, fishermen, palanqueros. The poler's wife is starting to worry that her husband may have fallen victim to this allure. She worries this because everyone knows about the village man who fell in love with a liwa and would visit her every night when the moon was full, until he was found in a creek with blood coming from his nose and ears, a sure sign. She worries because she cannot get a straight answer from her brother, a Miskitu who acts ladino, who will only say that there was an argument where they dropped the tourists off at the trail, that Erwin told him vete al carajo and he took a ride back downriver with a family of gold panners. But when she asks him who this family is, he says he doesn't know them, says maybe they came from another village, or the settlement upstream that is too small for a name, and when she asks him what the argument was about he says he doesn't remember, just that he is going to the pulpería for something to drink and perhaps to watch the película, and then he is gone in the gathering dark, taking the answers to her questions with him. She doesn't follow. She doesn't follow because she is alone and with child and afraid of the spirits of the forest, though she is not sure she believes in them, though she is equally afraid of becoming a widowed mother, for here such a woman is considered old and burdensome even if she is still young, but in the morning there is cacao to pick and ferment, bread to bake with cassava and coconut over sheet metal and hot coals from the recipe a Garifuna woman taught her.

Baking bread is her passion.

But before this, at first light, she will do what she should have done today when there was still time; she will walk into the village to speak to El Presidente del Turismo de Las Marías. He will get to the bottom of things, may even contact the gringo tour operator in Ceiba, who is there now having dinner at a Garifuna restaurant near the Río Cangrejal, the river down which he sometimes arranges whitewater rafting expeditions. Chabelita's has an air-conditioned dining room but the evening is fair and the expatriate and his wife and the Russian developer for whom he works are having their ceviche and conch soup in a small brick courtyard out back. Oleg is buying. Oleg always buys. He is a short stocky man who shaves his head and wears shirts as loud as his voice, who was once in the Soviet infantry and served in Afghanistan as a teenager. He likes to buy and to talk while he is scrolling his phone—you cannot get between him and his phone—but the expatriate is not interested tonight in hearing about the Phase Two lots, about transfer taxes and the mujahideen and land mines and night raids; he is thinking about the tourists and the guide and the interpreter, about the polers as well, and about the men who wear Armani and jewellery and too much *eau de parfum*, the ones you see in Ceiba, in San Pedro, in

Brus, in the capital, and now even on the island. He has seen them with the developer but did not expect to be approached by them himself. They like to buy as well, and all he has to do is nothing, not do or say anything to anyone for twenty-four hours no matter what, that is all they ask, they intend no harm, and he took their word and the money that bore their scent—half of it anyway, the rest payable when the agreed-upon interval has passed—but it feels as though he has sold more than his silence.

"I want to buy an island," the developer says. The expatriate nods and looks at his wife. She is sullen and picks at her plate. She used to smile on hearing the developer's strangely accented Spanish, was doing so much better, helping out with the business which was half her idea, but she has been like this lately, withdrawn, moody, has trouble sleeping, and when she doesn't she has dreams worse than insomnia. And lately she won't have him. He'd hoped they were past that, or as beyond it as anyone in their situation can perhaps expect to be—always in the dark, like campesinos; he has never seen her undress—but her mother still has a small house in Tegus and cannot make ends meet because she must pay what the maras call rent, the ones who shot her eighty-two-year-old neighbour's dog and nailed it to his door when he couldn't come up with fifteen dollars a week. Is this what brought the dreams back?

The expatriate's wife goes to church and thanks God she doesn't have a sister, that her brother is already with Him. She goes there with little else to thank Him for, carrying her Bible, and the expatriate is afraid she will ultimately retreat into its pages, into long skirts and abstinence not just from him, but everything. She talks about sending her family to Mexico—there is an asylum program in Tapachula—but Mexico costs money and the maquila has cut her hours, so when the men you smell before you see approached in their Armani and their Swiss watches, he breathed deeply and took—it is only fitting they foot the bill, it was men like them who made women like her—and he listens now not to the developer but to the jet plane passing over their heads and imagines himself aboard with his wife and what remains of her family, bound for wherever it is going, leaving the bad dreams behind. The plane is in fact bound for Houston but is not the plane Number Nineteen's girlfriend is on, which departed Roatan in the early afternoon and is now in a holding pattern over George Bush Intercontinental while airport officials wait for a storm front to pass through. Nineteen's girlfriend sits patiently in coach—first class was all booked up for the return flight, so perhaps it is just as well he is not here, what with his legs and back, though at the moment she is trying not to think of him, is trying not to think, nursing a cup of tea, Carrie Underwood in the provided headphones, grateful the seat next to her is unoccupied, not worried at the moment about storm fronts or about missing her connection, but uncharacteristically content to be in a holding pattern, in a state of postponement, reprieve, not even exchanging war stories with the stewardess—she never had a problem with that word—let alone mentioning that the airlines are downsizing, reducing pensions, that she was still on food stamps her first year in the air, that these days you need to think about a second source of income, a fallback (*I see you've noticed the pin*) and it only costs two hundred dollars with no quotas, no territories, and a ninety-percent buy-back guarantee.

You have to ask ten to get one (preferably a stay-at-home mother with good credit, maybe some college, or waitress or cashier anyone with skin really a hundred unit members and you can breathe again *I'd like you to be my guest at Emerald Seminar* meet the Nationals mythic creatures wearing The Suit with half a million in wholesale orders with twenty-six percent commissions getting paid to eat lunch and talk on the phone with co-pays and second jobs for the insurance and ex-husbands and drink in hand pining for the good old days another saying there were none) but it can be done, she is living proof God wants you to drive the Escalade.

If He could just let her not think Pink for five minutes.

The song is called "Jesus, Take the Wheel."

But it is about so much more than selling superior beauty products, it is about encouraging, enriching, empowering, eliminating animal testing in all but one of twenty-five international markets (China, where it is mandatory), achieving zero landfill status at its U.S. facilities, donating twenty-two million dollars to cancer research, fifty million to ending domestic violence, a subject she has been on intimate terms with (but is it domestic if you're not at home? ha ha if you got out of the way in time maybe he missed on purpose at Seminar they said there are some people you're going to have to lose in order to find yourself but is he one he never I mean he was drinking so full of hope only to have it maybe she was wrong to say all those years of Sundays of course it would have taken you can't just walk out on someone when and just but this strange trip he's embarked upon she should tell someone they have a right to know, his family—at least those he's not estranged from. The children).

The Captain's voice in her ears, displacing the music: "So, ladies and gentlemen, if you'll take a look outside at about your three o'clock position . . ."

She looks, thinking about his kids. The tops of the clouds are calm and sunlit and she has to remind herself that underneath it is hurricane season. Some storms never subside. The middle child, then, strong and stoic as middle children often are. Getting a degree in architecture, rolled her eyes at the suggestion of throwing a Your Skin party, but she is athletic and athletic girls are generally less interested in makeup. But she will spread the word, she will tell her mother, the ex, whom she met once, who is so pale and dislikes Florida but will remain there until her youngest graduates, the son Nineteen's girlfriend has met more than once (though once was enough, you could tell right away not that she has a problem with it times have changed so many things so much better in so many but how does anyone else not know unless they do and just keep it to themselves or pretend it is in the nature of families and especially fathers always the last to know or to admit they do) and what about the eldest, the first-born, whose whereabouts are uncertain and who rarely returns calls, and then cryptically, who is now kneeling in a motel room in Jacksonville, under the underbelly of the storm front, a stranger's hand on her head and his penis in her mouth (these days actors in pornography must often resort to prostitution to make a living) in trade for another fragment of the crystalline substance for which she has developed a ferocious appetite, the vast bulk of which is supplied to her country by the same interests who smuggle other product up from South America by land, sea, and air through Panama, Costa Rica, Nicaragua, through Honduras, where a man now sits in some remote place, in a room, alone, off any map, tied to a chair with a bag over his head?

Some kind of cloth. Soft, almost opaque. Its stale, almost choking smell, and that of his own breath, a pocket of fetid air he seemed trapped in. And there was something else, the must of sweat but not that of a hard-fought game, an honest day's work; more pungent, more offensive, that of a stranger. Someone you never want to be.

He heard voices, muffled, as through a wall. Spanish, outside, and where was outside?

He could turn his head, and that was all. Sought to calm himself with a deep breath. A tightness at his chest and abdomen. He tried to move again and now learned the full extent of his restraint: hands tied or cuffed behind the backrest of a chair, his ankles bound to its legs, knees tied together, a rope or something wound so tightly around his ribs that every breath came up short, his heart laboured to beat. His feet bare on bare wood.

He was thirsty.

He didn't know how long he'd been there, felt sure he was alone. He could not know where the others might be. He supposed he was frightened but for the moment felt strangely detached from fear; it seemed beside the point. Was he afraid to be afraid? He was aware he was not gagged, had a voice and could use it, but could not make up his mind to do so. Whoever had put him here would probably not need to be summoned.

He drew breath anyway, sucking cloth, but the sound it made was an impotent cracked whisper. He tried to wet his tongue, his throat, but could not muster the spit to swallow. Tried again and managed a sort of word—*Hey*—but the only response was the muted buzzing of flies. Then he remembered the ones in the canister and in the imperfect darkness saw the dragon carved in the rock and the Canadian's ashen face and knew now what it felt if not why.

He didn't quite hear them come in.

A movement of air, a shift in the darkness behind the cloth. Felt steps confused with the thudding in his head and chest. Someone removed the bag, carefully, like lifting the cover off a birdcage.

Light and air. Three of them. He wondered if they'd somehow been there all along. The door behind them was closed so the only illumination—more bracing than blinding—came from the window to their side, a lattice of crossed slats like spokes. Wooden floor, vertical plank walls. A rougher version of the room in which they'd taken their meals in Las Marías, but Nineteen didn't think he was in Las Marías.

Camera equipment in a corner; if not a dream then a film.

They'd let him keep his wig.

Three of them, all wearing masks—balaclavas, like the police at the clinic, but these were not police. The one he took to be in charge stood before him, just out of arm's reach. Wore the proverbial rubber boots, camouflage trousers, a sweat-salted red t-shirt, slight paunch. A machete in a sheath on one side, holstered pistol on the other. Paramilitary—was that it? All you could see of his face were the bridge of his nose, the tops of his cheeks, and his close-set brown eyes, the black holes of his pupils too big like those of someone who could see in the dark. It was good to have the bag off, but the eyes . . . A man of about forty, Nineteen thought.

He said something Nineteen didn't understand.

The other two were also in jungle mode but without camouflage. They stood behind the figure in the red shirt, hips slightly cocked, and did not move. Dried mud on denim. Other, darker stains. They too wore machetes and pistols, and one held what looked like a shotgun, shouldered up, the other an assault rifle pointing down. The familiar curved magazine, black metal, wood stock. A spike bayonet affixed to the muzzle. Their dull eyes looked beyond him, and the one with the rifle seemed to be a woman.

The other was holding a puppy.

None of this, of course, was happening.

The one in front spoke again. It was English and his voice was calm but the accent heavy and Nineteen still didn't understand. It sounded like a question.

"Water," he answered in his parched whisper. He had the idea the one with the dog was smiling. Or had fangs and fucking lipstick for all he knew.

"I say do you know who Kaibiles are?"

Nineteen thought. "Where is everyone?" he said and the man with the question stepped forward.

The last time Nineteen had been slapped he was a boy who inadvertently shook the beer he'd been sent to fetch. He'd wanted to yell *Fuck!* but had cried instead. This time there were no tears.

The man in the red t-shirt straightened. "I say look at me."

Nineteen turned his burning cheek.

"Do you know who Kaibiles are?" the man said again and Nineteen thought it prudent to shake his head. The man took a step back. He rubbed his hand. "Kaibil was a Maya king the Spanish could not capture. A warrior—do you pay attention?" He waited. "Kaibiles are warrior too, Guatemala army, but are not just regular soldiers. They say a motto: 'If I advance, follow me. If I stop, urge me on. If I retreat, kill me.'"

The puppy squirmed. Nineteen wasn't sure of the breed— brown baggy skin, dark muzzle, bloodhound maybe—but he'd seen others like it, often on a cell phone screen, posted, watched, adored, lavished with comment by an audience of millions; dozing, dressed in sailor suits, at play with kittens and infant children, not yet anybody's weapon.

"When the U.S. want their Green Beret to be better killers, they send them to Kaibiles," the man said. "Same for Great

Britain, China, Peru, Mexico . . ." His tone became formal, instructive. It did not suit him. "Many soldier want to be Kaibile. To try to qualify take eight weeks. First three, no hay pedo: theory, map-reading, interrogation, weapons, counter-intelligence . . ." He shrugged, dismissive, turned and took the puppy in both hands, held it like an object. A cratered scar on his arm like a rough navel. "Second stage they go to the jungle. El Infierno. Five weeks. Hand-to-hand combat, ambush training, survival, demolition, escape, scuba, obstacle. They are allow no more than three hours' sleep a day, and they must earn it. Are allow thirty seconds to eat a meal, and have to earn. They learn to eat anything—snake, ants, root—they drink the little drops from leaves. They are shot with live bullet in the arm or leg, then must learn to perform field surgery on themself."

He threw the dog in Nineteen's lap. Nineteen grunted.

The other two were still as scarecrows.

"Last week in El Infierno is only in underwear, barefoot. Last two days they spend in the river, up to the neck. Sleep is no permiso." Nineteen felt life insisting upon itself in his lap, tapping its tiny paws, sniffing at the slow ache in his crotch, at his legs, now his chest, looking up at him with unconditional hunger or what might be called love. He remembered that here people were not sentimental about dogs.

". . . Out of sixty-four candidate, maybe five will wear the beretta. Maybe one. Maybe nadie . . ."

It made him think of training camp. End of summer. The lowrounders, the aging veterans, the undrafted free agents like him, guys with no life to crawl back to, sitting on the edges of furniture after the last exhibition, the last game some would ever play, listening for that phone call or the knock on the dorm room door, the assistant saying Coach wanted to see you—and bring your playbook.

There was movement. The one holding the assault rifle was scratching the back of her leg with the toe of her boot. She did so just discreetly enough to suggest a human being, and in this Nineteen took some small comfort.

When he looked up the man before him was pointing a gun at his face. He hadn't even seen him draw it.

"How long?" the man said.

Nineteen stared at him. He didn't stare at the gun. To do so might bring the bullet.

"How long?" he said.

"How long do I say in the *yungle*? Kaibiles."

The dog stretching, sniffing his neck. The pistol looked almost like a silver toy but he believed in it. He began to believe in all of it.

"You don't know?" The tone was still cool. "You don't listen?"

It hurt to answer; his throat and mouth felt filled with sand. Didn't know there'd be a pop quiz on this shit. Had to say it again. The gun went away and the lecture resumed.

"But they train Kaibiles too well. They make Kaibiles not to be robot. They make a monster." He was standing over Nineteen now, barely sweating. The black cloth spoke. "The little dog is loyal to master and family. This is not trained. Man is a different dog: he is loyal to himself. Kaibiles don't just fight for the government, they fight for themself. And fight for the highest bidder . . . Kaibiles don't just train American, Peruvian, Chino, they train who pay. Train Zeta, train Cachiros. They train us." Nineteen felt the dog's unconditional tongue on his face, his neck. "We are not Kaibile. We are not Maya. We are not Los Zetas and we are not Los Valles. We are what comes after." The man in the red shirt seemed to ponder. "Maybe someone will be come after us."

His eyes watched the dog. "He likes you, but this perrito is yungle dog. Breed from Brasil. When he lick your throat, is not affection. When slave escape from Brasileño plantation, this one hunt him, catch him, hold him by the neck till owner is come." He reached down. "You don't mind." He scooped it up with both hands, showed it to his subordinates as if for the first time—*muy bonito*, except for one foreleg slightly shorter than the other—then turned abruptly back to Nineteen and said, "I almost forgot."

Though he was sure of nothing else, Nineteen doubted anything had been forgotten. The timing was slightly off but it was still a performance, perhaps even this ineptitude rehearsed. He'd seen versions of it before in locker rooms, on practice fields, at podia, just as he'd seen villains onscreen fondling pets while ordering up yet another slow death. The bag and chair. Behind him a supporting cast in rough symmetry. It had no place here but here it was, the further outrage of melodrama, another sentimentality, another corruption of imagination. Bad actors spilling B-movie blood, even when the camera isn't running.

He remembered the Canadian's drained face.

"I forget to tell you something else about Kaibiles: at the beginning of their training, they each one is give a puppy just like him." He held it up to his face, let it sniff at the mask. "They must raise it, feed it, nurture, bond with. To the dog, Kaibile is both master and mother. He knows no other." He rubbed the animal's flank on his cheek. "Then, at the end of his training, for his last test, the soldier must kill the animal and eat it."

The man in the red t-shirt curled his hand around the dog's throat and held it there above Nineteen's head. The dog squeaked and Nineteen wondered if it thought they were still playing. If it is all play, for better or for worse.

"Don't . . ."

"Lo importante," the man said. "We can do whatever we want, and what nobody ever want to do. If you ask questions, you will not like the answer. You maybe don't believe this is happening, but this bad dream have rules and you will follow them. We are not Zeta, we are not Barrio, we are not gangbanger playing soldier. We are what we are. ¿Entiendes? Is understood?"

It was not, but Nineteen nodded urgently. The man brought the puppy back into his chest and held it to his heart. He gave a terse order and the figures behind him came to life.

The little dog sucked his finger.

They gave him water from a canteen before they covered his head again, put his boots on for him as if he were a child, then cut him loose and stood him up. Buried pain erupted in the ball and socket of his shoulder but he didn't mean to cry out. His hands were still bound behind him; they held him hooked at the elbows. The steps down were the hardest part, then they were outside. Mud underfoot, smell of woodsmoke. When a change in direction was required, they jerked and shouldered him into it. The pain almost quenched his fear.

"¡Anda! Puto." Only one of them spoke, though he couldn't tell which.

It was very warm but not as hot as it would become and he thought it might be midmorning. He thought he felt the sun. Smelled roasting meat. A big dog barked. A terse word and the barking stopped. He slowed and someone cuffed the back of his head. Enough. He stopped and kicked out in the direction he thought the blow had come from, kicked nothing and overbalanced so that they just let him fall on his face, the ground knocking the wind out of him. Someone stepped on his back and then he felt a metal point pushing into his neck. No one spoke. He concentrated on breathing. When a tacit agreement between spike and flesh was reached, they hauled him up and got on with it.

For a moment there were loose boards under his feet. They stopped.

Keys jangled, rasp of metal and wood. Then: "*Honey, I home!*" He heard laughter and was shoved into another darkness. A foul smell. A sudden cool edge of metal on his wrist and his hands were free. The bag yanked off so that his head whipped back. There was light coming from somewhere but he couldn't make anyone out at first. His hands floated to his eyes. Nobody spoke till the door was shut, the latch locked.

"You're all right?"

"He looks okay." They seemed to be trying to keep their voices low.

"How was the orientation?" The Canadian, a flat tone new to him. "They ask you the question?"

Nineteen blinked. He did not want to sit. He saw now they were in a kind of hut or shed, dirt floor, bright cracks between old wooden boards. But most of the light came through a small hole in the pitched rusty roof and he saw that they were all there, all on their feet except for the guide, who sat on her boots in a corner, looking up.

"You shouldn't be standing," the Canadian woman said, but she was talking to her husband who said his legs were fine. She turned to Nineteen again. He was glad to see her, to see all of them—and they him, he supposed—but there was no spirit of reunion, they looked beyond that, and he realized once again there were missing pieces. Perhaps he should tell them.

She said, "This is really happening, by the way."

"Are you all right?" the interpreter asked again.

Hurt, not injured, he thought, and nodded. Recirculating blood sang in his veins.

"¿Está bien?" the guide said, and the interpreter told her he was.

Nineteen found their dirty dishevelment painful to look at. "And you . . ."

"Define all right," the Canadian wife said. "Tell us they didn't kill the puppy."

"Fuck the puppy," her husband said.

She sounded suddenly on the verge of tears. "You know I don't blame you."

Nineteen told her they hadn't killed the puppy, felt absurd saying so, then again tried to speak to all of them. "He talked about . . . some kind of training . . ."

"Kaibiles," the interpreter said, and the guide nodded. "Más Kaibiles."

"Killbillies," the Canadian man said. "We all heard that crap."

"Not all of us," his wife said, and she glanced at the guide and interpreter.

The guide said nothing.

"So he didn't put you to the question." Something sounded wrong with the husband's mouth. "*El jefe?*"

"What question?" Nineteen said.

"The finger or the dog?" The Canadian man stepped closer to the light and Nineteen saw his face clearly. He was almost grateful he'd only been slapped.

"You need to sit down," his wife said and he said he didn't but she took him in her hands and he sat.

Nineteen felt lightheaded and shaky, squatted in spite of himself. Smelled wood rot and dirt, above all the stench that had struck him upon entering—too human, ammoniac, and he saw the bucket in the farthest corner. It was too dark to see the flies he heard.

He covered his mouth and nose. "We have to use that?"

A moment, then the Canadian husband said, "I think you were the first . . . You don't remember?"

Maybe he should tell them. "There's a lot I don't remember," Nineteen said, thinking maybe he should. He heard himself speaking, then could not quite believe he was.

Occasional laughter outside, neither near nor far. Someone was playing music, faint but raucous. Accordion. There were two square shapes on either side of the door, windows with crude wooden shutters that looked permanently closed. Nineteen heard himself stop.

"Blackout," the interpreter said, as if he'd learned a new word, and said to the guide, "*Oscurecimiento.*"

"Concussions?" the Canadian husband asked.

"Probably."

"From your playing days?"

Nineteen looked at him and the Canadian said, "They know. They told us." He brought his hand to his mouth but didn't touch it. "I'm sure you had your reasons."

His wife muttered.

"You remember how we come?" the interpreter said

"I told you what I know."

They filled in the gaps for him as well as they could. He was glad enough he'd missed it, though his body remembered in its way: hours on foot, a forced march upriver from the petroglyphs. Prodded by boot and bayonet. Crammed into an inland cave after sundown, enduring an endless, sleepless night in a dank ossuary emptied even of bones by looters.

"They had a boat," the Canadian wife said. It had an outboard motor but wasn't big enough to accommodate the entire party—ten in all—and one of them had taken it upstream. "They were so . . ." She searched for a word, couldn't find it. ". . . Bitch fucking kicked me!"

"I thought you couldn't use a motor up here."

"This part the river is more calmer, and deep enough," the interpreter said. They didn't know where the boat was. They'd arrived at the camp or compound or whatever it was after first light. No one had yet seen it—their heads were covered when they were brought to the shed. Then, except for the guide and interpreter, one by one, to the room where Nineteen had found himself.

"One at a time." Nineteen recalled sitting in the chair. "Why not all together?"

"Psychology," the interpreter said.

"But not all of us," the Canadian wife said again.

"*Path*ology," her husband said, carefully negotiating the syllables. Nineteen watched him speak. Half his upper lip distended so that it swallowed the lower, the jaw on that side puffed and dark with bruising or dried blood. A broken tooth.

"You put up a fight?" The thought was comforting.

"I answered a question."

"Motherfuckers," the wife said.

"They said they would kill the puppy. They asked if I would be willing to lose a finger to save it."

"Christ." Nineteen didn't look at the husband's hand. "What did you say?"

"What any red-blooded Canadian would. I offered them money."

"There wasn't going to be a right answer," the wife said.

"They told me they would take my money whenever they wanted. So the jefe asked me again." He sort of vomited laughter. "I told them go ahead kill the little son of a bitch."

They'd hit him in the face with a rifle butt.

"I'm sure it didn't matter what you said." She was near tears again. "His tooth."

"I'll take that over a finger. There are worse things you could . . ." He didn't finish.

His wife glanced in the corner. "I know what *she'd* have said," and they looked to where the guide sat with her knees drawn up in her arms and her eyes closed.

"I think," Nineteen said, "it's time to let that go." The guide's eyes were closed and her lips were moving. A dialogue with the unseen. Her cap was on her knee.

"The hell is she doing?" the Canadian woman said. She softened a little. "Praying?"

"She speaks to the spirits of the forest," the interpreter said.

"How about that."

"I wonder how they knew," Nineteen was wondering.

"They who?"

"*Them*. About me, I mean. I mean can you just Google someone out here?"

"Why not?" the interpreter said. "Or they might be in touch with someone who can. They have our passports."

Voices crowded his head; he couldn't always tell who said what.

"Maybe they Google all their hostages," the Canadian man said.

Nineteen blanched; he would not yet consign them to that category. Hostages were gaunt pale men in low-res video, whiskered, crouching in jungles or anonymous rooms, reading prepared statements, obligatory denunciations, imploring governments to cooperate. Professing love to loved ones with fanatic knives at their throats.

"Could they be terrorists?" he made himself ask.

The interpreter scoffed through his nose. "Don't look like idealist to me."

"God save us from idealists," the Canadian man said.

"Guerillas . . ." the wife thought aloud. "Vigilantes . . ."

". . . and messiahs and visionaries." Her husband had difficulty speaking again, but not because of his damaged mouth. "We do bad well enough on our own."

"A-fucking-men," she said. Then: "Are you okay?"

He didn't answer, and even in the dimness you could see his sudden pallor. The way he'd looked at the Place of Small Carved Rocks.

"He said they weren't Zetas, though," Nineteen remembered. "He said they were what comes after." What lay beyond the end of the alphabet.

"Doesn't mean they not narcos," the interpreter said. "Narco don't just drug-traffic. Narco does kidnap, extortion, sell baby on the black market. Traffic *people*." He thought. "Maybe they do this now."

"Do what exactly?" the Canadian wife said.

Nineteen looked at her. She'd taken off her shirt, tied it around her waist in that way. You could buy anything on the deep dark Web. Someone's daughter. He turned away. "Maybe it's just a wrong place wrong time situation," she said. "Maybe once they've done whatever they need to do . . . I mean, they don't usually . . ." She didn't look at the interpreter.

"Kill gringos?" You could imagine him sort of smiling in his allotted shadow. "Maybe you're in luck, then."

The husband giggled. He seemed unable to help himself.

"This doesn't seem like any accident to me," Nineteen said. "The satellite phone, the masks, that . . . lecture."

In the movies, masks meant they would keep you alive.

"They didn't ask me the question. Didn't even tie me up," the wife said. "They're so . . ."

"They not gentlemen."

"I won't let them hurt you!" the Canadian man said abruptly. He had to catch his breath. "That poler. The brother-in-law. He seemed pretty adept for a beginner."

"Adept at stealing phones."

Nineteen rose. He would stand till standing started to hurt again. "Phone or no phone, we were due back yesterday, right? They should have missed us by now." He shifted weight off his ankle till he would have to shift it back. "They'll be looking, right?"

"So where are they?"

The interpreter sounded uncertain. "Search in Moskitia takes time. Has to organize. Aeroplane can't fly in bad weather, and is hard to see through canopy. To search on foot is muy difficult."

"Does she have to do that?" The Canadian woman was looking at the interpreter. "Have the spirits got back to her yet? Would she like to share?"

The guide ceased her communion. The interpreter said something to her. Listened. "She remind to keep our voice down. We know at least one speak English."

He pointed to the shadow in the gap under the door.

"She have any idea where we are?" Nineteen said.

"Deep jungle. Río Cuyamel area, maybe."

"What about this place?"

A long exchange in the ancestral tongue. "This bodega maybe use for cooking once. Or workshop. Was maybe settlement, or cowboy *finca*. Cowboy be please to cooperate."

The Canadian husband was looking at the base of the wall, where the boards were nailed to runners perched on stones. "How long does she think it will take to find us?"

"El Presidente in Las Marías has to notify tour operator in Ceiba if we go missing or late. Tour operator has to notify authority."

Nineteen remembered now: only the expatriate had known.

The Canadian wife had stood. "What authority? The army? What do they do then?"

The interpreter waited. "We not sure exactly. This doesn't happen before."

She made a sound and sat. Something skittered in the dampness and she stood again.

"Maybe we can dig our way out," her husband said softly.

"So we don't even know if they're looking for us?" Nineteen said.

Another tribal dialogue. A people who sing, but they weren't singing.

"Doesn't matter."

"How doesn't it matter?"

"Doesn't matter what we can't control. Doesn't matter if cuñado steal the phone or not. If they plan for us or we just come at the wrong time. They give water, wear masks so they want to keep us alive—maybe some of us. If they want money, going to take some time. They know somebody gonna be come look for us. We has to be ready."

"Ready for what, exactly?" Nineteen said.

"This ground is soft," the Canadian husband said.

"Ready for what?"

"Opportunity."

"What opportunity?"

"We can dig our way out," the Canadian man said.

His wife looked at him. "And go where?" She raised her hand. "'Don't mind us, just stretchin our legs.'"

Nineteen said, "What about the boat?"

"¿Qué dijo?" the guide said, and the interpreter told her.

"Is it just me or . . . ?" The wife suddenly clawed the air by her face as if at a web. "God I hate that music."

The interpreter translated. "Would have to find out where is in the day. If it's here—if we still here. We could try for in the night."

"If *we're* still here?" the Canadian wife said. "We have to be able to see, too. We're going to stumble around in the jungle in the dark?"

"She has done this. Even without moon." Nineteen imagined the guide leading them with supernatural grace, hand by hand by hand, in the dark. Dodging trees, roots, rocks, obstacles beyond the threshold of perception. The feet must have eyes.

"If she can, so can they. And how far will we get with us slowing her down? If these guys are red berets or whatever the fuck?"

"If," Nineteen said.

"'When you're pushed,'" the husband said, quoting from the film they'd shown in the village, "'killing's as easy as breathing.'" His rendition was credibly deep and dumb and he made a sound that was meant to be laughter.

"Oh, God," the Canadian wife said. She listened. The music had stopped. "Why is it so quiet out there? What are they doing? We need water."

"She say we should conserve energy," the interpreter said.

"Maybe she should just keep praying," the wife said. She looked up. "Maybe God'll drop a litre of Dasani through the hole. Tell her where a boat is."

She coughed. Her husband said, "Well He just told me we don't need Him, we've got the next best thing right here with us."

"What do we have?" his wife said.

"It's just too fucking obvious," he said.

263

"What do we have?"

Nineteen had wondered when this would happen.

"Sorry, just can't resist a good metaphor. Or is it a bad one?" He sounded giddy and apologetic. "Fourth and long, right?—Americans get four chances, right?—so let's huddle up. Make the call . . . No disrespect."

"Oh, God," his wife said.

"It's okay," Nineteen said, though it wasn't. "Somebody has to."

"The ground is soft, let's draw it up in the dirt."

"Old boy, don't lose your shit."

"I can't help it. Exes and Os, right?"

"That's high school stuff, actually."

"I kid. No offense. Or should I say, no *off*ense." He giggled. Nineteen almost laughed. He thought about Lawrence Taylor sacking Theismann on Monday Night, folding his lower leg in half for all the world to see, wrecking his career. *You ain't in Canada no more motherfucker.* And then he thought about the Canadian's bloodless face and said, "What happened in the forest?"

The husband sobered a little but did not answer. Nineteen repeated it.

"What happened in the forest," the husband said carefully.

"Back at the rocks. What made you shit yourself?"

"He didn't shit himself," the wife said. "Don't go back there."

"What happened, then? *Eh?*"

"Leave him be!" She lowered her voice. ". . . snatch that fuckin thing off your head."

"You think you're the only one entitled to amnesia?" the Canadian man said, finally, softly. "What happened in the jungle," he said, "stays in the jungle."

"We're dying in here," his wife said. "Maybe we shouldn't talk."

Nineteen looked at the foul bucket, the age-stained wood, the gash of light in the corrugated ceiling and thought, What the hell . . . 3 Out Hum In Left, he thought. Looked at the bucket again, the light pouring through rust and said, "2 Fake Lag Right, Naked." He looked at the husband: "3 Hip Hum In, Fake Halfback Around Left Boot."

"That's what I'm talking about."

The Canadian wife put her face in her hands.

"Zing 2 Flip Wide, Fake Pitch 49 Naked Y Strike. On One. Ready?"

"I'm ready. What else you got?

The guide started praying again.

Later God or someone dropped a twenty-ounce clear plastic bottle through the hole in the roof. It was passed around in a tight clutching circle, mouth to mouth, a swallow each, till it was empty. They hadn't eaten in a day or so nor were they hungry yet. Still later, before dark, they heard a plane taking off somewhere nearby.

Thunder. He started over.

Monday you couldn't take it easy. Monday you had to keep the arm loose, the blood flowing, or pay the bill in full. Training room opened at six. Ice a hip pointer—a nail driving from your inside out. Relocate your ribs. But not just your body; took all day to get over a loss—not even your wife knew how to look at you. Had to recover from a win in another way. And the ones you never got over.

The puppy or the finger. He'd forgotten something.

Monday you couldn't let up, Tuesday you were supposed to. Play golf, hang out, see a movie. Get laid. Tuesday the only film he saw was Sunday, only pages turned were in the playbook, sitting in a tub full of ice. Wednesday the cafeteria opened at six. Wednesday you lifted weights. Wednesday you got the game plan, tied to a chair, bag on your head, breathing your own foul breath.

Monday was Monday. Weight room at seven. Coaches' meeting from seven to eight and you got the game plan at nine. He'd forgotten special teams meeting at eight. Cafeteria opened at six on Wednesday. By nine they had a game plan, film room at nine-forty-five. Watch the same play seventy times, the good ones only once. Dig out the bullet, work on first and second down at practice. Lunch at two. Thursday the cafeteria opened at six. Eat the little dog in the dining room. Thursday was third down, Friday was red zone. Meeting, media, meetings, meat. Saturday wasn't Friday. Tuesday dig out the bullet. Walk-through, hotel, chapel, curfew. Saturday ask you the question. Game-plan review.

There were roaches in the mud, the only things that didn't bite. More thunder.

He'd arrived at Sunday, Game Day, but it didn't matter; he was still awake, it wasn't working. Try the playbook then, Coach's script. He'd committed it to memory in less than a week—you had to know the rules before you could break them. Satellite Dorito Double Delta . . . Absurd, or was all language code? Something else then, not sports—this was not a game, unless everything was. Unoriginal, but what if. Thumbs up or down in the Coliseum, bored patrician faces. Maya elite. You didn't go to Disneyland, you went to the afterlife. What difference?

He thought of the jargon of his former profession. The language of mortality: Live ball. Sudden death. Kill the clock. The purpose of play was to end play.

Thunder, no lightning. He lay on his side in the damp and dark, head pressed to his arm, hearing it. He shivered, didn't know the jungle could get so cold. No one spoke, but could anyone sleep? Maybe the guide. They lay close, head to feet, away from the bucket and the hole in the roof. It was not a large space. You shifted from discomfort to discomfort. A tentative rattling of drops like coins, multiplying into the barrage of a downpour. God, that's loud. He felt drops on his face then but there was nowhere left to crawl to. The whole place leaked. Open your mouth and swallow some; they'd been watered but it was never enough. The air felt heavy now. At least the rain would clear it for a time of jungle night pandemonium, of things that flew and bit and quenched their own thirst, but it wouldn't clear your mind. Nor the stink. Nor the ground of things that lived there.

Roaches didn't bite, but scorpions, spiders, snakes . . . People worst of all, hands down.

He heard the spatter of water sluicing through the hole and felt it, rolled over to put his back to it. They'd decided against digging because she'd heard someone rounding the shed at intervals, as if checking for this. *In the dark I would know thy* The rain might make a hole, do their digging for them. When he was a kid they said you would come out in China. Later he'd found this to be geographically true.

The good news was that his symptoms were indistinguishable from the general misery of his condition. The bad news was everything else.

And what was in *their* heads? The interpreter, the Canadians— whom did they love, or know, now, that they did? Who spoke their names? They'd mentioned no children. The guide had six. Her exquisite mongrel humanity. He'd heard her squatting over the bucket, but she seemed incapable of indignity. Surely she missed them but why couldn't he think of his own? A palpable absence. Find a way back to them then, but the leak grew louder, dug a hole in his head. The playbook was empty. No Great Escape, just humming disorder, just staying alive. He'd need more to work with but all he had was a hard-on—not quite what he'd prayed for; no torment went unobtained here.

Something happened to time, or had happened. Had he slept? It wasn't raining. The dark was not as dark anymore, a stillness in charcoal grey. Cracks of first light. Wet wood and earth. He listened for the rooster's crow—maybe he was a farmer after all—but heard instead a sudden pounding at the door and in his chest.

The occupants stirred, drew themselves up and in the confining dimness rose fitfully like marionettes strung to some amateur hand. More pounding at the door and a voice in Spanish shouting orders. A warning.

"He say stand, face the wall," the interpreter said and they complied hurriedly like children in punishment while behind them was the clink of the hasp just before the door banged open.

A brightening at the edges of vision. "¡No te des la vuelta!" and the interpreter, as if still in their employ, said they weren't to turn around. Footsteps and movement at their exposed backs. A soft thud. Nineteen wondered how many and, for some reason, if the woman was among them. He heard Spanish again and the interpreter said, "Don't turn around until door is close," but even then Nineteen hesitated; things had been done the Canadian was still unable to talk about, and would they see now what he'd seen then?

Breakfast. A large scratched plastic bowl of rice sat in the middle of the dirt floor and, embedded in the rice like champagne in a bucket—someone's sense of humour?—a litre of water with the label torn off.

The bottle went around once and the guide picked up the bowl in both hands, sniffed warily at it and nodded. She said something in Miskitu. Perhaps Grace. Undercooked rice laced with bits of maybe meat too small to readily identify and they ate with their fingers, dropped nothing. After they'd washed it down, a swallow each, the guide dabbed up the last few white grains still clinging to the plastic, offered them around, kissing them from her fingers when these were declined, then wiping out the empty bowl with the hem of her shirt.

"She does their dishes," the Canadian woman murmured through her teeth.

"She does this for herself," the interpreter said, and the guide placed the scarred bowl by the door and they retired to the walls and sat in glum silence, filthy, rumpled, matted, legs folded under them or knees drawn up, marking time by a narrow shaft of sunlight that angled through the ragged hole. The sounds of day disclosed. The barking dog. The light grew stronger, the rotting wooden box grew warmer. They avoided eye contact like passengers in an elevator. A wasp had entered through the hole and was building its grey fluted nest in an upper corner, making a tinny nasal whining like a trapped soul. The interpreter excused himself to the fly-ridden corner where nobody looked unless they had to, where even the dim early light looked defiled, poisoned. Nineteen heard only fluid and almost thanked his god everyone thus far was apparently too scared to shit.

No one had spoken since their meal and the Canadian husband was making some prefatory sound but only coughed and wheezed and said, "Mildew." Then the door thumped anew with its promise of fresh hell. The routine preceding the meal was repeated, the room entered and a voice spoken which Nineteen recognized as the first he'd heard in this place, setting forth the curriculum of an apprenticeship with death.

It invited them in cordial English to turn around and sit.

His shirt was now grey as if signifying some occasion but once again the thick arms, the gut, the pitted cheeks the balaclava didn't quite conceal. Accompanying him another of his faceless soldiers, wearing a fatigue cap and a bandana of dark colour below his eyes, covering them with a rifle, its stock folded. Another figure lingered in the doorway, perhaps their sentry, all in black so as to be one with his weapon.

The jefe held the cloth bag in his hands and looked around in appraisal, less voluble than he'd been the previous day but his predilection for theatrics unabated. Saw the empty bowl and nodded approvingly. Turned to contemplate the bucket in the corner, gesturing there to his subordinates and shaking his head as at the squalor of his tenants. Finally, looking at each of them in turn as if in some process of selection; no one looked back. He settled on Nineteen then, and tossed the bag in his lap.

Nineteen looked at him without picking it up.

The guide leaned forward slightly: "Por favor, señor." The man in the grey shirt turned absently, not to the guide but toward the corner near which the interpreter sat, as if he had spoken. "¿Puedo hacer una pregunta?" the guide asked, and without hesitation or apparent anger the man in the grey shirt spun and delivered a roundhouse kick to the side of the interpreter's face, as if this were the request and he was merely complying. The interpreter threw up an arm, bounced off the adjoining wall and fell sideways in the dirt.

The Canadian woman screamed but the interpreter did not make a sound.

"The fuck!" Nineteen drew up as if to stand and the bandana came forward, holding the rifle like a pistol, the muzzle suddenly close enough to grab, its black hole, black eye, black mouth that sucked the breath from you.

The interpreter sat up immediately and resumed his position against the wall, one hand over his face but not touching it. One eye was shut. The guide leaned toward him but it was the interpreter who stayed her with his other hand.

"I sorry!" The jefe gestured, almost solicitous, slightly out of breath. "I don't like them you know, this guns. I prefer to use other . . ." He turned his head slightly to consult the interpreter but did not look at him. "¿Cómo se dice *herramienta*?" And when there was no answer, said louder, "Difícil de traducir con una mandíbula rota" in a tone of wit, but his men seemed not obligated to react.

"'Tool'!" he said suddenly, brightly. "Prefer to use other *tool*— hand, foot . . . what else I can find." The black cloth smiled. "I sorry. What was the question?" Now he affected distraction. "Would someone more like to have question? One answer for all," and once again Nineteen felt he'd seen this all somewhere before. "Maybe you, *pantera*?" the man in the grey shirt said and looked at the wife who was trying to breathe without sobbing, and she turned away, and he did not.

"Sí, los veo entre lágrimas: For why they do this things? What do they want, these bad guys? What is going to happen to us?"

"Leave her alone," her husband said, almost choking on it and because he had to. The jefe ignored him but the figure in the doorway took a step inside. "Maybe you wonder about the little dog. The *cachorro*. You wonder if is okay—maybe you care more about animal than people."

The wife shook her head without looking at him.

"You are so a liar. Let me put your mind to peace." His cheeks rose under his mask and he knelt to her. "You no have to worry no more about him. The yungle is not a good place for perrito. And one with the short leg. But I am glad to tell you he has found a new home." He glanced at the empty bowl by the door. "Can you guess where is it?"

The wasp harvested mud from the floor, making its industrious noise.

"Maybe I'm just fuck with you. Or maybe a snake eat him this morning. Or . . ." He looked at the husband. "Maybe soon I have other question for you."

He shrugged, as if a mystery even to himself, and stood, pointed to the cloth bag. Nineteen considered his pitted pitiless face, the sudden improbable blur of the kick. The wasp, its long, jointed legs hanging in the light.

The image is steady, as though the camera were mounted on a tripod. The shot is composed so we can't see what is above his head or below his knees. We see almost nothing of the room he is in. There is light coming from somewhere above—harsh, unshaded, the impression is of a bare bulb. His clothes are dirty. He looks as though he has not slept. His hair is dishevelled, and doesn't look like hair. He is not alone—two figures stand behind him, apparently men. Their faces are not in frame but we see automatic weapons held at high carry, tactical vests. The man tied to the chair looks neither frightened nor calm, but in a state of suspension. He does not know what to expect, nor do we.

We hear a kind of chugging sound, distant; the impression is of a small motor. Then a man's voice, deep, accented, speaking English. It asks the man in the chair what his name is, and the man in the chair tells us his name. It asks the man in the chair if he is a policeman, and the man in the chair says he is not. (He speaks deliberately, in a low monotone, without emotion, without movement. His name is somewhat more familiar than his face.)

And he does not work for any law enforcement agency or military or government organization in any capacity? the voice asks.

He does not.

What then, the voice asks, if he is not a policeman, does he do for a living? and the man tied to the chair says he is retired.

And from what has he retired? the voice wishes to know, and the man in the chair tells us he was a professional athlete.

A pause. Then he is asked if he knows where he is.

The former professional athlete says he is not sure.

Does he know who his hosts are?

He does not.

Does he know why he came to this country? the voice asks.

The former professional athlete begins to answer when there is a jump, as of deleted or unrecorded footage. "Yes," he is saying when the video resumes. "I came to the island to get treatment for a medical condition."

What sort of medical condition?

From injuries he received playing professional football, the former athlete says.

Was he able to receive this treatment?

He was not.

Why was he not able to receive this treatment?

The former professional football player says the clinic where he was to undergo treatment was shut down on the day of his appointment.

Why was it shut down?

The clinic was closed, the former football player says, until further notice by those he refers to as "the authorities." (He stumbles over the syllables of the last word.)

Which authority?

The police, the former football player says.

And for what reason? the voice asks.

The former professional football player says the clinic was allegedly involved in some form of illegal activity. (He pronounces the last two words very carefully.)

Doesn't the clinic perform a valuable service?

Yes.

Is it expensive?

The former football player says it offers services that aren't available in the States.

Does it cater only to wealthy tourists?

No, the former football player says. It is there for the whole community, he says somewhat stiffly. Rich and poor alike.

Does he think the authorities have the right to shut down a place that performs a valuable service?

He does not.

So, if the government left citizens alone to do as they wished with their own money, the clinic would still be helping people and he could have gotten his treatment?

(The former professional football player concurs, and begins to add nor would he be in the situation in which he now finds himself, when there is another gap in continuity. The former football player looks somewhat discomfited when replay resumes, but there is no visual or auditory evidence as to why.)

What exactly is the condition for which he sought treatment? Does it have a name?

The former football player has difficulty answering.

He has a condition he can't even pronounce?

The former player says the disease affects speech as well as memory—if he has it.

If he has it? Why would he seek treatment for a disease he doesn't know he has?

There's no way to test for it in a living person, the former football player says.

Is he sure he hasn't gone to the clinic for some other reason?

Yes, he is sure.

He is not a policeman?

He is not a policeman.

He went there for treatment?

Yes.

Treatment or cure?

The former football player says there is no cure.

Does the football Liga take responsibility for this condition he cannot pronounce that has no cure, that he is not even sure he has?

(A slight shift, another gap.)

So he is not famous?

The former player admits to having had some success, a degree of fame.

But he never won a world championship?

No.

Has he played in one?

He has not.

So if he were Tom Brady or John [sic] Montana, would his life be of more value to this situation?

The former player says it shouldn't make any difference.

And if he were Ronaldo?

It shouldn't make any difference, the former football player insists.

Does he know who Ronaldo is? the voice wonders.

The former football player believes he does.

Does he think American football is better than fútbol?

(The former player's response is interrupted by his interlocutor.)

So if he played soccer, his life shouldn't be of less value to the situation?

No.

And if he were Hondureño, Lenca, Garifuna, mestizo, his life shouldn't be of less value?

No, the former professional football player says. A life is a life.

A life is a life?

(Burst of white noise, the image momentarily distorted, incandescent.)

And how is he being treated? the voice asks.

They have food and shelter.

And how are the others?

The others are alive and well, the former football player says.

(Pause.) Is there anything else he cares to say? To the authorities? To those he loves?

The former professional football player hesitates, his eyes cast briefly down. Then he assures us that he is "fine," that all are "fine," that their release is imminent so long as the terms of those behind the chair, behind the camera, are satisfied, though he doesn't state explicitly what said terms are, nor the consequences if said unspecified terms are not met, nor does he speak directly to anyone, by name or relation, nor use the word he knows is expected of him but would betray what it declares, and keeps averting his eyes, like someone who has caught a glimpse of the other side of the mirror, of whomever is or will be watching through that sudden window, at sixty frames per second, over three million pixels per frame, stranger or familiar, and he cannot bear it.

When he got back to the hut they were made to face the walls again. After the door was locked and they could turn around, they saw the interpreter was gone. Apparently it was his turn. Then Nineteen's eyes adjusted and he saw the guide was missing as well.

"One of them took her to empty the slop pail," the Canadian woman said.

"So talk to us," the husband said. "What happened?"

"How long have they been gone?" Nineteen did not want to sit again.

"Maybe fifteen minutes."

"Please," the wife said. "Half an hour easy."

"So what do they want?" the Canadian man said.

"They could have taken one of us to empty it." His wife's voice brimmed but not with the guilt of privilege.

"You know what you sound like."

"Don't call me that again. I'm just considering."

"Would you feel better if he kicked *her* in the face?"

"Don't be an ass. I'm just . . . How long does it take to empty a fucking bucket?"

Nineteen noted the wasp was gone, or had finished its work. "How long has it been?"

"Maybe they took her to the river to clean it," the husband said. "Maybe she'll see something."

"What river?" his wife said, and sniffed distastefully at her armpit.

The husband gave her his back. "So what happened? What do they . . . or should I say how much?"

Nineteen was anxious about the guide, but told them while he still remembered. He would pray for her.

"So they're making a ransom tape," the husband said.

"You know you can be one too, old boy."

"Are they keeping us here?"

"They didn't say." The woman had held the camera, sleek and steady in her hand, weaponry. "It ain't exactly a Q&A. They'll give you the answers and then ask the questions."

"God, I do hope she's all right," the Canadian wife said. "You know that, don't you?"

"They have a figure in mind?"

"I don't even know if it's money. If it is I hope they're not barking up my tree." Nineteen crouched. "There ain't no tree."

A considered silence. Then the Canadian man said, "Fame and fortune are not hostage requirements."

"Oh God, that word," the wife said. "Doesn't it hurt your mouth to say that?" But he spoke with less difficulty than he had the day before.

"We wouldn't have even known if . . . I mean, the American— the operator—never said a thing."

Nineteen had forgotten they were relative foreigners. "I asked him not to. It just gets in the way anymore."

"You had your reasons. We understand."

"What do you understand?"

"Okay. I understand that we don't understand."

"'We,'" the wife said, in her tremor of a voice. "Gets in the way of what? Pretending to be a regular slob and all?"

Nineteen looked at her straight on. "So how'd you two meet?" One regular slob to another.

"Everyone asks us that. At a First Nations rally in Ottawa."

"Bullshit," the husband said. "Decaf soy latte with an extra shot and cream."

"'Frack Off! Respect Native Rights.'" She mimed holding a sign. "Would a cunt do something like that?"

"That was before me," her husband said. "People like hearing that, though."

"You should think about it," she said. "You have shit to make up for, old boy."

"I don't apologize for making a living." He scoffed. "I'm not gonna freeze my ass off on some pipeline but I write a cheque now and then. And I won't state the obvious."

"Then I won't either," his young wife said, and redirected to Nineteen. "So. Now that you know everything, how's it working out for you, mere mortality?"

"Feeling pretty fuckin mortal at the moment, thank you." He looked nowhere. Couldn't even remember her name. "I don't guess you're a fan."

"I find basketball to be more fluid. But still." Her voice had lost its shrill edge. "It must have been something." She asked him almost kindly then: "Was it worth it?"

"This really isn't the time or place," the husband, of all people, said.

But now, if ever a time or place was . . . "It was never a job. To the last tick. Not even the bad times," when he was last to leave the locker room, head in his hands for twenty minutes.

The Canadian wife was saying something but was drowned out by ninety thousand voices singing his name. Monday Night forever. Moments of pure celebration that transcended even this darkness eating his memory alive. And off the field, chatting with senators, flirting with actresses. Taking a shit in a billionaire's bathroom. Shaking hands with Jim Brown, greatest to ever wear the uniform, at a post-season party at one of the owner's homes, a ten-thousand-square-foot chateau-style mansion with fountains and a private beach. Drove there with the Mystery Girl in an SUV bought with guaranteed money, after his starting season. Agents were not invited. Inside were nine bedrooms and ten baths, stone fireplaces carved in France, turret rooms that were once servants' quarters. Stucco and dark wood. The owner's wife, a stage actress who'd ended her career in a horror film franchise, gave Nineteen and the Mystery Girl the tour, showed them the indoor pool, private theatre, the bowling alley and gym in the basement.

The owner, ascot and cane, still sounding like the Brooklyn of his birth: "Rooney only does this for his players when they win." He'd bought the team on a short sale—same as the house—thirty years earlier.

Now the servants went home at night.

He'd led them into the great room where all fifty-three men on the roster were waiting—even Number Fifteen, whose job he'd borrowed and kept. A wall of windows looking out on a darkness concealing the great frozen lake. Many of the guests were employed by the team (coaches, the front of the front office; the accountants, the ball boy, the groundskeepers would get their own party), but there was also the mayor, a state senator, a Gold Glove shortstop, another mayor, a producer in town scouting locations ("I love a sexy old infrastructure"). Everyone was happy to see him, his dark eyes and Homeric nose broken in the divisional round, everyone congratulating and consoling, wishing him luck next year. ("Game slowing down for you?" "I'd like to speed it up some." "What's it like in the huddle?" "A lot of farting, tell you the truth.") He was only uncomfortable at first. Fielded flattery, rubbed shoulders, discovered canapés, shook hands with future business and golf partners, with steel and finance, with Hollywood, construction, with delicate lovely women who solved the mystery of the Mystery Girl (she was a dietitian in Training and Medical), who might have asked other questions had he come alone.

He shook hands with Jim Brown.

"Don't break his knuckles now. You wouldn't believe what I paid for them," the owner said, drifting away.

"Sometimes you almost forget someone owns you," Jim Brown said, his grip mild, nothing to prove. His head was shaved.

"Well I wouldn't bite the hand," Nineteen said.

"So who's feeding who?"

We all answer to somebody, Nineteen might have said but was too starstruck. Jim Brown, who'd had an affair with Gloria Steinem and was once accused of throwing his wife off a balcony, said, "I don't know how you pull it off."

"I could say the same of you."

"To do so much with so little."

"Can I take that as a compliment?"

"Take it any way you want."

"It's seventy-five percent mental."

"Tell me about it. I played with Frank Ryan."

"I heard he was some kind of math teacher."

"We're not talking high school algebra now. The man lectured at Yale."

"Renaissance man."

"Now you're talking Robeson."

"You could say I have a head for numbers."

"Nobody's just meat," The Greatest To Ever Wear The Uniform said, looking at the Mystery Girl.

He left early, and Nineteen went looking for teammates—it would have been impolitic to ignore his pass protection, or the starting defense, a winner's bread and butter. They were not hard to find, bigger than everyone else, bulging blazers and twenty-inch necks, in their best dress and on their best behaviour—even the animals, the berserkers every winning team requires—but sometimes it was just in the way they moved, or held their space. A displacement in the gravitational field.

After dinner there was a club DJ. Number Twenty-Nine, a cornerback so feared only seven passes had been thrown his way all year, did a backflip, danced on his hands. Sixty-Six, who aspired to the stage, committing suicide as Othello. Special teams gunner Number Eighteen showing the owner's wife how he could bend his little finger at a right angle and back. Their starting quarterback killer surrounded by women he had no interest in. Things loosened up but not too much ("Look where you are man, this ain't the Crazy Horse"). Still later, before the guests had thinned to an inner circle, Nineteen, comfortably champagned, his right hand feeling permanently squeezed (thank God he was a lefty), returning from one of the bathrooms, slightly lost, the music now slightly remote so that between the beats he heard another melody; the chiming of a piano. It led him down a hall where languished Goya and Turner, bought only to be sold, through arched portals of luxury and privilege to the dark wood-panelled library where he saw a figure there on the bench, alone, brown hair shining in the light of one lamp, playing with one hand, her back to him.

He had not seen her before but knew who she was, that she was adopted, that she didn't like crowds, and he remembered thinking he should leave but couldn't, that this was true music and true mystery because it wasn't trying to be; something simple in a simple dress, no chords, the pedal down so that each note became an infinite moment, another future, and he'd wondered if it was something of her own improvisation, not to be repeated, that he might be its first and last audience. He felt chosen.

He couldn't remember the colour of the dress, but remembered her head starting to turn then, as if she were becoming gradually aware, at the same time lifting her left hand, bringing it down on the keyboard, but the sound he heard was not hammer and string, but hammer and cartridge, as if to signal the end of the reverie. Then they heard another gunshot, signalling the start of something else.

Shouting. Near, then not. Boots at a run pounded the ground beneath them and the Canadian woman stood. They moved away from the door and closer to each other. More running and shouting. The commotion veered close to the shed again and the Canadians held each other. Figures strobed past the chinks and cracks in the walls. Nineteen held his breath but the better to hear; he tried to relearn the lessons of composure. Terror and hope.

"*¡Darse prisa! ¡Mueve tu trasero! !No puede estar lejos!*"

They did not speak till there was silence. A strange protracted vacuum, as if the site had been suddenly deserted. Nineteen tried to see between the boards. He put his ear to the door but couldn't tell if anyone still guarded it.

"The shots." The Canadian wife whispered. "They sounded . . . You think someone?"

It was impossible to say how much time passed before they heard the rattle of the lock. They stepped back. The door. Light— too much light. Then it was shut again before they could see who it had been.

It was impossible to say how much time passed before they heard the dogs.

The image is very still, as though the camera were mounted on a tripod. The shot is composed so we can't see what is above his head or below his feet. He is apparently outside. His hair is dishevelled, his face dirty, his jaw red and swollen as with recent injury. He looks like he has not slept. We can't see what is in the background because of the figures standing behind him. Their faces are out of frame but you see Kevlar and denim, black t-shirts, holstered pistols. The customary rifles are missing, as if the men standing behind him will require the use of their hands.

The man tied to the chair is naked.

(We are not sure why we came here. We are fairly certain we are doing nothing illegal. We have taken precautions, unplugged our external devices, blinded the little eye that watches us watch. Downloaded and installed, configured and clicked. We have connected to the server, run the browser and peeled the layers of encryption, read the disclaimer and clicked ourselves here, where he is, tied to a chair, looking into the camera, into us, as if in accusation, though we are certain we are doing nothing wrong.)

The image is steady. There is a sort of chugging sound, fairly loud; the impression is of a small motor. It is not too loud, though, to keep us from hearing a man's voice, deep, speaking Spanish. We do not speak Spanish (we can't help wondering if someone might have thought to furnish subtitles) but know from the accompanying description what the voice is saying, that he is asking the man in the chair his name and occupation.

"Soy traductor y a veces guía en el Moskitia," the man in the chair says. (His wrists are zip-tied to the armrests.) He speaks carefully, perhaps painfully, out of one side of his mouth, sounds calmer than you might expect but, still, the eyes.

So he is not a policeman?

"No soy policía."

Does he know who he is talking to?

"Lo sé ahora, sí."

Does he know where he is?

(Slight pause.) "No."

Does he live in La Moskitia?

"No."

But he is from La Moskitia?

"Soy de Brus, pero ahora vivo en Ceiba."

And he does not work for any law enforcement agency or military or government organization in any capacity?

"No."

And he is not a paid informer?

"Yo no."

Because if the police are paying him, it is now he who must pay.

( ).

Does he know he is a trespasser?

(Pause.) "Lo sé ahora."

But he calls himself a guide?

"Soy más un intérprete."

So he was not the guide for these other trespassers now in their custody? (The Canadians, the American, mentioned in the accompanying description.)

"No."

Where is the guide, then?

"No sé."

But the guide is never supposed to leave those she is guiding, is that true?

"Sí."

Why is she hiding, then?

"No lo sé, estuve aquí cuando—"

Does he know where she might be hiding?

"No."

Does he know where she might try to go?

"No."

Does he know how much pain even the smallest part of the human body can feel?

(We are not sure why we have come here, to this place that is not a place, but are fairly certain it is only to confirm what we already suspect, that this is only myth, urban legend, another horror film, another hoax to be debunked. Nor is this something we would pay to watch; we are more than certain we are not that kind of person, whatever kind of person we are.)

A man enters the foreground from beyond the frame, presumably the interrogator. We cannot see his face. He wears a grey t-shirt and is holding a small pair of pliers. He looms over the man in the chair and delicately places the tip of his fourth finger in the jaws of the pliers.

Does he know where the guide is hiding?

"No."

The man in the grey shirt moves the pliers to a nipple, dark and lightly haired.

Does he know?

(A quickening of breath.) "Soy traductor y a veces guía en el Moskitia . . ."

At sixty frames per second, over three million pixels per frame, the man in the grey shirt removes the pliers and steps momentarily offscreen. He returns holding a pair of clamps with plastic handles and serrated copper teeth. One is red and one is black, and each is connected by a long, heavy-gauge cord to something we cannot see. The man in grey touches one clamp to the other and there is a pop and a snap and a burst of sparks.

The man in the chair winces. "Soy de Brus," *he says again and the man in the grey shirt attaches the red clamp where the pliers were and the man in the chair gasps at the bite of it. Then the other. The man in the grey shirt leans to the right, partly out of the frame. The man in the chair speaks faster.*

"Soy de Brus, pero ahora vivo en—"

He abruptly stiffens and convulses but his injured jaw is tightly set and the sound it makes him make is a tremulous hum that at first seems to come from somewhere else.

Does he know?

He can only shake his head.

Again.

"Mi padre es Pech, mi madre es Miskito," the man in the chair says when he can speak again, eyes shut tight. Tears. "Madre de Dios."

Where is she?

It is not too late, we tell ourselves. We can still touch the screen. It is fake, we tell ourselves. Whatever is going to happen, has happened. We tell ourselves we owe it to ourselves, to him, to watch, to witness, to look at his genitals. To see. We can still touch the screen; it is too late for him if not for us.

The man in the chair speaks carefully and with great difficulty, as though it were important he be understood: "Soy traductor . . . pero me gano la vida . . . haciendo trabajos esporádicos en La Ceiba."

They move one to his tongue, then his ears, his penis. They are called crocodile clips, we remember in spite of ourselves. A puddle appears under him, spilling over the seat and spattering. (We heard it before we saw it.)

Does he know?

We remember in spite of ourselves. One is red, one is black. The image is steady. We are not that kind of person. The image is still. Whatever has happened is. We remember we are not. We are tied to our chair. It is red and black. Do we know?

"This is on her," the man in the grey t-shirt said, walking ahead. He seemed to be starting in the middle. "He should have know better, but a man will be a man," he said, and they realized he wasn't talking about the interpreter. "This is on her."

It hadn't rained for a while but the ground was still wet. It looked to be late in the afternoon; their shadows led them. Their boots sucked in and out of the muck and their hands were once again bound behind with zip cuffs—there seemed an unlimited supply—but their heads weren't covered and they did not know what this meant.

What was on her?

The sounds they'd heard in the shed could have come from man or woman.

"I know this man—he would not have initiate. She offer herself to him, because this is what a woman does in this position, when she have nothing else to give, doesn't even know if she gets in return." He still wore his mask, as did the three men who walked behind them, dark-eyed, thick-bodied, their boots and pants painted in mud as if they'd been knee-deep in it. Short-barrelled rifles at low carry. One bare-skinned under a Kevlar vest with pale keloids patterned on his arms like the scars where tattoos had been. "But sometime when you drop your pants, you drop your guard." Jungle wisdom.

Nineteen wondered what the Kaibiles would say. Apparently their rigorous training did not adequately prepare you for someone who offered to suck your dick, and bit down, or tossed a bucket of shit and piss in your face and took her chances in the river. Kaibiles my ass. God bless her. It was almost good to be outside again.

They were on a winding path. On one side a hill crudely embanked with stones, on the other a small field of withered cornstalks behind a barbed-wire fence. The jungle was close. They passed a henhouse of bamboo and chicken wire, vacant but for congealed white feathers and empty cardboard egg trays. A pen of widely spaced boards with feed boxes nailed outside, something big inside that growled and moved with them gap to gap. A thin haze of smoke. Duckboard wobbling in mud. Under a tarp draped over a wooden frame stood a cane press with rollers and a hand-crank like an old laundry mangle and no one wondered aloud for what it might be repurposed. Low wooden fence enclosing a skeletal carcass that might have been a pig, a corridor where they pushed through banana leaves four feet long, the only surviving crop. But for all its overgrowth the place did not look long abandoned, nor did the man in the grey shirt say what had become of the original tenants; he was their guide now.

The path opened onto a rolling meadow where there was a long, open shelter with a palm roof on pitched rafters. Hammocks hung from the rafters and posts and some were occupied and the tourists did not look at the occupants. Beyond this a single-storey house with a low peaked roof and gutters and a simple porch, small but sturdy, and Nineteen thought this must be the place of the chair and camera, where it had all begun for him. They did not stop. On the side of the house a weathered tarp was stretched taut from the eaves and staked to the ground and beneath it a cookstove and a pair of canvas stools and a small generator. A woman in camouflage pants was there, and he was certain he'd seen her before. She wasn't tending the stove, but was practicing knots with a length of paracord—over and under, over and through—her fingers so deft they couldn't help but look till she looked back. *Pantera.*

A soccer ball in the grass.

Behind the house was a lean, canted wooden shack that must have once been a privy, and beyond it, in place of pasture or cultivated field, a long stretch of grassless earth like a dirt road they realized was an airstrip.

They did not see a plane, but they had not come for that. They had not come for the outhouse; the man in the grey shirt was looking behind them.

"He should have know better and he will have to pay, but so will everyone," the jefe was saying. The men who'd accompanied them were beside them now and he was saying This was on her as he pointed to the back of the house and they turned.

They'd walked right by it. The sun was gone but there was just enough light, there was too much. They'd walked right by. The sun was gone.

"Look."

How neatly arranged, sorted and aligned like a display in a meat case. Symmetry and proportion. There was surprisingly little blood. Hands and feet resting upon the chest. The arms and legs in four pieces each, on either end of the trunk. Cross-section of bone like white eyes. Centred in front was the head, leaning back on the side of the torso like a lover at a picnic, eyes open and cast down, lips slightly apart. One ear was missing. Then they saw it had been shoved in his mouth, the better to hear his own screams.

"Luz," the jefe said, and one of his men drew from a holster an LED torch like yet another weapon and they saw it in the colourless glow, nested in the grass before the head as if ranked in the order of anatomy, looking strangely alive, snail-like, a separate organism escaped and in search of another host to which it would attach.

"See."

A short-stemmed blue flower sprung from the hole in his forehead.

"Traduce eso." More footsteps now, coming from around the corner.

Full night came quickly now and, when they could keep their feet, Nineteen and the Canadian husband were flanked as if to be led away, but the Canadian wife told, in not so many words, to stay. Rooted, transfixed by that merciless white light, she looked incapable of anything else, let alone resistance, but her husband was in a marginally better state. He turned with effort.

"No. You're not," he managed in a raw whisper, lurched toward her with his bound hands, was tripped and fell on his face, rifle-butted on top of his head when he rolled onto his side and tried to rise, drew up his knees to try again and was clubbed again and didn't get back up.

They dragged him to the shed while the other gringo, who had not tried to intervene, was detained and made to carry the remains into the surrounding forest, piece by piece, his captors scrupulous in the disposal of their refuse.

The divisional playoff went into overtime. The sun buried in the field of ice and stillness the lake had become, the stadium lights already on. The captains met at midfield and did not shake hands. San Diego called it and won. The clock set for fifteen minutes but whoever scores first scores last. Sudden death in January. The players on the sidelines in their long hooded cloaks, helmets atop heads, heaters roaring like jet engines with live flame. Corrugated air. Fleece turtlenecks. A constant urge to pee. The sky was fading blue and the field had been more or less cleared but it was on the ground everywhere else in town, dirty city snow.

The numbers were dismal. Nothing over thirteen yards, less than five a throw. Thirty below with the wind chill. The wind had also taken away his deep ball and the team that lived in California sunshine went man-to-man, got away with murder. His wideout, Eighty-Eight, appealing to the line judge: "What about hands-on after five, your honour?"

"We call it if it's big."

It was never big enough but the temperature kept dropping and receivers dropping balls like unwanted gifts. And Number Ten, his backup, kicked in the hand holding for the extra point that tied it, wouldn't be returning; they'd only dressed two quarterbacks.

An old man wandered the sideline. The special teams coach had brought his grandfather, a World War I veteran who'd played for the Dayton Triangles. Under his parka he wore a team jersey with the number that bespoke his age: Ninety-Nine.

A series of drives to nowhere. Stalemate of punts. Never too cold to talk shit.

"Play clean and I'll let you wash my jock."

"I don't kiss ass, I suck pussy."

"I guess you are what you eat."

"Are we alive?" Nineteen was calmly outraged in the huddle. No speeches, just formation, motion, play, count, and they clapped and broke and followed him upfield, staying on the ground, off-tackle, crawling in icy bitter increments to the Chargers' thirty-eight. Ten more yards they could think about a field goal. Nineteen did not want to think about a field goal. The crowd warmed him.

At the line. Big on big. Knuckles in icy turf, vapouring breaths like a team of horses. Nineteen pointed at the Mike backer creeping up and the Mike pointed back. The centre said "Diesel" and passed it down the line but Nineteen had the last word: "White, *hut!*"

Animal grunts in the pit, thud of bodies enforcing Newton's Second Law. Within two steps of his drop, he knew the lightning bolts were coming. Heard Coach on the sideline: "Tight window!" and felt the outside linebacker's feet pounding through the 2 hole, stood in and delivered the ball into double coverage, aiming to thread the needle once again. Number Fifty-Five, face concealed in a dark visor like the Black Knight, t-boned him from the right (*as he throws!*), torquing him mouth-down into ice-hard sod so that he cracked his front teeth on his own face-guard. Myriad motions like tiny clear worms on his eyeballs. He couldn't see what became of the ball but eighty thousand voices told him; you knew an interception when you heard it. His first in five games.

That low moan of collective despair, like wind in a narrow space.

"You too pretty for this game." The linebacker danced. "You're bleeding." He offered a hand. Nineteen knocked it away. Pulled off his helmet and steam came off his head.

Sitting on the electric bench near midfield, the trainer putting his lip back together with superglue. No one else would look at him except the assistant's grandfather, who had drifted near: "We had a Chinese running back named Aichu. Called him Sneeze." But the booth was already filling his ears in the headset.

"Since when are you not perfect? You should've ate the sack."

"Fifty-Five in the Pro Bowl? He's soakin up a double-team and still makes the play."

"You want his fuckin autograph? He's wearing a white jersey."

"Just shake that shit off, get rid of it," the grandfather said, his nurse tugging him gently away. "Ninety-nine years I ain't seen one easy yet."

Nineteen looked at the playbook while the Chargers drove the ball he'd given them. Fuck off, old man.

Coach stalking his defense from the sideline, throwing his headset, tripping over the cord. "I need some thump! I need some thump here!"

His parents sat next to the mayor at the fifty-yard line, mother fingering her rosary, but He was apparently a Chargers fan and let them drive all the way to the six with short passes in the flat. A twenty-three-yard kick. Easy money, sudden death. They lined up. Nineteen prayed again, another perfunctory negotiation. The crowd rumbled volcanically. The snap. The hold. His father drinking Canadian whisky disguised as coffee.

Wide to the right! The local radio voice sang it like an aria. The enveloping roar of white noise from the stands, a wave you could ride. Sudden life.

"God, that almost happened," his mother said.

"Beside the game, is everything okay?" the mayor asked, and she looked at him like what else was there.

Nineteen pulled down his helmet.

"Let's put something together," he said in the huddle with his broken mouth. "Dig deep," and don't forget to love playing this game, he was going to say, but instead said, "Fuck California."

On second down Number Seventy-Eight spat in the DT's face mask, and the official who wore the white cap and was an insurance underwriter the rest of the week spread his arms, palms down. Unsportsmanlike, fifteen yards. Their tenth penalty. "He fuckin punched me in the throat," Seventy-Eight explained in the huddle and Nineteen said, "16 Zeus Colour Check With Me, on Two," and at the line saw the Chargers had left only three men in the box so he yelled "Zorro!" and backpedalled into shotgun with Number Thirty on his right, and when the ball came he gave it to Thirty who started up the middle and here came the secondary, biting hard, and Thirty turned and pitched the ball back to Nineteen with Eighty-Four streaking down the left numbers and it might have gone all the way if Fifty-Five hadn't been up in his helmet like he had all day, but as it was they got all of it back and ten more, past midfield, first down, with someone's blood on the ball.

A naked man ran out on the field.

The drive stalled at the San Diego forty. (His mother: "Gosh. They're measuring again?") Fourth and one, thirty-seven below with the wind chill.

"Fuck it. Right here, right now," he said, and he waved the punting unit back to the sideline. Coach agreed and so did everyone else—in the seats, in twenty million living rooms, drivers running red lights with the radio on, coaches' stoic wives drinking mai tais in a private box. Layoffs, dead batteries, homeless sleeping on sidewalk steam grates, mothers trading children for a piece of white crystal, but we all agree. All we ask of the universe is one yard.

"Mary Left, Mary Left," he chanted over the centre's back.

"Where'd she go?" the defense said.

"Set   set   set . . ."

"Not today," the defense said, but jumped anyway because they were trying too hard not to and Nineteen got them five when they needed one without having to run a play. That sound they all lived for. Coach yelled "Feed off it" and the first quarter of overtime expired. The clock didn't matter. They would play one more and if no one scored there would be another coin toss and another kickoff, and in this manner the game would continue, quarter after quarter, day after day, as if the point of play were not to win but to keep on playing, a forever game, neither forfeit nor surrender an option. Amen.

The kicker kicked into a net, warming his leg.

Nineteen asked for a new ball. The kid wearing a red X tossed one to the umpire. After four hours the defense were riding on rims, tapping their helmets for substitution, and on second and four at the Chargers' twenty-two Coach tried to take advantage of this, called two straight running plays that netted a total of one yard. A forty-yard field goal for the win then, well within Number Two's range, and the wind at his back, but he'd already missed one from thirty-six, and an extra point, which was why they were in this mess; there were no chip shots in the Arctic blast, no sure things.

With Ten out Nineteen would have to hold, as he had when he was third string and no one knew his name, fetching coffee for everyone in the quarterback room.

Right now, right here. Nine men on the line, second and third team receivers—no-names—at the ends for containment. Nineteen on one knee seven yards back, Two behind him toward the left hash. (*For the win*) A silent count—Nineteen would signal with his arms, the long snapper would see it through his legs— and the Chargers called time to ice them. Good cruel football. Through the window of the uprights you could see the bleachers, cheapest seats in the house, now priceless, populated with the hardcore, drunks and rowdies, blankets and wool, kids wearing only warpaint like Halloween in January.

They lined up again. Set. That stillness just before.

He bobbles the snap! Nineteen on his feet!

He picked it up off the frozen ground, rose yelling "Fire!" so that everyone knew it was the disaster they'd drilled for, the kicker no longer to kick, shifting up front to block or get open, promptly levelled, Nineteen rolling left, looking left, in what was for him a sprint, pads cups and epaulets flapping like wings some flightless bird bringing the defense with him leaving Eighty-Five a nameless backup to a backup wouldn't even make the roster next year angling for the corner just alone enough waving hello hello me me at Nineteen in the air throwing back across his body putting whatever he could on it shoulders hips breath belief and he knew as soon as the ball rolled off his last fingertip, spinning ten times per second. Almost a perfect spiral.

Maybe maybe maybe

"That is not a catch! That is not a catch! Is that a . . . It's a *hey!*"

A hundred and thirty decibels of forgiveness. Coach blowing kisses. You didn't even have to kick the point after.

Later, interviewed by NBC in the shouting unheated locker room. Bare-shouldered in a towel, not muscular but toned, crediting only the team through his swollen mouth, his broken heroic nose.

But how did you stay so cool? For a second it looked like

Best mistake I ever made

NBC laughed in admiration, then wished them luck next week with Kansas City, again, at home, where they would knock on the door to the Superdome, the Last Sunday, and lose again by the same exact score, Hollywood and Wall Street watching from the sideline, from luxury suites with wet bars and fireplaces and glass walls.

The guide came to him in the shed. She had not abandoned them after all. It was full night but he could see her plain as day. Bare feet, bare legs, midriff, panties, the upper half of her shirt in tatters. As she came closer he saw the cloth had been deliberately cut, in even strips like some ceremonial dress, that her face bore strange markings, face paint or tattoos. She stood or knelt over him and leaned down; she was going to tell him something—how to get out of here, where the boat was hidden—and she opened her mouth and he saw that her teeth had been sharpened into the fine points of her ancestors.

She licked his ear, then bit it off.

He thought he might scream but the bite was strangely painless. Her lips on his cheek, her teeth; she swallowed another piece
of him without chewing. Again he felt nothing, only a hardness
gathering at his centre. His lips then, his neck, chest, a nipple.
He knew he should stop her before there was nothing left of him
but his hands and feet were bound, the rapture of being eaten
alive overpowering. She might digest him, shit him, regurgitate
and rebirth him, clothe him in ritual flesh so they could do it all
over again, her manner not savage but somehow loving.

His belly, then below . . .

When he woke he became aware of someone lying or sitting
nearby, but it was not the guide. Then he remembered. There was
nothing he could have done, he reminded himself.

They'd said little in her absence. The husband half-conscious
much of that time, possibly concussed, Nineteen speaking only
to keep him awake. Listening. They hadn't heard much beyond
the occasional whine of a dog, remote voices, music, were at the
mercy of the mind's eye and ear. The same few thoughts rattling like dice around the skull. (But if it were just another video,
another "interview," why was it taking so long?) The music was
the worst. Its abrupt cessation. The waiting was different then
but it was still dark when they heard the fist at the door, the
harsh command, and when they turned from the wall she was
standing just inside the hut, in a glare of lanterns behind which
her escort were silent and almost invisible.

She'd stood still for a moment, not speaking. The lights
remained in the doorway as if to show she wasn't hurt in any way
you could see. Her shirt buttoned, though misaligned, one sleeve
torn, or had it been? Mosquito bites but what else had bitten her?

She wasn't looking at anyone. She'd turned this way and that, like someone about to cross a street but not crossing it. Her husband had approached cautiously, as if afraid to touch her. Then he did. Took her shoulders, then all of her, in all of him, but couldn't coax her from the place she was hiding. She endured it stiffly but would not requite, wouldn't hear what he implored softly in her ear, couldn't find anything to look at.

A familiar voice spoke from the light.

They were fed again later in the morning, given a litre of water. Just white rice and beans this time—as far as they could tell—for which Nineteen was grateful but wary, trying not to think of the interpreter, trying not for God's sake to taste before he swallowed. He felt guilty at the strength of his appetite, nor did the Canadian reject his portion. The water tasted of iodine.

They reeked of the mould that colonized their damp clothes in white patches, and of their own bodies.

The wife displayed no appetite. Her husband coaxed her into taking a mouthful, eating from his hand like some feral creature lulled into tentative trust. She barely chewed, breathed around the food sitting in her half-open mouth, bits of rice clinging to her chin. She showed somewhat more interest in the water, and still hadn't spoken since she'd returned. Her husband, still nursing his battered skull, spoke only to her, in whispers. Stayed as close as he could without touching—she'd shrugged off his arm like a child who will not be appeased by affection. He cried. She didn't. Their boots had been taken and Nineteen made his way gingerly to the plastic bucket to relieve himself. The husband asked his wife if she needed help, then saw she had voided in the corner where she sat.

No one came for the bowl.

. . .

It rained. Poured through the hole above in a ragged spout, forming mud puddles and creeping rivulets so that the hostages—there was no better word—retreated to shrinking patches of relative dryness. For the Canadian man's wife, though, one spot would have been as good as another had her husband not prodded her, gently at first.

At some point she started to make a sound, a low unmodulated note made without moving her face, mouth slightly open, eyes dry, some animal precursor to grief. She would do it from time to time, though you couldn't be sure when she'd stopped or was drowned out by the rain.

"Since she loves the perro so much," the light in the doorway had said, "we see how much he love her."

The wasp did not return. He thought it might be the rain that kept her from finishing her nest—she stayed away at night—but had he looked closer, and had there been more light, he would have seen that the nest was completed, the fluted cells sealed off, and had the guide been there she might have told them the wasp was a mud dauber, that she was a solitary creature who lived off nectar and sang while she worked and was peaceful unless provoked, that she had filled the nest with the bodies of paralyzed spiders her brood would feed upon once they'd hatched, remaining cocooned in the nest for a year or so before emerging as fully formed adults. God's perfect little children.

Nineteen lived on a farm and didn't need the guide to tell him what a mud dauber was, but they needed her in other ways, and he prayed for her and wondered what had become of her, as he wondered over other things, such as why they hadn't heard the sound of a search plane, why the masked men seemed in no particular hurry and why they wore masks at all, and when he wondered aloud he elicited no response from the Canadian, who, except for the furtive whispering to his wife, shared her silence, a silence Nineteen understood as a punishment he didn't deserve. He did not think of himself as a coward.

"Fútbol is not the only sport of Honduras," the jefe said. It had stopped raining late in the day and you could still hear something dripping slowly somewhere. He wore his balaclava (some smooth shiny fabric, breathable, perhaps Lycra) and once again, his red shirt, team colour; was again accompanied by the pair Nineteen thought he recognized from the occasion of the chair, the bag, the Kaibiles, though he couldn't remember exactly how long it had been nor which one had held the puppy.

The guns, the masks, the postured menace, the replay sameness of it; they could peel your face off with a pocketknife and stitch it to a soccer ball, and they were also a profound fucking bore.

She had a scar at the corner of one eye.

"Tennis, *básquetbol*, Olympic, we like even American football . . ." He looked at Nineteen. "We have a national baseball team, in the Confederación. I play soccer in school but I love baseball, dream to play in America in the major liga." He shrugged. "Dreams. Here a young person have two choices if he want to make a living: the police or the army. I join the army. Then I find other choice."

"This is a choice?"

The Canadian man's voice was only slightly tremulous, his pink white-whiskered face impassive. His arms were looped protectively around his wife and the question provoked the one with the scar to square her feet and raise her weapon but the man in the red shirt checked her with a hand. "Quién puede culparlo," he said. "In his position I be the same. I would not respect him as a man otherwise."

"I don't want your respect."

"I know. I know what you want. Entiendo. I understand. But do you?"

The dripping. The Canadian looking as if to say *Try me.*

"So." The man in the red shirt picked up the empty bowl, looking down into it as he spoke. "So say I come from el barrio, San Pedro. Maybe my father a drunk, my mother prostituta. This a better story for you?" For once it did not sound scripted, even if it was made up. "Say I come from Mexico City, come from the street, or come from campesinos. Say I come from decent peoples. Parents work hard, nobody touch me wrong . . . I like to play shortstop, then join el militar. Then I eat someone's flesh in tamale make from banana leaves. What is better for you to understand?" He shrugged, looked for something in the bowl. "Some say taste sweet, like veal. Some say strong pork, more bitter. But only way to really know, like anything else, you have to eat yourself. Then you understand." He looked up. "Then maybe is too late . . ." He held the bowl, sighed. "Maybe I talk too much. But understand now: tomorrow, if the weather hold, the aeroplane be come. You going to put on it. Don't ask where you going, or why; you will know everything when come the time."

He spoke to his lieutenants. The Canadian woman removed herself from her husband's embrace. He seemed to need it more than she.

They took the bowl and still had not returned their boots.

On the third and last night he sat with his back to damp wood, trying to draft a prayer. He'd made deals with God before but, even when his request was granted, had often found the terms unmanageable in the long haul. So you eventually either paid the bill, or filed a kind of spiritual bankruptcy and tried to re-establish your credit in small ways (and there was always the devil). But there was apparently no limit to how many times you could step to the mountain, and here he was again, unworthy, insolvent, trying to beg without bargaining, and how surprised he was to receive an answer so soon, though he was momentarily puzzled when He spoke in a Canadian accent, and was saying something about a boat.

"What?"

A flat tone, of patient explanation. "I said they were under the boat."

"Who . . . ? Boat . . ." The husband hadn't spoken to him the entire day. They couldn't see each other.

"You asked me about what happened in the forest. At the petroglyphs."

"Okay." He supposed he had, but wasn't sure he wanted to know anymore. "How's your head?"

"I found the boat, the canoe, when I went to . . . It was over-turned. The hull was cracked."

"In the jungle."

A long hoarse breath. "I flipped it over—I didn't really want to. You knew something was . . . There was already a smell . . . flies coming out of their mouths."

Under the boat.

"Funny." Nineteen didn't ask what was funny. "At first it looked like they were buried up to the neck. But they were just . . . three of them. Eyes open, closed . . . What day is this?"

"What day is it?"

"It's Sunday, isn't it?"

He felt his unshaven face. "Sunday, sure." Sunday was as good a day as any.

Another long, slow breath. Slight change of voice. "It's going on two days then. You think she got anywhere?"

Nineteen kept seeing three heads under a boat, flies in their mouths like the speech of the dead. He seized on the change of subject. "She's on foot."

"She'd be faster alone."

He thought of the gunfire they'd heard. "She might be wounded."

"If she's wounded they'd have got her. They used—" Nineteen wondered if he was going to say dogs. "She'd have run into someone by now. Notified somebody."

"Maybe she did. It's been raining. You heard: the wheels turn slow here."

"Even for Americans? Lawyers, guns and money?" Now deadpan comic: "Exchange rate's just under eighty percent. I'm worth almost as much as you."

"That supposed to be funny?"

"Not to mention Canucks make better hostages. So agreeable."

"That's not funny."

"Who's laughing? They don't seem to be in much of a hurry. Maybe they grease those wheels, buy some time. Maybe they take us to a safe house somewhere we can't be found."

Men with briefcases. The polers' heads.

"You got an idea, I'm listening. Otherwise . . . The weather just cleared. Maybe in the morning . . ."

"In the morning what? You think you're gonna hear the 'Ride of the Valkyries' or something?"

Nineteen was almost embarrassed; in the stock footage of his imagination he'd seen something like a Vietnam-era gunship, hovering, whirling blades flattening the grass while American-trained special forces rappelled to the rescue.

"'On your way to ratfuck some baby democracy? Mind if we hitch a ride?'"

"The hell are you talking about? What are *you* going to hear?"

"A plane."

"Right, that's what he said. A plane."

"I'm thinking Beechcraft Bonanza, something like that."

"So you know planes."

"I know a single-engine piston when I hear one. If that's what they have to use, there can't be more than a thousand feet of runway there."

"You heard all that?"

The wife stirred in what they hoped was sleep. You couldn't see her, nor even hear her breathe. But she was completely there, wielding some great silent power over them.

"You got a pilot's license or something? You're just telling me now?"

"Listen. The G36 has a ground roll less than a thousand feet and it carries six occupants max."

"Did you tell me and I forgot? I told you about my memory."

"That's three of us, the pilot, two guards."

"Okay . . . Two guards, but."

"At most. Maybe they don't fill the plane. Maybe there's other cargo, so just one guy with a gun."

"So you're thinking . . ."

"It would have to happen in the air, then."

"We'll still be cuffed."

"Probably."

"If we could . . . find something maybe to cut with. Hide it till we need it."

"Maybe our feet'll be free."

"Something with an edge . . . sharp stone . . ."

". . . use my fuckin teeth if I have to." The husband didn't seem to be talking about plastic.

"Where would we go?"

"Doesn't matter. Just high enough to get on radar."

"If it's one guy we have a shot." Fucking A. Let's roll.

"If it's carrying drugs as well, I'm thinking one guy."

"Pray for drugs then. Even if you don't pray—cover all the bases . . . if he's telling the truth."

"Why wouldn't he?"

"I don't know . . . To fuck with us?"

"Why would he?"

"You tell me. Why would he tell us anything? He doesn't have to."

"I don't know. Latinos like to talk. I'm assuming a plane."

"Okay, a plane. If it's one guy we have a shot. The hell is *that*?"

Another sound from the jungle, an eerie ululation they hadn't heard before, so close and clear it might have been inside with them. A witch's cackle.

Late in the morning they were watered but not fed, forced into their boots and prodded to address the bucket one last time. Hands duct-taped behind them—it seemed their wardens had finally run out of plastic. Brief thought of the woman practicing knots. It was good to be rid of this place, and nothing more. The grey nest. Outside were small high clouds and sun, wet green, the always-sodden ground. Two guns behind, two before—one wearing a boonie, which to Nineteen had once conveyed a certain goofball ease, someone called by a nickname—the other with a cigarillo poking out of his ski mask. They were led through a narrow corridor of low trees and tall brown grasses that might have been sugar cane and Nineteen felt a stab of fear when he saw none of the scant outbuildings they'd passed was it two days before? Then he realized they were on a different path, that it would take them to the far end of the airstrip and thank God not by the house again.

The pista was more or less a dirt-and-grass road, scrupulously cleared—was that what they did all day? It was not all they did. Narrow, maybe fifty feet wide, harder to say how long—three football fields if the Canadian man was right. White wooden markers along the edges. They did not see the man in his red or grey shirt nor the girl practicing ropework nor anyone else. Jungle on the other side. Nineteen thought of fairways. Of course; he'd seen a man divided into fifteen pieces, stood now next to a woman coupled with dogs in an act you might pay per view through some black peephole in cyberspace; of course he thought of fairways.

In his back pocket was a shard of stone he'd pried from the rocks at the base of the shed. He had prayed they wouldn't be searched.

They waited at the edge of the strip near its dead end—sideline, red zone (it never let up). Their escorts behind and ahead, wearing tactical vests, radios, magazine belts; their stance relaxed but always, somewhere in there, the coiled readiness. Rounds chambered. There was no plane. Nineteen looked over their heads, toward the mountains at the far end of the pista. The Being whom he had petitioned in the night is reputed to move in mysterious ways, as do the servants He'd enlisted to enact His will. Where was it? Suppose it wasn't coming, suppose this was just some ruse, a final cruelty, a more subtle torture consisting not of the violation of flesh but of hope after its tentative mocking presentment, their escort in fact their executioners.

The illogic of this premise had not yet occurred to him when the plane came from behind them, not from the mountains as he'd expected. West? South? The sun was out but it was high and he couldn't be sure. They heard it first. The same low buzzing they'd heard on the river, at the carved rocks. It flew low, a darkness flickering over them and everyone looked up and turned their heads to track its progress, except for the Canadian woman, who looked as if she'd already gotten wherever they were going and was waiting for night to fall again.

Single engine, fixed landing gear; the husband had been right and Nineteen tried to catch his eye. What had he called it? Beechcraft? Cessna was all Nineteen knew. During his starting season, when his teammates were beginning to believe, Number Fifty-Eight, a middle linebacker who'd engaged a hypnotist to increase his sense of aggression and had also a license to fly, had taken them up in his 182 Skylane, dragged their shadow over the stadium, the lake, the city centre, from a height that had felt like home. Now he watched the plane fly away from them over the jungle, parallel to the strip. It dwindled and banked, dipping its wings, curving back toward them.

Later Fifty-Eight found true love and happiness and lost his game.

One of the guards behind spoke. "La ave madre viene a sacar sus pollitos del nido." Some witticism; they seemed to allow themselves to enjoy their work when their chief was absent. The one wearing the boonie gestured with his hand. It reminded Nineteen of the signals he would use at the line to send a man in motion. It seemed aimed at the jungle across the pista; someone must be there after all. Disguised coverage.

The plane centred itself over the approach to the runway and dropped steadily, slowing, louder, growing. No faster than a cruising car now. At the verge of the landing strip and just a couple of feet off the ground, into a headwind, it seemed to hesitate, the pitch of its engine rising with an abrupt burst of power. Then it touched down, reuniting with its shadow, bouncing slightly, the wheel struts bending outward, and rolled toward them. It looked terribly fragile. Two metal tanks hung like weapons from its wings and Nineteen realized this must be extra fuel, tried once again to get the Canadian's attention; perhaps this was the weight they were hoping for.

The husband wouldn't look at him.

Maybe they were just blowing smoke. He could give a shit less. If death was coming he would meet it halfway. The D tells you what to do.

When the edge of the wing swung past, their forward guard turned and faced his rank and ragged charges, looked them in the bloodshot eye and spoke into his radio. The plane trundled to a stop not fifty feet away, prop spinning, to set about the tricky business of turning around. The radio didn't answer but someone somewhere was shouting. Then, closer, a sound like an amplified sneeze and Nineteen thought he saw a small white object darting out the corner of his eye just before the plane exploded, one wing flapping straight up, not quite detaching, as in some hapless parody of flight.

The fuel tanks burst an instant later with a bright orange bass thump and the Canadian wife was already on her knees, pulling her husband with her. The man in the ski mask did likewise but the other turned at the moment of the explosion, not meaning to shield Nineteen from the spray of burning fuel that ignited his own clothing shirt to shoes, going to the ground where he rolled in a mute frenzy, fire in his throat, setting the grass alight. Small flashes now winking from the forest at the other side of the runway, the high percussion of rounds per second, that broken cadence.

The one wearing the ski mask belly-flopped into the only cover he could find on no notice, propped himself on his elbows and started shooting back. His ground pulverized, blades of grass springing up as if by invisible scythe. He'd lost his little cigar. Nineteen crouched, eyes panning everywhere, frantic with adrenaline, seeing everything but the husband and wife. Shouting all around now, the jackhammer of automatic weapons behind, a booming that must have been a shotgun and hot debris just starting to rain. Spent brass. A burnt chemical smell. A piece of something human fell, charred but wet. The one somehow still wearing his boonie smouldered in the blackened grass, trying to retch up the inside of himself in strangely orgasmic convulsions. Then Nineteen caught a glimpse of them angling out of the kill zone for the other side of the strip and he tried to follow, hiding in the acrid black smoke now drifting from the wreckage, doing what he had done so badly as a player, hands behind him, one leg held together with plates, screws, a piece of bone borrowed from his pelvis.

Someone grabbed at it and he kicked free.

Then they were in it. No path or clearing, just leaf and branch, ankle-deep underbrush. Rustling footfalls and sawing breath. Exhilarated terror. They ran without room to run, hunched down with heads low for balance and to protect their faces, eyes, from the incessant laceration. The sound of guns was already muted by distance and bush and seemed directionless. So did they. Nineteen was half-aware of the Canadians ahead and to the side, all bodiless motion. He tried to jump a log, stumbled but kept his feet. Another stuttered burst, deep-voiced, large calibre—feed the big dog—then something moving toward him from somewhere close, a displacement in the green tangle, and he reversed and rolled back over the log and under it, wedging himself in the dank depression where snakes are known to live.

Why hadn't he grabbed the rifle?

Because your hands are tied behind your back, dumbfuck.

He felt the tread of boots now, heard the crash of vegetation, a barking voice—"*Vuelvesalpista*"—and shut his eyes, willfully compressing as if to retract his limbs and hide within himself. Tried not to breathe. Then the log pushed down on his ribs and it was no longer even an option. They were stepping all over him. Toe of a boot, bayonet stab, an end you don't hear or see coming, but they kept moving, past him. Away. He opened his eyes, scraped himself out from under and spent two full minutes learning to stand with his hands behind his back, every side blind.

He couldn't see the Canadians. Maybe they'd yet to emerge from cover and he waited, afraid to use his voice, and would they use theirs? He turned. Could they have been taken? He'd heard nothing. Turning . . . there: not twenty feet, a shifting in the foliage, if anything at all. Moving away from him, if at all . . . He started toward it—you could no longer call it running—trying to get closer to something he wasn't sure he'd seen, farther from the smell of gunsmoke and burning fuel. Burnt flesh. Still not calling out.

It hurt to be alone this way. He didn't yet feel it was every man for himself, but that every step in this ravelled wilderness led further into mutual desertion. His throat burned, his limbs felt bloodless, but the need to keep on, to hide in motion, would not be denied. The shooting was distant again and remote in another way. Snare drums at halftime. Someone else's war. He wondered with vague alarm if he might happen upon the site where they'd been held; if you could become lost trying to find something, you could be found by what you were trying to lose. The idea stopped him in a narrow glade where he knelt in the damp decomposing heart of something, heaving, shaking, lightheaded, suddenly aware of an unfamiliar stinging sensation in his leg, looking down at the scorched patch on the thigh of his trousers. He'd caught fire without knowing it.

The birds were talking to each other again. All he could think of now was quenching his thirst—he might have licked the sweat off his arms if he could reach them, but to do so he would have to free his hands. He looked around, not for anyone but for a sharp edge or point, something to cut or pierce. Tried not to think machete. Then he remembered the piece of stone and his throat managed a dry whisper of gratitude—not just that it was still in his pocket, but that it was still in his mind to recall.

He worked it out carefully and felt for the best edge, using his fingers in a way he never had and each of which he'd broken at least once. Just start sawing away then but it became a minute gashing; he couldn't tell if he was accomplishing anything.

Biting flies. Patchwork light. Vines knotted as if by hand.

Who were they? He hadn't actually seen them but dismissed the possibility of the police or military out of hand—he didn't think they would have destroyed the plane. Nor did it seem like a rescue operation, unless a gloriously fucked-up one, a black comedy, not an action-adventure where skill and good intentions trump bad luck and everyone gets what they have coming.

Safer to assume a rival group then, competitors with similar ends and, God help them, similar means. But if they'd wanted to appropriate the airfield, would they litter it with burning wreckage? Maybe they'd turned on each other. A business decision. Or maybe they were something else—maybe they were *what comes after*.

Where had he heard that phrase?

He dropped the stone. Grunting with self-disgust, he stood and toed the dead brown leaves for it, then thought to check his progress first. His fingers could not find a tear but when he twisted and pulled his wrists there seemed a give, a looseness he hadn't felt before. So twist and pull. The sweat helped.

The gunfire had become sporadic, as if the fight were winding down. Someone had to lose, there was no third category here, no OT, but plenty of sudden death. Or not so sudden. Coach said a tie is like kissing your sister. He pushed further conjecture from his mind. Who won or lost mattered only to them. Anonymous men (and at least one woman) with masks and machetes and no compunction. Assume the winners were worse. He simply could not let himself be found.

Without realizing it, he'd begun to lift his hands as high as he could behind himself, bringing them down hard against his spine, spreading his elbows.

The effort cost. Everything began to be about water again. An acrid taste on his tongue, but his thirst could tie everything together. There were vines filled with water. Or a stream, a creek, tributary. The river. Hadn't she said that was where they should go? The Canadians would be looking for water. Better to look for a common object than each other. (And for all he knew they were sitting ten feet away, thinking his thoughts.) You were supposed to wait for rescue but waiting was not on the list. Head down-stream then, meet a search party on the way, or somebody with a boat. Speaking of which, where was anybody anyway? His mind rewound, tried to count days, and even this effort seemed consuming. Three? Four? The explosion of the plane had blown a hole in time.

Even before his hands came free he was looking around for a way to go, and for something that might serve as a walking stick. For all he knew they were ten steps away.

It was to be a surprise.

Garbage Day in the subdivision, two-wheeled bins at the curbs. No trees or sidewalks. A dog barking ceaselessly some-where. A local news team was interviewing the family on the pretense of a proposed recycling initiative when Nineteen rang their doorbell with the foundation's wish coordinator, a local personal injury attorney with whom he played handball. When the boy came to the door, he was wearing a sideline cap and a jersey with Nineteen's number on it. He was very small but his head was large and filled the cap tightly. The jersey hung like a gown. Nineteen had brought another of each, autographed, and a ball and cleats, also inscribed.

"It's you," the boy said flatly in a high, thin voice, hollow-eyed, his skin almost translucent and wizened to the contours of his skull. His nose was pinched and beaklike. You couldn't tell if he was smiling.

"No, it's me," Nineteen said, immediately wishing he hadn't. He shook the boy's hand, a slight cold object.

The wish coordinator, who was also a personal injury attorney, was familiar to the family from a series of local television ads in which he personally appeared and concluded with the tagline, "Bad fall? Give us a call!" Now he simply said hello and goodbye, his celebrity outshone; he would return at the scheduled time to pick Nineteen up. Nineteen watched him leave; he'd been known on occasion to leave his business card on furniture.

The boy had been stricken with a genetic disorder that causes children to age at eight to ten times the normal rate.

He lived in a ranch home with sponge-painted walls and sectional furniture buried in pillows. Artificial plants. The parents were dressed in team regalia. The boy's father documented Nineteen's arrival on a camcorder with considerable formality, then returned to the backyard, where he was smoking a brisket. The mother shook hands but kept a distance. She wore a ball cap with a ponytail hanging out the back and a great deal of makeup. "Would you like some Gatorade? We have lemon-lime and orange." Nineteen politely declined; he didn't like the taste and only drank it during games. He wondered if she was joking.

The cameraman followed them into the boy's bedroom. A full-length poster of Nineteen dropping back covered the closet door. The boy's father, a manager at Kinko's, had had an image of his son in helmet and uniform superimposed so that he appeared to be an eligible receiver. He was an only child.

"You keep the monsters in the closet," he told Nineteen.

"I'm honoured," Nineteen said. "Is that your dog?"

"No," the boy said. "But he never stops."

They went outside to play catch with the autographed ball. It had never been used. The boy's mother wielded the camcorder while the father basted meat with a spray bottle filled with apple cider. Nineteen gave the boy some throwing tips in a simple rhyme he had devised: "These two for grip, this one's for guide, the little one's just kind of along for the ride . . ." There was also a basketball hoop in the driveway and a Ping-Pong table in the garage, but the boy quickly tired and they repaired to the living room to play video games.

The mother brought aspirin. "So I don't get a heart attack," the boy said, swallowing with difficulty.

Nineteen did not play video games and was content to watch. The boy's disappointment seemed short-lived. The game was licensed by the League and Players Association to use both numbers and names, but the boy had the courtesy not to feature his guest, for which Nineteen was grateful.

"I knew it was you at the door," the boy said, squeezing a controller.

"You're too smart for us," Nineteen said.

"Dying makes you smarter in a way. You can tell when people are lying."

"How about I do a little coaching?" Nineteen offered, but the game's jerky passing mechanics were insufficiently nuanced to warrant any realistic advice, and the boy didn't seem to need it anyway. He'd won seven Super Bowls with his thumbs.

"Maybe you should give *me* some pointers," Nineteen joked. It was the summer before his shoulder separation and he was on the covers of *Sports Illustrated* and *Details*. But the reply was earnest.

"You're my favourite player because you do the same things as guys that have a lot more talent. You don't make mistakes. The only things that can hurt you are what you don't control." He kept his eyes on the screen. His voice was calm but he squeezed the controller relentlessly. "All you have to do is stay perfect."

"Veteran wisdom," Nineteen said after a moment. The dog barked.

The boy took off his cap. His head was hairless, bulbous, veined. "I'm over a hundred of your earth years old," he said in his high thin voice. He was twelve.

Afterward they ate dinner at a picnic table in the yard. The dog barked through Grace, the joining of hands. The boy's father was revered in the neighbourhood for his brisket. A fifteen-pound packer's cut he'd smoked for twenty-four hours over chunks of soaked hickory, barely sleeping, getting out of bed every hour to check the thermometer, spraying it with the cider to keep it moist.

"That steak got more rest than I did," he said, and served it with pasta salad and pork and beans, buns and pickles if you wanted to make a sandwich. He made his own sauce. "The best for the best."

The dog lived next door behind a tall picket fence so you could only hear it. You would still be hearing it, Nineteen supposed, when the boy was gone.

"Maybe you should throw him a slice," he said.

"Sure. Got some special sauce just for him." The father winked but didn't smile.

"Don't take it out on the dog, give it to *them*," the mother said. "Throw it in their hot tub."

The yard was big. An empty table and benches stood nearby as if to honour the uninvited, but a stipulation of the visit was immediate family only. Nineteen had also insisted that there be no discussion of his playing. He quoted dialogue from *Forrest Gump*, and they talked baseball, about which the mother proved quite knowledgeable. She was especially impressed with the Indians' use of relievers. The boy was inappetent.

Nineteen ended the visit taking pictures with everyone. Before he left, the boy gave him a gift of books by his favourite authors: Jules Verne and Roald Dahl.

"It's good to have a sense of humour," he said, "when your birthday's in dog years."

"No Goosebumps?" Nineteen said.

"They don't scare me anymore."

Nineteen thanked the boy and embraced what remained of him and could be seen losing his composure mid-sentence on the local news, at six and then again at eleven. He had lately a reputation for coldness with the media. On the ride back the wish coordinator who was also a personal injury attorney said, "Kinda puts things in perspective, doesn't it?"

"You always say that."

"I hear Young only sees Mormon kids."

"That supposed to be funny?"

"Mormons have four secret handshakes to get into heaven," the wish coordinator said.

The following week Nineteen would visit a ninety-four-year-old woman in a nursing home and give her a sideline pass to the next home game. He thought it would be easier because she was dying on schedule, but he kept hearing the dog bark.

He was climbing another hill—the third? fourth?—when he heard a voice. He stopped, took a knee, listened with everything he had left.

At first he could not tell where it was coming from but it was a man's, in what else but Spanish. There had to be more of them unless he was talking to himself. Nineteen looked around and behind, and the grim advantage of his condition was that he lacked the energy to panic; for a moment he could almost forget about his thirst. The vise in which his skull was clamped.

He listened. A voice could mean water, rescue, but this one did not sound beneficent. Nineteen held a walking stick he'd made of a slender bough, one end still jagged where he'd broken it off. A fist-sized rock in his pocket and whatever remained of his accuracy. Promises to himself he was not sure he could keep. Now he heard the voice again and it was somewhere above and ahead and didn't seem to be moving. It did not sound aware of him. There was no safe distance here but the forest was thick enough to hide in without hiding. He reached in his pocket.

Holding the stick, the rock, he went down on all fours and crawled like a supplicant to an altar. Winced at the soft crepitation of his progress, every inch a mistake, but he had not far to go. At the top a half-embedded shelf of damp rock afforded him some cover, and he stopped and listened, counting, then slowly rose and looked. Counted again.

Six of them, in a rough patch of sun, and he had enough depth perception left to know twenty yards when he saw it. Two men were on their knees, facing more or less his way, hands behind them. More or less surrounded by the other four; rifles, blades, a camouflage patrol cap. Someone cradling a big gun with folded tripod. No one wore a mask. One was squat with dark cropped hair and could have passed for a man except for the web belt-straps crossed between her breasts.

Nineteen wondered if any of them could be called idealists, but all he knew was that some were on their feet and some on their knees.

Two of them might have been Miskitu. The speaker wore cut-off sleeves and a goatee and, though brandishing a pistol and blade, sounded now like a reasonable man. Someone you might even approach for directions in a strange place. Or ask for water.

No one filming with a phone. Did this make them the good guys?

"Dame una razón por la que debería dejarte vivir." The other three looked on impassively, like jurors in some verdant court. They seemed unconcerned that they might be seen or heard. Nineteen couldn't help noticing their canteens. "¿Qué harías en mi lugar? Estoy escuchando."

The prisoners looked jungle-torn, flesh and fabric. Dried blood, dirt and sweat. Faces bruised and puffy. One had been wounded, a dark wet hole in his thigh, seeping. The other was missing half an ear but looked calm, beyond defiance, while his companion trembled with desperation—whatever training he might have had, however rigorous, it had not adequately prepared him for this moment. If anything could. Nineteen looked and listened for something familiar—voice, tattoo, a red shirt—something he could remember and hate enough to watch this unwatchable unfold. He realized he could not tell one player from another. Whoever they were, one was ready to trade his soul, if it was still in his possession, for another breath, while the other shook flies from his face.

The man with the pistol now stood before the man with the hole in his leg and spoke an abridged version of what he'd already said. The answer was so diffident as to be almost inaudible, and must have been unsatisfactory, for the man who otherwise seemed reasonable did something with the tip of his machete that Nineteen couldn't see, but he dropped his head at the sound it made the wounded man make.

Something in the jungle screamed back. Small holes eaten in leaves.

When he looked again the sleeveless man was standing beside the frightened one. He asked again. This time the reply came in a burst, much louder and longer than the first, denial or confession, one no more adequate than the other and which the man with the pistol punctuated in midstream, pulling the trigger on the question that has one answer.

Nineteen turned away at the bang of it but he'd already seen the eyes leap from their sockets, one still attached to the stalk of the optic nerve, and now they were everywhere. It seemed he never heard the body fall to ground.

One of them was crossing himself. Red spatter on leaves, trembling. A dissipating puff of grey smoke like a departing spirit. This moment of silence brought to you by The Realm of Perfect Indifference.

Now the other captive, who had flinched at the shot but otherwise maintained his demeanour. Now one man standing behind yet another at his feet. Gently resting the barrel on the blood-caked edge of gristle that was left of his ear so that the prisoner winced with white teeth, sucked breath then composed himself again.

"Última oportunidad," the man standing said.

"¿Cómo? No escucho tan bien de ese lado," the man who was about to be killed said, and the man who was about to kill him said "No importa" and gave the pistol to the woman Nineteen had mistaken for another kind of human being, who took it uncertainly, and then the man on his knees looked up slightly and saw Nineteen, saw Nineteen seeing him and it was already too late to turn away or try to run or do anything but look him back in the eye in mutual witness as if held there wholly by the will of the other.

The woman was hesitant. The man on his knees seemed to know this and spoke calmly. "En la parte posterior de la cabeza, en la base. No hay nada más que entender." He spat out a bug and Nineteen was certain he had not been given away.

The sudden halo of smoke, that jarring fracture of air. The jolt of it though you know it's coming.

Nineteen sank behind the rock again. He knew he should keep them in sight but he stayed low, trying to listen. He stayed low because the man could have but had not and Nineteen did not know why. He only knew at which point the man had stopped seeing him, and he the man, though now he saw him in a way he did not yet understand. For lack of anything better, he crossed himself.

Aftermath of calm voices. The jungle's eulogy of the unspeakable. Then the voices were moving.

Still he didn't rise. They were not coming his way. He wondered what might happen if he tried to follow, if they might lead him to water, but knew he wouldn't attempt it. When he finally looked they were gone but he stayed a moment longer, crossed himself again then went to see if the Lord had left him anything to quench his thirst.

. . .

Low growth, scrub. Still, he was in over his head. A narrow passage between walls of leaves, trying to remember to march, lift his knees and stamp down the brush, but it hurt to move that way. Stung, bitten, some kind of burning rash on his neck. Forget about the bad guys, here every living thing was locked and loaded. When the knotted vines became impassable, he had to try and skirt, double back to a point of departure he couldn't find. The jungle created itself as he went, he couldn't keep up.

He came upon a cluster of high stalks, segmented like bamboo but vivid red. Did beauty signify poison? He grabbed anyway, bending, twisting, breaking, looking for the wet stuff. Nothing but a vile stickiness.

It hurt to move this way and it was worse on the slopes, where his ankle was constantly bent and felt permanently deformed, his foot about to detach itself. Not to mention the rest of him. He was no longer sure which pains were new, nor which he could blame on his body's drought. *Hidrata tu cuerpo.* In camp he'd kept his hurts a secret and avoided the training room—he was an unsigned free agent, and the trainers kept tabs. Near the end it was the same thing all over again.

A rainforest without rain. Who was the governing spirit here? Would like a word with. She'd said land always fell to water but every declivity he tried was only another dry ditch to climb out of. Seemed he'd had a plan he couldn't quite remember; he was moving just to move. Getting hard to tell up from down anyway; the paths he saw were only in his mind, then not even there. *Hidrata tu mente.* He'd seen it on a bottle, now his head pounded with it. A broken grinding like defective machinery. Tongue welded to the roof of his mouth. Sometime today he'd pissed a burning trickle, a troubling dark amber. Couldn't catch his breath, his heart wouldn't slow even at rest. He seemed to be barely sweating anymore. But the cloud of mosquitoes that accompanied him like an emanation were well quenched, drinking him dry. God bless.

Was this the "little spring" they'd been promised? Only two seasons here, wet and not so. Leaves that never changed colour. How he'd miss autumn and what it brought to life. Birds barnstorming in tight flocks, red maples you could see in the dark. Radiance of decay, the season within the season. He'd done what no one before him had: beat the black and gold in their own backyard. Monday Night, Indian summer. Grace under pressure under bright lights rimming a black-hole void. The owner embracing him in the locker room, still in his underwear. Cashmere and cane. Gave him his daughter like a signing bonus. A helicopter overhead trying to get pictures, famous guests hiding under umbrellas. *The newlyweds will honeymoon at an undisclosed location.*

A spiderweb netted his face, architect and engineer lurking somewhere out of sight. Knee-high grass here and whatever it might hide: snakes, ants, ticks, some unknown species he would crush underfoot before it was even discovered. My bad. If it ain't us I hope it's you. He saw a dead tree, its hollow grey trunk filled with coiled vines or roots like some intestinal parasite, and his stomach turned. Exotic multiform orchids like alien pudenda. Faces made of foliage. The greener greening green greenness, humming in his head. Allow me to introduce my aunties, Flora and Fauna. (Spinsters my ass, I hear they do each other.)

He had his stick and his stone. Stumbled over nothing and fell. Reached up for a little help and no one gave it to him. *All I had, boys, all I had.* Something new was wrong; he worked off his boot and there was blood. The metal screw that held his ankle together, protruding through skin and sock. Mad doctor's monster. A failed experiment.

It started after Minnesota, when X-rays showed he'd played the second half—and won—with a fractured tibia. Vikings fans like extras in a German opera. The good years were behind him then. They'd knocked at the door twice, sorry wrong address. He'd done everything right, played virtually perfect games but still . . . A missed point after, a Hail Mary at zero. Not this year, not that year, not ever. He'd consoled himself in her dank soft undergrowth, her perfect hollow, *but you only let me in when you're losing.* Had she let him in at all? The heart is an undisclosed location.

Hail Mary, full of . . . What was she full of again?

He was moving along the spine of a ridge now, the going easier, but he wasn't thinking about that, nor even his consuming thirst—it was now a condition of being. Every cell a desert. He remembered the survival shows he'd seen on his flatscreen, Discovery Channel, men and sometimes women stranded by producers in jungles and arid wastes. They would find water. Hack open vines and drink as if from a garden hose, dig it out of the earth with their bare hands, devise ingenious vessels for its collection and purification.

He took a deep breath, trying to pull moisture from heavy air. Stopped to rest, putting his head to a tree trunk as if to transfer the chaos of memory to it.

She'd waited till he was up north on the farm before serving him with papers. He refused to sign the Acceptance of Service. She sent them via certified mail and he refused to sign the return receipt. She tried a process server, then the county sheriff, then resorted to publishing her complaint in the local daily, a full-page ad citing as the basis for dissolution his *increasingly bizarre and erratic behavior*, that he'd *irrationally and irresponsibly given away monies, property, corporate interests, and other assets to family and friends*, that yet he travelled by private jet and enjoyed lavish vacations, that he was or had been addicted to painkillers, alcohol, and internet pornography.

Was that before or after his father's funeral? He'd attended but wasn't there. A rustling overhead.

He looked up . . . Bird? Monkey? Some hungry thing? He couldn't tell; the light was going and it was a long ride home. He sat in the back with his sister, still in pads, his father complaining into the mirror.

"Fuckinass wing-t. All them niggers know is run. Two lousy points and you'd be in the sub-regionals."

Stopping outside a bar in Ashland. Said he had to use the bathroom but he was gone for an hour. Nobody went in to get him. Nineteen in the back with his sister, willing his mother to slide over, get behind the wheel and drive, just drive away.

Can't we think of something else to think of?

The assistant with soft hands, calling him Snake. Showed some of the boys dirty movies, then put them in one. Hung himself when they found out . . . Next.

Her hair hung over one shoulder, baring her neck. The first time he'd lost himself there, no longer needing to breathe. She guided his finger, making things moister and softer the harder he got. *Did her daddy say you could do that?*

He hadn't felt like a mistake.

The top of the ridge narrowed; he did not want to fight another hillside. He squinted. In the draining light he could still see enough to make out a sort of path, maybe a natural culvert, a game trail, cutting down the slope in front of him. He could follow it down when it was light again, on hands and knees if he couldn't walk. He turned.

Light comes out of the ground. Anyone knows that.

Something, a big pale rock projecting from the shrubs, above him. He touched it. Chalky. Limestone? What interested him was the recessed darkness beneath. Cave enough. He crawled in when he was as sure as he was going to get that nothing else had crawled in first. Obviously he was meant to; a little later and he wouldn't have seen it at all.

Soft dampness beneath him, damp hardness everywhere else. Close quarters. He lay on his side with his stick and his stone, wedged. Rubbed slick surfaces clothed in moss, licked his fingers. A chalky, bitter mistake. He could still see out the opening, had a sense of spiders, snakes, bats. Something sat on his head like a nest and he remembered what it was, but could not bring himself to remove it. It had justified every claim of durability and fastness its manufacturer made, if not authenticity, and seemed likely at this rate to survive its wearer, to be found decorating a skull otherwise picked clean by time and the jungle it might also outlast, yet another souvenir of yet another cancelled empire.

Some kind of helmet or ceremonial headdress. What say you, Dr. Jones?

I say he couldn't get the fucking thing off.

He thought he maybe heard something moving outside then and was still alive enough to be frightened. A big cat, maybe. Did jaguars make lairs of caves? Returning to find an uninvited guest in its home. Who's been licking my rock? Well since you're here you might as well stay for supper. Really very kind of you but I should be *No I insist.*

(Awful wet affection of its muzzle in your neck. Intimate but nothing personal.)

Had the roast puppy for lunch but I sure could use something to wash it down.

Sorry sir, this cave doesn't have bottle service. Go suck a stone.

Do I know you?

"I've got important information for you."

I knew it. Thought I recognized that blue tongue.

You were hoping for someone else?

Wouldn't kick a healer out of my huddle. Can you make it rain?

Somebody wants his two bucks' worth. What's in it for me?

I swear on my . . . I'll . . . Fuck it, just fill in the blanks.

Might want to call your bank, bro.

Is there someone else I can pray to?

Sure, but trust me, you don't want to mess with them.

Man I've golfed with presidents.

The terms are harsh. Muerte pura.

I thought all you wanted was our shit.

Your heart, bloody and beating from its cage . . .

You know I used to be a god myself . . .

. . . limbs, faces . . . your balls . . . and that's just for starters.

. . . self-made, you could say.

(yawn) Isn't everyone?

I just never found a place to put the love I had for the game.

If I could've worn your jock for a day, I'da found a place to put it. This tongue ain't blue for nothing.

She came the closest.

Never were much on debauchery, were you?

A little goes a long way with me. It was enough to be desired. Sort of.

Well, worship ain't love—not that I give a shit. Something big is going down.

They say it's the little things that count, I just don't remember any. But I tried to give back . . . visited a boy dying of old age . . . I've given blood . . .

There's never enough blood, and it's getting late. You might want to speak up a little.

Maybe I used the wrong word. She used to call it . . . semi-god?

Demi-, dummy.

That's it.

And I can barely hear you. The night is loud.

Achilles, all that shit . . .

I can't even see your lips move. Will you listen to those frogs sing, though.

He did. They were drowning out everything, even his delirium. There were frogs so small here they could sit on the pad of your finger. Others slicked with poison that could kill at a touch. And what did they sing about?

Demigods, she'd said, then waited till he was up north on business before serving him with papers. Yet he lost consciousness trying not to think of her.

The thunder didn't wake him but the rain did. Red lightning behind his eyes.

By daybreak it had stopped and the channel that furrowed the slope below the overhang was reduced to a trickle. It had become a small torrent during the storm but Nineteen hadn't needed it; he'd had only to cup his hands in the liquid curtain that dropped from the edge of the overhang and they filled in seconds. He did not count how many handfuls he poured into himself, but after its ineffable succour blessed his mouth and throat it seemed to flow to some hollow of his body he could not fill, nor was he certain there was no hazard in drinking rainwater nor did he care and drank till he was near to vomiting, stopping only to breathe and whisper thanks, then cupping his hands again.

He would drink the sky dry.

Now he looked at the dwindling stream and wondered if he should nurse from what remained, on hands and knees and belly, against future privation. If you waited till game time it was usually too late. He looked around. The limestone outcropping centred things, but beyond it no further progress could be made; it was up or down or back. The lack of choice was helpful and he recovered his stick and commenced downward, hoping the trickle would serve another purpose: land fell to water, someone had told them, though he couldn't remember who nor did it matter, and the deliberate wandering of the previous day, forgotten in the throes of dehydration, was again in effect.

Small steps, like an old man or a small child negotiating a stairway. He fell only once. By then it was just a muddy path, twisting down to form the bottom of another gully, profusion of wet ferns and vines on either side. Now a cascade of broken stone he descended clumsily to a thin strand of water, stagnant—without rain would it dry up like the one that had fed it?—but rather than climb once again out of a ditch, Nineteen decided he would follow what you couldn't even call a trickle and see if it led to something there was a name for, something that made a sound. Do what you wouldn't do.

He fought not to turn back. The ravine narrowed—he could almost touch either side at once—but there was no level ground, and he tried to straddle the bottom for better purchase with a foot on each side, the stick another leg. Grabbing tree roots embedded like veins in the cross-section. God, his ankle . . . God, everything. He decided to walk directly in the streambed, if you could call it that, if you could call it walking, amid slick green rocks and fallen tangled branches still clustered with leaves, patches of red clay appearing so that Nineteen wondered if he was getting close and continued to struggle down, in as much pain as hope, and was still listening for the sound of moving water when he was given something else. Something from above.

He stopped. It was still faint and remote, but there was no mistaking it. Look up. The edges of the gully cropped his vision, leaves and boughs crowding shards of bright grey sky; it was not enough. He had a voice he hadn't spoken in over a day and he shouted then, or tried to, a guttural rasp trapped in his throat in this slit of earth. Its impotence shocked him. Higher ground, it told him now, find a clearing. He quickly judged either side of this slanted muddy trench to be non-negotiable and began to backtrack.

Beating machine blades. Closer.

It took him so long he expected it to have passed by the time he got to the ridge where he'd sheltered, but the sound of it faded then grew louder by turns, as if it were circling. The sun had emerged somewhere. He was out of breath but not adrenaline and the pain in his leg had become an abstraction, a debt deferred till the blood sugar ran out. He stabbed the earth with his stick and hobbled on, looking up; visibility was only slightly better here, he had to find the open. It occurred to him the last aircraft he'd seen had not been on a rescue mission, but he somehow had the idea that bad guys didn't use helicopters. Then he came to a gap in the trees he thought big enough to be seen in from above and waited. He was shaking now.

A shadow flickered over him.

There. A dragonfly shape, already passing beyond the edge of the canopy. Before he could wave there was nothing to wave at, nothing to shout and jump at—if he could have—but a sound, and as he waited for it to come back around he had a second thought. The pilot would probably never hear you but someone else might and in his excitement he'd forgotten about *them*. Then forgot again. He waited for it to circle back, looking for insignia, something blue and white, but could only see its belly. He used his voice. It was stronger now, and in his state it took him a moment to realize there'd been a response, that it was not an echo nor some avian mimicry but had come from a human being.

He listened.

The chopper was fading again.

He shouted. The chopper was fading. He listened for more, heard nothing, then yelled again as if to hear himself. The reply was distant but he did not think it Spanish—he was not sure why it mattered—was sure enough, anyway, to try again—and there was more. He held his breath the better to hear. The chopper had faded. He shouted again, and listened, and shouted, and there began an exchange, a half-intelligible call and response, and Nineteen began to move accordingly, scrabbling for the source, getting closer and farther by turns, a children's game in a living maze, and it did not occur to him to stop and wonder whether he was being guided or lured.

There were two of them, a man and a woman. They stood in a grassy flat and he remembered a similar place at the end of a gruelling trek. The strange distant peak, gunshots. He thought there'd been others as well, fellow travellers, but he could not place these two among them. His throat burned with nothing to say. The helicopter was gone.

The man said something and took a step forward. He seemed too eager to Nineteen, who hobbled a step back and showed them the pointed end of his walking stick. He was breathing hard.

The man stopped and glanced at the woman, who was much younger and stood off his shoulder, not quite behind him. He looked back at Nineteen from this uncertain place, looked him up and down and said, "Your leg."

"What about it?" Nineteen wondered if they were even real— the visitations of the night before were still fresh. Perhaps they wondered the same.

"You hurt yourself?" the man said. It wasn't really a question.

"Around twenty years ago, thanks." Nineteen held the stick in both hands and realized what the man had said at his arrival. "How do you know my name?"

The man opened his mouth, then closed it. He was sweating and his face was pink except for a greenish bruise around his mouth, his white hair festooned with foliage like Roman laurels. It might have been camouflage. He and the girl looked as though they'd been dipped in mud to their necks. A canteen hung by a strap from his shoulder.

"You're lost like we are," he said finally. "That chopper might be looking for us."

Nineteen pretended to understand. "You think they saw us?"

"I think maybe we shouldn't have yelled."

"Maybe." But why shouldn't they have? "Maybe we didn't have any choice." He couldn't stop looking at the canteen. "Did you see it?"

The pink and white head nodded. Glanced around uneasily. "They didn't see us back."

"How do you know?"

"They didn't signal."

"What kind of signal?"

"I don't know. Planes dip their wings. A helicopter can probably do something like that. Or drop a flare, a line . . ." He muttered. ". . . drop some fucking toilet paper."

Nineteen couldn't help himself and pointed with the stick. "God I'm thirsty."

"Lower that spear and you can have some." The man unshouldered the strap. "Just take it easy, it's all we've got for now. And it's rainwater, not purified."

Nineteen made himself stop after three swallows. He could see the man trying to control his hands. The woman watched them both. She had not spoken.

"I'll take the shits over dying of thirst any time." He handed it back.

"You can die of the shits out here," the man said. "It's not the first you've had, is it?"

It seemed he was being asked for a story, but his mind kept jumping around, finding things then losing them. It jumped to the young woman, who studied him with a sort of relentless patience from which he would look away. She was bare-armed in a sports bra and had fashioned a head scarf from another shirt. She seemed connected to the man in some way—besides being caked in the same monochrome filth—and perhaps that was why she still hadn't said a word. He wondered if she was in danger. "Is that your daughter?"

A wry face. "Next question."

"Is she okay?"

"We should go." The man took a step in front of her. "They might still be around."

"Who?"

"You really don't know."

Running through the jungle, dancing on the edge of a firefight. "Go where?"

"Out of the open for a start."

"I just need to rest my leg a minute," Nineteen said, though he needed much more than that.

They moved into the trees. Tall ferns, the ground thick with roots, a lone spiky red flower. Nineteen sat carefully with his back to a white sapling. When he looked up the man was vigilant.

"How do you know my name?" he said as if for the first time.

The man waited, then asked in earnest, "How do you think?"

Laughter of invisible birds. "There was shooting yesterday," Nineteen remembered.

"I think that part of it's over."

Two men on their knees surrounded by guns. "Who do you think they are?"

"'What comes after'?" the man said, looking pained by the question. He waited for a reaction. "More of the same, far as I can tell. Not that it matters—they all eat each other eventually, don't they?" He looked about again. "I've no intention of finding out. I don't want to understand; I—we—want what comes after the helicopter."

Nineteen found it hard to pay attention. Somebody smelled like shit. He wondered if it was them or him, or everyone. He looked at the canteen again, but not because he was thirsty.

"We found it in the jungle," the man said. He considered something. "After the landing strip . . . You remember the landing strip?"

"The landing strip." Nineteen wondered if the canteen had been attached to a body.

"Are you looking for the river?" he asked suddenly.

The man nodded, encouraged. "I remembered from when they took us"—he watched Nineteen carefully—"it seemed like we were heading east. So we went the other way—at least tried to. Bloody sun wasn't much help. What I wouldn't give for a compass."

He kept saying "we," as if every step were subject to some mute consultation.

"I thought we got close. There were pools of water, then it turned into . . . swamp, marsh . . . is there a difference?" The woman nodded, as if there were a difference, or just nodding. "Black water. We tried . . . Not a chance without a fucking machete. God I didn't think we'd ever—" He looked down, and the woman reached out to him. The words congealed in his throat. "You don't feel them but you know they're on you." She lowered her hand. He didn't speak till he'd extricated himself all over again. Lifted his shirt, showing his tan hairless belly, scattered red welts with pinkish halos. His voice was matter-of-fact. "You can just sort of pinch them off. Doesn't hurt but they itch like hell."

They'd spent the night not a hundred feet away. Had managed a shelter of sorts, a lean-to made of sticks and palms. He'd hated to destroy it.

"How's the leg?" he said abruptly, either with concern or assessing a liability. "Is that a burn? From the airstrip?"

"Minnesota," Nineteen said. "Played a whole half with it." He struggled up to check its status and then they were at his sides, helping. It was almost an embrace.

"There's aloe around if it hurts. Have you eaten?" They'd found what looked like a zapote tree, just as they heard the helicopter, before that some sour leaves—"the ones she showed us"—and though Nineteen wasn't sure of these strangers, he recalled *her*. Still with them after all. Guiding now from memory or death.

They'd eaten worms.

"Not bad at all. You gag at first but mainly from the idea. Kind of almondy, really. And after what you've eaten . . ." He stopped himself and the woman proffered Nineteen his stick. He hadn't realized he'd set it aside, but taking it galvanized him, as if she'd relayed an unspoken message. She might need his help. Maybe the white-haired man wouldn't let her talk, maybe she wanted him to . . . He looked at the man. Looked at his belly, his chest. The point might break. Nineteen tightened his grip. The neck, then. The throat.

". . . could wait around for the chopper," the man droned on, "but . . ." But he'd given water, promised food. Healing of sorts. Maybe, Nineteen thought, for now, he would sing for his supper, even if it wasn't demanded of him.

"Show me the tree," he sang, "and I'll show you this stream or whatever it is I found."

The throat, the eye.

They had trouble finding the zapote tree but not the vicious black ants protecting it, some of which invaded their boots and whose sting felt like hot needles to the flesh. They fled to other fruit, what looked and tasted like wild raspberries, and then a rotted log from which they extracted a handful of thick yellow grub worms two finger joints long. They tore the heads off and sucked the pasty innards from the end, or tore them open lengthwise with their teeth. The worms tasted like what the worms had eaten. The woman swallowed the skins.

Now they made their way to the ravine below the outcrop where he'd passed the night. The thread of wetness at the bottom had all but dried up but, perhaps fed by groundwater, gained seep and flow as they followed it with great and painful difficulty for what might have been an hour to the bottom and what it emptied into. Clear and shallow, broken by sandbars covered with small stones, this was not the river but what might lead to it. The spring they'd followed gushed out through a layer of shale. She had told them this was a natural filter and they filled the canteen. It seemed to be midday.

It was decided they would head upstream. They stayed in it; the banks were impassably overgrown and they could be more readily spotted from above. They would also be visible to other eyes if other eyes were looking, but the banks were dense with forest to the edges and so they stayed in it.

The water deepened as they sloshed through and began to fill their boots. Stones on the bottom, slippery, or sharp and painful even through the rubber. Their sticks in the air. A drizzle began, perhaps precluding an air search but not relieving them of the numberless insects suspended above the water in thrall of breath and body heat. Wariness of snakes and crocodiles, of leeches and parasitic fish so small one could swim through the most intimate bodily opening, employing spines to lodge itself therein to the great agony of its host.

Submerged pissing. Diarrhea. He had known of players so fearful of being substituted they refused to return to the locker room during play, but stuffed a towel into their uniform pants and relieved themselves there on the sideline.

The channel curved and looped, they were in it now up past their waists and the grip of gravity loosened, easing tormented joints and muscles. They heard a deep familiar roar but were beyond terror by now and looked up only in expectation. A tribe perched in the upper boughs of two big trees, eating leaves and some kind of fruit. A dozen or so, black with golden mantle, downturned grim mouths, tails as long as their bodies. Some of them stopped eating to watch three more of the strange big primates they saw from time to time, now inexplicably fording a creek. One, the biggest and closest, perhaps the Monkey God himself, roared again and threw a pit the size of a stone at the passing trio. No one is sure why they howl.

The rusty taste of their brains.

Sometime in the afternoon a path took shape along the bank and they left the water. It had stopped drizzling and there were blue gaps in the overcast, but they wondered if it was already too late for deliverance from the air. Water poured from their boots as they wrested them off, peeled and wrung out socks, inspected feet whitened and rivelled like raw dough, sat briefly, then reversed the whole process and got on with it.

The path held and they wondered if it could be natural or sign of human presence, and the second possibility was a two-edged thought. Not long before sunset the banks opened into the Plátano. It announced itself but did not greet them; there could be no mistaking it, sudden breadth and rush, patches of whiteness and foam, but they felt no less lost, didn't know if they were above the carved rocks or below them, whether it would do them good or ill. Nothing looked familiar and everything looked the same. All they could be sure of was that they would have to spend the night here, and about ten yards inland they found a tree arrested in the process of falling so that its narrow trunk slanted over the ground at an angle of about thirty degrees. The husband and wife set about gathering fallen branches and boughs, the woman with wordless inscrutable efficiency.

Nineteen watched for a time as they lay the longest branches against the trunk, using it as a centre pole. The man spoke as he worked. "We built our cabin together on Marean Lake. Sixty-seven logs, western white cedar."

Nineteen nodded. An inflection in the man's voice he thought he recognized. He wasn't sure when he'd realized they were married, nor did he know why the woman wouldn't speak. He watched them as if waiting to be asked, then asked if he could help.

The husband turned but looked past him. "Something to be said for it, isn't there?"

"You're making a shelter."

But he was looking across the river. Over the trees the clouds were solid and dark grey and ribbed like the ceiling of a vast cave, the gash of sunset its distant pink mouth. "Why rage against it? I can think of worse ways to go."

"I asked if you needed help."

They needed insulation. Dead leaves, bark, whatever he could find, and Nineteen brought them what he gathered then went in search of dry foliage for bedding while they added another layer of limbs and the dying of the light proceeded, uncontested.

There was just enough left to see a lopsided crude A-frame when they'd finished, but it looked solid and perhaps wide enough to hold three. Nineteen was surprised; he hadn't been sure exactly who was to be sheltered. He crawled in beside them and lay on a bed of leaves and spongy moss the husband had found on the riverbank. He had his pointed stick. The woman didn't seem to object to his presence but wouldn't lie between them.

She would let her husband close but wouldn't suffer his embrace.

The men on their backs, the woman on her side, face out. Their clothes were still very damp and issued a rank fungal smell. All was blackness, and outside the orchestra tuned up endlessly, its own conductor, the mantled howler its first chair.

In the shelter a sort of vacuum had obtained. An almost suffocating closeness of bodily warmth, the fermenting smell, but the jungle night would grow cold. The woman said something. It didn't make sense, and then it did, and Nineteen realized why she only spoke in her sleep. He remembered. Not everything, but enough.

"It's Tuesday, isn't it?" he said, all he could think of to say. Tears in his eyes.

Something woke him in the night. He wasn't sure if he'd only dreamt what he thought he'd heard, or if he'd slept at all, but by morning he'd forgotten it and the Canadian man said nothing. It hadn't rained overnight and they rose in a grey dawn. They continued downriver but hadn't gone far when the trail, such as it was, abruptly ended. A big fallen tree, ganglion of roots at its upended base packed with black dirt and moss. They stood.

The Canadian looked toward the other bank. A rough line of half-submerged rocks broke the current and he seemed to be assessing the gaps. "We could see if there's anything on the other side." A pattern of red bites formed an almost perfect circle on his forehead.

Nineteen looked straight ahead, along the bank. "It doesn't look that bad if we stay close to the river," he said, though actually he couldn't tell.

The woman examined the fallen tree.

"We need to get out in the open where we can be spotted," the Canadian husband said.

"So where are they? It isn't even raining."

"It's raining somewhere. Maybe they can't take off yet," the husband said. His wife was looking at something on the trunk.

"I could go myself. Check it out and come back—if you don't want to get wet."

In truth Nineteen didn't—he would settle for lingering dampness—but now he was looking at what the wife was touching. Three vertical scratches in the bark of the tree. Hard to tell how recent they were, but they had not been made by ancients.

The husband joined. "Maybe claw marks?" he said, and then, "Where do you think you're—" because his wife had straddled the tree and now swung her leg to the other side, stood peering into the jungle along the river. Nineteen watched her till he saw them.

"Look." He pointed to another tree perhaps ten feet in, a cluster of mushrooms like tiny white parasols sprung from its bark, another set of scratches above. The Canadian man said nothing. They joined the woman, went a little deeper and found more, went a little deeper, and then the husband spoke to his wife and without discussion they began to follow the markings deliberately.

Breaking brush. The canopy dropped and opened and the jungle floor, fed by light and leaf rot, sprouted green and snarled once again, but the sign persisted and so did they. Stumble and sweat, curtains of vines, crowded slender trunks of secondary growth. The canteen sloshed half empty, half full. They stopped to rest. The dried mud that had helped protect the Canadians from bites had washed off and they were blood meal once again. Reset and restart, Nineteen lagging in his cloud of pain. Insect hum. Outbursts of spade grass. No more scratches now but branches broken at eye level, at regular intervals and on the same side, and twice were strips of some unidentified cloth tied around young boughs. Cut vines. The brush so thick the river could barely be seen and sometimes they veered away from it or above it but always they heard it; it ran in them like blood. They'd forgotten to be hungry.

Stopped again. The Plátano was visible here, wider and calmer, but there were no more markings, no more sign. They stood looking, dead-ended, and didn't speak, and stood and looked without speaking till there was something else to see.

Blood and the river.

Just a drop, dried, brown-red, on a leaf just ankle-high. Then again, on a rock the size of the one Nineteen had carried in his pocket but lost somewhere along the way. Still one more. They moved slowly. A small spatter, ants probing. They stopped.

"That could be anything," the Canadian husband said.

"Like hell."

"Maybe it's an animal."

"We could follow it and find out."

"Find out what?" the husband said. His wife was looking toward the river.

Nineteen remembered. The blood brought it back. "You hear anything last night?"

"Like what?"

"I don't know. Something woke me up. You must have been asleep."

"If you want to call it that."

"I thought maybe . . . a gunshot. But I might've dreamt it."

"You're telling me this now?"

"It wasn't close. But you didn't hear anything."

The husband was shaking his head. "Maybe it's a hunter. Maybe he left a trail so he could . . . Jesus Fuck." His wife was gone. He called her name. "What if it's . . . ?" He looked around, not quite frantic. "Where'd she get to?"

Nineteen pointed. She'd drifted off toward the water's edge and stood bent over something on the other side of a shrub. Her husband called to her and she looked up briefly, then down again. They moved toward her and joined her and saw what she'd found.

"Jesus fuck me," the Canadian husband said.

Maybe six feet long, and four wide, half-concealed, made of balsa and bamboo. The limbs of uneven length, uncut or jagged at the ends as though they'd been snapped off. The longer boughs were sandwiched between four straight branches acting as crosspieces, the whole thing lashed together with deftly tied vines. There was a lone loose pole for pushing and steering; the current would do the rest. There was no blood on it.

The Canadian husband said it again and then they dragged it out of the shade onto the pebbled bank. A sturdy weight. They looked at it and could have wept, not just for the gift of it but for the artless perfection of its making, in which Nineteen thought he recognized the hand of its maker.

"You think this is her?" he said, with less certainty than he felt.

The Canadian man took a moment to realize who he meant. "I've no idea . . . Then where is she?"

"She might still be around. Maybe we should . . ."

"What?" The husband warily scanned the riverbank. "Should what?"

"I don't know. Follow the blood. Maybe she's wounded."

"Follow the blood. To where? Why would she leave?"

"We could find out."

"What if it isn't her?"

"Then we know."

"And if it isn't her?"

Nineteen looked down as if she lay there before them embodied.

"If she made this thing, why is it still here?" the Canadian man said. "Last I saw, she was empty-handed. How'd she build this without . . . at least an axe? How'd she cut the vines? With her teeth?"

"Maybe." The will makes the skill.

"And left a trail so she could be followed? It doesn't make sense."

"I know. I don't know. Nothing makes sense. But look at it."

"I don't know either. But here's the thing: I don't give a fuck who made it. The universe fucking made it, okay? Maybe it's abandoned—I don't see a hair of anyone else around. All I know for sure is it's here. We should use it while we can." He took in the sky. "Who knows how long before it starts pissing down again."

Downriver the water curved out of view, changed colour; you could hear it running faster. Sound of salvation. Nineteen regarded the raft now in another way, nodding.

The Canadian looked at his wife. "I have her to think of."

"Okay," Nineteen said, and nodded. She was studying the oar. "Then take her home."

"Damn right." The husband seemed at first not to realize they had stopped arguing. "We could use another paddle."

Nineteen stopped nodding. "Actually, one should do."

The husband looked at him.

"I'll stay close to the water, keep moving downriver."

"What?"

"You should leave now—while the weather holds, like you said. Maybe you get spotted from the air." He glanced up. "Say hello to the universe for me."

"What are you talking about? You're not gonna . . . ? It's a thousand to one it's her."

"It's not about her." Nineteen looked at the raft again. "Looks to me like it'll carry two at the most—if that doesn't sink it."

"Well let's give it a try. See what happens."

"I wouldn't take the chance. I'll stay close to the river."

The Canadian husband opened his mouth and said nothing.

"You should leave now. It wants you to. Take her home."

"It wouldn't hurt just to try. The extra weight might help in the . . ." But he seemed to be trying to convince himself now, while Nineteen spoke to the ground.

"I'll keep the river close. We know they're looking . . . just don't forget me . . ." He tried to smile to himself. "Fucking universe."

"We don't want to leave you here," the husband said, and you knew that didn't mean he wouldn't.

"Maybe I eat some more worms . . . Body of Christ, right?"

"If it swamps at least we'll have tried."

" . . . rub two sticks together, make fire. Maybe I even run into a healer."

The Canadian man wasn't looking at Nineteen. "Wouldn't that be . . . I don't know." He shook his head. "I don't know." But he did. He looked at the raft, his wife, the river, then his wife, the raft, and finally Nineteen again. "You'll stay by the Plátano then?"

"Take her home, man."

They would leave him the canteen. Send back help if they found it first. Nothing left to say. She watched them embrace.

They dragged the raft to a patch of sand and mud and put halfway in. The woman stepped aboard without being told and sat in the front. Her husband gave her the oar and he and Nineteen got on either side and pushed. You felt the water take hold as it welled up in the gaps between the logs and your boots sloshed in the shallow. The Canadian man lifted a leg and said, "I'll take her from here," and the terrific clap of sound that accompanied his last word was so jolting and disconcerting Nineteen wasn't sure what had happened nor to whom till the husband pitched languidly forward as if pushed and, with an unspectacular splash, gave himself to that sudden good night, lay facedown in it with his arms out, bubbling but no longer moving, the hole in his back much smaller than the one in his heart.

His wife sat patiently in the raft, watching her husband float alongside.

Nineteen turned, head ringing, legs rubber. The first thing he saw was a camouflage t-shirt. Its wearer stood on the bank halfway between the river and the jungle and was holding a rifle but seemed unable to keep it steady, as if pulling the trigger had expended an effort from which she needed to recover. Her face was pressed into the stock of the weapon and hard to make out but for the scar under the eye, the eye red and unfocused. The shirt was torn at the neck and mucked with filth and one leg of her pants had been cut off and bandaged around her knee, stained yellow and red, the leg below distended, starting to blacken as if not only injured but grossly infected.

Her mouth moved but you heard nothing; either she was too weak to be audible or Nineteen had been deafened by the shot.

He glanced back. The bubbles had stopped. The raft was in the current's grip and drifting toward the middle of the river, the faster water around the bend, its lone passenger still in the bow, dwindling. Their eyes met but he did not know what she saw.

He turned again toward the jungle, wondering why he hadn't been shot. The barrel was lowered, the gunman still unsteady and now struggling with something on the side of her weapon, some kind of lever or bolt and Nineteen thought of the bulge he'd carried in his pocket but no longer felt so now he was doing what he wouldn't two steps three now on dry land maybe it was jammed or she was even reloading did you build it or wait while she did it for you you son of a bitch four feet three the barrel coming up again diving at the knees straight up like a club it must be jammed or wet down to the knees aiming for the bad one because that's how you do it hurt them where it already hurts like any good defender doing what he wasn't born to not even sure who she was in all her glorious damage nor whom he was trying to save

O kay, let's get our party started! First, I'd like to present our Hostess with her gift: a travel-size bottle of TimeWise® Age-Fighting Moisturizer! Some of you may not know that the leading cause of wrinkles, besides the natural aging process, is not keeping your skin well hydrated! This gift contains powerful antioxidants and gives you ten hours of moisturization! And it's also for having me over and sharing your friends with me, which is such a privilege . . .

Now I want to meet everyone. Tell us your name, what you do for a living, and your favourite thing about our Hostess with the Mostest. Then I'd like you to tell me about your skin.

Home, she waited over the weekend. She thought he'd said he would be back Monday, but when she didn't hear from him she wasn't surprised—a little worried, maybe, but she didn't try to call him. She gave him his space. People need their space.

Now I know everybody says it but, honestly, I never thought I'd see myself doing Mary Kay. I've had more jobs than I can count—I was even a stewardess when you were still allowed to call them that, and a little while before that—just a little—I thought I was going to be the next Tammy Wynette.

Tuesday she called. Instead of a ring she heard three ascending beeps, then a voice that said his number was disconnected or out of service. She called his daughter then—the younger one, the responsible one—who said she hadn't heard from him in a week, which was not unusual.

First the bad news: the aging process starts in our twenties and doesn't let up. As you can see, I'm living proof of that. Excuse me? Well thank you! That's very sweet of you! So the good news is I owe a lot of that to the TimeWise® Miracle Set, which is the number one best-selling skincare product today. More good news: your skin is constantly regenerating itself, and our products just speed that process up. Now turn to pages six and seven of your Beauty Books.

Tuesday she called the police to file a missing persons report. The police advised her that, since she'd last seen him in a foreign country, she should call the State Department.

Mary Kay Ash put God first, family second, and career third. She started her company the year JFK was assassinated, right after her husband died of a heart attack, at a time when women made fifty cents on the dollar that men made doing the same job.

The State Department said they could find out easily enough if he'd left the country, but contacting the tour operator could take some time. She did not know the tour operator's name. They asked her if she was familiar with the Privacy Act. They asked if she was aware of the Travel Advisory they'd issued in regards to American citizens visiting certain countries.

She asked if they knew who he was—he wasn't just anyone.

Of course not, they said. No one is.

They would be in touch.

For a free prize, can anyone tell me at what age a woman's skin stops naturally producing its own collagen? That's right, we do prizes at Big Pink. That's how we roll.

She did not hear from the State Department again, so she called the American Embassy in the capital, which had a name she could barely pronounce, and spoke to a specialist in Citizen Services. She told him everything she had told the State Department. The specialist in Citizen Services was aware of the situation and was in touch with Honduran authorities, from whom he was now waiting for a reply. She asked him which Honduran authorities he was in touch with.

Now imagine you've been on a deserted island for forty days and you haven't washed your face or taken a shower. (I know, isn't it?) Then you hear that a boat is on its way and the man of your dreams is on the boat and he's coming to rescue you! Write his name on the back of your profile card. Now I want you to think of the one *glamour product you would want to use before he arrives on the island to rescue you. Write the product down next to his name.*

The specialist in Citizen Services called back. The Honduran authorities with whom he'd been in touch had been in touch with the tour operator, who said the tour was not just a day trip but an upriver trek that involved several nights' camping. They were not due back in the city till Saturday.

She told the specialist she was sure he'd said Monday, but could not always be certain of his state of mind and supposed he may have misspoken. Was it possible to verify the tour operator's statement?

You have a chance to get this product for free from me tonight! Think of friends who would love a free facial and makeover, and write their names and numbers on the back of your profile card. (What do you mean? Of course you have friends!) Whoever has the most names at the end of two minutes gets their glamour product for free tonight!

And where was Lost Marias?

What was the Rio Cuyamel?

Everyone was in touch with everyone else. It was Thursday.

And if you don't like the Desert Island Game, wait till we play the Purse Game!

The specialist from the American Embassy called again. He had spoken with a specialist from the Canadian Embassy, who had informed the specialist from the American Embassy that a Canadian couple had also been reported missing, that they too had been expected back Monday, that it was believed they had embarked on the same tour as the missing American. Honduran authorities were now trying to locate the tour operator, who had not returned their calls and may have left La Ceiba, but they now believed the missing persons had gone to the Mosquitia.

There'd been reports of gunfire.

She asked how long it took to mount a search, was told it depended upon the weather. Had she heard of the Mosquito Coast? Perhaps she'd heard of the film, starring Harrison Ford?

And whatever you do, do not mix product; you don't want to wage chemical warfare on your face. And you'll want to replace your mascara every three months; there's more bacteria in that tight little black tube than there is inside a toilet bowl. And do not pump—wiggle the wand inside. That's right, I said wiggle the wand inside. Mary Kay also has a sense of humour.

Local television news affiliates caught wind.

But does anyone know we also carry products for him?

By the time they got back to her she'd already heard. Seen it, actually. Fucking Yahoo. (She got all her news on the internet.) Well excuse her language but . . . Yes, alone on a boat. Really? Sticks and vines. Maybe, but he really wasn't very good at that kind of thing. Well, that was true. Yes, she'd heard. It was just so fucking sad (she'd thought he was her father at first). Was she going to be all right? Still? Maybe she could write something down. Of course. Delicate. Not a third-degree type of situation. It must have been very traumatic, yes. Well God bless her, good for her. No, of course she wasn't. Yes, she knew how. Of course she was. For all of them. God fucking bless them.

. . .

Now I'm going to come around with a cotton ball and you're going to tell me if you want to be pink and pretty or bronze and sun-kissed.

She wore the Bright Your Way look for the local television news affiliate. (Chromafusion® Eye Shadow in Starry Night, Translucent Loose Powder to give your look staying power.) Too soon to tell, she told the local television news affiliate. But she had faith, and it would not surprise her in the least if he came walking through that door as she spoke, if that was His will. On the other hand, it might also be His will that she go back down there to that awful place and find him herself—even if she had to take a leave of absence. (God first, family second, etc.) But of course it was too soon to tell. (She did not mention other possible outcomes that might also be His will.) Meanwhile, she had her work to keep her occupied. (She knew he would want it that way.) Meanwhile, there were people who depended on her. But it would not surprise her in the least. Right there on camera. And she looked offscreen, presumably at the door through which he would return to her at any moment.

So, ladies. Pull your mirrors up out of your trays and hold them at arm's-length. This is how the rest of the world will see you. You are the queen of your castle. Now find some love in your heart and repeat after me: I am beautiful.

You are beautiful. Smile at yourself so you can see how beautiful you are. Now look inside.

The American Embassy called.

They never said why. All they gave her was thirty days' notice, and under the terms of the Agreement that was all they had to. She was a Future Executive Senior Sales Director, a National-in-Qualification, with eleven first-line offspring sales directors, nine second-line, so you would think they would have told her why. She suspected why, of course, more than suspected—she'd only asked for some time away, she wasn't sure how much she'd need—but of course they wouldn't say so, just that *After careful consideration we have decided it would be in the best interest of both parties* and offered to repurchase all repurchasable Company products at ninety percent (90%) of the original net cost provided they'd been purchased within one (1) year prior to return. She would have to pay for shipping.

In a way they'd done her a favour—it wasn't just something you could do in your spare time. They'd found a small place in town (one bedroom was enough) till he got back on his feet— literally, he could barely walk, was on a cane for God's sake. And of course there was nothing to forgive, he'd been punished enough—wasn't that the purpose of the whole ordeal? His ways aren't always so mysterious. And someone had to give care when he needed it, walk him to the bathroom when he couldn't, manage the medicines, the doses, the diet, manage the calls, the interviews, the appointments, reactivate his social media; someone had to screen publishers, agents, producers, possible co-authors (and what a book it would be: *Hail Mary: From NFL Star to Jungle Hostage, as told to*).

The cane was probably, hopefully, temporary. He'd had his ankle fusion taken down in favour of total replacement, now they were pointing scalpels at his hip and spine; plastic, metal, bone. He was in physical therapy, and there was another kind of therapy for the screaming dreams, the ambush of sudden recall, but nothing to be done for what wouldn't come back—memories of memories—nor for the vertigo, insomnia, confusion, raging moods and migraines, the strange volatile weather within. They were even thinking stem cells again—other clinics, other countries, risky unapproved treatments crowdfunded by the kindness of strangers—but that would have to wait as well. What a gift just to have him back. She'd been given this.

News tickers scrolling over endlessly looping clips: standing in the pocket, patting the ball, looking for the open man. *Found on a riverbank by a family of prospectors, holding an assault rifle, his skull fractured,* looking for the open man.

But what a book it would be. No wonder they all wanted at him. But she was more than just a gatekeeper now, she'd been chosen (if not court-appointed), given the keys to his kingdom; you would have to wait your turn. God first (and He has a private line), family second—even if they blamed her. He'd spoken several times with his ex-wife but saw her only once, at his son's graduation (in the company of a woman, if you could call her that, you could see where it came from, just saying, all His children, but if that's what you wanted you might as well have kept him in the first place). His younger daughter, the shortstop, fledgling architect, visited on holidays and semester break, and though he had yet to hear from the older so had everyone else, God knew, and then there was everyone else, not just news and government, but the most distant relatives, teammates, old business acquaintances, coaches, a professor of philosophy, a producer of documentaries (with a theory about the actors who'd ambushed the compound), people he hadn't spoken to in a long time and some he didn't remember and didn't know if he should pretend to. Even when the ripples subsided somewhat, his lapses and newly acquired stutter making speaking engagements problematic ("I need to mow the driveway," he'd said and the audience resorted to laughter, default noise of incomprehension), the proposed book dwindling to a magazine article, there were calls. That Florida-tanned charlatan, under investigation for use of non-addictive opioids, for fraud, malpractice, patent infringement, left a message she decided it best to delete. His old friend the restaurateur wanted to theme a steakhouse after him, and this call he returned. (His involvement would be purely nominal but there would be eponymous menu items, and memorabilia, displayed as tastefully as memorabilia can be displayed.) The old friend and restaurateur offered a one-time fee but Nineteen's girlfriend negotiated residuals; the GoFundMe funds (people were so generous) had all but dried up and they were living off the proceeds from the sale of his farm. She was thinking of opening a beauty salon: Studio 19. She was thinking of giving guitar lessons again, fostering a migrant child.

He would wander parking lots, forgetting where he'd left the car. He couldn't explain the rifle. Sometimes spoke of a guide.

But what a movie it could be. *The Last Comeback: From NFL Star to Jungle Hostage* (adults, TV-MA). Abduction. Torture. Escape. Bodies all over the Mosquitia. A traumatized woman who had lost her husband and the power of speech (and wasn't granting interviews), braving Class III rapids alone on a makeshift raft . . . Some of it, of course, would have to be pieced together. Some things were probably better left unremembered. He'd told everyone everything he could, and not just once; the Hondurans, the Americans, the Canadians, the Mexicans, not to mention the DEA, the CIA (such neatly dressed, self-contained men, and one woman), the FBI, CBS, CNN; all the abbreviations. A gunshot on the riverbank, then fractured time, mystery galore. They would have to fill in the gaps. The raft, for instance. He was fairly certain they'd found it, but wasn't it more interesting to think they'd built it? It wasn't really lying. Sometimes the gaps fill in themselves, she'd been told. Some things are too good not to be true.

The truth was the guide was still missing (the search effort had been hampered by torrential weather, her body thought to have been washed away in a flash flood, or buried in a mudslide), but the good news was he hadn't had any more blackouts. The good news was she no longer blamed his family for blaming her, for calling her out in the cyber schoolyard, unfriending and unforgiving and blocking and deleting. The big yellow thumb down. She understood. She supposed she might have felt the same—that she'd abandoned him to that awful place when he'd needed her most—not having all the facts. But to call her his warden, to say she was holding him hostage all over again . . . They would come around, if that was His will. She didn't hold it against them that they held it against her. The good news was that there was no more bad news.

And some things, in fact, were better than before. One bedroom was enough, and sometimes it was more than that. A gift. Sometimes he needed it more than ever—the best medicine of all—and she liked taking the top and feeling him hold on to her hips and breasts, looking like everything was about to come back to him, and afterward she would play her Taylor Rosewood and sing and sometimes he would try and join his voice to hers, and it didn't really matter if he couldn't carry a tune in a bucket, nor if he didn't know the words and made up his own, or just sat there and looked like he was listening. It didn't matter because she'd been chosen for this, because, as the founder of the Big Pink had said, *Most people live and die with their music still unplayed.* She could sing for both of them.

He sees her in Bakery. Or thinks he does.

Organic produce, Parmigiano-Reggiano, responsibly farmed salmon, meat that isn't meat. Attractive, well-dressed, whole customers. It is not the sort of place he would have gone to in his before—Giant Eagle, Walmart, when he grocery-shopped at all— but he likes to think he's a different person now, and not just in the bad way, and his girlfriend shops here with the passion of the recently converted. Not to mention all the free samples.

Not to mention the bar serving craft beer and wine, with a fifty-five-inch TV and NCAA, but he is strangely uninterested; he would much prefer wandering the aisles, the departments, cruising the shelves filled with packages that have labels, reading the labels, studying the packages like a scholar of the arcane.

Looking at something till it is nothing but the centre of everything, till it is a pork chop or a jar of organic tahini once again, and he can move on.

She is cooking for eleven tomorrow—Thanksgiving, more than a year since his return. Former teammates will be there, Numbers Twenty-Nine and Forty-Four, and so will Coach, wheel-chaired and accompanied by his wife, giving thanks without speaking; the sportswriter gal has also said yes, and the AM radio host on whose show Nineteen had a weekly call-in segment until that portion of the show was cancelled—due to time constraints, he was assured, not the increasing difficulty he had answering questions on-air—and *all* his children, because he has heard from a young woman calling herself his eldest child, returning from a wilderness of her own, she has promised, warning him she may not be the same as he remembers her, which he is not sure he does anyway, which doesn't matter because someone can remember for him, as long as she is there, which she has promised to be.

Only one guest declined his invitation. She would love to, she typed, but maybe next year, when it is done, when the baby whose name he can't remember can walk and talk, the child she is raising in what she calls the Territories without the use of her voice, without a father, with solar power and propane; he will be sure to include her in his saying of Grace, which he must remember not to substitute with the Pledge of Allegiance, as he sometimes does, and he tries to remember what her book will be about, if there is a book, if he is not confusing it with the child, but what a book it will be if there is one.

Kombucha, Vegan Vitamins, Whole Trade, electric car charging ports in the parking lot. Tomorrow, in deference to their guests, an eighteen-pound antibiotic-free turkey, a hen who lived most of her five months in relative free-range happiness, beak and toes and snood intact (a healthy bird is a happy bird, and better-tasting), bought at a considerable savings on an organic

farm whose owner invites customers to participate in the process-
ing (slaughter) of their purchases, and so she did, cutting veins and
arteries cleanly, humanely, one side of the neck to the other, the
hen held inverted in a metal cone, but she has also weaned him
almost entirely off red meat, freed him of gluten and dairy. You
are what you eat—perhaps that's the answer. He is amino acids
then, fish oils, Omega 3, 6, 9 . . . He is also notoriously underfoot
and unhelpful in these situations, and she kisses him gently and
tells him they are sampling chicken tacos at the poultry counter.

"Don't get lost," she says, half joking, half begging.

Pearled barley, dragon fruit, ladies in long sweaters and tights.

"You can substitute zucchini for the chicken if you want veg-
etarian," the woman administering the samples says, but he is
looking at someone else. Standing in Bakery with her back to him,
inspecting artisanal breads. More compact than short, dark pants
and a denim jacket, dark hair in a tight bun. Holding an empty
basket. It makes him think of someone. She is one-quarter profile
to him so that all he can see of her face is the curve of cheekbone,
shade of skin, faint dark fuzz over the upper lip, but it is enough
to make him think of someone, though he doesn't know who.

Cannibals, pirates, runaway slaves. What made him think of
that?

He chews whole wheat crust, and swallows.

Returning, he finds his girlfriend in the wine department, talking to the sommelier. He smiles to himself: she may not be his
girlfriend much longer, and what a surprise it will be. No one else
knows. But sometime between dinner and dessert, he will stand,
take a knee, open the little velvet box in his pocket . . . A moment
of panic, till he feels it still there. (Sometimes it is, and sometimes
it isn't.) He should not carry it around, he knows; he loses things,

like his phone. She keeps that for him now. The possibility of loss terrifies him.

"Madame Liberté Brut," the sommelier recommends. Sparkling, perfect for celebration. He proffers a taste.

"I like the green apple notes," she says.

He is no longer smiling. That doesn't sound like her, has he made a mistake? If so, where is she? Has she already left, left him behind? Perhaps it isn't too late; if he can find the checkout stands . . . He finds them, but there are so many, and then he sees her again—not her, *her*—moving through the long aisle past the stands, from Produce to Prepared Foods. He catches only a glimpse of her face but it is full on, it is enough, too much, and he remembers now, though, even at this stage, he knows it isn't possible.

Still, he has to make sure.

Limping now in his joggers, he follows her through the market tables. Heat lamps, smell of rosemary, curry. People in green aprons. Amazon Rewards—logo like an arrowed grin, but it reminds him of something else. If he could just get in front of her, get another look. Hear her voice.

He bumps into someone in a jersey bearing the number four. His hands in sudden fists, but why should a number so enrage him? The man looks at him oddly, as if to say Where's yours? but when he looks down at his sweatshirt there is only blankness. He looks up.

The man is gone.

Someone says, "Is 'sell by' the same as 'use by'?"

She keeps moving. She glides. There is a way to walk in the jungle. Round the corner is Dairy, coconut milk and Pure Irish Butter, but she doesn't stop in Dairy, she is entering the corridor where the restrooms are. Her basket is still empty. He could call to her, get her to turn around, but what will he say? He doesn't want to see that it's her, only to confirm that it isn't.

She pushes through the door, and before it swings shut he follows, entering the serpent's maw. A sudden heat, and for a second he thinks he's in the kitchen. There are walls but no ceiling. Rough, mossy, stained. A fetid dampness, overpowering; it does not smell like a kitchen. He takes a step and kicks something: a mask, stone or wood. A face that is part man, part jaguar, shaman in a transformed spirit state.

A shaman is a healer. He touches it. Shall he wear it?

There are other things on the floor, crawling and slithering. The walls move. Something flutters. He moves deliberately now, toward light and air, finds himself at the top of the pyramid. Above the trees. The steps greying, crumbling, fissured with roots, but some are still a timeless white, almost glowing. Limestone, perhaps. Still others faced with carved skulls as if he were standing upon tiers of the dead.

Then he looks down and sees it.

The long green field flanked by long slanted walls. Knee-high grass. At the end of the field another set of risers, broad and low and fairly intact. They are not part of a pyramid and he realizes they are not steps but seats. He tries to imagine then how the game was played, seems to remember someone trying to tell him once; something difficult, but simple, and the simplest ones are always the best.

The sun is a ball in play. So is the moon.

His hand goes into his pocket. The ring is there, and not there.

And now a woman's voice, calling him by name, saying, "What are you doing here?"

The author wishes to thank those whose generosity helped make this book possible:

Robin Maxwell, Eric Raymond, Rose and Klaus Marten, Sue and Keith Hunt, Kimberly King Parsons, Ken Baumann, John Baker.